SHELTER

SHELTER
A NOVEL

BY
DOUGLAS LLOYD JENKINS

BATEMAN
BOOKS

Published in 2022 by David Bateman Ltd,
Unit 2/5 Workspace Drive, Hobsonville,
Auckland 0618, New Zealand
www.batemanbooks.co.nz
ISBN: 978-1-98-853868-6

A catalogue record for this book is available from the
National Library of New Zealand.

Cover design: Keely O'Shannessy
Text design: Tina Delceg
Printed in China

'To love and win is the best thing.
To love and lose, the next best.'

William Makepeace Thackeray

CHAPTER 1
PART 1 — 1994

Joe wanted to get into the right-hand lane. It seemed to be moving slightly faster. There was nothing much in it, but shifting lanes was something to do. The radio DJ was saying a truck had overturned on the motorway.

'Motorists should expect delays.'

'No shit,' he said out loud to the radio as he punched the off button. There was already a slight gap. It would depend on whether the guy opposite was going to be a tool. Joe watched. The driver had a book propped up against the steering wheel. This should be easy. He flicked on his indicator. The space between the two vehicles grew slowly.

Once over, Joe looked in the rear-view mirror hoping to catch the driver's attention — say thanks. The guy didn't look up, but from where Joe sat he looked attractive. Leaning out the driver's window, he adjusted his towing mirror to get a better view, but as he did the traffic moved a little. After he'd taken up the slack, he looked again into the wide rectangular screen of his rear-view mirror. The driver swept thick, uncooperative waves of black hair back from his forehead only to have them tumble back again a second later. His forehead was broad but his eyes, focused on his book, were lost under thick, purposeful brows. The sharp morning light picked out the line of his nose, which at this inclined angle, looked somewhere between that of an anteater and a movie star.

Joe decided to try something. After checking the road ahead, he edged his ute forward. Just enough so the driver behind would have to move up but not so much that someone else could squeeze in and ruin his view. Looking into the mirror he started counting — *one, two, three* — yes that was a great nose, a Mel Gibson nose — *six, seven, eight*. The ute behind moved up, but still the driver hadn't stopped reading. Eight seconds — a lifetime on an Auckland motorway — it must be a good book, probably Stephen King. Looking again into the towing mirror, the alignment of the two vehicles now provided a clear sight line into the cab of the ute behind. He watched as once again the reader pushed his hair out of his eyes. His cheekbones were high and gave way to hollow cheeks. Where the opposing lines of his jaw met, it formed a vertical dimple resting between the two small pillows of flesh that framed his chin. Joe sighed.

A moment later, as if aware he was being watched, the reader slowly ran his tongue across full, pink lips — lips that in Joe's other mirror remained obscured by the arc of the steering wheel. Joe sighed again, deeper this time. He was probably a model — *one, two, three* — but then models weren't usually sitting in old utes in the early morning jam — *six, seven, eight*. He was pleased he'd bought the towing mirror. He punched the radio button back on.

'With Venus in the sky over Auckland early this year, this looks likely to be the *real* summer of love,' said the DJ with way too much enthusiasm.

'You're right,' replied a woman, clearly high on the same stash. 'This seems to be *the* January for a little action from the love planet.'

'Ah, but Jackie, men are from Mars—'

'Morons.' He turned the radio off again. Fuck Venus, fuck Mars. He was twenty-one, his time was running out. Some of his friends were already engaged or married. So, the planets or fate determined things, or there was a being who had the job of matching one person to every other person; why couldn't they just get on with it? After all, if it was already written who was meant to be together — why the delayed delivery? Was it all bullshit? He looked in his side mirror at the driver and then in the rear-view mirror at himself.

'How long have you known?' he asked his reflection, doing his best impression of Paul Holmes, who always asked *just* that sort of question on TV every night.

'Really,' he answered in his own voice, pausing for effect, 'I've known all my life.' He had practised that line a million times — in the bathroom, in traffic, even at work — in his head and out loud when no one was around. That's what he was going to say when people asked. Once he'd come out and found himself a boyfriend. *One, two, three, four* — how can you drive on a motorway without ever looking up? — *five, six, seven, eight.*

That, the coming out thing, hadn't happened yet but plenty of other, pretty legit gay things had. He'd fallen in love at primary school, but the family had moved to Australia. He'd survived two bloody miserable years with the same homophobic form teacher at Te Atatū Intermediate. At Rutherford High, he'd met Kurt, a blue-eyed, dark-haired Dungeon and Dragons player. Joe had fancied him but he hadn't risked anything. Instead, he and Kurt danced. He'd made Kurt dance even when there were no girls around. When Joe left for 'tech, Kurt had gone to university, early, on an IT scholarship. That last summer, before they went their separate ways, Joe had thought something might happen between them at last, but instead they pretty much stopped hanging out altogether.

Joe figured that was how it worked — he fell in love and then they left. Not that he was a virgin or anything, far from it, but Kurt was years ago now, when he was a teenager. His age bugged him — twenty-one felt old — but he was, he felt sure, still attractive. His shoulders were wide and, more importantly, square. He had a great thatch of thick light brown hair that had, as always, gone blond this summer. He leant forward, examining his fringe in the mirror, and after mussing it a little he took another quick glimpse at the driver behind — still reading. He looked again into the side mirror, catching the flex of the driver's bare arm as he turned a page. He was a big guy and if the rest of him was anything like his top half, an impressive slab of man. Nah, 'slab' made him sound dumb. He didn't look dumb, and what about the book?

One, two, three — he wasn't sure he'd ever seen anyone reading on the motorway before — *eight, nine, ten* — the driver behind followed in tiny steps, as if they were locked arm in arm in a slow, shuffling dance.

Yes, that's what he was, plain and simple, — a ten — or perhaps even an eleven?

Mesmerised, Joe lifted himself slightly from his seat and tugged at his shorts. He then busied himself, happily switching between the long letterbox slot panorama of his rear-view and the magnified portrait in his towing mirror, all the time silently urging the driver to look up — eye contact, *come on*. The thing was, long ago, Joe had realised he wanted love rather than just sex. *Come on, look up!* — how could you possibly fall in love with someone without seeing their eyes? Joe realised that he really, desperately wanted to fall in love, even momentarily, even just on his way to work.

Lost in his slow dance, Joe was late noticing that the two lanes ahead had cleared. Momentarily embarrassed, he floored it. *Fuck Tuesday*, he thought, as he pushed the accelerator home. Nothing ever happens on a Tuesday, and it seemed that this Tuesday was going to be particularly shit. He was already late and yesterday, last thing, some dickwad driver had dumped a whole truckload of timber in the wrong place. With the apprentice away, the foreman had asked him to move it — no forklift and no help, just him. It would take most of the day, and it looked like it was going to be a scorcher.

It was 11 o'clock and already hot. Joe pulled off his t-shirt. He figured he'd made a good start at shifting the bundles of framing. The ghettoblaster was playing the same station he had been listening to in his ute, but with the morning hosts gone it had settled into a steady stream of decent tunes. As he lifted the lengths of timber onto his shoulders, three at a time, he moved his hips to the music, his load bouncing in time with him. He set off for the far side of the site where he was restacking the timber into bundles identical to those he was dismantling. Returning, he noticed a builder he had never seen before sitting on the load of timber he was partway through moving. The guy was tanned and dressed only in a pair of small brown work shorts. For a second Joe thought the guy appeared entirely naked and, although immediately recognising that as an improbability, he allowed himself to be distracted by the possibility. It took him a moment then before he recognised the builder before him as *the reader*.

'Hey, I saw you on the motorway this morning. You let me in — thanks,' said Joe.

'No problem.' The guy gave a nonchalant shrug and then, without looking up, he took a small screwdriver from the tool belt at his side and set about dismantling his nail gun. Joe watched for a moment.

'My name's Joe.'

'Leo.' Still, the guy didn't look up.

'What were you reading?'

'Huh?'

'What were you reading on the motorway?'

'*Candide*. Voltaire.' At last, he looked up. His eyes were heavily lidded and in close-up they made his face seem even more attractive than it had in the rear-view mirror. 'Mean anything to you?' Joe shook his head. 'Didn't think so. Look, I got to fix this.' Leo turned away, and Joe left him to his gun. Joe needed to shift the bundle of timber Leo was sitting on, but rather than ask him to move, he stepped over and cut the bindings of the next bundle.

When he turned back, Leo had gone.

At lunchtime, Joe asked the others, 'Who's the new guy?'

'He's a wanker,' said Hayden.

'Yeah, he's been to varsity,' said another with a sneer.

'Right, as I said, he's a *wanker*,' repeated Hayden.

'His name is Leo Bridge. I worked with him on that hotel job last year,' said Steve. You could rely on Steve, Joe thought, so he turned to look at him to encourage him to continue. 'He's been working in the UK, doing restoration stuff. He got back recently. He's okay.'

'Restoration stuff. What'd I tell you? Up himself.' Hayden looked directly at Joe. 'Why you asking?

Joe shrugged and turned away. He knew Hayden. Hayden was a

dick. If he got wind of Joe's interest in Leo he wouldn't let it go. He wandered off and sat down in the sun, his back against the stack of timber he was moving. There, he ate his lunch, hoping all the time that Leo would reappear.

After lunch, Joe finished moving the timber quickly and then spent the last hour of the day doing very little else other than scout around for Leo. It wasn't until just before knock off that he saw him again, crouched down, carefully scribing a piece of wide skirting board and fitting it into a corner. He had a t-shirt on now that strained across his back, and Joe stood behind him for a long while, watching, running his eyes over Leo's squatting form and watching his massive lats work. Then, figuring he didn't want to be caught standing there, should Leo turn around, he cleared his throat.

'Hi again.' It took a moment before Leo stood and faced him, a length of skirting board in one hand and a chisel in the other. Where his face had glowed with the sheen of a morning razor shave in the traffic, his chin and jaw now had a distinct black scruff that made him look more than a little dangerous. Joe hesitated. 'It must have been good.' Leo frowned and shook his head slightly to indicate that he had no idea what Joe might be talking about.

'Candide Voltaire — your book.' Leo raised his hand and pushed the hair off his forehead, the action lifting his eyelids at the same time. There they were, the eyes Joe hadn't been able to catch that morning. The eyes he'd waited all day to see. They were strangely, almost disappointingly, grey but, despite their heavy lids, or perhaps because of them, they flashed for a second with a strange intensity. He wondered if the look was a warning, or simply a dismissal.

Joe's gaze then wandered down Leo's arm to the line of a vein that, emerging from under the cuff of his t-shirt, stood proud, then trickled across his bicep and down his forearm before crisscrossing with other veins like a river delta across the broad, powerful hand that clutched the chisel. It took only a few seconds for Joe's gaze to make the journey, but at the end of it, he knew — the universe had at last seen fit to deliver.

Joe thought about those eyes and their strangeness again that night as, standing in his underwear, he looked at himself in the mirrored door of his wardrobe. He'd tried to follow Leo on the way home, just to get some idea of where he lived, but as the radio began mocking him with an old Andrew Fagan song he'd changed stations and somehow lost Leo's ute. Neither of his flatmates, Suze and Marie, had heard of Candide Voltaire. They wondered if she might be a French movie star, but Joe somehow thought it unlikely that Leo would read that kind of book.

Now, slipping out of his underwear, Joe idly ran his fingers across his chest, down his torso and along the sharply defined curve of his Adonis belt. Stopping, he dropped his hands and turned sideways, looking at his reflected profile. He could be taller, he supposed, but his body was lithe rather than skinny. He was pretty much all muscle, and still pretty good for twenty-one. His was, he guessed, a football body. Leo's was a rugby body — the attraction of opposites.

Moments later, as he lay in his bed, he thought that despite all odds, for once a Tuesday had worked out pretty good. The parcel for which he'd been waiting, although delayed, had been delivered and it was the complete package, one for which he'd happily sign. As he turned off the light, the only problem he could see now was that although nothing like the other guys, or like any bloke he had ever met, nothing, except maybe the reading thing, suggested Leo was gay.

The foreman had asked Joe to pick up some stuff from Carter Holt and now, on the way back, standing in line at the bakery, he was looking at the guy next to him in the queue. He was wearing one of those orange vests that guys were beginning to wear on site. He was surprised builders had started going for them — fluoro had always seemed to Joe solely the domain of the stop-go men that manned roadworks — generally guys of the slack-jawed and pot-bellied variety. This guy, however, was attractive, but as Joe looked him up and down he couldn't help but compare him to Leo, and he just wasn't in the same league. In fact, for Joe, Leo had a whole league of his own, one that hadn't existed a fortnight ago.

Leo was magnetic, attractive in a way that Joe had never encountered before in another human being. Magnetic, because Leo didn't seem to do anything to attract attention; instead he pretty much sleepwalked through the day. He seldom spoke, moved only as required, expended no additional energy, and expressed no unnecessary emotion. Still, Joe could not keep from staring. More than that he felt as if he were trying to *absorb* Leo, soak him up with his eyes, and breathe him in through his nose. He wanted, if he could just figure how to do it, to bring *all* his senses together so that they might draw Leo into his very being.

'Faggot.' Fluoro guy slammed hard into Joe's shoulder. Joe lost his footing and stumbled backwards, hitting the drinks fridge, which rattled noisily. The woman behind the counter looked annoyed. Joe blushed. Watching the guy now as he strode out, he wanted to follow. He wanted to run down the street after him and shout, 'You might think you're hot but you look *stupid* in that vest! You're nothing, a big fucking nothing!'

A few minutes later, calmer, climbing into his truck, Joe sat for a moment. Leo was driving him nuts. He had, since that Tuesday, tried to create some basic connection but his target had resisted every attempt at conversation. When he'd asked what he'd done last Thursday, on Waitangi Day, Leo had answered 'I was busy.' It was as if he was there in body, but that was it. Leo projected *nothing* except total indifference.

Another problem was getting near him at all. It was a big site and Leo did finishing work. That meant he worked on another part of the project to Joe. He ate his lunch in the cab of his truck. So, all Joe could do was hope to be assigned somewhere close and just be around when Leo asked for a hand, but so far that hadn't happened.

Then there was the whole gay thing. Leo didn't seem any more gay than he had originally, so why was Joe even persisting? Then again, Leo was so unlike other guys, there had to be something . . . no, there *was,* there was definitely something about him that made all this worthwhile. At the very least, Joe was going to pursue it until he found out for sure.

Joe pulled up onto the site. There was a gap next to Leo's ute, and so he parked in it. No one was watching. Climbing down from his cab, he put his face to the passenger window. Pressing against the glass, he placed his hand on the top, cutting through the glare of the sun so that he could see into the cabin. It was a mess of battered black paperbacks, strewn among sunglasses, chopsticks and other discarded junk. At least he knew now that *Candide* was a book by someone called Voltaire. No wonder Leo had looked at him that way. He searched for music. He figured that was the best way to start a conversation, but the mess of tapes on the front seat was mystifying. There was no Nirvana or Pearl Jam. No Oasis or Blur. Not even Pulp, who tossers were always raving about. Sighing, he leant back against his own ute and, looking up at the blue late February sky, he added this new information to the little he knew about Leo. Leo was older. Leo had been to university. Leo had been to England. He read books. He listened to unusual music. The food he ate was weird. He used chopsticks. All this, strange and threatening, added up to one thing. Joe had quickly figured that the intensity of the guy scared the shit out of him. Leo's strangeness intoxicated him. He represented the possibility of an entirely different life that Joe knew existed outside that of a tradie's life in West Auckland, but it was one he knew almost nothing about. It was one he might like, mind you, if it meant they could share it. That would mean convincing Leo he wasn't stupid. A cloud covered the sun, and the sudden chill broke his train of thought. Grabbing the boss's stuff from the tray, he headed off to the site office.

The next morning over smoko Joe had an opportunity. Leo was there, for once, so Joe took a deep breath and had a go at starting a philosophical discussion among the guys.

'Do you sometimes think the universe might be fucking with you?' There was no response from anyone so he continued. 'You know, do you ever have the feeling that fate is just screwing you around 'cause it can?'

He looked toward Leo, but he didn't raise his head from the newspaper at his feet. After a moment Hayden answered.

'Sure. Yup, I think it is, particularly with you.'

'Really, why?' Joe leant in, happy at last to get his attempt at an intellectual discussion off the ground.

'Dude, why else did the universe tell you to buy that Holden when real men drive Fords?' The others laughed and Joe's face burned hot with annoyance. Leo raised his eyes from his newspaper at last, a look of cynical amusement on his face, but he didn't speak. That was a relief, at least.

Joe could have kicked himself. What a dick. He'd made a fool of himself again. Why did he have to be so dumb? Why was Leo, so smart and so totally hot, so determined to keep to himself. Perhaps this whole thing — Leo getting under his skin so badly — was just that — another cosmic joke at his expense.

Two weeks later, standing in the little shed where the guys stored their gear, Joe reflected on the fact that he was out of time. It was the last day of the job and on Monday the teams would be split up and relocated. He might never see Leo again. Still, he had nothing. In fact, he had less than nothing because bloody Hayden was following him to the next job. The more he thought about it, the more he knew this was not how things were supposed to be.

He glanced back over his shoulder to make sure no one was around and then turned back to the row of hooks. There was Leo's black jacket. He stepped forward and buried his face in its lining and inhaled the scent. The honest, earthy masculinity that swelled up into his nose had the joint effect of awakening his crotch and causing his knees to buckle beneath him. Suddenly, without a second thought, high on this new secret pleasure, he exchanged his keys for those in Leo's jacket pocket then hurried out to rejoin the others.

It was later than usual, but the guys were only now finishing cleaning up the site — throwing the last scraps of timber onto a bonfire that burned not far from the shed. One by one they were beginning to collect around the fire, opening beers and awaiting the arrival of the fish and chips the foreman always put on at the end of a job. The day had been overcast, and the light was now failing rapidly. It was going to be an early winter.

Joe realised his luck was in when Steve, the biggest and — after Leo — the quietest guy on site, called across to Leo as he walked towards the shed.

'Staying for a drink?'

Leo paused on the doorsill. Joe waited. It seemed forever before Leo responded. 'No, not tonight thanks.'

As the words tore through his head, Joe took a long swig of his beer. Watching as Leo reached for his jacket, hanging on the first hook inside the door, he felt a wave of old beer and new desperation rise in his throat.

'Come on,' Steve gestured at the group. 'Last chance to have a drink with your mates.'

Joe couldn't trust himself to say a word. He'd never been this scared. His entire future seemed tied up in this moment. He looked at the others. They were mostly looking at the ground or busying themselves with pointless tasks — none of them were the slightest bit interested whether Leo stayed or went. He wanted to punch them out, one by one, knock them down like bowling pins. Leo was worth more than the lot of them put together.

Now, jacket in hand, Leo was scanning his eyes over the group. Who was he looking for? Then Joe noticed Hayden staring right at him from over Leo's shoulder. Joe looked at the ground. He hated himself. He was a stupid, gutless loser.

Then, just as Joe decided that Hayden's suspicions and opinions didn't matter and that he would man up, Leo spoke.

'Okay,' was all he said as he placed his jacket back on the hook and took the beer Steve offered him.

An hour later, after the last round of beers had been opened and the newspaper from the chips stuffed into the ashes of the fire, provoking a last pyramid of orange-tinged flame, Joe still hadn't spoken more than a word or two to Leo. He couldn't, something paralysed him, releasing him only long enough to say something even more banal or stupid.

Now it was getting dark. He had been talking to a few of the guys, but the conversation had petered out. He turned around to face the fire. Looking across the flames, there was Leo, holding his jacket and saying 'goodnight' — the first to go.

Joe quickly said his goodbyes and shook a few hands before making his way to the shed for his jacket. His head thumped. He didn't know what to do but it was certain that if anything were about to change, he and Leo needed to be alone. If he let him go now there might never be another chance.

He wasn't sure what he was going to say or do when he got to the carpark. Leo could probably snap him in two if he wanted. Or he could call out, have the others do it for him. They wouldn't need much provocation. The guys had often talked about what they'd do to a queer if they got one alone, or if one ever touched *them*. Still, he figured it would be worth the risk.

There he was, leaning back against the door of his ute, squatting slightly, legs apart, as if sitting on an invisible bar stool. He was staring at the keys in his hand.

Joe called out. 'They're mine.' Leo looked confused. Joe held out the keys and then, grasping Leo's right hand — the hand Leo would naturally use to punch — he occupied it with a complicated switching of the two sets of keys. 'Sorry, don't know what happened.'

With Leo trapped in a semi-squat against the ute, Joe pushed himself between his parted legs. He could feel the hard muscles of Leo's thighs through the denim of his jeans as he pressed against them. Leo did nothing. He made no attempt to move.

Joe placed his free hand on the edge of the ute's roof. As he leant in, he caught Leo's gaze directly. For a moment they looked at each other, eyes unblinking. Leo's lips were open, either in surprise or readiness, Joe didn't care which. Joe kissed him, long and hard, with a force that

Leo responded to willingly. As they broke apart, Joe clocked only the slightest upturn of the corners of Leo's mouth, as if slightly amused.

Joe pulled the cardboard lining from the plastic cassette cover and wrote on the spine 'Dusty in Memphis'. It was one of his mother's. He liked it the most out of all her old records, kept in neat compartments under the three-in-one stereo in the living room. It was mostly Sixties stuff — Dusty Springfield, Shirley Bassey, Gene Pitney. Some of it had been his grandmother's — Sinatra, Johnny Mathis, Julie London. He'd heard them all his life, and he wondered why he'd never made a tape of them before. He couldn't be bothered writing out the track listings. It didn't matter much. Nothing mattered. He'd kissed Leo, but Leo hadn't *done* anything in response. He hadn't *said* anything. He could've said *something*. Instead, Joe, waiting, expecting, had watched as Leo had gotten into his ute and driven off.

The thing was, Joe wanted Leo even more now than before. At first, relying on the universe, he had hoped he would simply run into him. For a month now, Joe had slowed down around building sites and scanned any hardware shop or builder's supply yard for him. There'd been no sign. He had never quite figured where Leo lived so it wasn't like he could accidentally run into him.

As he put the tape back into the case and snapped it shut, he thought about how it would be Anzac weekend soon. After that, it would be winter proper. The job, cold mornings, wet days, would turn to shit. Yep, the tape was perfect. It meant he wouldn't have to listen to moronic morning radio DJs high on their crap ideas about love.

It was the Friday before the long weekend. None of his mates seemed to have plans. Marie and Suze had bailed back to their home towns for the weekend. He might as well stay — better that than go home to an empty flat. Most of the guys on site looked like they were settling in for a long session with a few boxes of beers. Hayden, as always, had a couple of joints. They were setting up, and he decided to change, get his good jeans and trainers from his ute. In the carpark, bending forward to retrieve them, he spotted something that made him jump. He hit his head hard against the door arch.

Ducking down, Joe rubbed the back of his head. After a few minutes, when he was sure that Leo, having walked up the drive, was now out of sight, he slammed the door and followed. Hanging back, his head still hurting, he lingered in the shadows listening, his heart pounding in his chest. Leo had arranged to borrow another chippie's trailer for the weekend. He waited till Leo had accepted a drink and then walked into the circle of builders. Catching sight of him, Leo raised his eyebrows in brief acknowledgement, then quickly averted his eyes.

'You two know each other?' asked one of the other builders. It was Hayden who answered.

'Yeah, they know each other.' Then, turning to Joe, Hayden added, 'Thought you were getting changed.'

'Changed my mind. Pass me a beer.' For the next thirty minutes, as Joe nursed that first beer, he and Leo took it in turns to look away whenever their eyes met.

They stayed in separate conversations, but when some of the guys announced they were going off to the local bar, Leo looked directly at him as he asked, 'May I tag along?'

The pub smelled of spilled beer, cigarette smoke and deep-fried food. The regular Friday night crowd was noisier than usual, and there seemed to be a lot of visitors — weird for a long weekend when town usually emptied out. A large television above the bar was playing videos. There a middle-aged woman, dressed in a cheerleader's outfit, was silently singing the praises of a boy called 'Mickey' as she had for as long as he could remember there being MTV. Genesis played over the bar's speaker system.

Looking at Leo it was as if every woman in the room had collected around him. One by one or in pairs they found a reason to sidle up and introduce themselves. Most were using the din as an excuse to speak suggestively into Leo's ear, placing their hands on his arm or shoulder as they reached up. What they were saying, he couldn't tell, but there was only one topic that night anyway. Kurt Cobain had shot himself a few days earlier. The girls in the bar were, he suspected, trying to tell Leo how devastated they were. They 'really needed someone to be with them right now.' He smiled. He might know almost nothing about Leo, but he knew without a doubt he'd think Cobain a tosser.

Occasionally Leo would look over at him with that same enigmatic half smile he'd seen in the carpark the night they'd kissed. It now suggested he wanted Joe's complete attention while he demonstrated his ability to pick up any of the women on offer. Joe realised Leo was right — he held all the cards — and for a moment allowed himself to hate him for it. Then, as he looked away, one of the hopefuls appeared at his side.

'That a friend of yours?' She gestured towards Leo.

'What friend?'

'The one you've been staring at.' She gave a slight smirk. 'Should I know him? Is he an All Black or a male model or something?'

'No, I don't think so.' He was trying to sound vague.

'Well, he should be.'

'Yes, he probably should,' he looked again at Leo.

'What's someone who looks like *that* doing here?' she asked, rattling the ice in the bottom of her empty glass with her straw. 'What's his name?'

Without taking his eyes off Leo, Joe replied, 'It's terrible about Cobain. It changes everything.'

The evening dragged on. Shit, there was Toni Basil again. He knew her name now, it was there along the bottom of the screen. Everything else was the same. Well, maybe the crowd was thinner. The bar was getting hot and smelt sweaty. He just needed to get his act together. First, he needed to get some air. He made for the door and a moment later stood in the carpark breathing in large exaggerated gulps of the crisp April night.

Then, from behind him, came a voice. 'Hey.'

Joe turned. Leo was standing there, same hooded eyes, same unreadable look on his face.

'You live around here?' Joe nodded. 'Well . . . what are we waiting for?'

As Leo bent over the doormat to remove his boots, Joe fumbled with the key in the front door lock. His heart was beating wildly.

They stood in the entrance hall together. Joe didn't dare take his eyes off Leo and just dropped his jacket where it fell. Leo followed suit. Then, without speaking, Leo stepped forward and kissed him. It was a long, searching kiss.

Pulling away, Joe led Leo into the lounge. There, grappling, they removed each other's t-shirts. That accomplished, Leo took over, pushing him against the back of the couch and unbuckling his belt. Leo pulled down his jeans, flinging them over the back of the armchair. Joe knelt forward onto the carpet in front of Leo to complete the same operation, but after he had unzipped Leo's fly and tugged on his jeans, they caught fast on Leo's large muscular thighs. Together they collapsed in a pile on the floor, laughing. After a minute or so, Leo obediently raised both legs in the air and waited. Joe tugged. At last, he flung the stubborn denim into the air. They both laughed again when the jeans came to rest on a dead pot plant by the hall door. Leo stood up and again kissed him — shorter, sharper, hungrier kisses this time — pushing him backwards down the hall. They stopped kissing at the bedroom door just long enough to remove their own socks and underwear. After a moment in which they had simply stood and looked, drinking in each other's naked bodies, Leo moved forward. Lifting Joe, he tossed him effortlessly in the air and onto the bed.

The sex was clumsy and awkward, brutal in the way known only to two young men intent on maximising their mutual pleasure for what they suspect will be the only time. When it was over, exhausted, half asleep, Joe lay wrapped in Leo's arms, his head against his chest as it rose and fell in a deep, steady rhythm. As they both stared at the ceiling, Leo spoke.

'You need to know something,' he said. 'I'm not gay.'

CHAPTER 2

It took the guys on site until morning smoko to figure out something had happened. They were sitting in a circle of old plastic chairs, their morning tea on upturned wooden nail boxes in front of them. Gavin, pouring boiling water over the teabag in his mug, was looking at no one in particular when he spoke.

'See, Joe? I reckon he got some this weekend.'

'Doubt it.' Hayden didn't look up.

'Just look at him. There's a kind of *stoopid* loved-up look on his face.'

'What's new? There's always a stupid look on his face.' Hayden laughed at his own joke and then took a bite from an ugly scone, following it immediately with a slug of Coke from the plastic bottle in his hand.

Gavin, mug in hand, was bending over now, getting in Joe's face, twisting his head from side to side, trying to catch Joe's eyeline. 'Shit, I'm right. Look how red he's gone.'

Ricky, clutching the 'Horny' mug he'd told them was a present from his fiancée, joined in. 'He's been walking mighty funny all morning.'

Joe's face was burning now. He could feel his skin tightening, creeping sideways across his face as if trying to find somewhere to hide.

'Ah *mate* — when did this happen?' Hayden's earlier doubt had evaporated, and he was now hoping the change of tack might encourage Joe to provide elaborate details.

'He was talking to that short chick at the pub.'

'And you left early, you dirty dog. Come on mate, spill.' Hayden was on his feet now, standing in front of him. 'High five.' He half stood and reluctantly raised his hand to meet Hayden's mid-air. The sting of flesh reminded him how much he disliked it, associating what had happened that weekend with such a stupid gesture, but he figured some things just had to be done in order to survive.

'Nah, it's nothing.' Then something occurred to him. 'Cobain means everyone's scoring. Sign of the times, best thing ever.' It worked. The conversation moved on. Gavin, Hayden and Ricky began thrashing out, yet again, just how different the world would be without Kurt Cobain.

By lunchtime they were back on the subject of Joe's recent score, digging for lurid detail that, when he failed to provide, they simply imagined out loud.

After taking a few more hits, Joe got up and, amid a hail of abuse, went out to the verge and ate his lunch alone. With his back against the retaining wall, he was too blissed out to care about the guys or much else either. At any rate, they weren't wrong. He did have 'a stupid loved-up look' on his face all right. Because he was in love and because he didn't have that much to think about except the obvious pleasures of the weekend, particular moments of which had flashed in and out of his mind all morning. Thinking about it now, watching the traffic drive by, he wasn't sure he knew any more about Leo than he had before. They had said surprisingly little of consequence during their time together. Now and then his mind strayed to pondering Leo's revelation about his sexuality. But even that didn't worry him much. Was *Joe himself* gay, *really gay*, if he wasn't out? Leo had enjoyed himself — Joe had the hickey to prove it. Luckily the guys hadn't spotted that. It might take Leo some time, but as far as Joe was concerned, Leo could take all the time in the world.

Leo was waiting, parked on the road outside his flat, when he got home. As Joe walked over, smiling broadly, his heart pounding, Leo rolled down the window.

'I knocked off early and thought you might want to talk about the weekend?' Leo gestured towards the passenger seat. 'Jump in.'

Joe looked at Leo and then down at his own shorts and boots. 'Can I get changed?'

'Sure.'

'Come in and wait.'

Leo glanced over at the cars parked in the driveway and shook his head. 'I'll wait here.'

Inside, Joe stripped quickly. There was no time for a shower. He sniffed his armpits, spraying them with deodorant before emptying the last lethargic puffs of the near-empty aerosol into his pubic hair. He pulled on the new underwear he'd been saving for a special occasion. Picking some black jeans and a black AC/DC t-shirt from the pile of laundry he'd done the previous night, he dressed quickly. In the bathroom, he squeezed some product onto his hand and massaged it through his hair and scrubbed his teeth. Back in his room, he changed into a different t-shirt. This time a two-tone black and blue Raglan sleeve that made his chest look bigger but clung to his stomach. He put on his good trainers and, leaving them unlaced, grabbed a jacket and headed for the door.

'Bye,' he called out to his flatmates as the door closed behind him with a bang.

As he opened the cab door, Leo brushed the contents of the front seat into the footwell with a single sweeping gesture. Joe climbed in, and for a moment they just looked, eyes darting across each other's body. Scouting around, checking no one was watching, Leo turned and, placing his hand on Joe's left shoulder, pulled his whole torso around into line with his and kissed him.

'Is it okay? To do that?'

'Hell, yes.'

Leo smiled. 'Where shall we go? You want food?'

Joe nodded. They didn't say much on the way — exchanging only occasional, nervous glances. After a while, Leo pulled up outside Canton Café, a little Chinese place in Kingsland. It wasn't exactly a restaurant, more of a takeaway. Bright lighting and just a couple of chairs and tables, but Leo was adamant the food was good. The woman behind the counter handed them a photocopied menu with tiny, fuzzy images of the dishes. Leo made some suggestions and they ordered.

'No license,' said Leo, collecting two ginger beers from the fridge. Sitting with their legs woven together under the little table, Leo asked Joe about himself. Joe talked about his mother, how his dad had walked out soon after he was born. About the schools he'd been to, about becoming a builder. How he'd left home at eighteen. He left out Kurt and what he knew about the universe. He couldn't have handled it if Leo had laughed. As he finished, the food arrived. He looked at the mass of glistening noodles and then at the table top.

'No forks.'

'Here, try these.' Leo passed him a pair of chopsticks from a small bamboo vase on the table. Joe frowned, taking the chopsticks and unwrapping them, holding them the best way he knew, like scissors. After a few minutes of struggling to get the noodles up off his plate, he hadn't managed a single mouthful.

'Shit,' Joe said as he rested the chopsticks on the edge of the bowl. Picking up a noodle with his fingers, which dangled over the edge, he popped it into his mouth. 'Don't laugh.'

'Why not? It's funny.'

Joe picked up the chopsticks and stabbed again at the noodles, but they still slipped from his grasp.

'Like this.' Leo demonstrated the efficient progress of his bowl of rice to his own mouth. 'You want some?' Leo offered him some rice. He shook his head, but then changing his mind, opened his mouth. Leo placed a prawn between his lips. Struck by the unexpected intimacy of the moment, Joe blushed.

'It's not fair, you use them every day,' he said, having swallowed the prawn. Shit, he thought momentarily, thinking Leo might wonder how he knew that particular detail. 'They were all over the floor of your ute — I just figured . . .' Leo didn't seem to care. Instead he took Joe's hand and placed the chopsticks in them.

'Here, try this. Hold one like . . . so.' He reached over and placed the chopstick between Joe's pointer, middle finger and thumb. 'The other . . . this way.'

26

Joe looked across at Leo. He didn't mind Leo teaching him stuff, not even in public, not if it meant being on the receiving end of his touch.

'You're good at it.'

'I grew up in South-East Asia.'

'Really?'

'On a boat. My parents were hippies. The sort of self-involved hippies that dump their kid in a private boarding school at ten.' Looking up from his food, Joe couldn't quite figure out from his expression whether Leo was simply stating facts or he was still mad about it.

'Where are they now?'

'They drowned in a storm when I was in the sixth form.'

'Shit, sorry.' He looked at Leo again more sympathetically, but Leo was looking down at the table top. Joe waited for him to look up.

'It was a long time ago. And I was here. If I were there, I would have drowned too. So, I figure, I'm grateful.'

There was a long silence. Joe watched as Leo ran his hand through his hair, brushing it back off his forehead. Leo's eyes, previously wide open, now appeared hooded and dark. Joe wanted to say something comforting, but he couldn't find the right words.

As he chased the food around his plate, he felt deflated. He wondered if he'd ever get the hang of chopsticks, wondered if he would ever be Leo's equal at anything? At last Leo spoke.

'You're doing well. That's the Chinese way. When you've mastered that I'll show you how the Japanese do it.'

'There's a difference?'

'Almost everything the Chinese and Japanese do is different. They make a point of it.'

'How old are you?'

'Twenty-five.'

'You?

'Twenty-one, last November.'

'I was pretty young when I lived with my parents, but one thing I do remember is we seldom wore any clothes.'

'Why doesn't that surprise me?' Leo looked confused. 'The first day I saw you. I didn't know they made shorts that small.' Joe leant in. 'But I like them — I like them a lot.' He smiled at Leo, but then glanced over at the woman behind the counter. Leo followed his gaze.

'She doesn't speak much English.'

'Good.' He slid his hand across the table, so the very tip of his index finger met the index finger of Leo's splayed hand.

'She's not blind though,' Leo added, and Joe quickly moved his hand back to the edge of the table. Leo's eyes darted back quickly, meeting Joe's, with an expression somewhere between mischief and guilt. 'No, I like it. I like it a lot.' Joe slipped his hand back across the table.

'Which school?'

Leo didn't answer immediately. Then, came the eventual reply, 'Can I *not* tell you that?'

'Sure.'

'It's just that I hated it and you'll draw automatic conclusions that will be wrong.' Leo looked at him. 'It's nothing personal. It's just that everyone does. I'll tell you if you *really* want to know.'

'No, that's okay.' Joe took his hand and slid it under the table. In response, Leo pushed his leg hard against Joe's. They looked at each other without speaking for a moment and then, as if on cue, they both turned back to their food. Eventually, Leo seemed to perk up.

'Nah, it wasn't that bad. I learnt a lot, not from school, but off my own bat. During the break I was usually the only one in the whole place. They had a good gym, a pool and an amazing library. I learnt German, extracurricular, only because it aggravated the masters to have to organise it. All they could ever do was talk about the war. It was my way of getting back at them and it worked for me. I kept it up at varsity because by then I had a thing about wanting to read Goethe in his own tongue.' Joe shrugged so Leo continued. 'Eighteenth-century German writer. *Prometheus* — that's sort of my thing. Sorry I was a wanker about Voltaire.'

'It's all right. I'm a bit thick sometimes.'

'I doubt that.' Leo looked down. His eyes skirted across the table top and then back up at Joe. 'Actually, I know that's not true. You know something?' He didn't wait for an answer. 'I think you're right about the universe, it does screw with us sometimes just because it can. Try reading Descartes or Spinoza.'

They talked for a while about the jobs they were working on and builders they knew, then they moved on to the project they'd worked on together. Eventually they realised how late it was. They'd been at the table a much longer time than their meals and a couple of bottles of ginger beer, all cleared long ago, warranted. Leo suggested they go. Joe reached over and took a sleeve of chopsticks from the vase.

'You reckon I can take these home? I want to practise.'

'No problem.' Leo turned to the woman behind the counter. 'Lan will be fine about it.' He motioned to the woman, demonstrating that Joe wanted the chopsticks and after a moment or two she smiled broadly.

'Yes, yes, take, take. Thank you.' Joe wondered if anyone ever said 'no' to Leo.

Back at the flat, Leo accepted Joe's invitation to come in. They crept through the front door and made their way quietly into the kitchen. Placing the chopsticks on the island countertop, Joe asked, 'Want a beer?'

'Sure. There's only so much ginger beer I can take.' He reached into the fridge and took out two red cans. Opening one, he handed it to Leo. They stood at the kitchen bench side by side, not saying much. Joe's hand played gently against Leo's thigh as together they listened to the fridge vibrate. Once Leo had finished his beer, Joe asked, 'You want to stay?'

Leo turned to look at him.

'Yes, but to be honest,' he glanced at the floor for a minute, 'I'm sort of sore. All of that . . . it's new for me.'

'Yeah, me too — sore that is.' Joe smiled and, moving in, kissed Leo gently on the lips.

Leo winced and put his hand to his face. 'Sore, remember?'

Joe slipped his arms around Leo's waist, placed his head on his chest and listened to his heartbeat. Reluctantly, he opened the front door for Leo to leave. Forgetting everything they'd said, they kissed and then kissed again, their scruff-burnt skin stinging. On kissing the third time, Leo bit long and hard on Joe's lower lip before pushing himself away with an exaggerated groan.

'See-yah. Tomorrow maybe?' Joe watched, his heart beating hard, as Leo climbed into his ute and closing the door slowly went back to the kitchen. Picking up the two empty cans he crushed them before placing them in the bin under the sink. He wiped down the already clean bench. He refolded the tea towel that hung over the oven door and turned off the light. Stopping, then turning back, he picked up the chopsticks from the bench.

As he passed through the entrance hall, Joe heard a slight tap on the door. Wind, he guessed, but he'd look anyway. It took less than a second to recognise the outline in the frosted glass. He opened it. Leo stood there, looking kind of glum, his eyes on the ground.

'Joe, sorry. I'm just not ready.'

'Yeah . . . I get it.' Joe felt his face fall, but he smiled wanly.

'No. I mean, I'm not ready to go home. Can I stay? Is it okay if we just sleep?'

Leo left before it was light, but he turned up on site at lunchtime. They ate together in Leo's ute at the end of a cul de sac, fronting a little reserve nearby. Leo played Joe one of his mixtapes. It was all punk stuff from before grunge and Britpop. Leo, although older than Joe, seemed too young for this music. Joe asked him about it.

'My height and facial hair got me into clubs before I was even fifteen. Mainstreet, the Gluepot, I saw a lot of this music live.'

'No shit! You actually went to those places?' he looked at Leo, a little in awe. 'Did you see the Sex Pistols?'

'No.' Leo frowned.

'Why, don't you like them?'

'They're great, but they never came here — they weren't really a touring band. Too chaotic.' There it was again, Leo's uncanny ability to make him feel dumb. Joe leant back against the headrest and stared straight ahead. He listened to the tape, some of it was poppy enough, even danceable, but most of it seemed brooding and angry. Leo placed his hand on Joe's bare knee and then slid it up onto his thigh.

'You hate Nirvana, right?' Joe asked.

Leo cocked his head suspiciously. 'Why? Do you like them?'

'No, not really, but I like that Cobain got us together.' Leo looked confused. 'It doesn't matter,' Joe added. He had a sudden flash of panic. 'We *are* together, right?'

'Yeah we're together,' Leo replied, then putting his hand on his chest like an All Black lining up to sing the national anthem said, 'though if I'm entirely honest, I don't know exactly what *this* is. From where I stand it's all pretty new and intense, but yes, we're in whatever this is together.' He smiled, raising both eyebrows and eyelids, so Joe saw the rare sparkle of his grey eyes.

'May I come over tonight?' Leo asked.

'Yes, great,' Joe said and then stopped, suddenly remembering, 'except my flatmates — they're having this work thing. It can get rowdy, go for a while.'

'Work thing?'

'Well, to be honest, it's a lingerie party. A whole lot of drunk women — it's not really something someone who looks like *you* wants to be around.' Leo cringed.

'No,' he answered abruptly. 'And will you be joining them?'

'Well they sort of don't mind me being there.'

'Can you bail?'

'Yeah, sure. Where? Your place?'

'My place?' The look on Leo's face caused Joe to wonder if maybe Leo might be hiding something. He feigned nonchalance.

'Sure, why not? Is there a problem?'

'It's small.'

Joe felt the relief wash over him. Was that all it was? He gave Leo a sultry smile. 'Space is not a requirement for what I'm planning.'

As Leo dropped him back at the site, he scribbled his address on a piece of paper and wrote something under it. His hand didn't linger as he handed it over. Joe was relieved, as high on the scaffolding the guys were watching.

Joe looked at the house and again at the paper in his hand. The address was right. Leo had described a big old two-storey house on Mount Eden Road. The note read 'down drive — gates and tennis court.' He climbed out of his ute. The drive was wide. It headed straight past the house as if it were a road leading somewhere in its own right. He walked down it cautiously, feeling the eyes of the neighbouring houses on him. There they were, the gates, huge, rusted iron things, on brick columns at the end of a high dark-green hedge separating the house from whatever lay beyond. They were open. Looking closer, he figured it had been a long time since they had last been closed. There it was, what he supposed had once been the tennis court, a large rectangle of unmown grass under the shade of two enormous oak trees. The roots had long since creased the playing surface but to one side stood a rusting umpire's stand. Over it, someone had strung fairy lights. Nestled under the trees was a small roughcast cottage painted the colour of a malt biscuit. French doors deeply recessed into the front façade of the building were picked out in the same white paint that still clung in shreds to its low veranda. He peered at the little house. How well it matched Leo — handsome, refined, but somehow a little scarred and all alone. As he stood there, taking it all in, Leo suddenly came bounding out of the front door towards him in big strides. He took him in his arms and kissed him vigorously.

'Welcome.'

'It's great,' Joe said, gesturing at the house.

'Yep. It's weird, like me, but I love it. It used to be a tennis pavilion. The big house is in four flats, but my place is pretty small. Come in. I'll give you the two-second tour.'

Small was an understatement. The whole thing was no bigger than the lounge of Joe's flat — smaller even. There was only one significant room and, walking in, it took just a second to accustom himself to its contents — a large bed, a pair of tall homemade stereo speakers, two bookcases — one big, one small — and an interior strewn with clothes and more books. Breathing in, it smelt strangely good. It smelt of man — not the leftover locker room variety, all old sweat and foot odour — but the fresh, earthy scent of a recently showered man and overlaid on top of that, the smell of one very particular man.

Leo led him through a narrow door to one side of a large, central fireplace. There was a small kitchen and a table, with just enough space for two, above which were pinned a whole lot of postcards — buildings, people and little flyers for films and gigs — some quite old now. Among them was a photograph of Leo, his face thinner, hair wilder, with his arms around a skinny girl. Leo caught his eye.

'That's England.'

Leo pointed out a tiny bathroom. 'It's best to shave in the kitchen sink.' The only additional room, entered from the far end of the worn wooden veranda, housed Leo's bike, his tools and some unfinished woodworking projects.

Back in the main room they sat together on the edge of the bed, which took up the lion's share of the space. It was a platform raised on wooden plinths.

'I made it,' Leo said, as Joe ran his hands admiringly over its surface. 'The joints, they're Japanese — traditional.' He stroked the figured sheet of plywood that extended a good width past the futon mattress. 'I hand-selected that and the headboard.' He turned to see a beautiful piece of figured plywood, but he laughed when he saw that Leo had clamped an old, black 1950s spun aluminium gooseneck reading light to the headboard. 'I've had that since the boat.' On the ledge, created by the plywood sheet along the two long sides of the bed, rested an array of glasses, used coffee cups and more books.

'You like books then?' Joe asked with a grin, looking at the bookcase and then at the piles on the floor.

'Books, music, building, there's not much else to me, I'm afraid.'

'Oh, there's a lot more to you than that.' Joe lay back on the bed.

Back in his own flat the next morning, Joe stood in the kitchen with his bowl of cereal. Before he'd seen Leo's place, he'd thought his own flat a good score. Looking now at the pink laminate cabinets with their pale grey bench tops and rimu edge, the microwave, the coffee plunger and the electric clock that, along with the fridge, never seemed to stop grunting and groaning, there was nothing to suggest anyone interesting lived there at all. He chucked his bowl in the dishwasher, closed the door and headed for work.

For the next week or two, Joe and Leo moved back and forth between the cottage and the flat. They saw each other every day and spent only one night apart when Joe went to have dinner with his mother. Leo turned up for lunch a couple of times, but Joe had to ask him to stop because, as 'the short girl' was nowhere to be seen, Hayden was starting to ask questions as to why Leo was hanging around all the time. Joe longed for the day that he and Leo might again be on a site together through the day and in bed together at night.

Joe climbed to the top of the umpire's stand and sat down in the seat, legs spread wide. It was colder now and getting dark, and the lights were on in one of the flats over the hedge. Through one window he could see a kitchen bench bathed in overhead light, but the rest of the old house was in darkness. Wandering over, Leo stepped up and balanced himself on the crossbar at the bottom of the stand. Reaching up to touch Joe's face, he missed his mark. Instead, his hand trailed slowly down Joe's chest and torso and came to rest on his groin. He squeezed the bulge in Joe's jeans hard and smiled up at him.

'Take 'em off.'

'What?'

'You heard.'

'Leo!' He gestured towards the flats.

'It doesn't matter. They can't see.'

Joe fumbled with the belt and then unhooked the stud at the top of his jeans and unzipped his fly. Leo grabbed the waistband of his trousers and pulled. The jeans caught around his knees and there Leo left them, their white pockets exposed to the fresh night air. Leo waited a second before pulling down Joe's underwear.

Joe leant forward, placing his two hands in the thick black mass of Leo's hair and guided him down but Leo reached up and brushed away his hands, beginning a long slow stroke into which Joe immediately gave in. Joe placed his hands above his head, gripping the top-most slat of the chair back, in order to anchor himself. He closed his eyes. When he opened them again a few minutes later, a man was standing at the sink of the brightly lit kitchen across the way, gazing out into the dusk.

Leo was working furiously now, and Joe's focus was fluctuating. Regaining his vision, he unintentionally caught the eye of the man in the window. Joe smiled involuntarily, and the man smiled back. Joe tried to compose his face and look as inconspicuous as possible, all the time hoping the hedge was high enough that he couldn't see Leo's bobbing head from where he stood at his kitchen bench. Still, their eyes met again and again. As the spasms took over, Joe forgot the man in the window and clamped his thighs hard on either side of Leo's head, trapping him between his legs.

A second later Leo, spluttering now, wrenched his legs apart. His head sprung up like that of a swimmer having reached the pool edge. His bemused expression made Joe grin broadly. Leo gave an exaggerated gulp — his Adam's apple bobbing in his throat — and then let out a gasp of relief. He laughed. Pulling himself up so he was face to face with Joe, Leo kissed him. Joe could taste himself on Leo's lips. He placed his forehead on Leo's.

'You're getting pretty good at that for a straight man — have you been practising?'

'Who said I'm straight?'

'Bisexual then?'

Leo sighed. 'What is it with labels? And before you say it, I'm not on any kind of spectrum either. In the end, aren't we all just men? And aren't all men really capable of all sorts of things? Men with men, meeting practical needs.'

'Is that what this is?' said Joe as he pulled up his jeans.

'Don't spoil things.'

'I won't. It's cold so come up here, keep me warm, and wave to the neighbours as they do the dishes.'

Leo took his place on the top of the stand, next to Joe.

'Were they there the whole time?'

'She's just arrived, but yep, he was.'

'Shit.'

Together they watched as the couple washed their dishes, marvelling at a domestic situation so different from their own. Leo put his arms around Joe.

'Stay.'

'I was going to.'

Taking Joe's hand in his, Leo said, 'No, I mean move in. You've seen it. There's not much room, but we can make it work.'

CHAPTER 3

There was a fire in the grate and the small room felt cozy. Leo, dressed only in a t-shirt and his underwear, was sprawled on the bed, staring at the ceiling, listening. The stereo was playing 'Seven Views of Jerusalem' by The Teardrop Explodes.

Wilder was the first of Leo's albums Joe had taken a real liking too. Still, he was bored. Taking a deep breath, he exhaled loudly. Leo looked up.

'What is it?'

'What's what?' Rolling back on the bed, Joe looked at Leo.

'Why the big sighs?'

'How do you get by without a television? Really? There must be times when you wish you had one.'

'What do you mean?'

'What do you do, when you're not, you know—'

'When I'm not at lingerie parties? I read or listen to music.'

'Yeah, I get that. Still, what about all the stuff you miss?'

'What stuff?' As Leo smiled, Joe knew already that he wasn't going to win this one. He didn't win any of them, but he'd keep going — it was something to do.

'The stuff that connects you and everybody else, so you've got things to talk about.'

'Give me an example?' Shit, what was it with Leo that a single glance could send almost everything fleeing from his mind? Every television programme he had ever watched had, in the second it had taken Leo to say those four words, somehow slunk away out of reach of his recall. He struggled for a long while before answering.

'*MASH.*'

'Is that still on?' Turning to the nearest bookcase, Leo reached over and tossed him a book. Joe caught it in mid-air and looked at the spine.

'*Catch-22*.' He stared quizzically at Leo.

'It's basically *MASH*.'

'Nah, we dodged this one at school.'

'Dodged?'

'The other form class got this.'

'What did you get?'

'*Oliver Twist*, I think.'

'What do you mean, "I think"?'

'We got it. Not sure if it was that year. All the same to me, I never really read it. Didn't have to, we watched the video in class. I got the gist. I liked some of the songs.'

'The book is great — one of the best and perfect for you.'

'How?'

'Well, you're both street urchins. Except he's East End and you're a Westie, but you're both always asking for more.'

Joe watched as Leo took down another book from the big bookcase and hurled it playfully, striking him in the stomach. Leo, ignoring Joe's 'death by book' act, had resumed his position on the bed and stretched over to scoop up his book from the waiting pile. The music had stopped and the fire was flickering out now. It was too hot to bother with another log.

'Read,' he instructed sternly. Lying next to Leo, on what was already *his* side of the bed, Joe held the book open at the first page. He stared at the words for a moment but his eyes soon strayed to the taut skin of Leo's forearms as he held up his book. Transfixed, Joe's eyes moved up along the line of Leo's bicep. Trapped by the cuff of his t-shirt, it bulged attractively. There was *that* vein. Joe put his hand out and with one finger lightly stroked the curving line of Leo's arm. With a mock forcefulness, Leo removed Joe's hand and placed it back on the surface of the bed. 'Read,' he repeated.

Joe stared blankly at the page. Leo would come around to his way of seeing things in a minute, he was sure of it. He began counting silently: *one, two, three*. When he got to one hundred he figured he'd better turn the page. At the top of the next page, he started again from zero. This was even more boring than before. Sitting up, he pulled off his shirt. Looking over, he surveyed the rise and fall of Leo's chest and sighed loudly.

'There will be a test.'

Joe groaned and lay down, returning to the book. This time he turned another page without counting. After a while, his eyes having skimmed the words erratically, he placed the book on the bed and yawned.

'Tough going?'

'Nah, it's okay.' He glanced at the cover of Leo's book. *The Courtier* by someone called Baldassare Castiglione. He thought for a moment what Hayden would do with that — Castrated Bald-ass — something like that. He watched Leo as he read for a while. It was clear he was engrossed in the book and unlikely to put it down anytime soon. Joe picked up his book again. Opening it a few pages in, he stared at the page.

'Changed books, I see?'

Joe looked at the front cover and then at the one on the bed — the two books had the same dull green hardcover bindings. He blushed hot with embarrassment and turned back to the first page of the original book and read: 'Among other public buildings in a certain town, which for many reasons it will be prudent to refrain from mentioning, and to which I will assign no fictitious name, there is one anciently common to most towns, great or small: to wit, a workhouse.'[1]

'Prudent?

'Wise.'

'To wit?'

'An adverb.'

'What do they do again?'

'Try namely or was.'

Joe nodded. 'Okay.'

'Did it work?'

'Yep.'

Leo returned to his book and, lying now on his back, settled further into the bed. Seeing an opportunity in Leo's shift of position, Joe moved closer, resting his book against the hard muscles of Leo's stomach. He draped his free hand across Leo's narrow hips. Leo raised his book higher to accommodate Joe.

Joe read on for a while then he ran his hands down the contours of Leo's unclothed legs. Finishing the return journey, he lightly stroked the bulge in Leo's underwear with his fingertip.

'There will be a test,' Leo repeated.

'That's how they ruin books, you know.' Joe lowered his head so his nose and mouth rested against Leo's stomach. He breathed in.

'What do you mean?'

'Tests.' The cotton of Leo's shirt, pressed against Joe's lips, muffled the word but Leo still heard.

'Well, a reward then.' Joe raised his head again, looking at Leo directly.

'People aren't really called "Thingummy", or "Bumble".'

'Aha. So, you *are* reading it this time?' Leo wasn't looking at him. His eyes were again following the lines of type on the page in front of him, so Joe gave in. He read to the end of the chapter. Then, congratulating himself, he moved on to the second.

'I'm up to that bit now.'

'Which bit?'

'Where he asks for more.' Joe looked imploringly at Leo. 'Please, Sir, can I have some more?' Leo smiled but returned to his book. Joe looked around.

'So, this is it, I've moved into a workhouse. All reading and no sex.' He delivered his best pout.

'Come here.' Leo took the book from him, but the kiss didn't come. Instead, he took up Oliver's story and began to read.

No one had read aloud to Joe since he'd sat on the mat at primary school. Being read to was weird, really uncomfortable. He wanted to laugh. He wanted to take the book back, but Leo's voice was serious. Then he began to concentrate on the deep, seductive sound and the warmth of his boyfriend's body. Placing his head on Leo's torso and draping his arms around him, he breathed in heartily. He drifted into the story. When eventually Leo put the book down, Joe took it up and without a word turned over with his back against Leo and continued reading.

That night as he lay back with his head against the pillow Joe thought for a moment about Ms Tring, his old English teacher. He realised now how hard she'd been trying, and he felt sorry for her. She'd told him he needed to 'pay attention in class' and that he was 'bright but that he needed to apply himself'. Back then nothing much captured his attention. His only goal had been to get into his trade course. He'd done that. But from the day he'd first met the man, book in hand, who now lay sleeping next to him, he had sensed that Leo was also disappointed in him, just as Ms Tring had been. 'Failing to meet his potential.' He'd heard that too, often enough.

He did worry that Leo might tire of him if all their relationship had going for it was sex, but he hadn't really known before what else he had to offer. Finishing *Oliver Twist* all of a sudden seemed critically important. Reading it properly and then picking up the next book Leo decided to hurl at him, whatever that might be. Leo needed to talk books with him, that was the crucial connection he needed to make. Then, as Joe began again to think about the universe and the improbability of its logic, he drifted into sleep.

Leo was restless, unusually so. He hadn't been able to settle on either a book or the right music. For the last half hour, he'd been pacing up and down at the end of his room. Then, standing in the doorway of the kitchen, hands on the doorframe, he leant in to stretch his pectorals. Then he'd turn and again walk the few short steps across the end of the bed to the front door. Suddenly, he reached for his jacket.

'Let's go out?'

Looking up, Joe asked, 'Where?' Not that it mattered. Joe knew he would go anywhere Leo asked. Beyond work, the supermarket, the little Chinese place, and a couple of movies, they hadn't really left the flat together in weeks. He hadn't met any of Leo's friends yet.

'The pub.'

Joe raised his eyebrows quizzically. 'You messing with me?'

Leo didn't like pubs, and Joe could guess why. Leo would get hit on. Leo got hit on most places — supermarkets were big — but pubs – well, he could imagine. Women, unattached or frustrated with their current attachments, would gravitate towards him. Then there'd be guys, who took one look at Leo and assumed he was an arrogant prick. They'd pick arguments to boost their egos or impress their women. The thing was Leo just wanted to be left alone. A pub wasn't going to be the best place to achieve that.

As they pulled out of the driveway, Leo turned left.

'Where are we going?'

'The city — there are some things I want to show you.' Joe put his feet on the dashboard in front of him and laced his shoes.

Leo parked his car in the shadow of a large, pale, stone church and gestured across the road at an old Victorian corner pub. Joe looked across. With its arched windows arranged in regimented lines, it was forbiddingly severe.

A moment later, standing on the footpath outside, Joe scanned the name in the glass above the door — Prince Arthur. Before he could ask who that had been, Leo ushered him in. There was no music. Instead, the TAB results played on a screen that at any moment was about to disappear into the cloud of blue smoke. The source of the smoke was a smattering of ancient old men who, arranged on stools along the bar, each had cigarettes clamped between their few teeth. Their hunched forms reminded Joe of a line of charred piles after a house fire he'd once seen. Although the barman and the punters seemed to recognise Leo, they either didn't notice or didn't care as, glasses in hand, Leo and Joe slipped through a pair of closed doors into the empty private bar.

Joe looked around and gathered his bearings. It made sense now. This was a pub Leo could drink in alone, undisturbed. Joe looked at the glass on the table in front of him, its surface etched by the pub's steriliser. Lifting it to his lips, he took a sip.

'I don't usually drink pints.'

'Really?' asked Leo.

'Haven't you noticed? Sometimes I've sort of got to watch myself — with this stuff.' He hesitated before adding, 'You know something?' He leant forward. 'If there's a girl around I'll order a shandy, and the barman will presume it's for her. You give her the other pint and just tell anyone who asks you're drinking Australian lager — but really no one asks.'

'So, you date the kind of girls who drink pints?'

'I don't date girls — but you know, camouflage, they have their uses.'

'Don't try it here.'

'What do you mean?'

'You're getting the next round.'

'Hell.' Looking into his glass, Joe wasn't sure what was scarier, the idea he might be required to drink another pint, or that he would have to navigate its purchase, but for the moment he concentrated on the contents of the glass in his hand and let Leo talk. He had figured early on that Leo, initially so silent, rather liked talking. He just didn't waste his time with the conversations encountered on building sites, or pretty much anywhere else.

Leo was talking now about the room they were in. Joe's eyes followed Leo's outstretched hand as he pointed to details high up, but the paint was so thick and yellow with nicotine, he struggled to see the finer details.

'I don't get it.'

'Get what?'

'Well, most builders do what they do because they're into building new, but it's this stuff you like.'

'I suppose it is, really.'

'How did you get into it? Building I mean.'

Leo leant back in his seat. 'I love books, but universities do weird things to them. They tear them apart until there's nothing left. Victorian lit, the stuff I like, they made sure you knew it was a dead end. They said you couldn't write books like that now, not if you wanted to be taken seriously. It seems no one wants to be simply told a story; they want to be emotionally involved in the journey with the characters. It's voyeuristic. You see I had thought I might . . .'

'Might?'

'Write. Then I gave up on that idea and took off to England. I got a job as a labourer and then did a sort of training course, half on site, half fast-track apprentice, designed for older guys. Funny, all I had was school woodwork, but I was really good at it. The thing is, I'd already discovered that they're the same, writing and building. Builders use their brains and their hands in just the same way as a writer or poet — creating something that lasts — or should last.'

Joe looked at him. 'And the old stuff?'

'In England, they don't pull things down, not much. You know, we worked on a job. It was a hospital, built in 1719, the same year *Robinson Crusoe* was published. The Germans missed it both times and so there it was. It wasn't big but adapted it was just as modern as any other hospital. Have you seen photographs of the old Auckland Hospital building?' Joe shook his head. 'They built it to be, that is, to *look like*, a Neapolitan palace. It was beautiful but, you know, they demolished it before it was even sixty years old. We do it all the time here — it's tragic. We'll regret it in the end when there's nothing left except glass.' He gestured at the room. 'All this is going.'

'Going?' Joe felt a sudden interest in the room that he had just so readily dismissed. He looked at Leo and then up at the ceiling, trying to remember what Leo had said about its patterned surface. As he did, he thought to himself: *read, look, listen, that's what matters, stupid*, but with the pint already swilling in his head, he suspected he wouldn't remember tomorrow. Joe snapped back as Leo spoke.

'I'll show you later. Building matters, you know, it's not just a job. You only really see the honesty in people, if there is any, in the things they create.' Leo took a drink. Joe sat back to think it all through. He had never really thought about building in those terms before. About how it all connected, as a means of expression.

Until now, building had been just a job, and not the most exciting one at that. Leo dropped his empty glass onto the table top with a clunk.

'Your turn.'

'Hell.' Joe drained the last of his glass in a single gulp. Wiping his lips, he stood, picking up the two empty glasses from the table.

'What are you doing?'

'Taking these back, why?'

'I wouldn't. They'll think you're trying to impress someone and the game will be up.'

Joe frowned and put the glasses down then made for the public bar. Last time the residents had all pretty much ignored him, now they all seemed to stare as he walked across the room. He stood in front of the bar, in what felt like a spotlight, for a while before the barman begrudgingly moved away from his conversation.

'Well?' the barman asked.

'Two pints of red.' The barman didn't move. Clearing his throat, Joe added. 'Please.' He knew immediately from the barman's sneer that the late addition of manners had been a mistake.

'ID?'

'What?'

'Identification. You got some, kid?' With the television screen between races, the last of the men in the bar turned towards him, keen to watch this new live show unfold. His face flushed red under their gaze. Reaching into his back pocket, he pulled out his wallet. Opening it, he presented it to the barman. Glancing at the licence, the barman grunted, and Joe put his wallet back in his jeans. Leaning forward, he poured two pints and placed them on the bar in front of him. Joe picked them up and turned towards the door.

'They're not free, you know.' The barman spoke loudly so that his audience would hear and on cue they chortled.

Joe turned. 'What?'

'Are you going to pay for them?' Joe trembled, causing the beers to slosh a little. 'Spill them after you've paid for them mate.'

One of the men at the bar laughed loudly and then began coughing, a deep wrenching cough that made it sound as if he was in danger of bringing up his lungs into the dirty handkerchief he had taken from his pocket. Placing the glasses back on the countertop, Joe again took out his wallet and this time extracted a note.

'You took a long time,' Leo remarked as Joe resumed his place at the table. 'Anything up?'

'He called me "kid" and asked for ID! I've been drinking in bars since I was seventeen. It's never happened before. Arsehole.'

'No, not in the bars you drink in, I don't imagine it has.'

'What does *that* mean.'

Leo leant forward and kissed him quickly. 'There you are, a first for me — kissing a boy in a pub.' So, *kid*, stop sulking and drink that quickly. We have things to do.' Joe looked at the volume of beer in front of him and shuddered.

The drop was greater than Joe had anticipated. He fell awkwardly, but Leo grabbed his upper arm before he hit the asphalt.

'Let's walk it off,' Leo suggested, pointing in the direction of the waterfront. Joe could do that. Concentrating hard, he put one foot carefully in front of the other. A moment later, finding his equilibrium, he fell into step alongside Leo. Until, unannounced, another wave of beer-fuelled unsteadiness overtook him and he swerved involuntarily, teetering on the edge of the footpath, pulling himself up just before he toppled over the kerb and into the gutter.

'Good idea, you can see more from there.'

'More of what?' asked Joe, gesturing vaguely at the near-empty street. Leo pointed up at the front of the buildings above the veranda line.

'Take a good look now because it's all going.'

'What do you mean?'

'As I was saying before — for the new casino. It's all getting ripped out for a giant towering sewer pipe right in the heart of the city. This whole side of the street — levelled. One day, sometime in the future, I suspect this whole street will be gone.'

Joe wasn't sure he'd ever driven this street, let alone walked it — no, he was sure he never had — but, regardless, he didn't want it to go. If it meant something to Leo, it meant something to him, and probably to hundreds of other people. Joe, his feet carefully following the line of the blue basalt blocks of the kerb, read out the names on the façades aloud.

'Leader Press. Hill and Plummer.'

'Printers. Hill and Plummer were wallpaper.'

Joe was starting to understand. He spied a building that looked very much like the one they'd just left. 'There's another old pub. Let's go in and look.'

'That's the Hobson. It's been closed up for years, but there is something great about it. Come.'

As they stood in front of the old hotel Joe climbed onto the low sill of one of the large windows but the old brown roller blinds were pulled down tight, and he couldn't see inside. Jumping down, he landed sprawling on the footpath. Grabbing him by the shoulders, Leo picked him up and half-marched, half-dragged Joe until he stood directly in front of a section of the wall.

'Spread 'em.' Placing his hands under Joe's upper arms, he lifted them above his head. Linking his foot around Joe's and pushing the other leg hard with his knee, he spread Joe's legs and pushed him against the side of the building.

'What, here?' Joe gasped in mock surprise.

'Press yourself against the building,' Leo instructed.

Joe complied. The entire length of his body rested against the concrete — like a criminal spread-eagled against a wall.

'It's warm, really warm.'

'The sun warms it in the day. Then it stays warm till late at night. What is it now, June? It's sort of like a night-store heater.'

Joe turned. Smiling at Leo, he lay with his back against the wall and gazed across the road.

'There's another pub.'

'The Empire. Another time. I think "the kid" has had enough. Come on.'

They crossed Victoria Street, still heading towards the waterfront. As they walked side by side, Leo started talking again. He spoke slowly, each sentence as crisp as the night air, both sobering and intoxicating at the same time.

'When I snuck out of the school dorm at night, I would just hang in town, especially after I had heard some good music. That was '83 or '84. You should have seen it then, Joe.' He walked a few paces. 'You should have seen it when I first saw it. Before the Eighties really kicked it in the guts. It was beautiful, an unbelievably romantic city.' Leo gestured up at the line of the street. 'Victorian buildings everywhere — department stores, theatres, cinemas, ballrooms, billiard halls — big Gothic things and little Classical temples side by side.' He stopped for a moment and, turning towards him, said, 'See, Joe, the men who built them, they believed in beauty and permanence. Even better or perhaps worse, I don't know, they believed the buildings they built would be there forever. Now most of them, they've been bowled and there's about to be another wave of it, I can feel it.' Leo stopped. He gestured at the building opposite. 'That used to be a department store. Farmers. It had a famous parrot, but when it comes to the past people always clutch at the wrong things. It wasn't the parrot that mattered.'

Joe could sense how much this stuff meant to Leo, how much he cared about the destruction of his beloved city. Then, from the depths of his memory, something flickered.

'I think I might have been here before — is that possible? Roof garden? Little trikes?'

'Yeah.' Leo put his arms around Joe's shoulders. 'Little trikes — that's what I mean.' They turned off, up a side street.

'What's that?' Joe gestured at a large church that had suddenly loomed up in front of him.

'St Patrick's Cathedral.'

'Auckland has a cathedral?'

'Two. And a synagogue.' Joe stopped for a moment. He rested on a low wall, hoping that it too was warm. Looking around, he marvelled for a moment at the beauty of the newly discovered city that surrounded him.

'This is really nice.' Leo smiled, and Joe felt the warmth of pleasure trickle through his veins.

'You know, I've been wondering something.'

'What's that?'

'Why I haven't met your friends. And now I have.'

'What do you mean?'

'These buildings. You speak about them as if they're your friends.'

Leo thought for a moment. 'They are my friends, friends who need rescuing. They're outcasts like me, caught in the wrong time and place.'

'All beauties, like you.'

'Don't.'

'Why don't you like it when I mention your looks? You are handsome, you're probably the most beautiful man I've ever seen.'

Leo scowled. 'It's not something I asked for, and I hate it.' He gestured at himself. 'I wouldn't wish handsome on my worst enemy. Do you know what I hate most of all about it? It delivers things I don't earn. My parents, they were like that, living off what they hadn't earned, things they hadn't made.'

Desperate to lift Leo's mood back to where it had been, Joe said, 'It delivered me, didn't it?'

'I'd like, like desperately, to think that was something else.'

'Let's go with the universe then.' They walked a few feet apart though at moments the uneven footpath brought them close together. Joe brushed his fingertips against Leo's hand. Then, suddenly, striding a few short steps ahead, Leo turned and began walking backwards so that he was facing Joe, still talking, gesturing left and right. Then he stopped. He pointed to the uppermost floor of the building on the opposite side of the street, which featured four half-round windows.

'They're Diocletian windows.'

'Come on then, let's look,' Joe replied as he darted across the street. Stopping only at the solid front door he pressed his face to the letter slot and peered in.

'Can't see much. Big space. Sort of open. There are columns.' Leo crouched next to him and looked up through the slot.

'High ceilings,' he said.

'This could be the reception, a hang-out space for the apartments, a café and on Saturday nights they could have a DJ — play a bit of lounge.'

'Come on.' Joe suddenly veered back across the road and craned his neck so as to get a good look through the Diocletian windows. 'Penthouses! Half a million each, Italian kitchens, downlights, a spa-bath — maybe a pool on the roof?'

'They've got pressed zinc ceilings.'

'Who wouldn't want to live here?' Joe looked at Leo, his profile outlined by the street light. 'We could do it, you know, Leo — turn this into something — show them how Auckland might be. We just need the cash.'

It became their weekend ritual, finding different beautiful old pubs to visit — the Empire, the Albion, the Aurora, the Naval & Family. Even once to an old bar unexpectedly full of drag queens. There, Leo caused a sensation where he was pawed as if he were a Ken doll. Afterwards, pissed off, he showed Joe the scratches and made it clear, architectural qualities aside, that they wouldn't be returning to that particular establishment. On those nights they'd drink or listen to music in near silence, not needing to speak, not daring to touch. At closing time, when they'd had enough, they'd walk those empty inner-city streets off the main routes, talking music, books or buildings in no particular order, sometimes all at once, until the cold air sobered them up. That the streets were deserted suited them just fine, but it perplexed Joe. How could such a beautiful city be so devoid of life?

On these nights, Joe liked to skirt by the warm surface of the Hobson Hotel and press against it. Joe never said, but the building reminded him of Leo, handsome, warm and sturdy.

Eventually, with their black duffle coats clasped against the wind, they would walk home up Hobson Street, along Karangahape Road and

Symonds Street. Then down Mount Eden Road until they reached their tiny flat and its big bed.

Joe lay on the white sand and watched as Leo, naked, walked up the deserted beach. They had spent almost every weekend of the spring and summer traversing Auckland. With their bikes on the back of the truck, they had explored the North Shore Beaches, the West Coast and the Hunua Ranges. At every vantage point, they'd looked back upon the city, surveying it from every angle. This weekend, the last before Christmas, building projects complete, they had packed their tent and taken a ferry to Rangitoto, only to find the whole island deserted as the rest of the city shopped and partied itself into a frenzy.

Now, having spent the afternoon clambering over the soft, green, rolling hills of Motutapu, Leo had gone in for a swim. Joe had opted instead to doze in the sun. Everything was good. Perfect in fact. He was getting blonder. Leo was getting browner. Almost always shirtless now, Leo seemed, if possible, more beautiful than ever.

Things were *almost* perfect, but for weeks now, whether they were on a sun-drenched beach or a bush-clad hillside, Joe had detected a faint vulnerability, a certain loneliness in Leo that made him seem unreachable. Whatever it was, it wasn't there on the nights they spent in town. Joe watched Leo, now doing handstands on the beach and, grabbing the disposable camera, he took a few lazy snaps. He'd tried to address it with Leo the previous night but Leo's answer, though entirely understandable, had somehow complicated everything. Maybe it was nothing but now, lying back in the sand, Joe once again ran the conversation back through his head.

Leo wanted to see the dawn break over Auckland from the top of Rangitoto. Getting up to the summit in the dark would be complicated, and they had considered camping up there, but the hard rock didn't seem very inviting. So, in the end, they had woken in the dark and set off in the pre-dawn light with a torch, making the top just as the night broke behind them in the east. They'd ended up sitting side by side on the top of the old concrete gun emplacement, on the summit, as the sun rose. In silence, they had watched as the rays of sun began to pick out the taller city buildings from the pre-dawn gloom. Joe had been the one to break the silence.

'You love the city, don't you?'

'Of course.'

'No, I mean more than you do nature — the beaches and stuff.'

'Yes. That's true.'

'Why?'

Leo didn't answer for a while. 'I grew up on a boat, that means an awful lot of wide, open sea. In the end it was nature, the sea, that took my parents. The city's close. Sometimes it can feel as if Auckland has her arms around you. It is as if the city is holding you tight against . . . well, you know . . . against everything.' Not for the first time, Joe was moved by Leo's eloquence and, reaching out, he placed his hand on Leo's leg. 'You've seen it, right, especially at night. The way she moves in close alongside you and sort of whispers in your ear.'

'Like a lover?'

'Yes, exactly, but a lover who is too trusting, too often taken for granted. It's an enticingly supine city — it gets misunderstood.'

'How do you mean?'

'Ravaged. You know the story, Joe, "the pretty girl was asking for it." You've heard them talk on sites, builders with their misogynistic opinions about women. When *we* know all she ever wanted was to be open to the possibilities of life.'

'I never really thought of cities as being like people. What happens to ugly girl cities?'

'Provincial towns. The real dogs become capitals.' Joe laughed and then stopped himself. 'You can laugh, Joe, it's okay.' Leo lay back on the concrete roof.

'It seems wrong somehow to talk about the city being "ravaged" with the dawn so busy bathing things in light, cleansing everything,' Joe spoke quietly. 'That's what it does, don't you think? Metaphorically. It brings a new start and offers up the world new again.'

'Nice idea, Joe. I think you're right.'

'You've always talked about Auckland like it's yours.'

Leo sighed and rolled onto his side, looking towards the city skyline. 'Mine? Not mine. Not really, but she adopted me, I suppose. I used to think we were both searching for something together — Auckland and me.'

'Did you find it?'

Leo didn't answer. The two men sat for a while, watching the changing view before Leo eventually spoke again.

'You, on the other hand, you're a native. This,' he gestured at the city now emerging from the dark, 'is yours. You're a kid from Te Atatū, an Aucklander. No one can argue with that — all this is your birthright.'

'Do you think so?'

'Yes. I hereby give it to you, *sicher aufbewahren*, as the Germans say, in safe keeping.'

'I am truly honoured, Mr Bridge,' Joe replied with a semblance of a bow.

Leo looked directly at him, serious now. 'Take it, Joe. You deserve it.'

Joe slipped his fingers into Leo's open hand. 'When you look at me, when you think of me, I am in paradise.'

Leo smiled. 'Are you talking about me or the city?'

'You. Always *you*. Well perhaps both, now that all this is mine too.'

'It's a nice line.'

'Not mine. It's William Thackeray Makepeace's. I've been thinking about it, about you, about us, ever since I read it.' Leo laughed. 'What's so funny?'

Leo leant over and pushed Joe flat against the concrete, and then, lifting himself over Joe's prone body, straddled him.

'It's William Makepeace Thackeray, *stoopid*.' Leo was grinning, but Joe couldn't help but feel hurt. Then Leo leant in and kissed him and, as if it were almost an afterthought, he said, 'I love you, Joe and I always will — I promise.'

Joe looked at Leo now, lying next to him, face down in the sand on a towel. Joe had been unable to stop himself blurting out declarations of love. At first Leo had just looked at him and smiled. Then with time he had learnt to repeat the words in an echo that left Joe warm but somehow not quite content. This was the first time Leo had taken the opportunity unprompted and the words burned through Joe's heart like a bolt of dawn lightning. But in the aftermath, in that 'I love you' and its attendant promise he sensed a tonal shift, not towards a newer deeper truth, but the faint spectre of a new distance, love as a full stop. Were Leo's words an embryonic act of goodbye, the end of something, or was it simply that he was beginning to realise there was a deep sadness in Leo? Maybe he didn't need to cure it. Perhaps it was simply an essential by-product of who Leo was. Maybe love would solve it for them. They had time.

Looking at the broad muscular planes of Leo's back, Joe again picked up the camera and took a shot. Fuck tone, he thought. He didn't even know what tone was before Leo. He never failed to be seduced away from serious thought by the broadness of Leo's back or the expanse of his chest. But best of all was the rarely glimpsed 3D moment. That place from a viewpoint slightly higher, where one got the swelling curve of his mighty shoulders and a view of both his back and chest. Seeing his opportunity, Joe repositioned himself to frame an ideal shot in the little viewfinder.

As the button clicked, Leo, still face down in the sand, said, 'They won't let you develop those, you know.'

'Ha! Where I take them, they'll keep a set for themselves.'

As the summer wore on, although happier than he'd ever been, Joe began to make space for bits of his old life that his sense of duty made him honour. Although Leo's parents had been Kiwis, he had neither family nor other friends, as far as Joe knew. Sometimes he would make Leo come out with his friends, barbecues mostly. Leo never enjoyed them. Joe knew he disliked the conversations and hated the music. He never said much. His friends, on the other hand, were curious. Who was Leo? How did he fit in? For Joe's part, he struggled to not show affection to Leo in public. He got pissed off when Leo inevitably got hit on by girls. This happened all the time, even among Joe's friends. He wished he could shout, 'Hands off, he's mine.' Worse, when asked, he always felt obliged to reply honestly, 'No, he doesn't have a girlfriend.' Leo, no help, would stand there, silently scowling. Invariably, he got moody and restless. One night, without a word, Leo had simply disappeared from the party. Joe had found him waiting at home later. He didn't give Leo a hard time about it because he understood.

Joe knew Leo craved his time alone. He suspected, on the rare occasions Leo went out alone, he didn't do much else than walk the streets — or sit at a bar surrounded by silent nicotine-stained men. Joe understood. The flat was tiny. It was possible to be in love and still get under each other's feet.

Yes, he and Leo were solid. They were joined more profoundly than other couples were. Leo loved him. He'd told him so. Joe knew it was true. He loved Leo too. They were soulmates — in this forever. So now, if Leo needed some time out, he was okay with it. That was, he figured, part of being an adult and in an adult relationship.

They certainly had their share of blissful togetherness. They established a nightly ritual. Leo, always home first, would turn on the fairy lights. When Joe walked through the door, he would throw back the covers to reveal his beautiful naked body, waiting for Joe to climb in beside him.

Together almost a year, the autumn nights again began to make their presence felt, having shared a birthday each and spent a Christmas together.

One night, Leo disappeared from a friend's birthday drinks. It wasn't anything unusual now, his disappearance almost a ritual in itself, something close to foreplay. Joe knew that once again Leo had simply met his limit of other people and that he'd be there, at the cottage, waiting for him in bed. This time, however, the white lights were not on. Confused, Joe lay on the bed, waiting. Hours later, Leo walked in the door. Joe had never seen him look this way. His expression seemed haunted and he wouldn't look Joe in the eye.

Before Joe could say a word, Leo turned to him, a look of pure anguish on his face, and he said simply, 'I can't do this anymore.'

Phil, his foreman at work, had a place in Grey Lynn. He'd invited Joe to a barbecue.

'There'll be guys from work,' he'd said. A week or two earlier Phil had delivered Joe a warning from management about absenteeism. It came in a haze of other inconsequential information. A warning about damage done to a future he didn't have.

He didn't care about anything other than Leo. He missed Leo's smile. He missed his voice. He missed Leo's arms around him. He missed his smell. It hurt like hell, but he didn't want the pain to stop. The pain was preferable to the risk of forgetting some crucial detail.

One day Phil had, with a flying tackle, stopped Joe walking into the swinging arm of a digger. When he asked, 'What the hell is going on?' Joe had no answer.

After that, Phil seemed to be watching. Sometimes he thought Phil knew, knew about him and Leo or just that Phil knew about him full stop. Other times he told himself Phil was just being nice. It was in this frame of mind that he had said 'yes' to the invitation. Still, he had no plan to front. He'd make an excuse the following Monday.

Late Saturday afternoon, however, he'd found himself parking in Phil's street. Then, slab in hand, making his way to the front door. Out the back, he'd taken one look at the crowd on the deck as it spilled into the garden and only then did he realise that this, the party, it wasn't something he could do. He'd told himself to try. He talked to a couple, but he couldn't stand their unexamined happiness. He wanted to scream at them. He'd drunk a bit. He might have coped with a small party, but this was way bigger than he'd expected. There were neighbours, people from the film industry in which Phil's partner worked, and some builders from the current job. He recognised an actor and some guys from earlier building gigs. He talked to one of them for a while about their new Holden and how the actor was probably a jerk.

Joe knew he should eat. Moving over to the food table, someone passed him a bag of potato chips. He ate them and drank some more. He hated the music. What was it? UB40. His beers were finished, had he drunk them all, had someone helped themselves, he didn't care, he would slip out.

Climbing into his ute, Joe knew he was boozed, but with no bigger problem than getting himself on to the Northwestern motorway, then off at Te Atatū, he'd be fine. It wasn't the first time. There were no cordons this time of year. He checked twice that his lights were on.

He'd been drinking a lot recently. It helped him stay numb. Puking helped too. Puking proved his emptiness. He wasn't going to chunder though, not yet. Not in his ute. Yes, lights were on — indicators too. Wrong lane. That was the exit there. He was travelling in the opposite direction now, away from the motorway. He parked his ute on an empty section of gravel next to a fence. The sign read 'Construction Zone'. It made sense. He'd head for the Empire. No reason other than they'd been there together. He looked in the direction of the Hobson but, like Leo, it had gone. He raised his hand to his forehead in a salute. Everyone was leaving.

He worried the barman might clock the fact he'd had too much but he figured he might as well give it a go. Beer in hand, he took up a position in the garden bar. He bummed a cigarette from a girl, even though he didn't smoke. Offered to repay her with a drink. She was pissed off when he delivered the beer then went off to find another spot.

'Wanker,' she'd called after him. He'd had enough, enough of girls, enough of other people. He stood in a corridor. Not outside the men's room, but close enough, so the crowd was thinner. He drank his pint. Then the crush grew. There was no space left. It started getting hot. The room swam. The lights pricked at his eyes. It was hard to breathe. He put his empty glass down. He headed for the door. There was a bottleneck, those leaving and new punters coming in.

'Joe?' Some guy in the squeeze was talking to him. He seemed familiar, school or somewhere, but he couldn't place him. He was with a group, smartly dressed businessmen and girls in high heels. 'Joe? You all right?'

Joe looked at him again through the haze. 'Leo?' he asked.

'It's me, Kurt.'

'I'm all right.' They made it through the door onto the footpath. Joe pushed at the guy. He didn't want people in his face. The guy's friends called out and he went with them. A blast of air hit. He felt sober for a second. He felt good. He'd walk. Find some music. Find Leo.

He wandered down the hill. That was the way the road was taking him. There was another pub. Not one he'd been in with Leo, but it looked the same, severe, grey, unpainted. There it was, the deeply recessed doorway over the same unnavigable concrete step. Unlike the Empire, there was no crowd outside, no one to push him here. Friendly. The interior was dark. He looked for a seat. There were no stools. The men stood at leaners or the bar. They looked rough. No rougher than in Leo's pubs. They were no doubt harmless. He was used to the looks he got as he walked to the bar now. Before he spoke, the barman leant towards him.

'Got ID?'

'Fuck you.' He wasn't sure why he said it. No, that wasn't true. He knew. He was sick of the shit the world delivered on him. Looking up at the barman, he smiled. He smiled a good smile. His best smile. He knew even then that it was a smile delivered at the wrong time and in the wrong place, but then, burning hot with the righteousness that comes free with a skinful of booze, he smiled again, even more broadly.

'What did you say, Sonny?'

'I said, fuck you. I'm twenty-two. I want a drink.'

The barman leant forward. Grabbing Joe by the front of his t-shirt, he hauled him across the bar. His body lifted into space for a moment before his feet found the foot rail. The barman pressed his face close to Joe's. He smelt the tang of booze and felt the shower of spit with which his words arrived.

'You, you little shite, can fuck right off out of my pub.' Then, with an almighty push, he sent Joe sprawling onto the floor, sliding into the heavy boots of a nearby drinker. The guy leant down and hauled him up by his shoulders.

He asked, 'You okay?' Just as Joe was about to reply, the guy pushed him hard, back in the direction of the bar. This time the brass foot rail of the bar whacked against his shins. His head fell forward. His chest hit the edge of the bar. Someone called out, 'Fight!'

'Nah, leave the ladyboy alone,' another voice replied. The crowd was laughing. Some gathered in a circle around Joe and the guy who'd pushed him.

'Apologise, you queer piece of shit.'

Turning from the bar, Joe said, 'Fuck you, arsehole. I got a right to drink here.' The guy stepped forward.

'Say that again.'

'Ian, forget it.' The barman gestured at two men who stood in the shadows nearby. 'Get him out — he's not worth another visit from the cops. Chuck him.' The two burly men grabbed him and dragged him, feet flailing, to the door. There, with a swinging motion, they threw him out. Just like when Leo had thrown him onto the bed that first night. For a brief moment he was flying, happy. Then he landed, face and hands first, sliding across the asphalt, the rough surface cutting into his hands and cheek. Getting up slowly, he looked down as the blood soaked onto the surface of his palms. He reached up to his forehead and winced. Turning, he made his way back towards the door. The two men blocked his way.

'Move!'

'Look, kid, you want to get yourself killed? Go back inside — fine by us.' They stepped apart. Joe took a step towards the pub door. He didn't see the punch coming, just a flash of something yellow in the light as it hit his cheekbone hard. He fell hard against the building, hitting his head. He slid down the wall in what seemed to him cartoon slow motion, collapsing onto the floor. The other man, sticking his boot in the small of Joe's back, lifted him on his foot and flicked him off onto the footpath. He landed hard and just lay there.

After a long while, he got it together enough to turn onto all fours. He watched as the blood from his cut cheek trickled onto the footpath under him. Then his stomach came up. He spewed. The vomit mixed with the blood. Then it came again more violently. He steadied himself but still swayed. There was blood in his eyes now. He couldn't see clearly. He could make out the arc of the streetlights and the dark grey concrete wall of the pub. He couldn't see the men. They must have gone. He spewed again.

Staggering towards the pub wall, he felt his way along until the smooth flat wall ended. Taking a few steps further he pulled himself up into a sitting position against a different building and in the dark he closed his eyes.

Two cops found him. The doctor in A&E said his teeth were okay. It was either a signet ring or a brass knuckleduster that had done the damage, but given where the incident had occurred he'd put his money on the latter. They'd kept him in overnight, given him morphine.

The next day, the doctor had asked, 'What were you doing at the Bridgeway? It's a bad pub, and you don't look the type.'

'What type am I?'

'Pretty normal. A good kid who maybe has some stuff happening.'

'Why does everyone call me kid?'

'Well, they won't after this?'

'Why?'

'You might be lucky, but I won't lie to you. This is likely to scar. No one's going to think you're a kid anymore.

Joe stood up and went into the bathroom again to look at the purple mess of bruise spilling around the bandage taped to his face. There were pills on the vanity top. They'd probably do it if he took them all. There were other pills too, his mother's, in the cupboard. He'd just drift off to sleep, and there'd be no Leo, no messed-up face, no mindless job, no fucked-up universe, no nothing, just stillness. All he needed was a bottle of vodka or bourbon — easy enough to get. He looked for his car keys, but he couldn't see them so, lying back down on his bed, pill bottle in his hand, he pulled his headphones over his head.

He hated that he'd had to move home, back to the bedroom he'd left the day after his eighteenth birthday, but he'd had nowhere else to go. The poster of three All Blacks clutching the World Cup that he'd pinned up when he was sixteen was still there. Steve McDowall reminded him a bit of Leo. Everything reminded him of Leo.

They'd argued for hours. Now, six weeks later, Leo's words were still circling endlessly in his mind: 'I still love you but not in that way'; 'It was love, but not *in* love'; that it had all got 'too intense'. He'd said they could build something better if Joe would just give him time. Numb at the time, Joe hadn't been able to make sense of any of it. They'd stayed awake all night, sitting in long silences, the gulf between them growing wider with each attempt at explanation. The next morning, Joe had moved out.

The music on his headphones was making everything worse. He looked up at the poster. He hated Steve McDowall, Sean Fitzpatrick and John Drake. All three looked down at him from the poster with contempt. It was simple. They were winners. He was a loser. A loser who picks fights in bars. He was a stupid, ordinary loser thinking about killing himself with pills. He took off his headphones. He *did* want to die.

Leo had gone to Christchurch — one of the neighbours in the front flat had told him. He'd pretty much left the day after Joe and movers had apparently put his stuff in storage, but Joe wasn't sure he believed it. Leo would be back — this was just a mistake.

Joe looked at the bottle and then, putting it on his table, he turned back to the poster. It pissed him off that they were so smug. Gesturing at it with a single raised middle finger, he said quietly, 'Go fuck yourself.' Standing up on the bed, he stood eye to eye with them now. Again, he raised his finger. This time he yelled it, 'Go *fuck* yourself!' His eyes watered. Then, reaching up, balancing on the uneven surface of his bed, he tore the poster from the wall and ripped it into pieces. That felt good. Shaking now, he placed his hand against the wall to steady himself.

There was still a corner of the poster stuck to the wall. He yanked it. A piece of the wallpaper tore away. He pulled at it. A long strip of the paper came off. He ran his fingernail down the seam. Pulling again, he peeled off a larger piece. He continued tearing strips of paper from the wall. Some he left hanging, others he threw across the room. He moved to the next wall, the long side of his bed, and tore a strip across it. Then he tore down to the top edge of the mattress. Jumping down, he pulled the bed away from the wall and, lying across it, tore the paper to the skirting.

He took the New Kids on the Block poster from above his headboard and screwed it up. Climbing on top of his bedside table, balancing for a moment, he booted the medicine bottle hard. It exploded as it hit the wall, showering the room with little green pills. Reaching up, he picked at the wallpaper just under the cornice and ripped.

Suddenly spent, the room in pieces around him, Joe sat for a moment on the floor, his head against his bed.

'What are you doing?' It was his mother. He knew her next question would be, 'Are you all right?' To which he would reply, 'Nothing. I'm fine,' like he'd said every time she'd asked in the last six weeks. Every time he'd come home pissed, every time he'd refused food or ignored her request to get out of bed, every time a simple task like doing the dishes or washing his ute had overwhelmed him.

This time, though, Joe couldn't help himself. He blurted out, 'Leo has left me and I am so in love with him that I don't know how I'm going to live without him.' His mother, leaning around his bedroom door, did her best.

'Leo? This is about another man?'

'I loved him. I *still* love him.' Joe turned away from his mum and arched his neck towards the ceiling. 'Mum, I'm gay.' His mum hesitated for a moment before answering.

'Well, it seems to me you've made a decision, and I respect that. It's your life, your choice, but Joe, so has he — Leo — and you need to respect him and his decision too.' With that, she turned and left the room. Despite that initial pause, she'd spoken quickly, as if she'd already had her reply worked out. He sat looking at the shredded wallpaper and poster, dotted with the little green pills. Leaning forward, crying now, tears mingling with snot, he reassembled the torn fragments of Steve McDowall's face.

CHAPTER 5

Friday night again — beer, dope, nothing new. The guys on site were being dickheads about queers — nothing ever changed there either.

'So, would you bash me if I told you I was a faggot?' He hadn't planned to do this, but something had made him speak crisply and clearly so that there would be no mistake in their hearing. They all laughed for a moment.

'Good joke,' one of them said. Then each of the others repeated it until, like a dying echo, their voices trailed off.

'Except I am. Queer as all fuck. I have been all my life.' None of them was man enough to do anything to him, and the group had quickly broken up.

Hayden was the last to go. He looked at Joe and, after spitting on the ground at his feet, said, 'You! A fucking fag. How, man? We were buds!'

Somehow Joe hadn't died and the world had kept turning. He even wondered for a moment if perhaps, despite everything, he'd been lucky. The mess, the cuts and grazes had cleared. The doctor told him the scar on his face had healed better than they'd expected. A thin white line now ran across his lip, buckling it, pulling it into the white skin of his face. It continued, only barely discernible, for a couple of centimetres across his left cheek before fading into the hollow under his cheekbone.

Another empty weekend ahead. He scanned his rearview mirror, hoping.

The following Monday, Joe discovered the joys of working with blowhard cowards with easy access to pink spray paint. Like everything else, though, the paint didn't kill him. It just took a while to scrub off. When a large day-glo pink hard-on was spray-painted over the bonnet of his ute, jism spurting where the driver's head appeared in the windscreen, he left it. He just couldn't find the energy. It stayed until a cop pulled him over and told him it had to go.

He figured if nothing was going to kill him and he couldn't kill himself, his only option was to stay alive and wait until Leo came back. He *would* come back. He had to. How could he just walk away from what they had? Joe understood about denial. He had lurked like an intruder among the self-help books in the central library. There he had read about loss and the stages of grief. This was different. He knew Leo loved him. They'd had so many plans. They'd talked about setting up in business together.

Eating lunch alone in his ute, Joe looked out at the handsome, refined façade of the old building they were tearing apart across the street. He decided then, if nothing else, he needed to make sure Leo didn't come back to a pile of rubble. Leo had gone — disappeared. The Hobson had gone — demolished. His old face had gone — disfigured. Even Hayden had gone, refusing to even look at Joe. This was his grim reality, but he figured it was up to him to build a brighter kind of future. No one else was going to hand it to him.

At home that night, sitting on the edge of his bed, Joe felt almost good. He looked about the still scarred room. He should really do something about it, his mother was doing her best and, after all, he had wrecked her house. His eye rested upon a brochure on the floor that had been handed to him by a woman at the door of the library. He picked it up and flicked through it and then, before he could change his mind, walked to the phone in the hall and rang, leaving a message, to sign himself up for a Continuing Education course called *An Appreciation of New Zealand Arts & Crafts Movement Houses.*

On the following eight Saturday afternoons he sat quietly in the basement of a university building, listening to the lectures. The tutor, having established he was a builder, frequently consulted him on issues of construction. The old ladies on the course nodded at him respectfully while complaining to each other about the draughty room and the hard wooden seats. Over tea and biscuits on the third Saturday, one woman tried to strike up a conversation.

'Are you one of the Wairarapa Wrights?'

Joe stared blankly at her, not understanding her meaning. Then, slowly, as if he had learning difficulties, she asked, 'Who-are-your-parents-and-where-did-you-come-from?'

He replied, 'My mother's name is Anna, and I've never met my father.' He could tell immediately that Te Atatū, even the Peninsula, wouldn't help.

On the final Saturday, a bus took the class on a tour of what the tutor called, 'The city's most prestigious homes.' Joe couldn't be bothered going. It was only at the last moment he'd changed his mind, hauled on his boots and thrown on a jacket, jumping on board just as the bus pulled out of the carpark. He was glad he had. He had found comfort in the dark, brooding houses, with their shuttered windows, panelled walls and sober finishes.

He became absorbed in the details, entranced as the dimly lit interiors came to life when a shaft of sunlight filtered through a tiny leadlight window, tracing its path across the floor. Moving his foot so that the sun fell across the toe of his boot, Joe wondered how these architects had created interiors so rich, resonant and full of feeling? What special magic had they possessed that he didn't? He ran his hands along the surface of a carved panel. It was only fruit and flowers, but his fingers tingled as if uncovering a buried treasure. The little bunch of carved apples, or perhaps they were berries, weren't at all lifelike though they seemed somehow imbued with life. They seemed to contain a message, delivered in an ancient language, one the craftsmen had left behind especially for him to decipher.

Reluctantly, Joe realised it was time to head towards the bus. As he bent down to the encaustic tiles to lace up his boots, Joe had a fleeting thought. Perhaps this house, the grandest of the tour, had been home to one of Leo's old classmates. He shook his head to dismiss the thought of Leo. When was Leo ever going to get out of his head? Frowning, he noticed a small redheaded boy dressed in an immaculate soccer kit standing on the doorstep at the house end of the entrance porch, watching him. Joe gave him a warm smile.

The kid turned slightly, bending over to rest his soccer ball in the crook between doorstep and open door, and strode towards him. Stopping in front of him, the kid pulled himself up straight and extended his hand.

'I am Master Andrew Campbell. I go to King's Prep.' Standing now, Joe took the boy's hand and shook it, all the time suppressing a smile at the boy's formal address.

'Nice to meet you, Master Campbell, my name is Joe.' Joe hesitated before correcting himself in keeping with the tone, 'That is, my name is Mr Joseph Wright.'

'It's all right, my friends call me Drew, and we're going to be friends, so Joe is okay.'

'Well, good. Then it's nice to meet you, Drew.'

'Joe,' Drew asked with a quizzical expression. 'Why are you wearing those boots? It takes you so long to get them on and off. You really should have thought about that.'

'You're right, they're not sensible, are they?' replied Joe, looking down at his grubby work boots.

'What kind of person are you?'

'What do you mean?' Joe replied. There was something about this kid — he had a precociousness that could only come from a private school education.

Drew touched his lip, tracing the line of Joe's scar on the surface of his own face. 'You look like a pirate.' Joe laughed and subconsciously raised his hand to his own lip. 'What do you do for a crust?'

Joe laughed again at the juxtaposition of a young boy using such an adult expression, probably borrowed from a father or a grandfather. 'Well, Drew, I'm a builder.'

'That explains the boots.'

'Yes, I suppose it does really.'

'What do you build?'

68

'All sorts. Houses and apartments mostly.'

'Houses like this one?'

'Well, I'd like to one day.' He looked around him and then settled again on the boy in front of him. 'You ask a lot of questions.'

'Well, we're friends. You need to know a lot about your friends.'

'Yes, well . . . that's true.'

'Joe, do you have a girlfriend?'

Joe laughed again. This kid had quite a knack for asking the curly questions. 'Ah, no . . . no, I don't.'

'Why not?' asked Drew.

'Um . . . it's complicated.'

'Don't you like girls?'

'Um . . . as I said, it's sort of complicated.'

'I don't like girls. I like boys. Like you. I like you a lot.'

'Well . . . I like you too, Drew.'

'Good. Will you be my boyfriend?'

Joe looked around nervously, unsure how to extract himself from the conversation without offending Drew. As he did so, one of the women from the bus tour by the name of Betty appeared alongside him.

Linking her arm in his, she asked, 'Take me into the garden, Doll. I'm getting a bit wobbly on it.'

'Sorry, Drew, I'm going to have to go.'

'That's okay, Joe, I have to go too. See you round.' He gave a small bow and, after retrieving his ball, ran down the driveway.

'Who was the little princeling?' Betty asked.

'His name is Drew. We're friends apparently,' Joe replied with a delighted grin.

As they set off, arm in arm, Betty guided Joe through the lines of standard roses.

'Margaret Merril, Scentasia, St Paul's Cathedral — she's a woman of taste, Veronica Campbell — not an Iceberg rose in sight. It's an easy mistake, falling for an Iceberg, but she's no beginner, you know?' Before Joe could ask what was so wrong with Iceberg roses, Betty gestured to the low hedge at their feet. 'Aren't the box hedges lovely? So neat, so precise.' He agreed with her. She pointed towards a pretty dovecote. 'Shall we investigate?' As Joe took a step across the lawn to where Betty pointed, his foot hit an uneven piece of paving. He stumbled and grabbed on to his older companion's arm.

'Aren't you supposed to be the one holding me up?' Before he could apologise, Betty took both of his hands in hers and said quietly, 'I lost my husband five years ago. There's not a day I don't miss him. I've been watching you these last few weeks. I get the feeling, well, let's just say, you have the look.'

Joe's mother peered around the bedroom door and gestured in an exaggerated fashion for him to take off his headphones. She'd clearly been calling him for a while.

'Telephone! A lady called Elizabeth Strauss. Posh voice, says she knows you.'

Pulling a face, Joe put down his book and stumbled into the hall to retrieve the phone.

'Hello?'

'Hello Joe, it's Betty, Betty Strauss.'

'Oh hi.'

'I got your number from the class list. I hope you don't mind?'

'No . . . not at all.' He ran his fingers through his hair absent-mindedly. What could Betty possibly want?

'I wondered if you would mind coming over and looking at a little job I have that needs doing? You're the only builder I know, and I don't want strangers in my house.'

Joe thought for a moment. Was he up to this? Didn't he always just do what his boss told him? He barely managed that some days. Then again, Betty had been sweet to him.

'When?'

'Next Saturday morning? 10 a.m.'

Betty's house was a pretty cottage in one of the tightly packed back streets above Freeman's Bay, overlooking the city. Its severe square front was positioned just a metre or so back from the road, but for some reason it lacked a veranda. In its place was a tiny porch with a tent-like iron roof. Below it was a lattice framework. Into this had been cut two large elegant oval openings — each framed in heavy wooden mouldings. On either side, big sad-eyed windows, filled with old silvery tear-stained glass, reflected a lavender hedge bristling with purple flowers.

Inside felt familiar to Joe. Not the home, but the house. He'd ripped out interiors like this on a job back when he first started working. The vibrant red walls, covered in paintings, contrasted with the doors and window frames, painstakingly stripped to their natural honey-coloured timber and then polished. He looked up, knowing the ceilings would be the same. Rich, dark, patterned rugs covered broad, flat floorboards. Once waxed, they were now scrubbed bare by the tread of feet. He gently scuffed the floor with the toe of his sneakers.

Solid dark mahogany sideboards covered with lines of red and blue vases. Were they Chinese or Japanese? Leo had never got around to explaining the difference in chopsticks, let alone pots, but he knew they made a point of being different — that he'd learnt. He stopped and stared for a moment. He liked the way they caught the soft light as it filtered through the front windows. The vases, arranged like a watching army, eyes on the road, made the room seem safe.

Further down the hall, as they headed towards the kitchen, Joe noticed the same light as it spilled in, gently stroking the surface of a patchwork counterpane on what appeared to be a spare bed. It was just like he'd pictured the room in which Oliver wakes at Mrs Maylie's. It seemed to him a happy house, but then again, what did he know about such things?

Joe looked at Betty as she scuttled ahead of him, gesturing at the rooms off the hall. She appeared nimbler than she had been a few weeks earlier. Leading him through to the back of the house, she stopped. Off a small kitchen there was a nook in which sat a scrubbed kauri table. On it, Joe's eyes caught a little cane tray containing lidded crystal pots filled with marmalade and jam and a set of salt and pepper shakers in the shape of hula dancers. Collected together on one edge, they suggested that this was where Betty had her breakfast. An old bentwood chair with a handmade cushion cover and discarded copies of the *Herald* neatly piled up with an unopened subscription copy of the *Listener* on top of the next chair confirmed his hunch. Next to the table a window looked out over a carefully tended garden, which ran down the slope of the long, narrow section. The window itself was clearly in an advanced state of decomposition. A leak had eaten away its substance.

The window rattled in its frame, even in the light breeze.

'It's lovely now, but in the winter it leaks. It's very draughty.' Extending her hand towards the window, Betty stopped short of the frame, lest it dissolve under her touch. 'I just don't know what to do about it.'

'It's easily fixed.' Joe put his hand gently on the window. It felt spongy. Glancing out, he let his eyes traverse the colourful garden spread out in front of him. Two little urns on pedestals reminded him for a moment of Leo's abandoned tennis court garden, but he could see from where he stood the formality was only momentary. After an old garden shed, it dissolved into meandering pathways that headed down the slope and out of sight. Looking at Betty and then out into the garden, he spoke. 'You know, you should really think of giving yourself a little deck just here,' he pointed to the space directly outside. 'French doors and then in summer you could sit out in the sun and have your breakfast in the garden. It could be a little deck in the style of the one out front.' He gestured in the direction from which they'd come. Joe stopped suddenly. He couldn't remember the last time he had spoken that much in one go. He lowered himself into a small chair.

'Regency — it's a Regency-style porch.' Betty's tone was indignant.

'Oh, okay, Regency.' He was confused by Betty's sudden change of mood. She stared at him, clearly upset. What had he done wrong? He stood up again. It was no skin off his nose. Maybe it was time to leave.

'I only want a repair. I haven't changed anything since . . . Joseph and I . . . we did everything together to this house. I love it just the way it is.' Joseph? Now he was beginning to understand. Was this why he was here? Her husband was called Joseph.

'Well, okay, no problem. I can fix the window for you. It'll take me a weekend.' Joe let his eyes wander again out to the garden. There was a long silence before Betty spoke.

'How long would it take to do a set of doors and a deck? Just a little one, mind you? Just big enough for a couple of friends.'

'If I could do it on my weekends, I might be able to get it done in six weeks. I'd have to get a door made, and we'd need to get the Council in on it.' There was another long silence.

Then Betty, slipping her hand into Joe's, said, 'Perhaps we could do it together, Joe, you and me. This might be just what we both need.'

'I am not having you waste away on my watch.'

It was their first Saturday on the project. Betty had already made Joe an enormous morning tea of scones and sandwiches. The tea had come in a cup with a saucer and a teaspoon. He'd drunk it without comment, even though, since Leo, he'd become a dedicated coffee drinker. There was something about Betty that made it impossible to say no to her.

Now, not two hours later, Joe was sitting in front of an even more substantial lunch of a homemade meat pie and a freshly iced cake. He smiled.

'Thank you. This looks nice.' He reached for the pie.

'Wait,' she said as she came to join him at the table. 'Okay, now you may help yourself.' Selecting a pre-cut slice of pie, Joe placed it on his plate and then picked up his fork in his right hand. She looked at him reproachfully. 'It's not a shovel, dear.'

Reaching over, she gently took the fork from his hand and transferred it to the right position in his left hand. She then handed him the knife. This lesson in table etiquette brought an instant pain to his heart and something in him unexpectedly crumbled.

'Silly me, I've forgotten napkins.' As she tottered off to the linen cupboard, Joe took a deep breath and wiped his eyes with the back of his hand. He hoped Betty didn't think he was too uncouth. Despite her admonishments, he liked her a lot. Returning, she placed the napkin in front of him.

'So, are we all right now — yes?'

'I think so.'

As they began to eat, Joe relaxed.

'Back straight. Food in the face, not face in the food — you're not defending it from the Mongol hordes.' Joe straightened up. 'Better. You're such a good-looking young man. You don't need to slouch as if you had something to hide, not when you have so much potential.'

There was no afternoon smoko, but at 4.30 p.m., after he'd cleaned up, Betty brought out two small crystal glasses on a silver tray and a plate of biscuits.

'Sherry,' she said as she passed him a glass. 'And wine biscuits.'

'I recognise those — Cheers!' Joe took a big mouthful of the sherry. Looking at Betty, he knew he had no option other than to swallow, which he did in a gulp. He was grateful for the blandness of the biscuit that followed.

'This is nice. Thanks.' He looked across the table at Betty as she sipped her glass politely. She beamed at the compliment. As his head began to throb, Joe took a second tentative sip. Nope, still disgusting.

'Now, tell me what happened. Who's responsible for your broken heart?'

Joe hesitated. How much of the truth about Leo would Betty be able to take? *Oh, what the hell*, he thought. He had nothing to lose. So, Joe started to talk about Leo, gingerly at first. He looked closely at Betty to see her reaction to the fact his heart had been broken by a man, but she didn't even blink, she just reached out and patted his hand. Betty talked too, about her husband Joseph.

'Wasn't he handsome?' she murmured as they pored over old photographs. Joe was pleased to see that he and Joseph looked nothing alike. She told him how Joseph had picked her out of a secretarial pool a few years after the war. How jealous the other girls had been. How they'd found an old building in which to set up business as importers of novelties and giftware, supplying shops and department stores. They'd decorated the place in the official colours of the recent coronation and impending royal tour and had even covered it in bunting, although knowing the royal tour wouldn't bring the new queen anywhere close enough to see it. Then, a few years later, they'd bought this little house long before people like them bought in Freeman's Bay. How all the neighbours had been Polynesian and how old friends had felt sorry for them for being so hard up, for *having* to live there. She told Joe how they'd done it up. They'd based the little porch on the illustration on the front cover of *Garden Open Tomorrow*, a favourite book by Beverly Nichols, one they'd read aloud to each other.

With no kids to keep them in Auckland, Betty and Joseph had planned to travel after retirement — they'd saved up a nest egg. Joseph Strauss retired on the dot of sixty-five. He had finished work on a Friday night. The following Monday morning he had died of a heart attack. Their retired life, the special life they had planned together over all those years, had lasted one weekend. Joe figured, since then, every Friday had reminded Betty of possibility and every Monday of her aloneness. In this state, Betty had lived on alone in their little house for the last five years, only occasionally venturing out for anything other than the essentials. The architecture lectures had been a big step for Betty, it seemed. And opening up to Joe, an even bigger step.

Joe began to really enjoy his afternoons at Betty's, working away in the sun. Gradually, Joe began to feel something in him start to change. It was coming up to a year since Leo's disappearance. Joe could, with Betty's help, tick off a list of advances he'd made in getting his life back on track, or at least holding himself together in public.

As the exact date approached, however, Joe could feel an unstoppable cloud of pain moving in and begin to clutch at him. In the fog, the ground he'd gained turned out to be quicksand. Having stopped for a moment, he found himself sinking fast. It was in this state of mind he now lay in his bed. It was Saturday. Betty would be expecting him, but she'd understand. She'd put the scones away in the airtight tin with the *Laughing Cavalier* on its stubborn lid, and she'd be okay. He spent the day in his room.

Rousing himself only long enough to get to the video shop, Joe whiled away the evening with *The Double Life of Veronique*. His mother had given up early, the subtitles driving her off to bed. He'd stayed up late listening to music and fallen asleep around 3 a.m., only to be woken late the next morning by a noise outside. He rolled over. There was another noise. He heard voices — closer now. He turned towards the door.

There she was. Betty, immaculately dressed, handbag over one arm, standing there in his bedroom, his mother hovering behind her at the door. He sat up fast.

'Get dressed,' she said and reached down to pick up a t-shirt off the floor. 'Here, put that on — and those.' She picked up a pair of shorts between thumb and forefinger and tossed them towards him, glancing as she did so at his mother. 'I saw his boots at the door. Tell him to put them on and I'll see him outside.'

'Outside?' he asked

'At your truck. What, did you think that I'd left the taxi waiting? You're driving me home. You have obligations, young man. So, get up. I'll be waiting.'

Sitting in the front passenger seat of his ute, Betty barely spoke to Joe on the way home but when she did finally say something, it was brutal.

'I'm just not having this, Joseph. Sulking is disrespectful to me, and above all to everything Leo and you had together. This behaviour, this feeling sorry for yourself, it stops here. Never again.'

Shamefaced, Joe had worked away in silence. After a rather sombre lunch, Betty had mumbled something about a radiogram then shuffled off inside. Shortly afterwards, through the newly made hole in the side of the house, came the sound of a strange operatic voice. A woman's singing unaccompanied, its warmth flowed through him, lifting him up until it deposited him, renewed, on the lawn again.

'Kathleen Ferrier,' Betty said, poking her head through the framing timbers. 'What do you think?'

'Crank it up, Betty, crank it up,' Joe replied, the previous frostiness between them all but forgotten. With this new voice floating out over the garden like a breeze, Joe felt new life flow into his body.

Joe began to look forward to his weekends with Betty. Drinking sherry, listening to crackly opera on the radiogram, the volume as loud as it could go — a year before he couldn't possibly have envisioned himself here, and yet here he was, almost happy again. When Joe finished the job, Betty threw a little party for a few of her friends and neighbours — a deck-warming party.

When asked by a neighbour whether Joe was her grandson, Betty had replied, 'No, he's my toy boy.'

Together they'd both laughed, giggled like naughty children — until, annoyed, the neighbour had walked away. Betty turned to him. 'Tears first, then comes laughter, always in that order, always.'

Slowly, Joe began to return to himself. The fog came less frequently. And now, when it did, he found he could still function. He got his act together at work. He joined a new firm, which meant more pink paint and new practical jokes, but he didn't pay it much attention. Instead, he just focused on the work. He took all the overtime going, private jobs, the lot.

He spent only a little of the money he earned on books and music. With Betty's help, he dressed a little less like a builder, especially on the nights when they went out together. He rather liked the way he felt in his new clothes. Betty took him to the opera and the ballet. He joined the gym. He toned the parts that didn't get toned on the job. He began to look at his scar less as an embarrassment and more as a badge of honour, a wound in the cosmic duel for love. He swore less. Betty even said he was becoming 'a very presentable young man.'

The big houses he loved lingered in Joe's imagination. For a while, he considered signing up for a degree in architecture. Instead, he enrolled across the road from the architecture school at a polytechnic. They were known to be easier on older students. Joe soon found he enjoyed studying. He began to seek out depths of knowledge that perplexed his younger classmates. Most of them seemed to simply want to graduate. He learnt not to ask questions during lectures but to stay on after class, talking to his tutors, mining them for knowledge.

He found his old energy returning. He could now focus completely on the task at hand. At work he found out studying was more offensive on a building site than being gay. After a while, his workmates forgot about the gay part. Instead they took the piss out of the studying. He ate his lunch alone in the cab of his ute with his textbooks in front of him and some thrashy old song of Leo's, now *his* love songs, on the stereo.

Two years out from Leo, Joe would, should he have been asked, said he was okay. Although, beyond Betty, there was no one to ask the question.

Joe went back to sex. Some hook-ups turned into boyfriends, but they didn't last long. He knew why. Love was off his list. He always tried to make it clear at the beginning, but some guys thought they might change him. It was always the end when they said 'I love you'.

The universe had had its little joke. It had dangled a perfect life in front of Joe and then snatched it away. So now he was no longer a player in that game. Its rules mystified him. He locked love away with the things he no longer understood or required and let business fill the emptiness. Now, business he understood.

Eventually, he went back to drinking too. He danced with old friends with whom he'd almost lost touch. He went to parties at his old foreman's house. He met some interesting people from the film world. Found out the actor wasn't a jerk. He even did an under-the-table job for him. Then for one of the actor's friends with whom he had a short fling. He told his friends he was gay. They all pretty much asked if Leo had been his boyfriend.

'Yes, but we broke up.'

'Sad,' they'd said. Suze and Marie said they'd always known. They'd seen how he looked at Leo, the once or twice they'd all been together.

They'd nicknamed him Joe's Candy — after Candide. Steve said his older brother was gay and that it was irrelevant to him.

He had some good heart-to-hearts with his mother. She admitted she had guessed about his sexuality a long time before and that it hadn't changed her feelings for him. She loved him dearly. She said she was sure he'd find someone. She liked having him back home, she said, and he could stay as long as he wished. Joe explained he didn't want to find someone else, not yet, perhaps not for a long while. She understood. Joe too understood his mother a little better now.

CHAPTER 6

Out of the blue, Joe had a phone call from Kurt. He said he wanted to meet for a drink. Joe hadn't thought much about Kurt in the last few years. He wasn't sure this was what he needed right now, but nevertheless had agreed to meet in a little upstairs bar in town.

Kurt was explaining how his firm Infusion Software had made a lot of money developing a new line of business programmes.

'I want to diversify, protect myself from any potential collapse of the dot-com sector, by putting some of the money I'm making into property development.' Joe arched an eyebrow, a little unsure why Kurt was telling him all this. By the look of Kurt's designer jacket, he was clearly doing well. 'I've been buying and selling, but I want to do bigger stuff. I've got a couple of sites.'

'And?' Joe asked. The bragging was getting boring. He glanced again at Kurt. Kurt who he'd once idolised. Sure, his blue eyes still sparkled from behind his black eyelashes, but the flame of teenage desire had somehow flickered out. He wondered for a moment what it was that had so captivated him? 'What's this got to do with me?'

'You're a builder. I can trust you — you've always been straight with me. Do you want to do something together? Split the profits?'

'Sure,' Joe said with a shrug. After all, what did he have to lose? It wasn't as if he had any other plans.

Their first project was a small block of three townhouses in Remuera. Since the 1940s a lone state house had sat marooned in the middle of the site's large mass of lawn. Kurt and Joe didn't hesitate to bowl it. Kurt had plans for the townhouses drawn up by a draughtsman. They weren't good — Joe could see that a mile away. They'd end up as one of those blocks where there was always a 'For Sale' sign on the fence, a moving truck in the drive and a skip on the verge, Joe was convinced. He spent his nights with a pencil, drawing over the plans. He tried cribbing bits from the big book on Frank Lloyd Wright Leo had given him for the one Christmas they had together. He thought a lot about Leo and what he liked in a building. He tried to channel Leo into the design, but nothing was working.

Intending to drop off an assignment to his tutor, Joe wedged his ute into an illegal park between two trees on Symonds Street. Right in front of him a sign read: 'School of Architecture, Property & Planning'. The plans of the townhouses were rolled up on his back seat. It was worth a try. Having struggled through the heavy glass doors, Joe looked around for an office of some type. A guy, older than Joe, shaven head and with the start of a gut, walked towards him with a polystyrene coffee cup in his hands.

'Hi.' Joe stepped directly into the man's path. Then, his words coming out in a rush, he explained, 'Look, I'm a builder. I need an architect — someone to look at these. They're shit, and I don't know what to do about it.' Joe rolled out the drawings onto a trestle table, the stained tablecloth indicating its use at some catering event the previous night. The guy peered closely at the plans.

'You're right, they are shite. Try this.' Taking a soft dark pencil from his trouser pocket, he drew a series of swift lines across the plan. He sketched new openings over the elevations and scored through others. 'That won't solve your problem, but it will help.'

Joe looked at the drawings. 'What do I owe you?'

'Nothing. But next time, come to me first. I don't have time for this. Fishing a card from his jacket pocket, he said, 'I'm John, by the way.'

'Joe.' The two men shook hands.

As he held open the heavy door to allow a group of students to come through, John called out an afterthought. 'Oh, and dump that monolithic cladding — there's bad news coming. Remuera? Try brick.'

Sitting with the drawings spread out on his mother's dining room table, it took Joe a while to puzzle it out. The lines John had drawn were dark and emphatic. They cut through the plan decisively, but they were also confusing.

After a while, Joe came to see that John had broken up larger spaces into defined rooms. He'd placed large windows where they were needed and the smaller openings corralled into elegant compositions that read crisply on the outside of the building. As he traced the lines onto a new copy of the plans, he made small innovations of his own. When he'd finished, the units looked somehow stylistically unified, in a way Joe thought likely to guarantee their appeal to their market. Kurt looked at Joe's sketches for a moment before agreeing to a redraw. Convincing him to change to a more expensive cladding, however, took a little longer.

'Architects cost you money and very seldom make you any,' Kurt explained. 'That's all I know.'

As the townhouses went up, Joe watched the rooms take on their form out of the flat grey nothing of the concrete floor slab. He had observed the process many times before. In the past it had been a visual aid allowing him to count down the days before a job was over. Now he took pleasure in the completion of each step. He began to feel a new confidence in the project. Once the walls were up and the roof on, he spent his weekends on site looking over the week's progress. He made small changes, corrected poor work and tested fittings and finishes. These rooms were already more satisfying to be in than most new build rooms. Each room was private, contained and safe. They were the type of shelter for which any couple, or family, might hope for. The three units nestled together so each caught the sun, but the residents wouldn't look into each other's lives. Outside, the red brick made them look solid. The choice of dark green aluminium joinery meant that in time the townhouses would not look out of place among their more stately neighbours. Joe ordered two large urns for the front gates. He planted specimen trees to provide real shade and to complete the graceful line-up that gave the old street its character. He borrowed piles of library books on house interiors. He made careful decisions. He found he was good at it. The rooms came together with enough personality to make them distinctive but not so much as to make you feel you were moving into someone else's house.

On auction day the first unit sold very well, but by the time the hammer came down on the third, thirty minutes later, the first appeared an unbelievable bargain.

As Joe guided Betty through the dwellings, before the new owners took possession, he explained he'd been tempted to buy one of them for himself. He'd imagined one day showing it off to Leo. Leo would understand he had applied honest principles to their construction, that he'd put in every ounce of himself. She'd patted his arm.

'There are better things to come for you. Trust me, doll.' He'd settled instead for a villa, a walkable distance down the hill from Betty, and a big mortgage.

Kurt was well pleased. After the success of their next two townhouse projects, undertaken concurrently, he suggested they make it official.

'What do you say, shall we form a company? Fifty-fifty?'

Betty had urged him to say yes. She had even — after a short, sharp discussion — offered her savings to solve Joe's shortfall in capital, and with that she became the new company's third shareholder.

Now the guy behind the desk wanted a name.

'What do you mean?'

'For the new entity. It has to have a name, legally. Something like "Joseph Wright Builders Limited".' He looked at Joe. 'Unless you have other ideas?' Joe felt himself redden. The name of the business — that was one thing he'd never given a moment's thought. He looked at Kurt who held up his hands.

'I'm strictly the back-room boy on this one.'

'Well then, how about Joseph Wright & Partners Construction.' The lawyer began to fill out the box.

'Wait . . . how about "Thackeray Makepeace"?'

'I like it.' Kurt repeated the name. 'Thackeray Makepeace. Sounds classy.'

The lawyer shrugged. 'No reason why not. Actually, it'll help if you go under — a less obvious connection back to you. You do know it's supposed to be the other way around though, don't you?' Joe nodded. 'Thackeray Makepeace Construction it is then.'

Joe credited becoming head of a construction firm, albeit a small one, as the moment a passion emerged in his life that rivalled the love he felt for Leo. He didn't stop thinking about Leo, not for a minute, but for now — thankfully — he had other things to focus on. Kurt possessed a knack for smoking out the worst house on the best street. Together they replaced a series of single rundown properties through the central and eastern suburbs with boutique townhouse developments. If the neighbours were unimpressed at the announcement of development next door, they seldom complained about the final results. With half a dozen projects under their belts, the firm began to look at larger projects. At first, they took on conversions, transforming old commercial properties on the city fringe to smart residential blocks. Joe eyed the central city sites he knew from years earlier, but for the moment they lay outside his grasp.

Where Joe had once seen only surfaces, he now saw structure. Looking beyond to the bones of a situation meant a satisfying conversion but also a good profit. Old finishes could be changed, improved or updated. Poor structure was bad business. He didn't believe everything needed preserving, but he made a promise to himself never to pull something down without first looking at restoration or conversion options. After the firm did their first small green-field apartment block, Joe tried to lure John from his position at the university. Demurring, John warned him no one retained in-house teams any longer. In the end, he promised to find him the right backroom technocrat to run his team and also to send his best graduates. Joe, in return, would give the young architects opportunities to shine.

When Thackeray Makepeace won their first award, for Best Small Developer, there had been a request for media. The young woman, a journalist, had left a telephone message describing them as: 'A firm with a flawless reputation run by two men from ordinary suburban backgrounds, yet to turn thirty and something of a mystery.' She'd wanted their thoughts on her summary before going to print. Kurt, who'd retrieved the message, handed the request on to Joe.

'I don't do media.'

Kurt rolled his eyes. 'Why? Because you're gay?'

Joe looked surprised. 'Well, I was going to say because I haven't done much in the way of media training and that we could do with someone to head PR, but yes . . . I'm gay and that's not necessarily good publicity for the firm.' There was a long pause before either of them spoke. 'How long have you known?'

'You always were, even when we were kids. I've been waiting for you to say something for years. That's why you're so good at this shit, you know the decorating and stuff. There were other builders. It's not a biggie.'

'But . . . I . . .'

'No biggie, seriously, forget media training. Just tell them whatever you want to tell them. You don't have to give them your life story. You've just won an award! This is an opportunity.' Joe got up to leave. 'Wait a minute, sit back down.' Kurt took a moment to compose his words and then, in a bland, matter-of-fact way, said simply, 'Joe, I'm not gay.'

'I know that *now*.'

'Wait a minute. Just listen. I'm not gay, but you and that stupid dancing you used to do, you made me do, it got me through it.'

'Through what?'

'Shit knows now. A crappy adolescence I sometimes felt I wasn't going to survive. I owe you big time.' Kurt had never before mentioned school days. Joe had always thought his focus was entirely on the future. That was what made him so good at software. This sudden nostalgia was feeling weird.

'There's more. I haven't been entirely straight with you.'

'About?'

Kurt spoke slowly. 'Joe, I've never asked you,' he hesitated, 'about your face.' Joe winced. 'I saw you once, in a pub, you were out of it. So out of it, you didn't know who I was. You called me Leo. I hadn't seen you since school, but there was no scar then — not that night. I felt shit for not doing anything after you'd done so much for me when I was, you know, lost. I felt bad for a long time. Joe said nothing. 'That's why

I rang you — for that first project, but I found out fast I'd made better than a pity choice. See, I don't have an imagination. As you proved on the first one, you do. Imagination is the rarest of all business resources. Most people in business fail because they don't have it.'

Joe felt relieved. The conversation had at last moved away from his personal life to the more comfortable territory of business. He asked, 'What about Infusion Software — that's imaginative, surely?'

'No, not really. It was at first. Now I buy it in. I pay a lot for it, but actually it's Infusion I want to talk to you about.' Joe was suddenly feeling a little sick in his stomach, and Kurt's choice of a slow reveal wasn't helping.

'And?'

'Infusion has just sold into four major American corporates, with two more to come. The money we're making, that I'm making, makes Thackeray Makepeace look small beer.' Things still weren't getting clearer to Joe. Did Kurt want to sell out? He asked the question. Kurt looked surprised.

'Shit, no. Quite the opposite. This firm relies on *your* work and *your* imagination. You got any big ideas, Joe? Because what I'm saying is, if you need it, there's big money there now. Just say the word.'

When Jacinta Jones, the smart blonde journalist, asked him about his wife and family, Joe took a deep breath and replied simply, 'I'm gay.' However, that detail hadn't made the final copy. Instead, the article, appearing next to a full-page advertisement for shower domes, reported that: 'Joseph Wright, a bachelor, prefers not to discuss his personal life.'

'Look, it's like this,' she explained from the couch in his office in a follow-up meeting. 'I got a Master's degree from Victoria, followed by four years in the UK with a top public relations firm handling major clients. I spent the last year at home in the provinces to find out Hastings is a hole and that my husband was an even bigger tool here than he was in London. Now I'm out of both. Do you imagine writing doo-doo for *NZ Property Investment* is really me?' Jacinta was, Joe was quickly discovering, rather fond of rhetorical questions — unnaturally so for a journalist, he thought.

'That was my last piece. Journalism is not my thing. I'm joining a new public relations agency, and I want to take one standout client with me — someone with great growth potential.'

'Who?' asked Joe.

'Spoken like the boy from Te Atatū. You can't be *that* naïve. Or are you?' she looked at him directly without appearing to blink. 'Perhaps that's all part of your charm. Yes, I think we can work with it.' She gave Joe a knowing smile. 'Don't get me wrong, it's all great material.' Jacinta adjusted her pencil skirt for the third time, this time smoothing it out against her legs and lowering it by a centimetre. She continued, 'Thackeray Makepeace is going places, everyone says so, but you haven't done anything truly notable yet. Investors need to see vision. The men behind the firm. Your buddy isn't playing ball, so it's you. They need to know who Joseph Wright is and to believe in him.'

Joe's first impression of Jacinta a few weeks earlier was certainly that she was ambitious, but now she exuded a hunger, which might, if handled correctly, indeed be helpful to the firm. It was true that he wanted to pursue bigger projects. He didn't much care she thought him naïve — he knew he wasn't, not when it came to business. However, looking a lot younger than he was meant there were plenty out there who mistook him for a sap. Those who tried usually came a cropper. The firm had recently bought up the remains of a smaller company run by an ageing Ozymandias who'd tried to outpace him.

'I'm not talking about the subscribers to *NZ Property Investment*, most of whom are suburban trolls,' she leant forward, allowing him a direct view down the front of her blouse. 'Shit, these people buy their property advice in the supermarket. If they're lucky, they might just cark it with enough in the bank for their kids to forgive their horrendous upbringings. You need someone to help you grab the big opportunities, to see that you make something of your potential. That's where I come in.'

It was amusing to Joe how some women in business were unable to turn off the tricks of the trade, even in the presence of a gay man. The tight skirt riding up her legs, the generous view of cleavage. Even now, as Jacinta looked down at her papers, she was twirling her long, blonde hair around her finger — classic flirting. He thought for a moment about how young men in business didn't wear overly tight pants or hoist up their packages or encourage a semi before walking through his office door. They never left an extra button undone or flexed their guns to close a deal. Kiwi men just weren't that savvy. For the moment, the sight of a good-looking woman working her way through an armoury of well-rehearsed, but in this case ultimately useless, weapons was entertaining for Joe.

Closing the portfolio in his hand and looking up, Joe announced, 'We are with Pulse PR for public relations.'

'How's that working for you?' Again, Jacinta showed no intention of waiting for an answer. 'I would say they're acceptable. After all, they got you into *NZ Property Investment*, smack bang next to the ad for Showerdomes. Forget Thackeray Makepeace for a moment. I'm talking Joseph Wright — the brand behind the company. I'm talking about running a personal PR profile alongside that of the firm. We need to get you in the *right* places, alongside the *right* people, profiled in the *right* media.'

Joe looked directly across the coffee table at Jacinta. 'So, let me get this straight. You gambled that the way to establish yourself as the best candidate for *my* PR person was to misrepresent the only personal thing I said in our first interview?'

'Not misrepresenting. Keeping the powder dry. If you want to come out as queer, I'll build you a Hero float. You can be the fairy on the top if you like, but if we do it, we do it where someone's going to notice.' Joe laughed. That idea he liked. Jacinta Jones' take-no-prisoners approach was certainly refreshing, but she wasn't done yet. 'Face it, though, the gay thing could easily piss off serious investors if it's not handled right. There are two sides to everything, but the style thing — we can get them with that. Thackeray Makepeace is a class act and, potentially, so are you.'

Joe grimaced slightly, but it was clear that nothing was going to stop Jacinta and that he liked. Both he and Kurt had learnt early that success in business was about employing people with complementary skills to your own, creating just enough diversity to cause positive friction. Joe suspected there was something about Jacinta Jones that would make her both a natural irritant and a likely positive fit with the firm. It was a combination he believed he could handle. After all, he'd got used to the pretentious sass of the pretty young architects John sent him. Gail, his doughnut-eating and consequently doughnut-shaped personal assistant kept him real, or so she told him. The men in the teams were old school construction workers with doom-laden opinions on any issue, and he could handle them. Sales were a mix of pansies, straight boys and younger, blonder, but less sharp, versions of the woman in front of him. That lot, in particular, might learn by having Jacinta Jones around the place.

'Tell you what. I'll go with you if you forget about the agency. Join Thackeray Makepeace as Head of Public Relations, Sales and Marketing. There's a vacancy. I'll make it worth your while. I want your full attention on us. You are right, the company *is* going places, but if you want to be part of the ride, you're going to have to be *on* the ride. Don't decide now. I'll put together a package. I'll have it to you within 24 hours. Let's just shake on it now — to let me know you'll at least think about it.' He stood up. He had for a moment stopped Jacinta Jones in her tracks. As she stood up from the couch, smoothing down her skirt once more, she extended her hand.

'Well, Joe, this is a surprise, and it is certainly something I'll consider very seriously.' Jacinta flicked an errant lock of hair away from her face. 'Very seriously indeed.' She gathered her stuff together, and Joe walked her to his office door. As he opened it, he extended his hand once more. 'Well, it's been a pleasure.'

Taking his hand, Jacinta asked. 'Just one thing, how committed are you to the name?'

He looked at her, a little perplexed.

'Thackeray Makepeace. I find it a bit weird and too long,' said Jacinta, in her characteristically direct manner.

'Now that,' Joe cocked his head, 'is solid.'

'I can work with it.'

'Good — pleased to hear it.' Then he added, 'Jacinta, Thackeray Makepeace needs to be big, really big, bigger than . . .' He didn't get to finish his sentence because before he had time to select the right word, Jacinta interjected.

'Yeah, I get it. You're going to conquer the property world. I've dealt with your type before.'

CHAPTER 7

Joe climbed onto the treadmill. Placing his water and his towel in the moulded plastic pockets of the console, he selected the manual programme. The machine asked for his workout time. *Thirty minutes.* It then requested his weight. *Seventy-five kilograms.* Next door to him, a young man with blond dreadlocks, having just completed the same series of questions, was running slowly, without enthusiasm. His feet, in sandshoes, slapped heavily against the belt. He looked back at his machine. Incline: *Zero.* Speed: *Six-point-five.* The belt stalled. Then, lurching slowly into life, climbed until it met the set speed. It was no more than a walk, but he liked to spend two minutes there. It was, he rationalised, his warm-up.

He looked at the guy on one of the rowing machines in front of him and then up to the newly installed television screens. SKY News was covering the flooding in Mozambique. Looking away from the devastation, he cast around for something more uplifting. The line of treadmills in front was filling up with young women in garish leotards. He hoped the last two spaces might provide him with somewhere more satisfactory to rest his eyes while he exercised. Increasing his speed, he began his run. Looking to his left, he wondered why the skinny Rasta kid bothered? He probably told his friends he'd 'done some cardio,' when, really, he'd strolled through his regime in a daze, listening to his Discman, his eyes on a dislocated screen. Better he got on the weights or did some squats, built up some semblance of glutes.

Out of the corner of his eye, Joe noticed someone climb on to the vacant treadmill to his right. He glanced over quickly. He hadn't seen the guy here before — biggish, dark skin, black hair — but Joe noted that he had set the speed on the machine to the point it had taken Joe ten minutes to achieve. Turning his head for a better look, he surveyed the guy who, oblivious to anything much, was now running alongside him. He was young, in his mid-twenties, and muscular. His loosely cut singlet offered tantalising side views of both back and torso. He was cute, all right, but he knew it. Yes, he was working it — the cute thing. Joe increased the speed on his belt, and a second later the guy followed. They ran some more. The guy was keeping pace beside him without much effort.

Joe wasn't used to being outrun. He pushed the button again and, as if in a mirror, his neighbour responded immediately. Joe caught the guy's eye and they both smiled. Joe dialled up again. He was running pretty fast now, his shoes hitting the belt in a steady rhythm as the clock ticked off the minutes. The guy matched him again. Joe didn't dare try and read his neighbour's monitor. If he stumbled at this speed, he'd likely fall and shoot off the end of the belt into the machine behind. He punched his speed up. He gave it five minutes, his feet barely touching the tread as he flew. He began to consider hitting the stop button. No, he couldn't do that. Not when the guy next to him was still only gliding. The guy punched the button again, and Joe followed.

Joe was running at near capacity now. His water bottle beckoned, but it was too risky a grab. *Twenty-seven minutes* — he punched the button up and then up again. The whole treadmill was shaking now. His feet scarcely kissed the belt, flying up behind him only to come back down and hit the treadmill again a millisecond later. His heart was pounding. His shirt, soaking wet, stuck to him and sweat stung his eyes. He kept running. Then, there it was, flashing in front of him: *COOL DOWN*.

The belt slowed and the speed started to reduce, but not fast enough for Joe's lungs. Hands on the rails, Joe jumped, placing his feet on the side of the still spinning rubber. He leant forward, lowered his head and breathed in deeply. His sweat dripped onto the belt, dotting it with bullet-sized drops. The guy next to him punched stop and slowed, jogging, then walking, until his treadmill came to a halt.

'Great workout, thanks!' He called over to Joe with a smile.

'Any time,' Joe panted back. The guy appeared barely warmed up, though his entire body glistened. There was no denying it, he was incredibly attractive. Joe glanced to his left. The Rasta had gone. He turned back to find his running mate extending his hand.

'Tony,' he said by way of introducing himself. 'And truly, thanks. I needed that — it's my first session in three days. I'm the barista, well, part owner really, at Biota on Jervois Road. You heard of it?'

'Think so,' Joe said breathlessly, still not quite recovered.

'Come see me sometime. I'll make you the best coffee you'll ever get.' Joe watched as Tony walked off, stopping to chat to one of the trainers, before heading for the free weights. For a moment Joe considered following, doing a few reps on the bench next door, but then he remembered how much he despised gym hook-ups. Well, the last one sure hadn't worked out well.

A couple of days later, Joe found himself still thinking about Tony, so he decided to have another look.

Joe *had* heard the buzz around Biota. The sign in front of him offered 'Organics sourced from the unique microclimate of Auckland.' It seemed, however, that the clientele were drawn to Biota less for the organics and more to see Tony. Most customers greeted him like an old friend. From behind the stainless steel bank of the coffee machine, Tony kept up a constant stream of 'ciao' and 'grazie', never forgetting a name or failing to remember a coffee.

Forming an adoring arc around the machine, Tony's disciples waited patiently for their coffee god to deliver. He didn't disappoint. Every cup came with a flirty smile or suggestive wink. Taking a seat, Joe watched Tony's performance. It was impressive, as were his looks. Tony's heritage was hard to place. While he pondered Tony's ethnic origins, Joe noticed Tony lean over and whisper something in the ear of his sidekick. He then came out from behind his hissing machine and made his way through the crowd, two coffees in hand. As he watched Tony approach, Joe realised just what he was. Tony was a prize, a prize Joe was about to award himself for getting this far. So, he asked him out — old school style.

The restaurant was new, smart, not somewhere Joe had ever tried before. Tony had suggested the place, and the staff appeared to know him well. The service, interspersed with lengthy revelations of restaurant world gossip, was super-attentive and a stream of diners, uninvited, greeted Tony at the table throughout the evening. Although he more often than not failed to introduce his visitors, after every interruption Tony feigned annoyance, making an exaggerated point of turning back to Joe to resume their conversation.

'What was I saying? Ah yes, I know. Hospitality since leaving school at fifteen, dishwasher, waiter and barman. Did I say that already?' Joe shrugged. 'These days most owners know I pull a big-spending crowd.'

'So you said.'

'I've scooped up major prizes in the barista awards three years running.' He'd mentioned that too, but Joe didn't mind. He was simply enjoying sitting across the table watching this hot man. 'I'm over being a Pavoni-pony, but my friends, the ones that own Biota, they got me in to establish it, you know, as a hot destination. They'll on-sell, with a potential profit split in it for me.'

'Potential? It looked pretty profitable to me.'

'Nothing on paper — you don't need to when it's friends. People are pretty honest, straight up, in the restaurant world.' Joe thought this unlikely, but he dared not interrupt. 'I've done it a few times before — set up places.' The cafés and restaurants he listed made Joe wonder how he'd never noticed him before. When Tony paused for a moment, he asked his burning question.

'I'm Italian. It's cool, everyone asks. We were circus people — well, my great-grandparents were. They came from Italy as part of a troupe of tumbling acrobats. My grandmother, well there weren't too many Italian marriage ops, and she was the youngest of twelve. It had to be a Catholic. It *always* has to be a Catholic.' Tony rolled his eyes. 'Are you Catholic?' Joe shook his head. 'So, she married the son of a Chinese Catholic market gardener. That's my grandfather. My mother, their daughter, married a Croatian mechanic. Their name was Gerbic but they changed it to Graham years ago.' As Tony turned to talk to another visitor to the table, Joe sipped at the cocktail he'd just been delivered. Turning back, Tony took to the restaurant menu and wine list in a way that suggested it would be the property developer rather than the barista who would be picking up the bill. Joe didn't mind — in fact he rather admired Tony's attitude. The food was excellent, but to every compliment, Tony responded by naming another restaurant, or another chef, that could do it better.

At the end of the evening Tony, stopping for a moment, said, 'I know nothing about you. Your place?'

For someone who worked in a café, Tony didn't seem to be a natural morning person. He slowly revived himself over a morning espresso he'd made on Joe's machine, having turned down the offer of breakfast. 'I'm the star act. Warm-ups do the breakfast shift. I gotta be there at 10.30 when the horny mothers start arriving. I'm there till 3pm. Then the gym — aerobics one day, weights the next — then party time. That's me. It's a pretty cool life, don't ya think?' Joe nodded.

At the front door, Tony turned. 'See ya. Love ya, babe.' Stopping in his tracks for a moment, Joe looked at the man already half out the front door, dressed in the clothes he'd arrived in the night before. A man who he somehow knew would be walking back in the same door that evening. He knew then he neither needed to believe it or reciprocate the emotion. He just had to say the words. There and then the obligation would end.

So, without further hesitation, Joe replied, 'I love you too, babe.'

This wasn't going to be deep, but Joe decided there and then it was going to be fun.

Tony's life was one big party and Joe had signed up as his permanent plus one. The plus one that picked up the tab, but Joe didn't care. He was enjoying reclaiming some of the years of his early twenties, those that the first time around he'd given up to mourning Leo. Tony wasn't Leo. There were similarities — the colour of their hair, the tendency of their skin to develop a dark tan — but beyond that they had little in common. Tony's music was dance floor music, a percussive progression of pulses without lyrics or an obvious end. Tony explained it kept him amped. There had never been anything amped about Leo. You couldn't talk to Tony about a book. He treated bookshelves as one would a line of rotting corpses, holding his breath and giving them a wide berth. Tony preferred his new PlayStation and sitting on the couch in his underwear, gaming console in hand, Tony looked hot. Because of that, Joe figured his books and music could wait for those evenings when Tony was out with his friends.

There were plenty of friends, all strategically placed. In busy restaurants, a table appeared immediately. In the most expensive restaurants, the best seats suddenly became vacant. The chef sent off-menu delicacies. The wine steward accidentally opened the superior vintage for which there would be no additional charge. At clubs, Tony didn't queue. Bouncers unclipped the velvet rope and moved aside as soon as they saw him approach. Barmen served him over the heads of the crush. His drug dealer was reliable. Standing on the curb, taxi drivers pulled in on the off-chance that Tony might require a ride. They did this because every one of them — waiter, bouncer, dealer, barman and taxi driver — considered Tony a great guy and their close friend. In return, Tony did an excellent job of remembering names and connections. He looked great propping up a bar. He could set a dance floor on fire. He looked good in photographs. He made restaurants hot and clubs cool. It was of little matter that his clothes were on appro and would have to be returned the next day to the friends who worked in his favourite boutiques. What mattered was that Tony turned up.

'This is more like it,' Jacinta said when Joe first introduced her to Tony. 'Well done. We can definitely do something with *him*.' It seemed to Joe that Jacinta was struggling to keep her hands off him, but Tony hadn't seemed at all perturbed. From that moment on his boyfriend and his publicist had become close friends.

Jacinta had, as Joe had suspected she would, proven a perfect fit for the firm. Joe was now a celebrity in the property pages and real estate supplements. He was well enough known to receive the nod of near recognition and partial smiles that Auckland café goers and supermarket shoppers reserve for those minor celebrities they think they know from somewhere. The smiles had recently gained a new intensity after Jacinta had positioned a series of billboards wherever commuters spent time stuck in long queues of rush-hour traffic. The billboards featured a smiling property developer encouraging Aucklanders from outlying suburbs to consider a move into the central city. Every morning thousands of frustrated drivers gazed at Joe's face for a longer time than they'd spent with their own in the bathroom mirror.

When the proofs had turned up at the office — he hadn't been sure. The airbrushed version of himself reminded him of a politician, or — worse — the victim of an experimental facelift, the result somewhere between a young Vince Martin and the Briscoe's lady. He asked them to pull back on the Photoshopping — make his face more real — but in the end he'd acquiesced. The first time he'd seen one, visible from the motorway as he approached the northbound Greenlane exit, he'd almost gone into the back of an old Galant as it crawled along doing seventy. He was used to them now. He told himself they weren't really of him. They were instead, as Jacinta was so fond of telling him, 'The highly profitable face of Thackeray Makepeace.'

In Tony, Jacinta now had a new playmate and ally. Together they nailed the company functions. Working together, they made them buzz. Tony's friends added style and glamour and the company's parties were considered *the* hot ticket. When a couple of Tony's friends bought units in Valmont, a small inner-city development, the project went off. All the remaining units quickly sold, aided by Jacinta's newspaper profile of them as 'the new cool' and the building as their 'fashion destination of choice'.

When Thackeray Makepeace entered their first float in the Hero Parade, it was Tony who gyrated on top. Around him danced four brave builders, some of the more obviously mincing boys from sales and the two young lesbians from accounts, all naked except for leather carpenters' aprons with the 'TMC' logo picked out in rivets.

For his part, Tony worked hard, in the only way he knew, delivering a stream of overheard café conversation, always beating the business pages of the *Herald* to the scoop. The quality and profitability of his business espionage improved greatly when, after the profit share in Biota had proved elusive, he'd moved on to maître d' at Samphire, a stylish new eatery popular with a lunching business crowd. Jacinta, whom he suspected of moonlighting on the new restaurant's publicity campaign, ensured Tony got photographed in a new round of street style features.

Tony and Joe were photographed together in the social pages of the newspaper alongside the rugby players and car dealers with their shared brand of bottle blondes. Jacinta got them profiled on a TV current affairs show as positive role models for gay youth. Tony parlayed it into a gig, guest-starring with a troupe of male strippers for a series of charity events. Joe joined the board of Rainbow Youth.

Joe knew that in a city almost defined by its obsession with both coffee and real estate, the celebrity barista and the celebrity property developer appeared an ideal pairing and he was, for a while, happy to believe the things he read in the colour supplements.

Joe flicked the cover of the photo album closed and reached for his wine. The coffee table was further away than he expected so he lifted himself out of the deep folds of the couch and perched on the edge as he poured himself another glass. Reaching for the stereo remote, he pressed play — the opening notes of Mahler's Symphony No. 1, dawn. Dawn for the third time tonight, but he didn't care. He looked at his watch. 10.35 p.m. Tony wasn't likely to be back much before 2 a.m. Joe took a sip of his wine and leant back to listen to the music, letting it wash over him.

All that — the good times — had been at least six months ago and not even re-reading Jacinta's clippings, stuck erratically behind the sticky plastic leaves of the album, could convince him any longer they were Auckland's perfect homo couple. He settled back into the embrace of the sofa. The music had come back to earth now and would soon return to the cosmic calm of the opening bars. Tony had moved in after a year and for a while it had worked. In fact, they were planning to spend their second anniversary together in Sydney. Joe had been trying to convince himself for a while now that the relationship had longevity, but he was starting to have his doubts. Joe glanced out at the view for a moment. He should get up and close the curtains, but what was the point? No one could see in.

The problem was that the emotional depth he yearned for did not exist, not in Tony. Whether on his gaming console or his phone, whether in a room full of people or climbing into the bed next to him, Tony always seemed somehow absent. It was as if wherever Tony was, whatever he was doing, his mind had already moved on to the next thing. Tony was never going to provide the closeness, the intimate connection, for which he yearned. Tony and his friends were devoted to one thing only — maintaining their positions as Auckland's A-list queens. That relied on them remaining unchanged, loyal to nothing, forever ready to pioneer the next big thing. They could never age. They could never risk saying anything someone might remember, lest it got held against them. They could never wear anything, do anything or go anywhere that the pack hadn't first preapproved. Tony's only lack of conformity within the group had been his refusal to grow a moustache. That act of individualism was it. There was nothing further to come.

As the second movement began, Joe's free hand swayed with the music. Was he being unfair about Tony? After all, it suited him not to delve too deeply within himself either. He never mentioned Leo to anyone. Revealing the story would only make Joe look like a loser, and he wasn't a loser.

As the wine and music, working in cahoots, swirled in his head, Joe admitted to himself that he thought about Leo a lot. It was to Leo that his mind wandered when he first woke and to whom his mind returned as he climbed into bed at the end of each day. He had neither seen nor heard a thing since Leo left. He had considered, once or twice, hiring a private detective, but he was never sure what he'd do with the information. Besides, he told himself that he had matured. He had moved on, become immune to the most painful aspects of his past.

In fact Joe was still heartbroken, lonely even, but there were times when he wondered if he might nevertheless be the winner in the situation. As different from Leo as it was possible to be, Tony made Joe realise that something within himself was real. The void of ordinariness and stupidity that he had felt when he was with Leo no longer existed. Those things, the books and music that he'd initially pursued to impress Leo, had somewhere along the path come to form the heart of his own world. They weren't something he could now give up to move closer to Tony. Music and books were as much part of who he was as were his sharp suits. The CD versions of Leo's scratchy old records didn't get played as often these days as the music he had discovered with Betty. The Mahler symphonies, this one currently mid an existential scream but about to subside into something close to a love song, those were *his* thing, not anyone else's. It was to these, or to opera, that he would listen while lying on the couch, with a wine glass in his hand and Tony out. In moments like these, he felt anything but ordinary.

Then there were books. No longer a reader of nineteenth-century novels, no longer falling for the sentimental tricks of Dickens or struggling to decide whether it was Hardy's villains or heroes he'd like to take or be taken by behind the nearest stable block. He had come to like novels set between the wars. Evelyn Waugh — those he read and reread, bathing in the extrapolation of romantic friendship that occurred between aristocratic youth in so many of the novels, all without the messy interference of sex, at least not on the page. He loved novels about people who in recovering from one world war were unknowingly about to face another. He imagined the lives of characters well after the last pages of the book. Thinking through their eventual fate in a war they couldn't foresee made him feel prepared for what the world might throw his way. He strayed further, into contemporary literature, at first choosing novels at random from the shortlists of literary prizes featuring in the window of the Women's Bookshop. He got his personal assistant to go in at lunchtime and buy them. He was grateful to Leo for introducing him to reading and music, and to architecture even, but what he listened to, what he read, wasn't Leo's anymore.

Determined to leave the last of the wine, Joe clambered out of the couch. He picked up the bottle and the glass and carried them to the bench. Turning off the kitchen lights, he walked over to the large doors that looked out onto the deck and, grabbing one side of the curtain, pulled it across and then stopped, curtain clutched in his hand. The music was in its final movement, beginning to rail against the cosmos. He liked this part — where the percussion goes wild and then in barges the orchestra. He stood and listened, looking at himself in the half reflection of the glass door, until the last notes had receded.

'Not many working-class boys from Te Atatū ended up living this life,' he thought. Still, Rutherford High didn't seem keen to have him back. They preferred the Kurts of the world. There was still something of the blokey builder about him who went partying with Tony at weekends, but the Joe who read books, loved ballet and more often than not preferred to hang out with the old lady who lived up the road — he was nothing the kid from Te Atatū could ever have imagined becoming. That kid, the teenage Joe, would have liked that he was successful, would have loved the Porsche he drove, but he would have thought his older self an impossibly pretentious poseur — a wanker. Perhaps he was. But this was his life now. It was one he rather liked, in fact, except that he had no one with whom he could share it with the same emotional and intellectual intensity, closeness and connection with which Leo had started him off on this path.

A relentless *unst, unst* spilled from the hangar along with a haze of coloured light that pulsed with the music. Inside, the cavernous space was thick with the haze of dry ice and reeked with the smell of a thousand male bodies sweating through expensive colognes. Joe was unsure if he'd come out to escape the music or the smell but, either way, the cooler open air was a welcome relief as he stepped outside. He soon became aware of new smells out here — the sweet smell of fast food and then the acrid stench of vomit. He turned. To his left, a kid in angel wings was throwing up. His friend, identically dressed in wings, lamé shorts and gold-painted Roman sandals, held back the large feathered appendages, lest the kid wearing them topple over into the puddle that, with each convulsion, grew around his feet.

The party was still ramping up. The star DJ was two or three sets away, but already the showground was full of those the party had ejected. Through that crowd, made up of damaged kids and leering old men, the occasional group of god-like creatures would prance, passing three-abreast like Auckland cyclists, similarly arrogant, similarly untouchable. Joe felt in the middle somewhere. Damaged certainly, occasionally leering, not in his twenties anymore but not yet old. Not an Adonis — he had never been an Adonis — but he knew he wasn't bad either. He checked himself over for about the tenth time that night. His silky black t-shirt stretched tight across his chest. It gripped his stomach. He knew it rose up as he danced, exposing his carefully maintained lower abs. His black shorts clung tight. His new underwear, purchased that day, placed his business where his business needed to be. He felt good. Better than those angel-kids anyway. Somewhere around here was Tony, his trophy boyfriend, who, for all his shit, was still super cute.

As a length of discarded tinsel tumbled past in the warm breeze, Joe took a deep breath and decided to venture back into the fray. He needed to find Tony, who had disappeared some time ago with his hospo mates. He didn't much like the moustachioed restaurant queens with whom Tony hung out. Joe referred to them privately as 'the fluffies' because it suited him to tease Tony a little, and because they were, to a man, all vacuous froth. It had genuinely pissed him off when the core fluffies appeared, coincidentally, at the same Oxford Street bar where they had joined the pre-party crowd. This was supposed to be *their* weekend in Sydney. He had chosen that bar because it was old school. It wasn't likely to be frequented by tourists. That hadn't meant a thing. The bar was packed wall to wall. All of Sydney was out for this one. Every bar on the strip heaved with bodies. Tony feigned ignorance, pointing out that every gay boy in Auckland was over for the party. From the immediate evidence, he might have been right. Still. Edging around the dance floor, he spotted Dave, a one-time hookup and now friend, dancing alone. Dave saw him too and beckoned.

'Where's Tony?' asked Dave over the music.

'I have no idea.' The music had momentarily surged, and so they were now both shouting.

'I wouldn't let that one out of my sight if I were you. He's trouble.'

Joe nodded in agreement and the two men danced together for a while, lost in the beat of the music. Then Dave put one hand on his shoulder and indicated with the other towards Tony among a group of men dancing in close formation on the floor. Stripped to their underwear, they were grinding hard against each other in time to the music. In the centre, a tall, sleek, muscular boy with a trim black beard and handlebar moustache jumped up and down. At the top of each high leap, he sprayed the others with the contents of his water bottle. The men below ran their hands over each other, massaging the rain of water across their warm, glistening bodies as they locked lips together in changing arrangements. Only as the water boy completed his highest leap yet did a flash of pendulous cock make it clear that the communal strip hadn't universally stopped at underwear. Joe watched Tony as the whole group bounced rhythmically together. Around them, an increasingly large group of men collected, half-dancing, half-watching the seething mass of sleek, muscled bodies. Tony always moved well, like a piece of silk in the wind, and he loved an audience. He knew too that he was feigning indifference to the circle of viewers around him.

'Hospos,' Joe explained to Dave with a roll of his eyes. 'The Fluffies.' Dave shrugged to indicate he hadn't understood. Joe waved his hand to show it didn't matter.

'Watch him,' warned Dave again.

'Ha. Why, half of Sydney is doing that for me?' Executing a sweeping 180-degree turn, he danced away from Dave, before spinning back and dancing towards him again.

'Trouble. Sexy, sexy trouble.'

Joe leant in close to Dave. 'What was that?' As he spoke he felt two arms circle his chest from behind. Searching fingers then ran down his stomach, across his abs and glanced off his thighs before disappearing. Next Joe felt someone begin to gyrate softly against him, rubbing themselves rhythmically against his backside. Turning, he encountered a slender young redhead — a kid of barely twenty — dressed in nothing but the skimpiest candy-striped blue and white togs, the narrow bars of which swum attractively across the curves of his pelvis. The kid smiled, oblivious to the possibility that someone might object to being so intimately frisked by a stranger.

Swaying back a few steps the boy continued his dance without speaking or in any other way acknowledging Joe, except with a beatific smile that radiated across his face. They danced together for a while. The kid was cute — young and cute. His body was alabaster white — the abraded line of muscle bumps on his torso cast grey shadows against his skin. A slash of freckles peppered his face and shoulders. Euphoric, the kid was in a trance, smiling and dancing in swooping gestures.

Dave tapped him on the shoulder. 'He likes you,' he gestured at the kid.

'Yep, seems like it. He's about eighteen, would be my guess,' Joe said, having adjusted his estimate down.

Dave nodded in agreement. 'Go for it. You know Tony would.' He gestured across the floor to where Tony's gyrations had led him into a semi-crouched position, from where he appeared to be simulating a blowjob. 'Any rate, have fun. I'm going outside.'

The boy leant forward, placing his hands on the back of Joe's neck, rubbing himself softly against his groin in a swirling motion in time with the music.

Then into his ear, barely audible, the boy said something indistinct. Joe signalled a state of incomprehension by furrowing his brow and placing his finger next to his ear to indicate that he hadn't heard. 'Jew,' the boy said, pointing to himself. It was still hard to hear him clearly. 'Jew,' he repeated. The act of pointing led the boy into another long pirouette across the floor. As Joe watched, he was unsure what this spontaneous declaration of faith had meant. The kid was still smiling and, judging from the outline in his speedo, what he said might be true.

'Okay,' Joe nodded and smiled as the kid again came into his orbit. 'Jew.'

The kid, smiling, spun away again in a big arc. Joe was going to tell him that he wasn't Jewish, that he wasn't really anything, but the kid had clearly moved on. Swaying with the music, he looked at Joe and grinned. As the DJ flooded the hangar with the opening beats of *Blue Monday*, a large crowd surged onto the dance floor, pushing him and his new dance partner together. Mouthing the lyrics 'I can and shall obey,' the redhead grinned broadly at him before meeting the verse again. 'But if it wasn't for your fortune, I'd be a heavenly person today.'

'That's not the line,' Joe started to say but, not wanting to ruin the moment, he allowed his voice to tail off. At any rate, there was no chance the kid could hear him. He smiled. This had been the only song that Leo had ever danced to in public. For a moment Joe lost himself completely in both that memory and the attractions of a new young man.

'What the fuck?'

'Tony.' The kid moved in, oblivious to Tony's presence. 'Just having fun.'

'He's, like, fifteen.'

'Twenty at least,' Joe said, reclaiming his original assessment. 'And, anyway, you seemed pretty occupied.' Tony looked at the kid who was dancing alone, still smiling, a few metres away, the crowd having again dispersed.

'Don't fool yourself that the kid's into you,' Tony said with a mean smirk. 'He's just fucked up — high. He'd do anyone about now.' The kid danced back into range. 'Fuck off,' snarled Tony.

'Shit, Tony, leave the kid alone.'

'I said FUCK OFF.' Tony pushed the kid square in the chest. He wobbled for a moment then, instead of falling, he spun off like a top across the floor. 'Aaron has scored some coke. Maybe I'll catch you later, back at the hotel?'

Joe wasn't good at drugs beyond the occasional joint. Once upon a time, he'd have been asked to join them, but these days Tony preferred to go it alone. That was fine. He watched as Tony re-joined his posse waiting by the entrance. The big guy, taking his time to climb back into his underwear, was collecting admiring glances. He looked around, but the kid had disappeared into the crowd. Joe danced alone for a while. It was getting light. He would head for the hotel room. Tony would follow. He usually did.

As Joe walked along the concourse littered with tinsel, the occasional discarded t-shirt, then a familiar pair of angel's wings, now bent and broken, he noticed the blue speedo kid sitting alone on a park bench. Walking up to him, he realised he didn't know his name.

'Are you all right?' There was no response. The kid looked like he might be asleep. Sitting down beside him, he turned and again asked, 'You okay?'

When the kid didn't respond a second time, Joe prodded his arm gently. 'What's your name?' Without making a sound, the kid fell awkwardly, his head landing with a thud on the park bench. He groaned. The kid was at least alive. Joe shifted slightly so the kid's head rested in his lap. Shit, he was completely out of it. He placed his hand gently on the boy's head and stroked his forehead. A loose lock of red hair captured his attention. Lifting it gently, he tucked it back behind the boy's ear. He was considering what to do when two young men — one blond and the other dark — approached the park bench.

'Hey, Mister, what the fuck?' asked the blond guy.

'Is he your friend? He's passed out,' replied Joe.

'Passed out with his face in your dick. Old perv.' said the dark-haired guy.

Recognising 'dick' rather than 'deek', Joe asked, 'Are you Kiwis?'

'Yep, he is,' replied the blond. 'I'm local. That's my cousin.' He gestured to the boy on Joe's lap. The guy gestured to his friend that he needed a hand and together the two guys lifted the comatose body off Joe's lap and balanced him between them.

'The wines were too various. It was neither the quality nor the quantity but the mixture.'[2] Looking at the blank faces of the two boys in front of him, Joe immediately regretted employing a literary allusion at 5 a.m., not when his audience were young party boys. To reclaim a little of his cool, he added, 'Well, it goes something like that.'

The dark-haired boy shook his head. 'Nah, it's the eccy — he's totally fucked up. He'll be okay tomorrow or the next day.' The redhead opened his eyes momentarily and mumbled something before passing out again. Together, the two friends set off down the concourse, half-carrying, half-dragging the limp body between them. Hopefully, he'd be all right.

Tony didn't reappear until the end of the following day. An after-party, he'd called it. What did Joe expect?

Later that day, they were sitting in their seats, complimentary glasses of champagne in hand, as the first of the economy passengers began trailing past. Tony jumped up to high-five some of them. At others he waved his champagne glass, shrieking, 'Move on, loser.' Just as Joe settled into his magazine, turning away from the spectacle of yet another scene, he started to plan 'the conversation' he knew he'd have to have with Tony. There was no point dragging out the inevitable.

Joe was fond of Gabriel Oaks, one of Thackeray Makepeace's smaller developments. Looking up at the two integrated rows, each consisting of four three-storey townhouses placed sharp end to the street, it felt to him like a revisit of the little schemes with which they had started out. The site had been Kurt's earliest purchase — acquired long before Joe had come onboard and he'd got the crucial section in a deal by which the elderly owner retained life-time occupancy — only to take longer than expected to depart. The development was currently only in block form, still roofless and exposed. It looked as severe as it was ever going to be and he wished they could somehow stop there. The floor under his shoes was wet and littered with leaves and small branches. Auckland had received another thorough beating. During a weekend storm, rainwater had poured in through the roof openings and where they had yet to fit windows and doors. He had used the weather as an excuse to check out any potential damage on the site before going into the office that morning. There was none. As the sun began to reach into the spaces, he was just killing time.

With some of their more recent developments, Joe had devised a personal mind game, naming projects after characters in old novels. It amused him greatly to sneak these past Jacinta. He'd gotten away with Rawdon Crawley, Valmont and Fifine. Jacinta had never bothered to ask who Gabriel might have been. She'd never read *Far from the Madding Crowd*. It was a small thing but, climbing the roughly formed concrete steps towards the sunlit roof of the southern block, he grinned, savouring his latest small victory over the all-conquering machine that was his publicist.

At the top of the stairs, Joe looked out over spectacular sea views that Kurt could only have guessed at when he'd bought the properties. The return on the two front units alone, commanding as they did the best views, would go a very long way to filling the Tony-sized hole in his bank balance. Looking down onto the unformed driveway of the neighbouring block, he glanced at a delivery truck as it pulled up. There was nothing special about it but he watched as the driver swung down from the open cab door. Suddenly something tore at the bottom of his stomach and moments later had moved on, taking a stranglehold on his heart. It thumped violently in his chest. He was sure. Damn sure. Yes, he was about to puke. He crouched on the ground. He placed his hand on his throat as if this could keep his entire insides from spilling out onto the rough concrete floor. With his other hand he reached out, steadying himself against the parapet wall. Crouching there, swaying unsteadily on the balls of his feet, he watched as Leo unloaded the truck.

As he stood up, his head was spinning. His entire body burned hot. Leaning back against the cool of the damp block wall, he inhaled deeply. Collecting his thoughts, he figured Leo was now in his mid-thirties. He was almost four years older than Joe, and it had been nearly ten years. Those years were supposed to have counted for something. The long hours imagining Leo's eventual return *should* have prepared him for this moment. Life had surely hardened him, but there in his chest, he could feel his heart beating violently. It was as if, having been released from a confined room, it was stretching itself in the warm sunshine for the first time in years. From the distance of the rooftop, Leo appeared unchanged. He was as magnetically handsome as he had been that first Tuesday morning when he had appeared in Joe's rear-view mirror. All Joe could think about now was once again lying next to Leo and exploring every inch of that body, checking this older Leo against the records of the younger man that he had stored for so long in the hard drive of his brain.

After a while making his way down to the ground, Joe moved slowly in the direction of the site manager's office. Years ago, he had needed to ask guys on site sly questions without wanting to appear too interested. Now he simply asked straight out.

'Can I see that delivery docket please?' The foreman handed over the green page, and Joe casually checked the details, while the foreman looked on nervously. 'Who was that driver — do you know?'

'No, never seen him before.'

'Find out, will you? The guy looks familiar. Somehow I recall a problem.'

When the foreman reported back a few days later, it seemed that Leo hadn't been doing so well. He'd been back from Christchurch for a couple of years. He'd worked a few different sites but was picky about projects. Soon after he'd arrived back, the luxury jobs had disappeared.

None of that sounded surprising to Joe. His firm had scaled back on the high-end projects of late too. In that, at least, Gabriel Oaks was something of a gamble based on a hunch that the luxury market was now in recovery. Apparently, Leo had been helping to restore a friend's classic boat, and sleeping on it too. He was doing part-time deliveries for a building firm. The foreman had nothing else.

One Saturday morning, a fortnight later, Joe caught sight of Leo walking down Ponsonby Road. Leo hadn't seen him, but with no time to gather his thoughts, Joe stepped out into his path like a flasher.

'Leo, I want to talk to you.'

Blindsided, Leo came to an abrupt stop. Joe suddenly recalled how big and commanding Leo's presence was. After a moment, Leo began to move again. Joe had always been nimbler than Leo, so he easily blocked Leo's attempts to step around him. Like a wild cat trapped in the corner of a shed, Leo recoiled. His eyes flashed.

'What do you want, Joe? I can't do this here.' His voice, a low growl, reminding Joe of his animal namesake. As Leo tried again to move around him, Joe reached out for his sleeve. Leo pushed Joe's hand aside. 'Don't.'

It took everything Joe had to get his words out. 'Hey man, I just wanted to say hello. It's great to see you. You're looking really good. That's all.' He stepped back slightly to give Leo some space. Leo looked warily at Joe, his hands thrust into his jeans pockets. He looked at the ground and then back up at Joe again.

'Joe, I *can't.*'

Joe's next words came a little more fluently. 'Relax, Leo. Look, I have a job for you. I heard a rumour that you're looking. I've got a spot for a builder — finishing work, nice project, pays well.' Leo looked even more uncomfortable at Joe's proposal. He looked again at the ground as he spoke.

'Ah, I don't think so. It's not a good idea. It's just not . . . not now.'

'You working at the moment?'

Leo shifted from one foot to the other. Still clearly pissed off, he answered. 'I've got a truck.'

'I mean building. Leo, are you building? Are you making things?'

Again, Leo looked at Joe directly for a moment, before answering. 'There's stuff coming up soon — stuff without complications. I'll be fine in a month or two.'

'Without complications? You mean without me?' Leo shrugged. With a little forward motion, he indicated that he just wanted to keep walking. At that moment Joe figured he had nothing to lose. Now the words came fast, not loud, but with all the strength of purpose he could muster.

'Okay. Truce. What's the problem here? We were *friends*. As far as I'm concerned, we still are. This isn't about fucking. This isn't about 1994. It's about now — a whole new century. It's about the fact that right now you *need* a friend who can help you out. From what I can see I might be the only one you've got. So stop being such a dick, Leo. Take the fucking job or—' Out of breath and words, Joe stalled.

'Or what?' Leo's flat tone dared Joe to make a threat.

'Just take the job, Leo.' Joe held out his hand for Leo to shake but, eyeing it suspiciously, Leo left it in mid-air. Joe stepped aside and, with a sweep of his rejected hand, Joe indicated that Leo was now free to continue his walk down the street. Pulling the collar of his jacket up around his neck, Leo walked off without looking back. Joe called down the street after him. 'Be at the office 7.30 a.m., Monday.' Only then did he dare take a deep breath and inhale what remained of Leo's lingering scent.

Joe walked through the door of the first café he saw. Looking at the heaving mass of people, he turned and walked out again. A few minutes later he found an unfashionable side street bakery café, where he figured he could think undisturbed. Joe collapsed into a seat. The adrenaline that had coursed through his system only moments earlier was now ebbing fast. He felt suddenly drained.

As the waiter brought the coffee he'd ordered, Joe asked for a second. He knew he'd need the caffeine. Beyond that, he wasn't sure of anything. He was confused. What had just happened? He had for a long time imagined being reunited with Leo. Of course he'd imagined that they would find a way to fall back into each other's arms. However, this encounter had made that scenario seem ridiculously unlikely.

Since first discovering Leo was in town, Joe had been periodically struck by a wave of feeling. It was as if his past had dumped his younger self, coughing and spluttering, back intact and alive onto the sands of his current life. Now it felt as though this younger Joe was sitting at the table next to him, awaiting the arrival of *his* coffee, keen to regain control of their situation. He could see him reflected in the café window, identifiable on his left profile. A face that lacked the small white scar that had come to symbolise both the stupidity of Joe's youth and his transition into something resembling adulthood.

Turning his head slightly, the kid was gone, replaced by the adult Joe. For weeks now, since Leo had reappeared, these two Joes had been locked in a battle that began every morning in the bathroom mirror, continued in the rear-view mirror of his car and the reflection of his computer screen, before a return performance in the bathroom mirror at night. Now, as he shifted his head slowly from side to side, Joe no longer cared how it might seem to passers-by. He was trying to find a way forward, something that made sense.

Years earlier, his younger self had stood silent in the carpark of an Avondale pub, waiting, wanting nothing other than for Leo to take him home. Back then he'd relied on the goodwill of the universe to make it happen. He wasn't now so naïve to believe that Leo was about to follow him home — that the cosmos cared much about him. Not after everything that had happened. Yet, his whole body yearned for that very same experience. The pain of desire that had come with Leo's return cut fresh and deep. The younger Joe just wanted to find the quickest path back to Leo's bed. The older Joe, the one who had faced Leo on the footpath a few moments earlier, now imagined himself back at the crossroads offered him in a carpark more or less a decade earlier and knew he wanted something else. He knew now he wanted the 'something better given time' that Leo had offered the night they'd split.

Joe congratulated himself. He told himself that, entirely unrehearsed, the words he'd managed to speak were the first emotionally adult words of his new life. Yes, there had been too much swearing, but at least he had managed to say what needed to be said. Leo needed a friend. There and then Joe had stepped into the gap. Although no oaths had been sworn, no contracts signed, Joe had offered a new pact to Leo, a declaration of love that delivered a second chance, a far more significant promise than that which had been on offer the first time around. Sure, Leo still had to actually turn up and, with the vision of his hand left hovering mid-air, Joe wasn't too hopeful about that. All Joe had to rely on was that Leo would search his soul and find something close to what *he* now felt.

Then there was Joe's next problem. They never had been friends. Back then, Joe had introduced Leo to his mates as, 'My friend Leo,' but in actual fact they weren't friends at all, they had been lovers. Now, having made a very public declaration of friendship, Joe wasn't quite sure he knew how to be friends with the guy. Not when a very significant part of himself really, desperately, wanted to have his clothes torn off and be thrown to the ground for a weekend of really hard lovemaking.

CHAPTER 9

Joe rested on the wooden bench, back against the lockers. The squash game had been hard. His new playing partner had opted out of a shower and jumped straight into his car. Joe didn't mind. If being naked in a locker room with Joe freaked the guy out for the moment, so be it. The guy was okay.

Getting up, sticky with sweat, Joe made his way slowly to the shower stall. Once inside, he threw his towel over the top of the door and turned on the water. After waiting a few moments, he walked into the warm stream, the hot cascade felt heavenly on his tired body. Five minutes later he hauled his towel down off the door, placed it over his head and began drying himself. As he was about to flick the lock on the door to 'open', he heard something that caught his attention. Two men had come out of the sauna and now stood talking. He held the towel to his chest, listening. The voices were loud and confident.

'One more and it's all ours. We should have knocked it off first but it won't be an issue. We might have to pay a little over the odds if he cottons on, but without that property, we don't have access.'

'He's got no idea?' asked a second, quieter, voice.

'It's a hat shop or something. Of course he has no bloody idea,' said the first voice. 'No, we're essentially home clear.'

Then the second voice, now even quieter, said, 'Careful. There's a lot riding on this. Remember, Wright plays here.' Until then, the conversation had been fascinating enough. It was good industry gossip of the sort that he'd missed since he and Tony had split after returning from Mardi Gras. However, at the mention of his own name, Joe's ears really pricked up. Silently, he placed his hands on the top of the partition walls and lifted his feet off the floor, bracing himself against the door in front of him, and hung on. If anyone checked under the door, the stall would appear empty, although the two men seemed too oblivious to their surroundings to care. They kept talking.

'No queer's going to get the better of me. I'm sick of that smug faggot. His face might be all over the papers, but he'll be gone in six months' time. They just don't have what it takes to make it in business.'

'Too busy with their hair and nails,' the second voice added and both men laughed.

The first voice resumed. 'You give me the name of one queer worth even $10 million. He's done a few small things but, Christ, would you do business with him? No one serious does. He minces around those little pansy developments, with their pretentious names, like there's a piece of reinforcing steel shoved up his arse. Fuck — they disgust me.' The second voice said something inaudible and the two men eventually moved off.

Lowering himself to the ground, Joe rubbed the blood back into his sore hands. Throwing his towel back over the door, he turned the shower back on.

'There's no hat shop, but there's a glove maker here.' Nick, from Legal, was pointing at the planning map. Joe had never quite understood Nick's choice in eyewear. His oversized frames were more *Tootsie* than you'd expect from a lawyer. 'It's what you're looking for, I'm sure. All the properties surrounding it have moved into new ownership in the last five years. Which normally you'd take to mean someone is accumulating, right? Interestingly, in this case, no two properties are owned by the same firm. Well, not on the surface of it, but I did some digging. They're all shell companies. They trace back to Honeywell, which is Todd Wilding and Bill Fowler, both members of your squash club.' Nick smiled broadly at Joe. 'I've compiled a dossier on them. It's been fun actually.' Tracing his fingers across the map, he continued. 'They need this property for access — all the other boundaries are small lanes. The increased traffic load on any of those means that, without the glove shop property, the Council would never okay a development big enough to deliver the necessary returns. It's the only possible place for an underground car park entrance. If I—' Nick stopped, corrected himself, and resumed, 'If *we* were doing this, I'd have secured that property first. Everything hangs on it.' Joe looked at Nick, whose skinny frame seemed to quiver with excitement, and then back down at the map.

'Thanks, Nick. You've been very thorough.'

'It's a rookie mistake.'

'Maybe, maybe not. I suspect these guys think the world is exclusively their playground. There are plenty out there just like them.' Joe looked up from the map. 'These two, however, consider themselves particularly entitled.'

'And they're not?' Nick said with a shrug. 'So, what next?'

'Let's just say the gloves are off.'

The sign read CLOSED, but Joe tried the handle. It turned in his hand and the door opened. An old shop bell tinkled above him as he stepped through the entranceway. He scanned the empty room. On either side of the shop were parallel wooden counters. Both of them were clad in old red and white Formica edged with a chrome strip. Behind both rose a large bank of cream painted shelves with a thin pinstripe of red to the edge of each shelf. Once filled with boxes, the shelves were now only sparsely populated. Those left exposed appeared coated with a blanket of grey dust. Joe coughed involuntarily.

Glancing to the left, he saw, hanging from the ceiling, a red and cream sign saying *Men's Gloves*. On the corresponding right-hand side, another sign read *Ladies' Gloves*. No one appeared, so Joe moved over to wait in the still empty shop in front of the men's counter. Spying a bell, he rang it.

After a moment or two, an elderly man dressed in a purple suit, the narrow lapels of which revealed its advanced age, emerged from the back. He took up what Joe felt sure was a position, long ago assigned, behind the counter.

'Can I help you, Sir?'

'Yes. Well, gloves, I suppose.'

'Oh, I am sorry. We don't do retail these days. I assumed you were here for something else,' he looked at Joe closely. 'Selling something, perhaps?' Without waiting for a response, the man continued. 'I'm just here tidying things up. We have some last orders, largely South Island, Ballantynes, but not much for Auckland. Then we're done.'

The old man gave the countertop a couple of short, sharp pats with his hand.

'What sort of gloves were you looking for?'

'To be honest, I'm not sure. I've never owned anything other than ski gloves. I didn't know there was a local glovemaker until yesterday.'

'Well, we're the last. This was my grandfather's firm. Founded 1902. In his day we supplied everyone. Even Edward, Prince of Wales, when he had a glove emergency on his tour in 1920.' The man gestured at a shabby cast papier mâché royal warrant that hung over the front door. Joe wondered what constituted 'a glove emergency', but the man interrupted his thoughts, asking, 'What type of glove?'

'Sorry?'

'What type of gloves do you require? What is the occasion?'

'What do you recommend?' The man turned around and took a long cardboard box down from the shelf.

'These should do you, quite general purpose, walking, driving, etc.' Lifting open the lid, he pulled back a layer of tissue. 'Donkey-grey kidskin.' He took the gloves from the box and placed them in Joe's hands. They were soft, and for a moment he ran them through his fingers.

'So, your son isn't taking over then?'

'I was, as we used to say, "not the marrying kind".' The man stopped as if on the point of saying something else.

'Me neither.' Joe looked up at the man and smiled.

'I guessed. Young men, young New Zealand men, don't normally buy gloves. They don't even consider them. They stick their hands in their pockets. They slouch around like baboons. You have a certain—' he stopped and looked Joe up and down before continuing, '—recognisable bearing.'

Joe smiled. 'Thank you.'

'Well, it's nice to see there are still men of taste out there, even if all this doesn't endure.' The man gestured towards the empty shelves and then turned again to face Joe. 'My name is Gerald Gilmore.'

'I'm Joe Wright. Nice to meet you.' Joe extended his hand. Rather than shake it, Gerald clasped it in his and stroked it gently.

'Nice hands,' Gerald said, then added, 'I think in your case, we might progress to doe skin.'

'Thanks.' Joe looked for a moment at his hands, newly discovered, before continuing, 'What will you do?' Gerald took the gloves and placed them back in the box. Folding over the leaf of white tissue, he replaced the lid and returned the carton to the shelf. Moving a little further along the shelves, he climbed a few steps up a small ladder. Taking down an almost identical box, he placed it on the counter. Only then did he answer Joe's question.

'I'll sell up, when I've sorted things. I've got a niece who lives in Melbourne. I don't want her burdened with this when I go. I've had an offer.' Gerald opened the second box. 'Now, I don't have grey in the doe skin, but I do have this yellow.' He handed the gloves to Joe. 'I'll see. I wouldn't mind retiring to Bali — it would be nice to put my feet up.'

Joe smiled. 'Really?'

'Does that surprise you?' Gerald eyed him suspiciously. Joe suspected the likely reason Honeywell had waited so long to buy the property was in the hope that Gerald might die in the interim. 'Frankly, they can pull it down if they want. It's no skin off my nose. The shop's had its day, much like me. It's liberating, in a way, to know the end is nigh. I'm not the sentimental type.' Joe had pulled the yellow glove over his right hand and was now inspecting it closely.

'That's too large for you. A glove must fit closely — like a second skin.' Gerald again took Joe's hand. Slipping the glove off, he laid it on top of its partner on the red countertop. He turned and took another pair from the box, checking the tiny label sewn into the cuff. 'Try this one.' He manoeuvred the glove carefully over Joe's palm, inching the glove across his hand. Then, pressing lightly on the space between each finger he positioned the quirk of the glove firmly against the base of each finger in turn. Finally, he moved his attention to the fit of the thumb. Stopping and standing back for a moment, Gerald looked pleased. Leaning in, he gave the glove a firm tug at the cuff and secured the button at the wrist. 'Perfect.' Gerald took Joe's other hand and repeated the process.

'Thank you.' Joe was looking down at his hands now clad in the bright yellow gloves, which indeed fitted like a second skin.

'Machine sewn. In some of those Johnny-come-lately menswear boutiques in the city, they will tell you handmade gloves are superior. Never believe it — machine sewing is finer and the look more elegant. These are unlined. The leather will play directly against your skin and meld to it.' He stood back. 'Yes, you look quite the flâneur.'

Joe appreciated the use of a word he'd read but never heard spoken, but he wasn't sure he'd be wearing the bright yellow gloves anytime soon. It would require a couple of stiff drinks before he would be likely to venture out in public wearing such obviously 'gay' gloves. As if reading Joe's mind, Gerald spoke. 'They were, you might be surprised to know, once considered a staple of any well-dressed man's wardrobe. In some more civilised countries, yellow gloves still are. You will find they go well with most ensembles.' Joe looked again at the gloves, which matched the pale grey of his pinstriped suit perfectly. 'Yes,' continued Gerald, 'yellow, burgundy, grey and blue, they are the building blocks of any glove collection . . . and of course white for the opera.'

'And brown?'

'Hmm.' Gerald frowned. 'Not since Mr Simpson. It's all changed.'

'You mean Mrs Simpson, surely? The Duchess of Windsor?' Joe asked, indicating the warrant over the door.

'No. I meant Mr Orange Juice Simpson. No respectable gentleman would appear in brown gloves for a decade or two after that.' Joe was going to say that he didn't think the 'OJ' in OJ Simpson stood for orange juice but looking again at Gerald he wondered perhaps if he might be being teased. Instead, he moved to the business at hand.

'I might be able to help. In fact, that's sort of why I came in.'

'Oh yes. Help with what?' Gerald looked intensely at Joe who met his gaze.

'I'd like to make you an offer.'

'And not on a pair of doeskins, I presume?'

'Well, yes — I will take the gloves. I might even take the whole box, but I am referring to another offer.'

'Our boxes of gloves are arranged in style, not size. As to quantity, a pair of Gilmore Gloves will last a gentleman a lifetime. You do not require a gross of them.' Gerald replaced the lid of the box. It felt for a moment as if Joe might be asked to leave, but then Gerald continued. 'But you seem like a good fellow and to be honest I have not had as good-looking a man as you through the doors in years.' Joe blushed. 'Hands.' Joe offered up his gloved hands and Gerald turned them palm up. He unbuttoned each cuff, then, one by one, he tugged lightly on the end of each finger in turn. Then, with an additional tug, the gloves, that a moment ago had fitted snugly, effortlessly slipped from his hands.

Gerald flattened the gloves. Then, folding the thumbs over the palms, he placed the pair, palms together, on the countertop. From underneath the counter he took a smooth sheet of red tissue paper, the name *Gilmore* printed across it, and wrapped the gloves before placing them in a small, cream cardboard pouch. This he sealed with an adhesive sticker featuring two intertwined Gs. 'Compliments of the management. Really, you were fortunate we had your size.' Gerald handed him the stylish parcel. 'Now come through. I'll make tea and we can talk.' As Joe admired the small parcel in his hands, Gerald, emerging from behind the counter, walked towards the front door. He turned over the sign so that it now read OPEN from the outside. Once Gerald had turned away, Joe discretely reversed the sign and silently activated the door lock. This was not a moment for interruptions.

The two men settled on either side of a large wooden table in what had once been a busy staffroom.

'So, you're gay?' Joe asked.

'My generation was never that forward, nor did we use that word — not in *that* context — but in answer to your question, yes I am.' Gerald was pouring tea from an old brown earthenware pot into two tannin-stained, lavender-toned Wedgewood cups. Joe recognised the shape and style from his mother's china cabinet, where they had sat admired but unused all his life.

'And you ran this business?'

'Well, one could, you know, in fashion. It was safe. Having a go at men in fashion and accessories was more difficult when Fred Allen, the All Black captain, was in dresses and Ron Don, the Head of the Rugby Union, was in lace. It was a different world then.'

'And they treated you well — those blokes?' Joe asked curiously.

'Not well, but tolerably. We got by,' Gerald said, sipping his tea. 'What business did you say you were in?'

'Property development.'

'Oh, that's tough, I'd imagine. And how did you get into that line of work?'

'Well, I've been a builder since I was seventeen.'

'Oh honey, how long ago was that?' asked Gerald, with a barely suppressed giggle. 'When did you know?'

'About?'

'When did you know you were one of the lavender set?'

Joe considered for a moment. 'As a child. Don't we all really know then?'

'Perhaps, but it's not a common perspective. Most parents like to hold on to the belief that their child is, well, *normal,* until the last possible minute. Until they're told otherwise, in fact. I'm not sure you can blame them for that. When did you do something about it?'

'At seventeen. In a ladder store.'

Gerald raised his eyebrows and laughed. 'Oh my, you're a confident one.'

Joe thought for a moment. 'Oh no, not a ladder *shop*, a lockup — a shed. He was older than I was.'

'You young ones. It's all Americanisms, ass not *arse*, store rather than shop.' Gerald stopped for a moment. 'They always are, you know, older, but under the skin, young or old, we're all the same — survivors.'

'That's kind of why I'm here — to prove that, young or old, together the pansies are tougher than the world thinks.'

'Now, that's a word I recognise.' Gerald, waved his teacup in salute.

'Someone's going to make you a good offer on this property.'

'They already have — I told you — I have a letter. They sent a minion to follow up. I am waiting to meet the principals. Indeed, when you first walked in, I thought you might be one of them. Let me guess — you want me to sell to you instead?'

'Yes, sell to me at the price they're offering now, but I'll also pay their eventual offer price.'

Gerald blinked slowly. 'Sorry. I'm confused. Are you saying you'll pay me twice?'

'Essentially. I'll pay their offer price now. Better still, I'll buy Gilmore Gloves from you too, as well as the property. I'll deal with everything. Then I'll broker what will look to them like a sale. On that I'll split the difference with you — fifty/fifty paid in annual instalments and at the current rate of interest.'

'Oh, on tick?'

'Yes, I suppose so. Property on,' Joe stopped for a moment to remember the term, 'my mother did it — oh yes, property on lay-by.'

'Not quite,' Gerald corrected him. 'In retail with lay-by, you don't get the goods until you've paid. That's why no one does it now — all that waiting before you get your hands on the goods. People just aren't interested in that, not now.'

'Perfect, lay-by then, no public record of the transfer of ownership until after the deal with Honeywell is done.'

'Why don't I just get the full price from them?' asked Gerald casually.

'Because I usually have a little more to offer than the price of a pair of gloves.' Gerald raised his eyebrows. 'Sorry, I wasn't trying to be rude.

We won't actually sell it to them. We're just going to have some fun. Think of it as me paying you to help me bring down a couple of smug homophobic arseholes.'

'Language.' Joe took the rebuke with a smile. He rather liked Gerald.

'These men, they owe you something?' asked Gerald from across the table.

'Yes. They owe us *both* a little respect.'

'Sounds fun.'

'It should be.'

Gerald again raised his teacup. 'Oh well, here's to a little late life activism. You know, I think there might be a bottle of gin here somewhere.'

Gerald was dressed in his best suit, a pale grey and pink windowpane check. Under it, he wore a green shirt and a soft lavender waistcoat with silver buttons. At his throat was a carefully tied cerise silk bow tie. His hair possessed a freshly crimped look, and his cologne was noticeable. In his buttonhole, he wore a pink carnation.

'Too much?' he gestured to the carnation.

'It's perfect. I only wish it connected to a microphone.'

'Or it squirted.'

Joe leant in. 'Are you wearing eyeliner?' Before Gerald could answer, the doorbell tinkled. Leaving the side door slightly open, Joe took up his position in what had once been the secretary's office. He stood behind the open door just long enough to hear the two voices from the racquet club as they moved mechanically through the empty rituals of a business greeting. Joe then relocated a little further into the office where, although better concealed, he could still hear most of the conversation. Gerald invited the two men to sit. Once they had settled, they resumed their conversation.

'As per our letter and the previous discussion, we're offering you $2 million,' said a voice he guessed was Bill Fowler.

'Oh, that's such a lot of money. I just don't know.' Gerald's tone was intentionally daffy and confused.

'You'll be able to retire a very happy man.'

'Of course, of course I could,' the pitch of Gerald's voice rose an octave. 'I just don't know what to do. Such a lot of history tied up in this building, you know? Family — three generations in fact.' Gerald began to launch into a long story regarding the founding of the business, but before he got much past the First World War, Fowler's voice interrupted him.

'We are authorised to go to $2.5 million.' If the threat of a long story was all it took for them to up their offer, then just how overexposed were Honeywell? Joe leant in closer.

'Oh, really? That's wonderful. Such a nice amount two-point-five, so very, very pretty, don't you think?'

'I suppose so?' said Fowler with a slightly bemused tone.

'Pretty like a pansy. You know, the flower. Do you like flowers, Mr Fowler?' There was a moment's silence. Joe's stomach tightened. This hadn't been part of the script they had practised earlier. Gerald was heading into potentially dangerous territory.

'Of course.' Fowler seemed a little confused, but before even a moment passed, Gerald followed up.

'Four would be better.' Gerald's voice had now dropped below its usual level. He was illustrating that he could indeed negotiate more than the price of a pair of gloves and up his own split of the profits. You had to respect the old guy.

'We could possibly go to three.' The gruff voice of Todd Wilding had entered the conversation.

'Oh yes?' Gerald paused for a long moment. 'You know that's a million more than your original offer?' Joe had no doubt towards whom that remark was addressed. 'Yes.' Gerald resumed the tone of his earlier scripted dialogue. 'I'd take *four* in a flash.' The two men said something Joe couldn't hear.

'We have a deal at four then?' Fowler asked.

'Oh yes, *we* have a deal.' Gerald almost squealed with excitement. The noise of chairs scraping against the wooden floor suggested that the two men had risen to shake on the arrangement. 'Yes, I would. I would take $4 million in a heartbeat but, sadly, I'm not the owner. I am not authorised to accept.' There was a moment's silence before Wilding spoke again.

'You're not? Gilmore Gloves owns the building surely?'

'Oh yes, they do.'

'And you're the proprietor of Gilmore Gloves?'

'Yes, in my family for three generations,' answered Gerald soberly and with a clear note of pride. 'As I was saying to you earlier, my grandfather was born—'

'Then you're the owner, Gerald Gilmore?' Wilding interrupted.

'Yes, I am Gerald Gilmore, but I just work here. Started in 1950 as the stock boy. Here I am fifty-something years later, less stock but still the boy. Gilmore Gloves and the property were sold a few weeks ago — on lay-by.'

Fowler and Wilding began talking to each other in low voices. The squeaking of springs suggested that Gerald had sat back down and was now leaning back in his chair to observe the confusion.

'Would you like to talk to the new owner?' Gerald asked.

'He's available?' the two men replied in unison.

'Oh yes, of course he's available. In fact, he's expecting you. I know he wants to sell just as much as I do. Would you like me to call him?'

'I'm not sure what you're playing at, Gilmore,' said Wilding sharply. 'Of course we would like to talk to this man . . . whoever he might be.'

'Surely. Just a moment.' As rehearsed, Gerald pressed the red button on his desk console and an old public address system took a moment to crackle into life. Then, for the last time, a series of trumpet-shaped Tannoy speakers relayed Gerald's words to every corner of the long silent factory.

'Mr Wright — if you could stop mincing around your latest *pansy* development — there are a couple of men down here who would like to talk to you.'

CHAPTER 10

Betty wanted to get a few things. So, having heard the rumours, Joe suggested a trip to the new Mega in Lincoln Road, Henderson. They hadn't even made it through the clacking turnstile before a burly greeter subjected him to his first raking head to toe assessment.

'Welcome to Mitre 10 Mega.'

'I'll need a big one.' The two men glanced knowingly at each other as Betty gestured at the line of shopping trolleys. Wrestling one out of the jam, Joe wondered which enlightened soul had come up with this place. Straight guys could have their supermarkets — they could point their bananas whichever way they liked — but here, wow! Gay tradie heaven and not more than a couple of miles from where he'd grown up. It was to him as if every man in range was in the process of cruising, looking, assessing possibilities and connecting.

Betty placed her handbag in the fold-down children's seat of the shopping trolley and took out her list. Two men passed by, looked him up and down, then turned to each other and laughed at some private joke. He leant over the end of the trolley, following them with his gaze, before realising that his rear was in the air. He clenched his gluteus tight and stretched out his leg behind him — hell, he'd worked long and hard on those calves.

It was a funny thing how people never really thought of tradies as gay. Men in shops were under suspicion, waiters for sure, fashion designers, ballet dancers always, but, in Joe's experience, ever since fluoro orange vests had caught on, there had been plenty of tradesmen looking for action. After all, it had been his tradies who had been the first to line up for the company's Hero float. And, all those years ago, it had been another builder, a polytech tutor, who had ushered his enthusiastic seventeen-year-old self into this world, after he'd been the last to hang up his gear in the ladder store.

Betty was now looking closely at a large display of kitchen gadgets hanging from metal hooks on a display wall. Joe had been shopping with her plenty of times in the past and knew that she would examine the items in front of her one by one, reading the labels in full and comparing quality and price.

'Are you all right there?' he asked her. 'Do you need any help?'

'I need a little spatula.'

Joe scanned the wall and then the aisle. No sign of a spatula. He knew it was going to take Betty some time to complete her search and there was no point hurrying her. He'd just have to wait. It was then that he noticed a young guy standing against the shelves, staring at him. Joe stared back. Now he was coming over. Joe looked at Betty — she was still preoccupied.

'Mate, are you Joe Wright, the developer, by any chance?' Before he had a chance to reply, the guy spoke again. 'From the billboards for wack-a-way and then make-peace.'

'Sorry?' He had never heard this variation of the company's name, but once he'd digested it, he smiled.

The guy produced a black marker pen. 'Can I have your autograph?'

'If you want, but I've got nothing to write on.'

'No matter.' The guy lifted his shirt and indicated his chest. Joe signed the smooth, recently waxed surface. He wondered for a moment whether he should add his phone number.

'Awesome, mate. Thanks so much,' said the guy as he lowered his shirt.

'You know I've never done that before — signed another human being.'

The guy laughed as he turned to walk off. 'My own personal tramp stamp — this is going to drive my boyfriend effin wild. I *love* this place.'

'Who was that?' asked Betty, clutching a large pink plastic spatula.

'Nobody. A fan.'

'I want a *little* rubber spatula. These are all too big.'

'What do you need a little one for?'

'Oh, they're very handy.' Betty resumed her search, intently examining the shelves again as if sure the missing item was concealed there somewhere.

Joe followed, leaning on the trolley as he pushed it slowly after her. Suddenly, Betty gave a small cry of glee and deposited a spatula, not much bigger than a ballpoint pen, carefully in the bottom of the large metal shopping trolley.

They turned into the next aisle — giftware. This was going to take a while. After all, Betty had spent her life selecting little gift items from import catalogues to supply department stores. He knew the recent flood of goods from China with their low prices and poor quality both disturbed and fascinated her.

Further along the aisle a couple caught Joe's eye. He was tall, muscular and dressed in a skin-tight pale blue rugby shirt, straight blue jeans and oversized white trainers. His girlfriend, a pretty blonde, was dressed identically. Together, the handsome couple were idly surveying the ceramic picture frames in front of them. Catching sight of Joe, the guy wedged his hand into the back pocket of his girlfriend's tight jeans, and she automatically nestled her head into his chest. Biting hard on his bottom lip, the guy scanned Joe's body. The hunger in his eyes was palpable — Joe thought the gaze of a stray dog at a butcher's shop window would seem more casual. He returned the compliment with a raking glance, indicating his appreciation with a smile. As their eyes met, the guy, losing his nerve, looked away.

Betty had disappeared. Joe looked about before spotting her through a gap in the two aisles. He wheeled the trolley with its lonely spatula, to catch up with her.

'Is there something unusual about this hardware shop?' Betty asked as he pulled up beside her.

'It's size, you mean?'

'No, something else.'

'As in?'

'The clientele — they seem somehow preoccupied.'

'Really — what with?'

'I'm not sure. It's probably nothing. I can't find it.'

'What?'

'Sandsoap. It should be here with the other cleaners.' As Betty looked about, a young female assistant appeared. She greeted them cheerfully.

'Can I help you find something?'

'Do you have sandsoap?'

The girl looked confused. 'Sandsoap?'

'You use it after you've cut up a chicken or been dealing with liver on a wooden bench.' The girl scanned the shelves before announcing.

'We have Solvol.'

Joe offered his two-cents worth. 'That's what mechanics use to get the grease off their hands.' He looked again at 'rugby shirt' and his girlfriend who had followed him round to this aisle. The girlfriend now clutched a picture frame with an image of a pre-made family in it. Rugby shirt seemed to have a sudden interest in cleaning products but equally seemed to be avoiding Joe's gaze. Joe sensed that every time he turned away those hungry eyes were upon him again.

'Chimney sweeps use it too, but it's not what I'm after,' added Betty.

'Sandsoap is quite different. Pearson's used to make it. It's in an orange box. Can you find out? You have everything else.'

The girl held up the Solvol. 'Sure you don't mean this? This box is orange.'

'That's red. It's a carbolic soap I'm looking for.'

'Carbolic, as in soft drink? We have Sodastream in aisle sixteen.'

'That's *carbonated*. They are *quite* different things. It's the same with suet, you know.' Joe wasn't sure if it was him or the shop assistant that Betty was talking to now. 'You can't get that anymore either — so how are you supposed to make a suet pudding?'

The girl looked at her blankly.

'You know, I went to six butchers last week. They all thought I meant dripping or lard.'

'So, you get it at the butcher's?' the girl said wearily. 'This is hardware. Have you tried Woolworths?'

'No, it's soap. Aunt Daisy swore by it for scrubbing down the kitchen table — in the Fifties — you know.'

The girl smiled.

'The 1950s? I'm seventeen, shall I get someone old?'

'Yes, please do that, doll. Get someone old.'

Betty turned to Joe.

'Should I buy one of those airtight plastic boxes to replace the old cake tin?'

'I like the *Laughing Cavalier* tin.'

'It's *The Blue Boy* — Gainsborough.'

'I like *The Blue Boy* even better.' A young man in a blue top and track pants grinned as he brushed past, well within reach. Joe turned his head, assessing the rear view as the guy also turned to look back over his shoulder. Tempted to find some excuse to abandon the trolley and follow, Joe instead reluctantly turned back to Betty.

'They're not very classy, plastic boxes.'

'Practical though, but they are expensive. Who knows if they'll last?'

'Only about 5000 years in landfill. Get one if you want, but I think you might have to give up on the soap.'

'Yes, I suspect so.' Betty placed the smallest of the plastic boxes in the trolley. 'Do they cut keys here?'

Sitting in the café next to the garden centre, Joe scanned the line-up of bromeliads, real plants trying hard to look plastic, while across the alleyway, tubs of silk flowers yearned to be mistaken for the real thing. They were waiting for tea among a crowd of mostly older women and young families. At a nearby table, two women Betty's age were engaged in an intense conversation. The sight of them made Joe reflective.

'Betty, did you ever have a girlfriend?'

'What do you mean?' The arrival of the tea delayed Joe's explanation, but once the tray had been cleared and slid down the side of their table, he answered.

'Someone to do girl things with — someone to confide in.'

'Gossip, you mean? No, not really. I worked all my life with Joseph. There was Mrs Klein, our landlady, but I wasn't much for afternoon teas and lunches with the girls.' Betty lifted the lid of the teapot and peered in. 'Oh, it's a tea bag. Well, I suppose it's the best they can do — poor things.' She replaced the lid and began to pour.

'I'm supposed to have one. It's the one thing I don't have.'

'What do you mean?'

'Gay men are supposed to have a close woman friend they tell everything to and who they advise on fashion.'

'I can remember when you could barely dress yourself — those horrible black t-shirts you used to wear — only good for dusters.'

'We tell them their backside looks big in things when their boyfriends and husbands are just too scared. In turn, they get us out of jams.'

'Ah! A beard.'

'Sorry?'

'A beard. A woman who specialises in stepping out with swishy young men to make them look a little less suspicious at dances or weddings. It was an early Sixties thing when there suddenly seemed to be a lot of swish.'

'Sounds good.' Joe smiled and repeated the new phrase 'a lot of swish', rolling the words around in his mouth. The two older women stared at him. Embarrassed, he took a long sip of his tea.

'Are you in a jam?'

'Hmm?' He dropped his teacup a little too noisily into his saucer.

'Well, I see no reason why I won't do. What is it? Do you need a wingman?' Betty motioned towards a young man in t-shirt and cargo pants sitting at the table opposite with a woman, probably his mother. Joe realised the young man had been staring. Was that what people saw when they looked at him and Betty? An attentive son out with his mother? How unlikely *his* mother would be to have noticed the boy opposite. Betty was the perfect wingman.

'Yes, but . . .'

'What is it?'

'Well, as you know, I'm trying to reconnect with Leo. Make it work as friends and . . . I'm unsure where to go.'

'Go?'

'Literally. Where can I take him. I told you he's working on one of the teams. I've seen him on site a few times. We've talked and it has gone okay, but I want to find somewhere we might go together — to talk, to give us a way back in to reconnecting more permanently.'

'To prove you're harmless, you mean?'

'Well, I suppose so, if you *have* to put it like that.'

'What were you thinking?'

'I'm not sure, but if we could just talk for a while, I know we'll be okay.'

'Sometimes it's the simplest settings that say the most.'

'I don't want to be in a crowd, but I don't want to ask him somewhere where we'll be alone. He can't come to my place. It needs to be neutral.'

'The museum? The art gallery? What about the pictures?'

'What, and sit in the dark?'

'What if I came too? I could play gooseberry.'

'Is that too pathetic?'

'*Finding Neverland* is showing at the Academy under the library and I rather like that Johnny Depp. No, better still, *Casablanca* is on at the old Berkley in Mission Bay. I'd love to see that again — Bogart and Bergman. Why don't you ask him to join you and your elderly friend for ice cream on the beach? Then, if you're getting on, I'll totter off to the movie and leave you to it. If it's all looking a bit grim, we can all go to the movies together, and I'll sit between the two of you.' Betty looked pleased with herself as she sipped at her tea and Joe resumed gazing at the man at the next table who smiled back a sympathetic 'out with mother' smile in return — no potential there.

As they left the café Betty beetled off in search of delphiniums to replace hers — slugs had gotten to the shoots. Promising to join her in a moment, Joe went to trade the shopping trolley, with only its minuscule spatula, a small plastic box and a newly cut key in the bottom, for a shopping basket. Parking it, he spied the blue boy with a young man, nineteen or so, shirtless, his shorts unquestionably pornographic. They were walking quickly through the checkout together, intent on getting somewhere fast. Once they were out of sight, Joe turned and made his way back to the garden centre. From out of the last aisle shot the young shop assistant they'd been talking to earlier.

'They don't make it anymore.'

'Sorry?'

'Sandsoap, Pearson's went out of business years ago.'

'Oh.' Joe didn't particularly care about the soap. Especially when he registered that just behind the shop assistant stood 'rugby shirt', now beardless. As Joe approached, the guy bent down and from the bucket at his feet took a branch of imitation japonica blossom.

Holding it out to Joe, he asked, 'Mate, know anything about these?'

Leo had looked wary when Joe invited him to join them the following Sunday. Joe had explained that he'd like him to meet Betty, but that she didn't like his new Lotus — it was too low to the ground, and it only seated two. So, Joe had said, if Leo wouldn't mind picking them up, perhaps they could go somewhere? Leo seemed on the verge of accepting until Joe had mentioned Mission Bay. For a moment Joe thought he'd put his foot in it. Trying for a recovery, he said, 'Look, we can take Betty to the movies. Hang for a while and then, in the merciless daylight of Mission Bay's rampant heterosexuality, a couple of old friends can have a quiet drink — catch-up properly. There'll be time to go elsewhere, if you prefer, and then come back, and pick her up.'

Eventually, Leo exchanged his phone number for Joe's address before getting back to work. Joe felt momentarily guilty. He had made Betty sound like an obligation, but if nothing else, he now had Leo's phone number in his pocket for the first time in a decade.

Joe was waiting outside when Leo pulled up in his old saloon. He pointed out Betty's house, visible from where they sat, and when they'd driven the half a kilometre, Joe jumped out and walked the few feet to her front door and knocked. Leo got out of the driver's seat and waited. After the introductions, Leo walked around to the passenger door and opened it for Betty. He then guided her gently into the seat, ensuring her head didn't collide with the hard edge of the roof, and pulled the seatbelt across for her before gently closing the door. A moment later the whole car shook as he slammed the driver's door.

'Sorry,' he said, turning to Betty. 'It's old, and you have to do that.'

Betty and Leo had hit it off immediately. Joe wondered why he'd ever worried that it might have gone differently. Sitting in the back seat, he occasionally caught Leo's glance in the mirror as Betty asked him a whole barrage of questions about himself. It was as if Leo had never been mentioned — where was he born, what had his parents done, where did he go to school? A question, Joe noted, Leo answered without hesitation. Betty already knew all the answers but still, there was the occasional gem of discovery, a detail or two, that surprised even Joe. When Betty asked, 'How do you two know each other?' There was a sudden uncomfortable silence.

'We worked together,' said Leo. 'Still do.'

Betty and Leo were still chatting away as, three rapidly melting ice creams in hand, they slid into the uncompromising bench seats of a barbecue table in the park opposite the cinema. It gave Joe a chance to look at Leo uninterrupted. He swore Leo hadn't changed much at all, but he stared at him all the same — enjoying the opportunity. Leo's jaw was still square, although probably not quite as much as it used to be — now it was more sculpted rather than chiselled. His black hair was flecked with the first grey hairs. He was still handsome, though, the rough surface of his muscular chest sparsely coated with black hair, visible through a gap in his open shirt. Were his abs still hard? If they were, it wasn't fair. Perhaps he could convince Leo to join him at the gym? Gym buddies, shooting the breeze as, turn and turn about, they recovered between reps. Nah, Leo had inherited what he had, and it seemed to be sticking around. He probably hadn't used the gym since boarding school.

Joe was watching Leo talk to Betty as he licked his ice cream, when, shifting slightly in his seat, their legs brushed together under the table.

The jolt was electric, and they jumped apart. His ice cream hit the sandy soil at the same time as Leo's legs whacked into the underside of the tabletop, which, bolted to the ground, shuddered.

'Sorry!' said Joe urgently.

'What happened?' asked Betty.

'Nothing.'

'What was that crash?'

'It was *nothing*. Forget it.' He bent down and picked up the remains of his ice cream, tossing it in the direction of the circling seagulls, whose angry screams only heightened the tension at the table. Leo scowled at him and he looked away. Betty changed the subject.

'Leo, since you're a builder, would you have time to look at my potting shed? It's getting rather disreputable.' Joe looked at her. It was as if the old reprobate was about to make a move on Leo. He stepped in.

'Leo's more a sort of specialist craftsman. I can look at your potting shed, Betty.'

'But you're too busy.'

'I'll send someone.'

'You can send Leo. He works for you, doesn't he?'

Leo, clearly still tense, spoke. 'I'd be delighted to help. I like old structures.'

'All settled then. Do you have a card, Leo?' Joe cautioned Betty with a look, but she pretended not to see. Leo produced a card from his battered wallet — a sad photocopied thing. Joe wondered fleetingly what Betty was up to. Then again, what did it matter? If Leo and Betty got on, was that such a bad thing? Just as he was considering this, Betty announced, 'I should go now — in case they're busy.'

'There's a good half an hour yet.'

'No, I want to go. The film is ninety minutes, I checked. So, I'll meet you both back here at 3.45.'

Once Betty had gone, Joe turned back to Leo. 'Thanks for coming.'

'My pleasure. She's nice.'

'And you're being nice.'

'Did you expect something else?'

'I didn't know what to expect.' The two men fell silent for a long time. The sun was hot, and the shade of the trees was some distance off. A few seagulls lingered, and Leo tossed the last of his cone in their direction. From the surrounding sky, the rest of the flock descended before a bird flew off, cone in its beak, the rest following.

'She sort of rescued me,' Joe said, out of the blue.

'From?'

'Myself, after—' He stopped. This was dangerous territory. 'Beware, though, she collects willing young builders.'

'Young?'

'Hey, I for one don't feel a dammed bit different from how I did at twenty-one.' Joe cringed. Argh, why had he said that? He looked at Leo, embarrassed, but Leo's expression was unchanged. 'Do you want to get a drink?'

'No, I'm happy here. The sun's good.'

'Mission Bay was her idea.'

'Ghastly, isn't it?' In perfect timing, an open-topped car full of young, overly tanned teenagers screeched to a stop at the crossing. Joe looked. Betty was safely on the other side of the road and heading into the doors of the cinema.

'Do you know what made me come? Why I said yes?' Leo cast him a sidelong look. 'The "merciless daylight of rampant heterosexuality".'

Joe laughed. 'This time, that one, it's mine,' he paused. 'How are you, Leo? How are you really?'

'I'm good. Thanks for the job.'

'Shit, it's nothing.'

'You've done well. Thackeray Makepeace, eh? You never could get that right. And now you have, you've made it something in itself.'

'Thanks. Most people never make the connection with Thackeray.'

'Poor Thackeray — entirely forgotten. Are you seeing anyone?'

'No . . . nothing serious.' Joe thought of telling him about Brendan, the rugby shirt, but no, he didn't want Leo to think he'd become a slut.

'It's a bit complicated — still figuring something out. You?'

'No one.'

They sat in silence as the sun bore down. Joe watched as a long stream of ants ran across the sticky tabletop in whirling, seemingly direction-less, patterns. Behind Leo, silhouetted against the bright sky, was the dark form of Rangitoto. He thought for a moment about their night there.

Leo slapped the back of his neck. The raw mechanics of the action drew Joe's eyes. He might have coped with that just fine, as he had with everything until that moment, had a sudden breeze not sent a strong gust of Leo's scent his way. It was the one thing that had always worked its way in deep, disabling his defenses, his drug of choice — the smell of Leo. Suddenly it all started to feel too much. Leo's open-necked shirt, straining across his chest, the deep 'v' exposing a triangle of skin towards which Joe's eyes kept straying, despite his best attempts at self-control. Teetering for a moment on the edge of declaring his undying devotion or, worse, starting to sob, in desperation Joe took the only possible escape and spoke up.

'Nice shirt,' Joe said.

Leo, suddenly uncomfortable, began buttoning up. 'Joe?'

'Hmm.' Joe was concentrating on his breathing, a self-administered inoculation that seemed to be working, as long as he could stay focused on something other than Leo right now.

'What do you want?'

'What do you mean? I don't want anything.'

Leo eyed him warily, his heavy eyes full of suspicion. 'Come on, Joe. I know you better than that.'

'I want us to be friends, that's all. Real friends.'

Leo looked hard at him. 'That's what you said on the street.' His voice was low and his tone unreadable.

'I meant it,' Joe said earnestly.

Leo looked up. 'Friendship is hard. Friendship gives more but demands less than love.'

Joe smiled and then bit his lip. 'I didn't think that subject would be coming up.'

'Which one?'

'Love.'

Leo looked away for a long moment, clearly going over something in his mind. He looked back and asked his question. 'I've been wondering something. How did you get that scar?'

Joe touched his lip and shrugged but didn't answer.

'Looks like we're even. There are things neither of us wants to talk about.' Leo looked at his watch. 'Come on, let's do something.'

'What?'

'You know, I wouldn't mind seeing that film. It's two o'clock now but there'll be shorts and if we run . . . ?'

'Last one pays.' Joe was already out from the confines of the barbecue table, but Leo struggled to untangle himself, before taking up the pursuit. They dodged tooting traffic and burst through the doors of the cinema at full speed, Joe still slightly in front. Pulling up hard at the ticket counter, they stopped to catch their breath.

Leo placed his arms around Joe's shoulders. 'Keep up, old man.'

'I was first by a mile.' Joe turned to the lemon-lipped woman behind the counter. 'Two please.'

'The feature has started. So I can't really let you in.'

Leo leant over the counter and smiled. 'Please?'

The cinema was almost empty and they quickly found Betty and took up seats next to her. Squeezed in his seat, between the two of them, Joe glanced down at the light of the screen as it played off Leo's thighs, his legs spread wide as if to catch its reflected sheen. Joe recalled all the times they had sat together in a cinema, pressing their legs hard against each other in an erotic battle of wills for seat space and to determine dominance in what inevitably came later. Then, just as *she* walked into *his* gin joint, Leo reached over and gripped his upper thigh, squeezing it hard. Turning in towards him and smiling, Leo whispered into Joe's ear. 'Watch the film.'

CHAPTER 11

Joe first met Danielle at a party. It had quickly become one of those tedious days in which even he, the boss, couldn't escape endless meetings. From the moment he'd walked in the door at 8 a.m. he'd sensed that there would be no cutting for the squash courts today.

It was now 5.30 p.m. Looking at his watch, Joe knew he wasn't going to get to Betty's in time to pick her up either. In a little more than an hour and a half, they would be flicking the switch to make the name Thackeray Makepeace light up in neon along the boom of a crane. With that, they would finally launch the Virginian, their most substantial development yet. It was a big deal. The site surrounding the glove factory had been bought up cheap after the collapse of the original developer. The Virginian had propelled Joe, Kurt and Thackeray Makepeace into the big time. It had also delivered him a new friend in Gerald — at this moment house hunting in Bali. In Gerald's absence, he and Kurt had asked Betty, the firm's minority shareholder, to throw the switch. She had graciously accepted the invitation.

Joe turned away from the group discussing the project redesign. He wandered over to the redheaded architecture graduate who was packing up his bag, ready to leave for the night.

'Would you be good enough to ask my PA to send a taxi to Freemans Bay to collect Betty Strauss and take her to the crane party? She knows the address.'

'I could pick her up for you,' the kid offered enthusiastically.

'What's your name?'

'Drew. An-*drew*,' the boy repeated his name in two distinct syllables. Joe thought for a moment. Betty wasn't fond of taxis. She considered them a waste of money and had never ceased to mention the cost of the taxi ride she'd taken to Te Atatū in order to haul him from his bed years earlier. She would just as likely send the driver away and walk. This kid seemed pleasant enough — she would like him.

'Are you sure?'

'Yes, I'm just finishing up.' Drew pulled the zip on his backpack firmly to ensure it was tightly closed.

'Here. Take my car,' Joe handed him the car keys. 'Less confusing for Betty.'

'Gee, thanks.'

'And come to the party yourself.'

'I am . . . I will . . . I mean we all are, but thanks for asking.' The kid's freckled face flushed red as he stumbled through his words.

'Of course,' Joe turned back to the table and the meeting.

They stood under the small marquee erected on the flat rooftop of the original glove factory building. The building would act as the site office and promotional suite until the initial tower was well advanced, and then it would be taken down. Joe had chosen the name of the firm's first significant high-rise development, and Auckland's only twin tower residential development, from a Thackeray novel, *The Virginians*.

For once the penny had dropped with Jacinta who had dumped the plural and parlayed it into an homage to an old television series that had starred a boyish cowboy. They'd had one hell of an argument over the change. 'No one cares about your literary references,' she'd argued.

No one cares about a television programme from before the dawn of time, he'd thought. Looking now at the nine-storey banner, its black and white image of a pouting lasso-carrying, gun-slinging beauty, supported with the words *No Other Name, just The Virginian* on the side of the blank face of the high rise opposite, he had to admit she'd been right.

Jacinta had gone all out on this one. The poster was in bus shelters and hoardings all over the city. The bill-sticking company had received a record number of requests for copies. Long before they had appeared, the tag 'No Other Name' had turned up as a stencilled graffiti in obscure parts of the inner city. The beautiful people in the clubs and then on the catwalks of Fashion Week had worn t-shirts of the cowboy image. She'd taken a deep breath before admitting that she'd used 'a still live connection,' with Tony to achieve that particular coup. The American actor, who starred in the series, now a semi-retired gas and oil businessman, had jumped at the opportunity to visit Auckland. Despite the series having been cancelled in 1971, before Joe had been born, the press treated the charming old actor like current Hollywood royalty. He had just a few days earlier finished a media tour by unfurling the very banner that he was now looking at live on breakfast television. At the same moment, a crew of graffiti artists added the leaning cowboy stencil above the original tagline on walls around the city. Legal was in a huge flap about it but Jacinta, he had to admit, knew her stuff.

There had never been a media storm like it around a new building, and that included either Metropolis or the Sky Tower.

Joe handed Betty a glass of champagne from the table. Her dress was an old one but of a classic cut. Over it, she was wearing a genuine mink jacket, much to the envy of some of the other guests. They were finding out first hand that neither Zambesi nor its southern cousin NOM*D could cut the early winter chill. Between Betty's dress and jacket, Joe caught the flash of two impressive Art Deco dress clips made of square cut diamonds.

'You're one hell of a classy dame, Betty Strauss, and this project is going to make you a very wealthy woman.' He raised his glass. 'Here's to you.'

'Thank you,' she replied. 'Now, that boy who picked me up, who was he? Whoever he was, he was delightful.'

'I thought you'd like him.'

'More to the point, doll, he likes you.'

'What?' Joe was only vaguely tuned in to what Betty was saying. It didn't help that the music had been cranked up a notch.

'He thinks you're tremendous. Didn't stop talking about you all the way here.'

'Sorry?'

'A crush on the boss, I think.' Betty took a sip of her champagne. 'You've met him before, I understand?'

'Hmm.' There was no point trying to have a meaningful conversation in among the madness of the party. Joe surveyed the crowd. He couldn't see Leo. In fact, all his senses were telling him he wasn't there. Bugger him and his 'give me some space' moods to which he still seemed to cling.

'Stay warm, Betty, I just need to find someone.' Spying the kid they'd just been talking about, Joe beckoned him over. 'Thanks for collecting her.' Drew, a green beer bottle in hand, made a gesture to suggest that it had been no trouble. 'Drew, isn't it?' he asked. Drew's face lit up with a broad smile. He nodded. 'Can you stay with Betty please? Just for a moment? I need to locate someone.'

Joe pushed his way through the crowd, stopping to accept congratulations from some guests and nodding hello to others. As he reached the edge of both the party and the rooftop, he looked out onto the street. It was empty except for a few stragglers making their way up the path between the line of large flaming braziers. He looked up at the building opposite. The figure of the Virginian, which towered over Auckland, now engulfed him. He'd been right. No Leo. Just this once he wished Leo would front for one of these events. He'd worked hard on reconstructing a friendship between the two of them. It had been rocky. There was so much unsaid, so many areas that neither wanted to be the first to broach. Opportunities for them to be together had been hard to find. At first, Leo had been suspicious of Joe's motivation, but slowly, tentatively, they'd got into the groove of meeting and talking. Sure, he was showing off, as much to Leo as to anyone else, but this event was something special. Bugger Leo for not recognising that and turning up. He was thinking about calling when a hand on his shoulder sent a simple base charge through his body. He turned.

'Leo, about time.' The two men hugged, but Joe noted that the push back came a little quicker and a little harder than usual.

'Joe, I'd like you to meet Danielle. We knew each other when I was in the UK.' Joe recognised her immediately from the photograph above the kitchen table in Leo's old flat.

'Hiya,' said Danielle in a shrill Northern English accent.

'Hello.' Joe extended his hand. 'It's very nice to meet you, Danielle.' Just as his tone had become suddenly formal, the smile that had just flashed across his face had been the official Thackeray Makepeace corporate greeting. Jacinta would be proud of him, but he felt dishonest.

'Call me Dani. Everyone else does.'

Keen to get back to something that felt a little more real, Joe turned to Leo.

'Come with me and let's do this.' Joe led the way back to the centre of the crowd where Betty and Drew stood chatting.

After the lighting ceremony, Betty became deeply involved in a conversation with Leo. Just beyond them, Drew appeared to be listening in. He looked up and smiled across at Joe who smiled back. Joe then turned for a moment to take in the new arrival. So, this was Dani. She'd been on the scene for a couple of weeks, but this was his first look at her. She was not what he had expected from the photo. When they had been together Leo never really mentioned her, although strictly speaking, she was his immediate predecessor. Back then, previous girlfriends were something to which Joe had given no thought. Now here was one in the flesh.

All Joe knew was that Leo had followed a Kiwi girl he'd met from London to Birmingham when she'd transferred to her firm's Midlands office. It was there he had got his first job with a construction firm. Dani had been the receptionist. He gathered it had got a bit messy with the first girl. Leo and Dani had dated for a while. Then he'd come home to Auckland not so long after they'd met.

Then, about six weeks ago, Dani had got in touch. She'd migrated to New Zealand with her widowed father. Since then, Leo had been seeing a bit of her. Joe suspected Leo and Dani had been discussing old times, a conversation perhaps a little less dangerous than *their* past.

Joe often wracked his brains to figure what sort of girlfriend would best suit Leo. Or, more truthfully, what type of girlfriend for Leo would best suit him. He'd never got far. However, he couldn't see this woman being the one. Danielle was a bit shorter than him and thin, very thin. Next to Leo, she was fragile and birdlike. Her clothes, inherently English in their conservatism, made her look plain and older than she was. He was still looking at her when Dani turned to face him.

'I've heard a lot about you. I've wanted to meet you,' she placed her hand on Joe's upper arm.

'Likewise.' He stepped back a little so that Dani's hand no longer rested on his arm and, surprised, she let it fall back against her side.

'Congratulations,' she gestured at the crane, the red and green neon of which cast a strange fairground pallor over the guests below. 'Leo says you're quite the business genius.'

'Oh, I wouldn't say that.' Joe's heart leapt at the rare compliment to be reported from Leo.

'And that you're his greatest creation.'

'Well, there might be some truth in that bit.' Joe again flashed his automatic smile but wondered for a moment whether Leo had said anything of the sort. In the time that they had reconnected, in which they'd been friends, he'd never once heard Leo take credit for any of his success.

'Seems to me he should have got shares.'

'Sorry?' He'd heard her right, he was sure, but he wanted confirmation.

'You know, in the whole thing — it would have been the *right* thing to do, don't you think? Given that you had the idea together?' Joe stopped for a moment. What did she know about Leo and him? 'It's not too late, you know. From what I understand you could still make him a partner.'

'If you'll excuse me, I've got to take care of some clients. You understand it's business first at these things.' As he turned, he brushed against Betty. She grabbed his arm and took the opportunity to declare in a stage whisper, clearly audible to everyone in the small group, 'Your Leo, I've figured it out, he looks just like Robert Mitchum, and we *all* fell in love with him back then.' Leo laughed. Dani, picking up on Betty's particular choice of words looked perplexed. Reaching out for Leo's hand she glanced at him nervously. Drew looked as if he'd just got the last piece of a jigsaw puzzle and took a long swig from his beer bottle. Joe, pretending not to have heard, made an excuse and moved off.

The crowd had thinned out. Joe, suddenly feeling exhausted, was taking a moment to sit on the building's parapet edge, concealed in a pool of shadow cast by a large pōhutukawa tree. He was looking over at the image of the leather-clad cowboy and watching as the first of the caterers and the last of his guests trickled away past the spluttering braziers below. Jacinta could take over now. Kurt had disappeared home long ago and in a while he'd head off.

'One last beer?' Roused from his thoughts, Joe raised his head to look. 'Thanks . . . Drew.'

Drew hoisted himself over the ledge, and took up a place on the parapet opposite him. 'Great night. You must be pleased?' Drew raised his beer in a toast, and the two clinked their bottles together in space midway between where they sat.

'Yeah, I am.' The two men were silent for a long time before Drew spoke again.

'He looks a bit like your friend.'

'Sorry?'

'The cowboy — he looks a bit like your friend. Leo, is it?'

'Yes, I suppose he does a bit. Not my idea.' Joe gestured at the image.

'But a very effective one.'

'Yes, damn her,' he looked in Jacinta's direction. 'Sorry, I shouldn't say that. She's very good at her job.'

Drew smiled. 'And you're my boss. Well, boss to both of us really.'

'Yup,' Joe smiled back. 'It's inappropriate.'

'He's the sort of guy you could fall in love with.'

'Who is?' asked Joe.

'The Virginian. What was his name?'

'Oh, sure.'

'I'd probably have fallen in love with him as he was in his heyday, rather than now. If you get what I mean.'

Together, they gazed at the cowboy. A squealing of tyres broke the silence as a car took the corner of the street below too fast. Skidding slightly and then correcting, the driver accelerated away aggressively.

'Actually, that's a bit shallow.'

'What is?'

'What I just said. Like, he seemed like a nice guy when she brought him to the office. And on television people liked him a lot.'

'Yup, they did.'

'And just 'cause some guy's way old, doesn't mean he's not hot.' Drew looked down over the side of the building. 'Sorry, I talk too much. I get told that all the time.'

Joe lifted his bottle and took a drink. As he did, he tapped it against Drew's. 'Not at all, it's refreshing to talk about something other than business.'

'Do you believe in love?' Drew asked.

'Strange question.'

'Do you think? I think it's a pretty ordinary question really.'

'Strange question to ask your boss then.'

'Maybe . . . but not out of context,' Drew said as he smiled broadly. 'Think of it as like mentoring. I'm mining you for wisdom.' After a minute or two, Joe answered.

'Yes,' he said slowly. 'I do believe in love.'

'But not with nine-storey cowboys?'

'No.'

'A bit pointless?'

'Futile, I think, is a better word.'

'And "the one"?'

'Which one?'

'Do you believe there's *one person* for each of us?' Drew asked. Joe frowned.

'Mentoring,' Drew reminded him.

'I used to really believe that.'

'And if you never meet that person?'

'You always meet that person. That's how it works. Then the trouble starts.'

'So, it doesn't always work out?'

'Eventually, yes, I think it does. Fate has a habit of throwing things in your way, things that blindside you, but you get there in the end. You just have to hold on to what you believe, what you really believe, until . . .'

'Things that blindside you. You mean like an age gap?'

'Yes, I suppose, like an age gap.'

'Or him being straight?' Joe didn't answer. He caught Drew's eye.

'Aren't you an architect?'

'Yep,' replied Drew. 'What made you ask that?'

'This isn't the normal architect conversation.'

'I'm probably not a very *normal* architect,' Drew countered. 'And any rate "to understand all is to forgive all."'[3] Joe recognised the quote, but Drew was talking again. 'Suppose you've just got to go for it when you find it?'

'You've lost me again. Find what?'

'Love — the right guy — you just have to take a risk.'

'Yup. I guess you do.'

'Where does it come from, do you think, that kind of courage?' asked Drew.

'I've never known,' Joe said with a slightly resigned sigh.

'But this development, even the papers are calling it courageous.'

'Well, now, that's courage of a different sort.' Joe gestured at the scene below them. 'Courage in business comes from a different place. That, you can learn. You end up knowing instinctively where and when to fight. You know your own weaknesses and your opponent's failings. I will tell you this for free — some actual useful mentoring — forget what people tell you, revenge is a great motivator. The other type of courage that you speak of — courage in love — that comes in a single moment, when something propels you. You'll have only one chance to act. That is when you absolutely *must* risk everything. Then, like adrenaline, the courage kicks in and it carries you through.'

'Suppose so.' Drew rolled his empty beer bottle between his hands.

'It can change you, you know, making that step, crossing the line, it can make you a whole new person. It releases something in you. For someone young, like you, it can be the point at which life, *real* life, actually begins.'

'There's an equation, you know.'

'For what?'

Drew gestured again at the cowboy. 'Age appropriateness.'

'Really?'

'You take your age and divide it by three and then add eight. That's it.'

'That's what?'

'The youngest person you can,' Drew lowered his voice and leant in, 'you know, fuck, and it be socially acceptable, like not disgusting or pervy.' Joe looked blank. 'Do the math, it's fun.'

'No, thanks, I've had too many of these for long division.' Joe indicated the empty bottle. Then, climbing carefully over onto the solid concrete of the roof, he added, 'Hey, Drew, it's been nice talking to you. Are you okay to get home?'

'Yeah, I'm fine, and likewise, it's been nice.' Standing up, Drew asked, 'And what about you?'

'I'm fine to drive, if that's what you mean.'

'You'll need these then.' Drew pulled Joe's car keys from his jacket pocket.

CHAPTER 12

Joe looked at the files on his desk. He was getting behind. He would have to delegate some of this if he were to make any progress. Turning his back on it for a moment or two, he glanced around his office at the new mid-century credenza, a line of universally ugly industry awards along its top and then up at the big Robert Ellis of Auckland's swirling motorways that he'd bought a couple of weeks earlier. Sighing, he turned back to his files. He was still searching for a good desk to replace this one. It had been his first, and indeed this recent revamp of his office was the first since the day they'd moved in. In those days they'd shared occupancy of the floor with a little graphic design studio — now they had the whole building. Yes, his desk had served him well, but it was time to replace it with something more stylish — Fifties or Sixties perhaps? He'd check the auction catalogues, talk to some dealers.

Joe reached over and picked up a file — 'Second Quarter Projections' and looked at it briefly before spotting the folder underneath — 'Potential Acquisitions'. Those he liked. Looking around, feeling slightly guilty, as if someone might spy him through the glass window of his office, he picked up the file. There was nothing like the thrill of a new building, a new project. He knew he should do the less interesting stuff first but since when had he ever done the expected? Most of them were dull, rectangular sections of flat land, one-time industrial sheds, plots drawn together from three or four old houses. Some he wouldn't touch. Some of it had potential, but nothing made his heart leap. Not that it mattered — there'd be heart palpitations enough as construction on the Virginian got more fully underway.

As he pulled the last page from the file, he heard a noise from down the hall. Was it *another* birthday morning tea?

The page was a real estate promotional sheet for a little building. He knew it. It was at the top of New North Road — a scruffy little box of a thing, Fifties, faded paint, tiny medallions of the Queen all over it — too small to be commercially viable and in the wrong part of town unless they could buy up around it. If they could do that then this might act as a cornerstone for something bigger. He stood up and walked over to the open door.

'What's going on, Theo?' he asked one of his staff, gesturing down the corridor towards the source of the noise.

'Don't know — sounds like when—'

Joe interrupted him with a clearing of his throat, suddenly remembering Theo's love of long conversations equating events to the plots of obscure movies.

'Give this to Drew, will you? Ask him to see what he can do with it.'

'Drew?'

'Redhead. Design team.'

'Oh, Sandra Dee?'

'Sorry?'

'That's what they used to call him. You know, hopelessly devoted.'

'Used to?'

'He's gone.' Theo made a swishing action with his hand as if Drew had been swept away in a storm. 'Left last week. They did a whip around — gave him the DVD. Can I give it to someone else?'

'No . . . ah . . . it's not important. Pop that back on my desk, will you?' Joe asked, handing the file to Theo, and heading off in the direction of the noise. He entered the reception to encounter two women he'd never met before, one of whom appeared to be struggling with his receptionist, Gail, over his leather-bound appointment book.

'What the *hell* is going on here?'

'They don't have an appointment,' answered Gail in an exasperated tone. Turning towards him, the woman suddenly released the book, sending Gail flying back into her chair. The two visitors were almost identical except that one had long, grey hair, the other a close-cropped buzz cut. Lining up beside each other they spoke in near unison.

'We're here to talk about the tree.'

'Tree?'

'The pōhutukawa on the Gilmore site.' Joe nodded sagely. He had long learnt it was best to meet with the locals early, but it was seldom easy.

'You'd better come in.'

As they followed him down the corridor, Joe racked his memory for the details. Gilmore's, and the sites surrounding it, had been light industrial, commercial properties, mostly dating from the boom in building after the war. There weren't many residential properties nearby, very little in the way of an existing neighbourhood. Where exactly did these two live, he wondered?

He remembered the streets of the city when they'd been empty of people, and that had at last begun to change. He'd sometimes parked for a moment in his car and watched as people threaded in and out of apartment buildings in the early evenings, returning home, leaving for a run, a bike ride, or off to a restaurant. Not that it had *all* gone right. He could barely bring himself to drive Hobson Street any longer, too many losses, too many memories gone, but he knew this development would be different. It would bring a new community of residents into the city, and already other developers were refitting some of the older factory buildings nearby for retail. They could see the likely extent of change the Virginian would bring. Taking all that into account, he hadn't expected anyone to turn up representing the community regarding this development. However, he'd do his best to keep the peace.

Entering his office, Joe ushered the women to the visitors' chairs on the outside of his desk. As he walked around to his own seat, he surveyed them. Both wore a grave expression, often assumed by the eternally and professionally aggrieved. Both in loose t-shirts, one in faded jeans, the other in a long skirt — all, it seemed, purchased in an op shop. It was only as they both plonked themselves down that he noticed their feet. He couldn't recall ever before taking a meeting with someone not wearing shoes. One barefoot, one in a pair of old sandals, the effect was the same. Legs crossed, each now dangled a filthy foot in front of him.

The short-haired woman spoke first, in a distinctly rehearsed line that came tumbling out at speed.

'Every tree matters, just like every child matters. Men like you build houses for the rich and run rough-shod over the children to do it.' Joe was just thinking this through, unsure when he'd last trampled a child to develop a property when the other woman spoke.

'It's *molestation*.' Joe looked directly at the woman with the long hair, who had just spoken. The word was a strange choice. It took him a moment, but then he got it, children, molestation, gay man. He grimaced inwardly, the collegiality of the rainbow was once again proving itself only skin deep. 'That's what it is, plain and simple. Molestation of the city. I've seen it before — you developers are all the same. As wimmin, we've seen it.' She stopped but only for a moment in order to power up her voice. 'Do you know what it's like to be molested, Mr Thackeray? Or are you Makepeace?' Before he could answer, the other woman interjected.

'It's the Tangata Whenua. That tree means something to Māori in a way you, as a Pākehā, couldn't—'

'Man. *You as a Pākehā man*,' Long Hair interrupted, correcting her companion's speech.

'Yes. It means something that you, as a Pākehā man, can never understand,' Short Hair continued. Joe wondered how these *Pākehā women* considered themselves so very capable of understanding.

'We,' Long Hair began, indicating herself and the woman next to her. '*We* feel it, you know. We're all one in this — us and the locals.' It was as if between them they had had a little pre-meeting discussion and decided he, 'the *gay* developer,' would need, first and foremost, a little educating. He repressed a smile.

'The locals, who are they exactly? I mean, who do you represent here?' Joe immediately regretted asking the question.

When the two women got up to leave an hour later, he had been lectured on the Treaty of Waitangi, child poverty, sow crates, palm oil, Waihopai Station, global warming, female circumcision and the inevitable beatification of Helen Clark. All of these were, in the minds of his uninvited guests, something intimately connected to the lone pōhutukawa tree in front of Gilmore Gloves.

As he walked the women to reception, as much to ensure they left the building as to shield his receptionist from any subsequent unpleasantness, Long Hair, who clutched an oversized woven kete to her long skirts, spoke.

'*Your* process, Mr Thackeray, is not *our* process.' On the 'our' she swirled her free hand in a circular gesture over one breast. For some reason, Joe found this meaningless gesture, intended to impart God only knew what, very funny. Stifling a laugh, he called 'goodbye' and closed the glass front doors behind them. He had an overwhelming urge to call out 'and don't forget the children', but managed to stop himself. One thing he had learnt over the last hour was that these women were painfully devoid of humour. He turned to Gail to see her dabbing at her eyes with a tissue. He stuck out his tongue and put his hands to his neck as if he was strangling himself, in an effort to make her laugh.

'They didn't have an appointment — all I asked was that they made an appointment,' Gail sniffed. 'They said *terrible* things.'

'Yes, I know. But they've gone now. They won't be back.'

She blew her nose and managed a small smile. 'I've cancelled your 11.00 and pushed back your lunch meeting to 1.00.'

'Thanks, Gail. You're an angel. Now can you do something else for me please?' She nodded and grabbed her pad and pencil. 'Hunt out where pubs get those "No shirts, No shoes, No service" signs.'

Joe had thought a lot about that tree but still, after work, he drove over to the site to look at it again. It might once have been a great tree, maybe one of Auckland's best, like those in the Domain or on Takapuna Beach. However, years of brutal pruning to ensure the safe passage of pedestrians and vehicles, the egress of telephone and power lines and the upward thrust of street lamps and road signs, coupled with repeated assaults by a neighbour determined to keep the tree out of his property's airspace, had turned it into a lopsided mutant. The only fully formed branches were those that grew directly over the roof of the old glove factory building. They might have kept it, but its spreading form would have compromised the design of the lower floors. Even then the tree would still have been a brutalised stump. Better in this case to plant new. Gerald had agreed.

A few days later, still amused by his encounter with the two hippies, Joe had told Leo about it over coffee. Leo's parents had been hippies but, as he'd explained, they had been wealthy hippies, clad in kaftans and bespoke sandals, more interested in foot massages and finding themselves than fighting for causes. Most of his parent's friends had been American draft dodgers, not environmental warriors.

'No advice from me, except for one thing. Hippies can be persistent. Hoping they say their piece then disappear might not be the most effective approach.'

The firm had gone through the standard processes regarding the tree. The Council had signed it off. There had been no objections from those in the various council departments concerned or from neighbouring property owners. The only submission was, as suspected, from the two women. Curiously, they hadn't fronted at the public hearing. Joe had assumed that, having made their point, they must have moved on to other causes. Working around the old glove factory, now the display suite, meant that the tree had not needed to go immediately. He realised later, however, that his act of kindness to a mutilated giant had been a mistake. Out of the blue had come an injunction to stop the removal of the tree, behind which was an environmental group calling themselves Tamariki o te Pōhutukawa. It had been a momentary nuisance, one the legal department had quickly sorted out. The District Court overturned the injunction, siding with the Council and the firm, which meant that the original decision for removal had stood. There and then it all should have gone away.

What Joe now had in front of him on his desk, however, was a notice of an appeal, lodged at the last possible moment in order to comply with the 'within fifteen days' requirement. The decision was now appealed to the Environment Court on the grounds that the significance of the tree to Tangata Whenua had not been duly considered in the original process. What was different now was that 'all work deemed potentially injurious to the welfare of the tree' must stop pending an appearance in the court and an eventual decision. The costs of such a stoppage would be enormous. Leo's words of warning, seemingly irrelevant when he'd spoken them a few weeks earlier, now rang in his ears: 'Hippies can be persistent.'

'All work has stopped on-site. I've sent the men home. Tomorrow we'll move them to other sites but after a week or so we'll be talking layoffs.'

'Right.' Joe had his foreman on the other end of the line. 'There's nothing further you can do. Get security on the site. As soon as we know anything, I'll call.' He put down the phone. In front of him sat Nick and Jacinta, heads of legal and public relations respectively. They both knew this was a council of war and had taken up their seats while Joe had been talking. Nick clutched a folder of documents; Jacinta, her handbag. It looked, Joe thought, glancing down at the blue snakeskin bag, as if she was about to go shopping.

'How can the hippies afford this? They're just a couple of penniless nutters.' Joe was addressing Nick seated in front of him.

'They *were* just a couple of penniless nutters — they've organised themselves. Lawyered up,' Nick answered.

'How could those two organise anything?'

'They have a history of protest,' Nick said as he checked his notes. 'Some of it quite legit — land marches, nuclear-free, gender politics and so on. Some good local community stuff — lighting in parks, cycleways, crisis centres, etc. . . .'

'But?'

'They appear to have been driven out of any organisation with which they have ever been involved. They're there on the ground at start-up but gone before anything gets achieved.'

'Pushed out?'

'Moved on, I suspect, so that some work gets done. It's kinder.'

'You're *my* lawyer. Forget kindness,' Joe said bluntly. 'Where's the money coming from then?' Joe could see that Nick was champing at the bit to tell him what he knew.

'They have the backing of a trust. One that has, until now, exclusively funded the restoration of an area of native forest north of Matakana—' Nick hesitated.

'And?' prompted Joe impatiently.

'North of Matakana,' Nick repeated, as if that answer should be more than sufficient.

'North of Matakana?' Joe threw up his hands. 'What's that supposed to mean?'

'Todd Wilding has property up there. The trust is essentially replanting the land surrounding his beach property as a charitable scheme. It's quite legit — a lot of wealthy people do it.'

'I thought the bankruptcy cleaned him out.'

'Honeywell, certainly. His family trusts, no. He is at arm's length on this, but he's there in the background all right. You can't ping him on it though because it looks like a completely natural extension of the Trust's environmental interests. Them wanting to save a significant tree. But as we well know, it's just—'

'Revenge,' interrupted Joe.

'I think you could say it's tit-for-tat, yes.'

Jacinta, who had been unusually quietly through the entire meeting, now spoke. 'It's simple. We can stop Wilding in his tracks, and we can do it this afternoon.'

'How?' asked Joe and Nick together.

'You need to take another meeting.'

'What do you mean?' asked Joe.

'One you won't want to take.'

'With whom?'

'Tony Graham.'

Joe bristled at the mention of his expensive ex-boyfriend's name. 'You know where I am on that.'

'He's useful and he wants to play ball.'

'You can play *that* ball!' Joe scowled, his volume rising.

Jacinta didn't flinch. 'I would — but they don't seem to cast straight men from that mould.'

'Oh, I wouldn't bet on that.'

Jacinta, seeming to ignore him, spoke again. 'Tony has an uncle. He's a chief or a kaumātua or something. He says this guy, the one they're bringing in on the appeal, is bullshit.'

'Hang on, the Pavoni-pony has a *Māori* uncle?'

'It turns out his grandmother on his dad's side was Māori. She married the Dally.'

'He never mentioned it to me,' Joe muttered under his breath.

'No. I suppose he never considered it worth much, until recently. Have you seen him?'

'No.'

'The "ciao" and "grazie" are all gone. It's "kia ora" all the way now.'

'No more "amore"? Now it's all "aroha"?' Joe tried to lighten his tone after his earlier bad-tempered remark.

'Exactly, and a very elaborate tribal tattoo down one arm,' Jacinta continued. 'Let's just say he's working it. The uncle has encountered this guy before. He's not the real deal, not from around here, essentially a Māori for hire. He regularly pisses off the locals by speaking on stuff that has nothing to do with him. Wilding knows they'll lose long term, but this is most certainly a stalling mechanism designed to cost you money.'

'Interesting, good to know.' Joe massaged his temples as if he'd been struck by an instant headache.

'They're waiting at reception.'

'Who are?'

'Tony and his uncle.'

'Jacinta! You can't spring shit on me like this.'

'I thought you of all people would see the need to act fast. You're losing thousands of dollars a day while that site is closed.'

Nick opened the folder before him and chimed in. 'She's right, you know, it's potentially going to cost us . . .' but the look Joe flashed him made him trail off.

'Joe, just talk to Tony. Meet the uncle. It's not going to kill you,' Jacinta said.

Joe shrugged. 'Doesn't look like I have a choice. Send them in then.' When Jacinta didn't move, he added, 'What's the delay?'

'I think you need to go out and meet them rather than summon them through me. It's more respectful.'

'You're fucking kidding me.'

As Joe walked down the corridor he caught Gail's eye. She looked nervous. She motioned towards Tony and two other men sitting in reception as if to say 'not my fault'. Tony and the older of the two men stood up as Joe walked in. Tony looked unchanged except for the tattoos and a pair of dark wrap-around sunglasses.

'Tony.'

'Kia ora, Joe, great to see you,' Tony grasped Joe's extended hand and shook it. 'This is my Uncle Tane. Joe shook hands with the elder man. 'And that,' Tony gestured at a young guy who sat with one of Apple's new iPods in his hand, 'is Pedro.'

Pedro didn't look up.

'Please come in.'

The two men moved towards the corridor. Pedro remained in his seat.

Tony's uncle was a tall, elegant older man with softly flowing grey hair. Dressed in a sharply tailored, grey wool tweed jacket and a black polo neck over black jeans, he clearly looked after himself. The family resemblance was remarkably apparent. Joe wondered now if there was in fact anything at all Italian about Tony.

'I've been spending some time on the marae,' Tony said sitting in one of the two chairs that Nick and Jacinta had vacated to take up more distant positions on Joe's office couch. 'Getting in touch with my whānau.' So, it seemed Tony, so manipulative and so shallow, had suddenly found a deep well of familial obligation. Joe would have laughed, it was so absurd, but he was still angry at being railroaded into this situation.

162

After the pleasantries were done, Tane spoke quietly but commandingly.

'This situation is a big concern for my people. We've been hauled into things with this imposter twice before. We don't want it to happen again. We're keen to stop it before it is presented to the courts.'

'Sorry, with all due respect, how does the situation concern you? Surely the environmental lobby group, Tamariki o te Pōhutukawa, are arguing for Māori?'

'That is, if you'll excuse me, a very Pākehā way of looking at things, to think there's only one Māori side to any argument.' Joe nodded as if to suggest he understood, though he didn't. *Ah, what the hell?* he thought. *Might as well be transparent.*

'There isn't?'

'No. There's our side, my whānau's side. The story Tamariki o te Pōhutukawa — or rather, the troublemaker, is spinning, is that a passing chief planted the tree. It was supposedly a marker for his people. The story is a blatant lie, but, worse than that, if we let it stand it implies that those people once had some status here. That can complicate things. We'd like you to stop it. You have the resources. Tony says you'll do the right thing — now you know who you're dealing with.' Tony grinned like a kid suddenly praised in class for accidentally answering a question correctly.

'I am trying to stop it, but I'm not sure how,' Joe replied. Turning his head slightly to look directly at Nick, he asked, 'Might the court throw this out as a nuisance thing if we can show that Wilding is behind it and given this other guy's history as a bogus complainant?'

'They might. Well, they almost certainly will, but it will take time,' said Nick from the couch.

'Speaking of time,' Tony jumped up from his chair. 'Uncle has another meeting — this one was a bit short notice, you see.' He glanced at Jacinta. Looking a little surprised, Tane rose slowly to his feet.

'I'll take my leave then, Mr Wright? It's been a pleasure, but I do, *it appears*, have another meeting.' Tane's handshake was firm. 'I'm sure you will take the appropriate action to resolve this situation.'

'Thanks, mātua kēkē.' Joe involuntarily raised an eyebrow at Tony's sudden fluency in te reo. 'Can you please ask Pedro to come in?' asked Tony. As Tane left the room, Joe looked at the sleeve of curling dark blue koru that now trailed down Tony's right arm.

'Why, Tony?'

'Why what?'

'Why are you here? What do you want?'

'What do you mean? We're bros, aren't we?'

'No, we're not, Tony. Not anymore.'

'Harsh,' Tony laughed. 'Come on, Joe — let bygones be bygones. We've got to stick together, bro. We're a whānau, really, the gay boys.' Joe wondered how Tony's new notion of whānau might play among the conservative old kuia on the marae.

'Take the glasses off, Tony,' Joe demanded. Tony complied reluctantly. 'And what's up with your uncle's quick exit? It looked to me like you suddenly didn't want him to be here.'

'He's busy — practically runs everything on the marae. We came separately, but he's relying on me more and more.' Tony slipped the sunglasses back on. 'You know, there is something that might help you get what you want, but I figured you wouldn't want to hear it from me.'

'You figured right, *bro*,' Joe responded sarcastically.

At that moment Pedro sloped into the room, iPod still in hand and headphones in his ears. He looked unimpressed at the occupied couch, before sitting down on the vacant chair. He was a pretty boy, slim-hipped, brown-skinned and with thick luscious lips, though somehow the name Pedro seemed unlikely.

'Pedro was a waiter for me at Samphire. Pedro has something to tell you.' Tony leant over and slapped Pedro on the arm. The kid looked up and shrugged his shoulders. He took off his headphones.

'Go on, bro,' urged Tony.

'That guy, the old one, paid me a hundred bucks to blow him out the back by the skip.' Pedro replaced the earphones and spun the dial of his iPod, which clicked rhythmically.

164

'What?' Joe asked, not quite sure what he'd heard, or indeed why he was hearing it.

'Todd Wilding paid him a hundy to give him a lunchtime blowie out the back of the restaurant.' Tony translated Pedro's words, adding in the missing but critical information. Nick moved to the edge of his seat as if about to stand but instead leant in, pushing his oversized glasses up his nose, not wanting to miss any further lascivious details. Jacinta sat back on the couch, smiling.

'Actually, bro, he's been doing it for years. He used to part-own a couple of restaurants. In those days he was well known for the other end of things, providing rather than receiving if you get my drift? Apparently, he wasn't always so ugly. Some ancient queen told me that everyone knew you could get off out back if Wilding was there. When I mentioned it to one of the other staff, they said he was still doing it. I knew you wouldn't believe it from me — so I brought Pedro along to tell you. Wilding knows what he's doing, Pedro gives great head — don't you, bro?' Pedro didn't respond. Nick was starting to look very uncomfortable on the edge of the couch. Joe wondered how much of this part of the detective story he'd be sharing with his wife over dinner.

'Smoking gun,' said Jacinta, after Tony and Pedro had left. 'What more do you require?' Joe was thinking and remained silent, so Jacinta spoke again.

'It's obvious, meet with Wilding, tell him what you know and it's all over — they'll withdraw their case.'

Joe took a while before he spoke. 'I won't do it.'

'Why the hell not?' asked Jacinta, apparently surprised that he was rejecting her perfect solution to their problem.

'Because what Todd Wilding does behind restaurant skips is his business. I am not going to use another man's sexual preferences against him in business.'

'Even after what he did to you?'

'What he *did* to me was to call me a faggot and not even to my face.

For that I took away his business. That's sufficient punishment, don't you think?'

'He's an angry closet queen that you've pissed off. He'd ruin your life at the drop of a hat. In fact, he's trying to now. He's going to run you into the ground fighting this in court. It's not like you're in planning for the building — you've already started. We've pre-sold apartments, including one of the penthouses. You don't have time to waste playing Mr Nice-guy.'

'I won't do it. An eye for an eye. It's done, Wilding and I, we're finished. It's over. I am not some Old Testament prophet raining down eternal plagues against this guy.'

'How the hell have you got so far? You're a complete pussy.'

'Okay, this is all very useful,' Nick interjected over Jacinta and then, turning to face Joe, he continued. 'Just so you know, there were only ten plagues brought down on Egypt in the Old Testament, and it was God rather than Moses . . .' Nick looked at the ground as if in apology. Joe had forgotten that Nick and his wife were churchgoers. That realisation made Jacinta's next comment more than a little uncomfortable.

'He's an ugly closet queen paying to get sucked off by twenty-year-old waiters in back alleys. That's *not* sexuality. That's *not* gay politics. That's just bad practice. You don't have too many other options but to grab this by the balls and run with it.' As Joe had expected, Nick was reaching something close to his limits. He now began to rein things in.

'Might we be we underplaying the Māori angle? Tony's uncle?' Nick asked grimly.

Jacinta interjected. 'Too long-winded. Too costly. I say we go with Pedro, we leak it to the media.'

'Oh yes? And which particular lifestyle section will you send that press release to? I can't see it in *Viva* — I won't out someone for profit.'

'And there could be libel issues,' Nick added.

'Not if we have Pedro and God knows how many others.'

'You want to destroy Todd Wilding because he's gay? I told you, Jacinta, it's not happening.'

'I want to hammer Todd Wilding because he's a dishonest arsehole, one who at the moment is pretty much sending my job and your business into the toilet.'

Ignoring Jacinta's virulence, Joe turned to look out his office window and down at the carpark. Wilding's indiscretions were certainly a gift. God only knew how many gay men's lives Wilding had made miserable, but what Jacinta was suggesting was below the belt. He definitely couldn't get his head around that as an option. Better Wilding realise the situation he was in and pull back on the appeal of his own accord, though he realised that was probably too much to expect. Nick broke the silence.

'If you look at the ethics of the situation, Joe has a point. That earlier business, that began with the squash club, morally and ethically, you could consider that to be over. Think of it as a contained experience. You might, if you like, think of it as a duel, a matter of honour, and you won. It was between the two of you, and it's over. To ramp it up again at this point would be wrong.'

'He's the one ramping it up.'

'You make a good point, Jacinta. On the other hand, it's not Joe's name on that injunction. It reads Thackeray Makepeace, which means that you, Joe, have an obligation to Thackeray Makepeace's shareholders to do all in your power, if not to maximise profits, to at least limit losses. At this point, he does seem to be the one taking it to another level, and Thackeray Makepeace needs to respond. This suit is a whole new game.'

'Game on, I say.'

Nick spoke slowly. 'All I am trying to say is that personal ethics and corporate ethics are not the same thing. The territory can get a little blurry. No one will judge you for doing what's best for the firm.'

Joe watched the street below as a driver tried to negotiate a parallel park. Having tried two or three times to get into the space front-on, the driver had then decided instead to try reversing. Now, apparently frustrated with that approach, they had given up and driven on in search of another park.

'Nick, what were they offering to bring to the table, resource-wise?'

'Ah sorry, who?'

'The marae.'

'Nothing really, support perhaps?'

'And Tony wants to impress his uncle.'

'Presumably.'

Joe turned back to the window. 'Jacinta, you've discussed this with Tony, I expect? Has he got anything more?'

'Like what?'

'Security video — most restaurants have that.'

'No . . . I don't think so, just the kid's word, but I can ask.'

Joe turned to look directly at her. 'Jacinta, when you find him, the guy just like Tony, remember to look closely at the soles of his feet.'

'Why?'

'Because, there in little tiny writing is stamped the word "user". It's the model number. Tony's a user, always was, from the day I met him. Always will be. Don't let the looks throw you. That charade he pulled — the one to get Uncle Tane out quick smart — ask yourself, why didn't Tony want the uncle here?' Joe leant back against the window frame. 'Why didn't he want Uncle there when it's Tony that has the solution that kindly old Uncle is looking for?' Nick and Jacinta looked blankly at him. Neither spoke. 'Tony's heard something about Wilding. It may or may not be true. So, he couldn't wait to big note with his uncle. He didn't tell Uncle what he knew. He told his uncle he could get to me and with that to Thackeray Makepeace's deep pockets. Uncle now expects me to solve the problem and, if I don't, I or if you prefer "we" — Thackeray Makepeace — will be the villains. It'll bite us in every resource application we ever present. The thing is, Tony has the solution but he's too gutless to tell his uncle — he'll use me to do it instead. I bet the uncle doesn't even know Tony's queer. That'll be it — our Tony just hasn't found the right girl yet. I wonder how he explained Pedro — some disadvantaged Māori kid he was going to offer to us for work experience. That or some other spurious bro bullshit.'

'This might well be, but none of this is solving our problem,' said Jacinta.

Joe knew she was right. There wasn't time to perfect a business solution. They needed to act. He would deal with the consequences later.

'You know what, Nick has a point. This whole thing with the uncle, Tony, Pedro, even Wilding, none of it has anything to do with me. When in Rome, do as the Romans do, as they say.'

'Sorry?'

'In Auckland, the right solution to the problem is always the one that's fastest and cheapest. It's a model I've largely tried to avoid but bugger it, I give in. When Nick says it has to do with the firm, he's right. I'm not the firm. Nick, you work on the bullshit angle. Jacinta, you work on Tony. Do it fast. No media, not a whiff of this in public. No rumours, nothing, do you hear me?' They nodded. 'Jacinta, do what you do best. Have lunch with somebody or whatever you need to do but make this go away.' Then, remembering the strange motion the hippie woman had made with her hand, Joe parodied it with one of his own.

'What the hell was that?' asked Jacinta.

Nick smiled, 'Pontius Pilate. We've got this.'

CHAPTER 13

Joe felt dazed. It was as if at this café table, jutting out above the sea of footpath pavers, his friendship with Leo had suddenly come to rest, like a ship caught on the rocks. Just as the mummies at the next table each clung to the illusion that the random scheduling of their antenatal group had created genuine friendships, the truth of Joe and Leo's connection seemed suddenly tenuous. Like those mummies, they were friends all right, but maybe only in that coffee-fuelled moment. For Joe and Leo there was the occasional game of squash, sometimes a drink, followed by a movie. They had no mutual friends whose barbecues they might both attend. There were no shared sporting interests that might constitute weekends in front of each other's television screens. There were sometimes Thackeray Makepeace parties. Leo did his best to avoid those, even though his name was permanently at the top of the corporate invitation list.

When asked why he so seldom came, Leo replied that he wouldn't be able to explain who he was or how he might have come to be there. Joe had heard all those excuses years before except that now they carried with them the ominous associations of his and Leo's shared history. Leo allowed Joe take him out to dinner on his birthday. Birthday and Christmas were the two occasions when he would accept a gift, albeit reluctantly. Joe couldn't see the point of having money if he couldn't spend it on those he cared about. Joe had even enjoyed spending money on Tony. With Leo, Joe wanted to spend big, but the way Leo behaved it was as if Joe were the devil trying to purchase his soul.

There had, after one particularly long, well-lubricated dinner, been a late-night stumble around some old city haunts, though these days looking up at buildings and assessing their potential seemed a little too much like work. At almost every building remaining from their youth, Leo would ask, 'So why hasn't "the Mistake" bought that one yet?' Joe hated it when Leo called Thackeray Makepeace that but Leo thought it was funny. Joe, however, could still recall the whole conversation — both the 'William Thackeray Makepeace' and the 'I love you' spoken moments apart. He was never sure which half of the conversation Leo considered the mistake.

He could only think of one way to make Leo's teasing stop. That was the problem. With a few wines or beers in him, Leo's arm across his shoulders on a city street, it became all too clear where Joe wanted to go next. On that subject, though, Leo was unwavering. And so it was that with no team, no code and no sport to share and to provide something that looked and perhaps felt like intimacy, it seemed to Joe that true friendship between the two men, two men not sharing a bed, was strangely out of reach.

Shaking himself out of his reverie, Joe registered that Leo had asked him something and was waiting for a reply. His expression was serious and he was looking Joe directly in the eye. Joe's confusion must have shown on his face because Leo repeated his question and this time there was no mistaking it. 'Should I marry Danielle?'

Joe knew he'd have to answer eventually. He tried to rationalise the situation, look at it with a little distance, assess it as he might a new property or investment. Danielle had, in some ways, made things easier. Her presence in Leo's life meant that Joe saw more of Leo. They were around the same age. They went out sometimes to pubs or clubs. Joe could always rustle up someone to make a fourth. She was okay. Dani was okay. Dani was just an ordinary English girl, no intellectual and no great fashionista, a fairly straightforward woman, albeit one with the voice of an amplified cheese grater. Dani was no threat. If she was the one Leo wanted to marry, then who was Joe to oppose it?

Though she was no threat to Joe, he did genuinely wonder if Dani was the one to make Leo happy. She didn't read. Her opinions came in airfreighted copies of *Hello* magazine. She watched *Coronation Street*. She complained that you couldn't buy 'proper' Mars Bars or Marmite here. She talked endlessly about football. She revelled in the financial and diplomatic successes of ex-Spice Girls. He knew he was being a snob. The voice in his head argued that Dani was no worse than he'd been when he'd met Leo. Dani was a version of what Joe would have been had he *not* met Leo. She was ordinary. When Leo could have what any 'You need to know, I'm not gay' man might want, Dani was an unusual, if not unfathomable, choice. For that reason, Joe suspected that Leo might actually be in love.

Leo had never mentioned love, but most days Dani (God he hated the way she shortened her name to a man's) — Danielle — didn't look even close to being a girl in love. In fact, sometimes she didn't seem to like Leo very much. It was as if Leo were an expensive bright pink sports car that had looked great in the sales yard. It had been a wild test drive, but now she had it home she was paying big to re-spray it grey because its uniqueness embarrassed her. The Leo Dani wanted was an ordinary suburban boyfriend. For all of those reasons and the fact that, if he were honest with himself, Joe just didn't like her, he'd always figured she'd be temporary. Temporary because marriage was a bullet they'd both dodged. Marriage was, he'd assumed, still somewhere on that list of ordinary things Leo had, until now, remembered to despise.

Returning to the moment, Joe answered the question that had lingered in the air for an uncomfortably long time. Looking directly at Leo he said, 'You can ask me anything, Leo, but you need to figure that one out yourself.'

After an initial look of surprise, Leo had resigned himself to Joe's answer. They sat in silence, until, as the mummies began to push past, one by one, their oversized black baby buggies, too big for the confined space, bumping the back of Joe's chair as they stopped to ogle Leo, he spoke.

'Will you be my best man?'

There the real negotiations had begun. Leo didn't want a bachelor party, nor would he accept any financial assistance to pay for the wedding. Her father's English pounds would pay for the whole thing — but without a family to speak of he wondered if Joe could help him rustle up a groomsman and some other mutual acquaintances that made him look less of a loner. Joe wondered when Leo had started worrying about things like that, but he used his friend's needs to bargain for his best man's rights. There *would* be a bachelor party. Initially, Joe suggested limos, strippers and lamp-post bondage so that Leo would eventually agree to a simple but elegant farewell to bachelorhood of Joe's creation. It worked.

They began with champagne on a deserted building site served on a stack of framing timber and ended with a port, bottled in the year Leo had been born. The port they drank, already at the end of tolerance, in the empty smoking room of a vine-covered Auckland club. It was there, after an evening of light-hearted fun they had begun to talk.

'First time?' Joe asked.

'First time what?'

'You know, *the first time*?'

'Okay. I was walking home from a Ramones concert.' He stopped. 'This is embarrassing.'

'Go on.' Joe waved his port glass in Leo's direction.

'I was in the halls of residence, my first year at varsity. They'd played the PowerStation, I was a little high and a little worse for wear. Nah, I'm not telling you.'

Joe refilled Leo's glass and then his own. 'Come . . . on! We're mates, and this is a bachelor party — there has to be *some* filth. Tell me, or I'll get on my phone and call that stripper.'

Leo sighed.

'There were these working girls, you know, out for a smoke.'

'Go on.'

'They offered,' Leo looked down and seemed about to speak directly to the tablecloth. He eventually looked up and said, 'to do me for free. They said they were sick of ugly old men.'

Joe laughed. 'I thought you didn't like the free stuff that comes with the looks, and *now* I find this out!'

'I don't, and this is exactly why, but back then it just seemed a good way to circumvent what, to an only child raised on a boat and sent to an all-male school, were the complexities of the opposite sex.'

'Was it, *you know*, worth it?'

'Hmm. Well, we couldn't go inside, so they took me around back into a rear garden. There was a pink PVC garden lounger they — it was kind of grotty.'

'But, every teenage boy's fantasy — a three first time.'

'Not really — it was pretty awful, but it changed something. Somehow sex got easier. I had university girlfriends but when I started building things amped up. Client's wives, daughters, *not* at the same time. I'm not proud of that either, starting out with hookers and housewives, but I had no-one I needed to explain my behaviour to except myself. Suppose I've been the same ever since, in that regard at least.' Joe refilled their glasses again and they both took another drink of the plum red sticky port.

'Well then, ask.'

'About what?'

'Mine.'

'In a ladder store — you tell *everyone* that story.'

'I don't.'

'Yes, you do — except perhaps Betty.' Grinning, Leo finished his glass. 'I knew, you know.'

'Knew what?'

'The keys — you had a new Holden and I had that ancient Toyota. I knew from the minute I put my hand in my pocket that you'd switched them.' Joe smiled broadly and sat back in his chair.

'And?'

'And I still walked off to the carpark *knowing* you'd follow.' Joe went to speak, but Leo stopped him. 'I decided when you kissed me that if I saw you again I would kiss you back.'

'Why?'

'Didn't know why. Not then. You weren't the first — not by a long shot.'

Joe jumped forward, leaning over the table. 'Sorry, *what* are you telling me?'

'You weren't the first guy to hit on me.'

'I didn't hit on you. I was too bloody frightened.'

'No, it was more of a dying swan act.'

'Sorry?' Joe refilled the two glasses again, emptying the bottle.

'You were like one of those looped video clips of the detonation of a high-rise building, the ones they use in the montages of rock videos. A little quiver and you'd crumble, only to pop back up again, smiling, ready and willing to do it all again. Didn't matter what shit I sent your way, you'd pop right back up, with a goofy look on your face.'

'Bullshit.'

'Yep, that was it. That and the stupid try-hard things you used to say.'

'Why, then?'

'Why, what?'

'Us.'

'You know the answer to that every bit as well as I do. I've drunk too much to keep talking,' Leo said as he slipped his hand into Joe's. 'You know something unbelievable?'

'What?'

'I'm getting married in three days.' They raised their glasses in a silent toast.

The wedding was in a marquee on the piece of land that Leo had bought years before with money left to him by his parents. Back then it had been on the very fringe of the city, but Auckland had, over the last twenty years, spread past it.

On the morning of the wedding, Leo and Joe got ready together in a nearby motel room, Danielle having insisted on a night's separation. They had then driven over in Joe's new Jaguar.

Joe watched as Leo undressed out of his regular gear and then dressed in his wedding suit. Joe took what he figured would be his last long look. He committed this latest version of his one-time lover to memory alongside many similar images he had stored away. Then, while Leo stood in his shirtsleeves, offering out his arm so that

Joe could insert a cufflink, Joe slipped an expensive vintage Rolex onto Leo's wrist.

'Take it. Something old, something new . . .' Leo looked at the watch, ran his finger once around its bezel, smiled and embraced Joe. Holding him close, Leo whispered, 'Thanks, thanks for everything.'

Dressed identically, the two friends stood side by side, with Steve, their old building mate, who'd surprised them all by flying back from Australia to be Leo's groomsman, on a grassy slope before a temporary arbour. As Danielle's father went through the protocol of giving away his daughter, Joe imagined himself letting Leo go too. In undeniable pain, he blanked out the 'if anyone can show just cause why this couple cannot lawfully be joined together in matrimony' bit by running the lyrics of an old Buzzcocks song about inappropriate choices in love through his head at full volume. Afterwards, his stomach churning, he smiled through what felt like hours of photographs with dull, plump and boring bridesmaids.

In the marquee, as Joe stood to make his speech, he noticed Danielle appeared nervous. He summoned all he had and smiled at her. She had nothing to fear from him. His speech stayed away from the groom's early experiments with love, although he knew it would have made great material. Instead, he poked good-humoured fun at the man he still loved more than any other before resuming his seat at the bridal table.

Later, as the bride and groom departed in a hired white vintage Rolls Royce, he walked back to the bridal table in search of a drink. Glad now he hadn't asked Betty to come, he took a bottle of champagne, along with the waiter who delivered it, over a small mound to the side of the house site that he'd once imagined he and Leo would build together. There, he allowed himself to get very, very drunk and give in to his base instincts.

After the wedding, Joe and Leo didn't see much of each other. It didn't matter. Business kept Joe busy. Thackeray Makepeace's latest project was proving time-consuming. Leo was presumably busy too, building his own house. At first, Danielle had gone with Leo as he shifted soil, laid out the profiles and began digging foundations. She came a little less often as he laid blocks and then positioned floor joists. Then eventually she'd stopped coming altogether. Leo worked weekends and evenings on the house alone.

After a few months, Joe had unexpectedly run into Leo on the street. Leo had casually mentioned that he was putting together a group of builder friends to help erect the enormous, laminated timber forms that would structure the central part of the house.

'They're good guys. We should knock it off pretty quick.'

'Why didn't you ask me?' Joe asked. 'Am I too faggy for your other builder friends?'

'Where the hell did that come from? You haven't been on the tools in years. I'd sort of forgotten.'

'Forgot I was a builder or forgot I was a friend?'

'Joe, you're screwed up sometimes, you really are.'

That Saturday morning Joe was in the yard and loading up a truck before it was light. By 7.30 a.m. he was driving the well-worn ruts of Leo's paddock, dressed in his gym shorts and a worn hoodie. His old work boots were on the seat next to him. As he got out, Leo walked up to him. Laughing, he pushed him firmly back against the side of the truck. Lifting his hood up over his head, he pulled the drawcords tight around Joe's face. Placing his index finger on Joe's chin, he lifted it up and looked into his eyes.

'Just keep your hands off my car keys, faggot.'

It was 9 a.m. No one else had showed. It was looking like it was going to be just the two of them. The job was a huge one, too. Wooden beams needed to be raised one by one into position using a series of ropes and pulleys and then fixed. He wondered for a moment if he should get on the phone and get a crane out there, but he didn't want to overstep the mark.

Before the pair of them started manoeuvring the first beam, Leo brought out a pair of old wooden speakers from the little tin shed on the property and set them out on the grass. Joe immediately recognised them from their flat. They had been the largest piece of furniture Leo had owned after his bed.

'Wait.' Leo disappeared into the shed. A moment later the first track of an old Teardrop Explodes album boomed out over the property. 'They live here now,' shouted Leo over the noise. 'Not much call for them at home.' Leo sang along for a moment or two, before adding, 'Now, let's do this.'

They worked together in perfect harmony, each guessing what the other needed in advance. A couple of times Leo left Joe straining at the end of a rope, saying, 'Gotta change sides' as he disappeared into the shed and flipped an old record. As the day got hotter, Joe barely noticed Leo strip down to his shorts. Joe pulled off his own t-shirt, thinking this might well have been the first time he'd had things other than Leo's state of undress on his mind.

Come 6 p.m., Joe had never felt more exhausted. Every part of his body ached. He was fit, but he was only gym-fit. Eleven hours on a building site was a different thing altogether.

As they finished, Leo said, 'Good day's work and I can't even offer you a beer — one of the others was supposed to be bringing those. A couple of the guys have assured me they'll be here tomorrow, so . . .'

'So, what? I'll be here too. Seven-thirty, right?'

'Are you sure? Well, I'm not going to argue — you've proven you can still cut it on a building site. But hey, tomorrow's Sunday. Let's make it 8 a.m.'

The next day Phil and Zane were there shortly after Joe, muttering brief apologies and long stories about demanding wives. The day wasn't the same as the day before had been. Phil and Zane were too aware that Joe headed a large firm. They tiptoed around him, making an exaggerated point of deferring to him on minor things. After a while they relaxed enough to tease him gently about getting old behind a desk. He almost wished they'd make some stupid fag builder joke. He could tell them a few that still did the rounds. In the end, he figured that they both knew they could be looking for a job from him anytime soon. For all their posturing they didn't have the guts to risk getting him offside.

Joe still remembered the day Hayden had turned up looking for a job. Thirty-five, too much of a dopehead to recall that he'd ended whatever friendship they'd once had the night he came out. He and Hayden hadn't spoken since that day and he hadn't given him a job. Not because he had said the things he had, but because of the dope. There wasn't much left, if there'd ever been much to start with, and he wasn't going to put other builders at risk.

Working that weekend on the house, and the occasional one after when Leo needed him, allowed the two men to talk music and books. Leo admitted how hard he now found it to find moments to read. Joe slipped him a few new books, reminding him that he had once holed up in the cab of his ute to read books at lunchtime. Leo confessed that he sometimes wondered if he was still the person Joe remembered. Joe assured him he found him almost entirely unchanged.

Joe realised Leo was someone he could say anything to. He could talk honestly about the things that were on his mind, even his relationships, brief as they might be. Leo might sometimes look askance, but he always listened. In the work context they anticipated each other's moves, finished each other's sentences, challenged each other, teased each other, and they flirted. Finally, in the high tide of those weekends, their friendship slipped off the rock that it had been marooned on for a long time and set off on a new and more definite course.

Curiously, Danielle began to turn up unexpectedly on site under some pretext or other. One day after two such visits, not more than half-an-hour apart and neither with apparent purpose, he asked Leo.

'What's going on?'

'I told her.'

'Told her what?'

'About us.'

'What about us?'

'You know, that we were lovers. That you're my ex-boyfriend.'

Joe had never heard himself described as an ex-boyfriend, which he liked, but he was too surprised to delight in the reference for long.

'Hell, Leo, when did you do that?'

'Just before we got married. It was the honest thing to do, to clear the air on everything.'

'And what did she say?'

'She freaked, but then she said she was okay with it.'

'And is she?'

'She was for a while, but she doesn't like it much that you and I are out here alone.'

'Out on Brokeback Mountain together you mean?' Leo looked confused. 'It's a short story about—'

'I get it, Joe. Not helpful but yes, something like that.'

Driving home, Joe realised that although he had arrived, perhaps inevitably, at the point at which he disliked Danielle — now he also felt sorry for her. Dealing with the regular presence of a husband's ex-girlfriend would be hard enough, but throwing an ex-boyfriend into the mix when you had previously thought your husband was straight, that was bound to mess with your head. What, he wondered, had Leo told her? That he was bisexual? Unlikely — Leo had always dodged that label. That Joe had seduced him into it? That it had been love? Honest, Leo would have been honest. Just how that honesty was going to play out though, Joe could only guess.

Hitting the first traffic lights as he headed into the city proper, Joe's thoughts wandered to a bigger problem. He didn't much like the house Leo was building. It didn't matter how much he worked on it, he couldn't get his head around the house in any way. He kept telling himself that Leo, with such exceptional taste, would build something wonderful, but he was starting to doubt. The curved laminated beams that he had helped to place, graceful in themselves, gave the interior space a cathedral-like grandeur, but the rectangular corrugated iron box around them made the house feel brutal and hard. The projecting wall of windows at one end overlooking the surrounding landscape appeared to him like a slack-jawed maw, gawping from the house's main façade. It rendered the house dumb and slow. The result looked like an awkward giant, hunched against the hillside, friendly enough but ultimately ugly. He played over and over in his mind what a good architect might have added to the site, still factoring in Leo's immensely satisfying sense of craft. It took him time to realise that Leo, the ultimate builder, had in the end built the ultimate builder's house, one that was proud, solid and ungainly. He knew he could never tell him any of this and the thought of keeping such a critical opinion to himself disturbed him greatly.

The phone rang — an internal transfer.

'Call from a Dani Bridge.'

She'd never rung him at work before. 'Put it through Gail,' he said cautiously.

'Hiya.'

'Hello Danielle, how might I help?'

'I wondered if you'd like to come down for the weekend? Just a few friends, for a sort of housewarming barbecue. Saturday night. Leo could do with the company.' Joe remembered her friends, with whom she worked at the drainage department of the local council, from the wedding. They hadn't precisely clicked then, especially not after the drunken episode with the waiter had turned into something close to a public spectacle. He couldn't help but feel that something about the invitation didn't ring true. When had Leo ever required company? Joe supposed Dani thought his presence made her look good. With the completion of the Virginian, once again a prime-time television show had profiled him. Joe was probably the closest she could get to a celebrity at the party, but if it made things easier for Leo, of course he would be there. He agreed to come.

Joe got to Leo's early. As the two men stood, beers in hand, Joe noticed that when Danielle's friends arrived, they swept through the handcrafted interior of the house to the far end of the living space where they stopped to admire the view. Turning, they had no words left for the house itself. Joe suspected that hurt Leo a lot. Danielle moved the conversation on by announcing to the small crowd that they were going to have a baby.

Joe took Leo aside and congratulated him, promising to spoil the kid rotten. Looking over at Danielle, deep in conversation with her female friends, Joe realised why she'd invited him. He was being put in his place. Danielle had wanted him there as they announced the one thing Joe could never do: give Leo a child.

There were complications. Danielle wasn't young, and was hospitalised several times during the pregnancy. Eventually, however, she gave birth to a healthy baby boy. They named him Taylor, but Leo always called him Tay.

CHAPTER 14

Joe played with the invitation in his hand. The script along the top of the card read: *A weekend to celebrate the reopening of Kudu Lodge as a luxury retreat*. He propped it against a presentation inkwell, given to him by a heritage group. The invite had come from another developer with whom Joe had a passing friendship based on mutual admiration. Where Joe's projects were central and eastern city residential, the other developers were high-end hospitality and rural-fringe lifestyle.

Everyone in property knew Kudu Lodge, the famed lakeside mansion of Sir Charles Bedford in the Southern Waikato. Born to New Zealand parents in South Africa, Bedford returned to New Zealand after the First World War and built a chain of pubs, hotels and other projects funded by a seemingly inexhaustible mining fortune. Kudu Lodge, Bedford's private home, had been designed by a London architectural firm and built by a team of English builders and Italian plasterers imported for the purpose. After Bedford's death, Kudu, although the subject of numerous advances, had been closed up. All in all, although famous, Kudu Lodge had long been a mystery, and this was to be its pre-season rebirth for a select group of the developer's friends and business associates.

He was going, there was no question about it, and it was Leo he wanted to take as his guest. But would he go? Joe knew Leo would love the house and if Joe caught him in the right frame of mind, he might *just* tolerate the people. There were other reasons. Although Joe had done his best to be a friend to Leo, there was a new distance between them as Leo had grappled with the consequences of fatherhood. There was less time in Leo's life for Joe. There also seemed to be less time in Leo's life for Leo, and Joe wanted to do something about that. He knew he wasn't being entirely selfless either. He could have sent Leo, with or without his family, on holiday almost anywhere in the world. That was providing Leo wasn't too stubborn to accept. A weekend away with Leo was needed to feed something in Joe, and he knew that most of all.

Joe had, on receiving the invitation, enquired immediately of the organiser. The retreat was expected to be full for the event and an additional room was unlikely. However, a twin room might be available, particularly as he had given them so much notice. Surely Leo could cope with that? One part of Joe imagined ceremoniously pushing the two beds further apart to ease Leo's concerns. Another tiny part of him wasn't past hoping that Leo might, at last, decide to push them closer together, but he knew that was unlikely. When, over the phone, he suggested to Leo that they go away for a weekend, he'd expected resistance. More than that, he'd expected a point-blank refusal. After the obvious questions, however, Leo had agreed quite quickly.

When Joe collected Leo from the house, Danielle hadn't been home.

'Thanks for this. I needed it,' said Leo as he locked the front door.

'Not too much grief, I hope?'

'Apparently, she needs a break too,' Leo's tone was resigned as he climbed into the car. 'She's taken Tay to her father's for the weekend.'

Joe could tell Leo was doing his best to appear unimpressed by his new Audi as he reversed quickly up Leo's long driveway.

'I'm driving from Mercer.'

'You wish,' Joe replied and they both laughed.

Leo seemed in good spirits as they coasted along — conversation flowed with relative ease. It was early spring, and the Waikato River was in flood. The low-lying ground on either side of the road was saturated. The rolling pastures were a verdant green and glowed supernaturally as the white car sped down first the expressway and then a series of narrow country roads. As they approached their destination, out of the corner of the windscreen, Joe could just make out the still, bare oak trees that lined Kudu Lodge's long drive and then the roof of the house itself nestled lakeside. He pointed it out to Leo.

As they drew closer it was quickly apparent that this was an impressive building. A steep, black slate-clad roof covered the main body of the house, from which another lower roof emerged to form a wing. Both swept down in a graceful line and curved out dramatically, just as they neared the ground. Joe's eyes followed the roofline to impressive hand-forged copper brackets, the concave curves of each holding up broad overhanging eaves. They gave the house a sleepy-eyed fairytale look. Small rustic casement windows, seemingly chiselled into the rough, plastered façade, shone with a warm inner light, suggesting to Joe that every bulb in the house was being employed to counter the effects of the cold late afternoon light.

Joe pulled into a park, an identical Audi roadster on either side.

'Okay, time to tell you the truth. I've brought you to an Audi owner's bash.' Turning he smiled at Leo. 'I apologise.'

Leo laughed, but quickly turned back to the house. He was clearly already lost in its grandeur.

'It's almost Charles Voysey. I hope they haven't wrecked the inside,' Leo said as he took his bag from the open boot.

The projecting porch sheltering the front doors opened into a large double-height entrance hall, lined with the trophy heads of the kudu, or antelope, from which the house took its name. Here a smartly dressed young public relations woman was waiting for them.

'Mr Joseph Wright of Thackeray Makepeace and . . .' she stopped, and, after taking an appreciative gawp at Leo, resumed with a newly inquisitive tone, 'and partner?'

'Friend. Mr Leopold Bridge,' Joe answered politely.

'Leo, please. It's just the star sign, nothing else.' Leo shot the comically annoyed glance he held in reserve for every time Joe extended his name to 'Leopold' or 'Leonardo', while shaking the young woman's hand.

'We have you both in room sixteen, top floor at the rear, lakeside. If you'd like to leave your bags here, you can collect your key from reception when you go up to your room. Some of the other guests are in the billiard room. Please, go through.'

The room number, executed in gold leaf, shone against the new white paint of the planked bedroom door. The key, the original, was a decorative iron piece to which was attached a large and inconvenient curtain tassel. Inside, the room was large, panelled to three-quarter height in a dark oak. Above this ran a simple line of rough white render. Along the shelf at the top of the panelling, a line-up of Imari plates politely shared the ledge with a series of polished brass candlesticks. A large red-brick fireplace took up a considerable space on one wall. Off to the far end of the room was what Joe assumed to be a bathroom. Along the same wall one of a pair of stable doors had been left open to reveal their luggage now neatly arranged in a built-in wardrobe. The room was luxuriously furnished, but Joe suspected it was not Kudu's best.

As he placed the key on the occasional table, next to a vase containing a large floral arrangement, he noticed propped against it a small book on the history and restoration of the house. On it, a small handwritten card caught his eye — *Kudu Lodge welcomes Mr & Mrs Leo and Jo Wright*. He took the card and put it in his pocket, but as he turned around, he quickly realised his next problem was not going to be solved by sleight of hand. Leo was standing at the bathroom door, having just looked inside. The cheerful demeanour of the afternoon's drive had evaporated. Leo looked thunderous.

'What's going on? This,' he gestured at the room, 'is not what we agreed.' There was, as Joe had noted immediately, very obviously only one large bed.

'No, it's not what I requested. Maybe it's one of those beds that splits and they've just forgotten to do it.' He walked over and lifted the mattress, but it and the base were one solid, immovable piece. He let the pile of bedding drop with a thud.

'I'm not sleeping with you, Joe.' Leo was pissed. Joe perched on the edge of the bed.

'I'll sort it. Just get dressed for dinner.'

'What?' Leo looked confused.

'It's formal. Don't worry, I have it all organised.' He walked over to the wardrobe and took out a black suit bag and hung it on the knob of the door. 'Shoes are in a box in the bag on the shelf.' He gestured at the wardrobe. Knowing Leo would never have accepted the invitation had he suspected it was black tie, he had meant the suit to be a surprise. It was intended as a present to cap off a perfect day spent together, but now he felt it had probably been a step too far.

'What the hell is going on here, Joe? This is not what you promised. The bed and now this,' he gestured at the suit.

'Nothing is going on. Get dressed, or you'll look like a slob at dinner, and while you're doing that, I'll sort out the bed situation.'

Twenty minutes later Leo emerged from the bathroom cleanly shaven and with a towel wrapped around his waist.

'Look, Leo, they can't do anything about the room. They're full. It's a mix-up, and they're sorry. I'm sorry.'

'I'll stay somewhere else.'

'Where? We're in the middle of nowhere.'

'I'll sleep in the car.'

'It's an Audi.'

'I'm *not* sleeping with you.'

'Okay, I get that. I'll sleep on the floor or in a chair. We'll figure it out. *I'll* sort it.' Before Leo could respond, Joe closed the bathroom door, undressed and climbed into the shower.

When he came out of the bathroom, Leo was standing, arm on the mantelpiece, with a glass of whiskey in his hand, looking every bit like the dapper Hollywood movie star. The new black dinner suit fitted well. Joe was pleased. He'd at least got that right. Throwing his towel over the back of one of the carefully distressed leather armchairs in front of the fire, he walked across the room in his underwear to grab his white shirt from the wardrobe rail.

'Pour me a drink,' Joe said as he pulled on his shirt and began doing up the buttons. Leo begrudgingly followed the instruction, pointedly looking away from Joe until he was fully dressed. By the time he was finished, Leo had downed his second scotch. Joe considered for a moment asking Leo to tie his bow tie but thought better of it. Instead, he used the mirror above the vase of flowers and tied it himself. Catching Leo's reflection, Joe could see that Leo hadn't calmed down. His eyes were barely open but they still seemed to flash with an inner fury. If Joe hadn't been directly in the path of the storm, he would have said Leo was at his most magnificent.

They walked down the hall in silence except for the squeak of Leo's new shoes. Joe paused at the top of the stairs. There the balustrade swept up in a dramatic curve terminating in a towering newel post well above their heads. This provided a protective screen that he figured had been for the house's original hostess to make last-minute private adjustments to her appearance before the very public descent to the crowd waiting below.

'Look, Leo,' Joe grabbed Leo's upper arm and turned him towards him. 'I didn't do this, you have to believe me.'

If things had gone to Joe's original plan, the room would have gone silent, and everyone would have turned and looked at them as they walked into the room. In reality, they stood there in the double doorway for a long minute before the host of the party stepped forward.

'Joseph Wright? Good to see you, and this is?'

'Leopol — *Leo* Bridge. Leo is something of a specialist on house restoration.'

'Well, my name's James Stone, Jim. Sorry I wasn't here earlier to meet you. I got caught up at the office. Anyway, great to meet you, Leo. I do hope you like what we've done here,' he said, shaking Leo's hand vigorously. 'This is my wife, Brenda.' He gestured at the woman next to him who was semi-engaged in polite conversation with another man. Having been interrupted, Brenda excused herself and turned around.

'Brenda, meet Joe and Leo.'

'Gosh, you're a handsome one,' Brenda said to Leo.

'You flatter me. It's simply a reflection of the company and of course the setting.'

'Oh and charming too,' twittered Brenda. 'Did you hear that Jim?'

'Hmmph.' The group of four laughed politely.

'Come through to the bar. Let's get you a drink.' Leaving her husband to greet late guests alone, Brenda took Leo by the arm and led him into the bar. Joe found himself trailing behind the two of them. So, this is how the evening was going to play out. It reminded him of that night years earlier in the pub. The night they'd first hooked up, when Leo had flirted with each of the female patrons without ever quite taking his eyes off him, reminding Joe that while he might have any woman in the room, Joe, on the other hand, couldn't have Leo.

As expected, Leo was utterly courteous and charming throughout the evening. He fetched drinks, complimented the women and listened to everyone's stories. One by one the women in the party took terms to present their individual charms. From time to time, Leo shot Joe the occasional dark look to remind him of unfinished business. Joe was left to talk shop. One man, a balding, overweight investor packed into an obviously hired dinner suit, sporting a red bow tie and cummerbund, had noted that his considerably younger wife had, after a long wait, come to the top of the list for Leo's attention. He turned away from the group of men he was talking to and looked at Joe.

'Your friend, he's a queer too, I assume?'

Pretending he hadn't heard, Joe enquired pleasantly, 'And is that your wife?' He gestured towards an overly tanned brunette in a leopard print dress, who at this moment had one arm around Leo's neck. The man nodded. 'He is *completely* queer.' The man looked satisfied and, turning his back to Joe, resumed his conversation.

Deciding to leave the party where it was, Joe turned and walked towards the partially open doors of the dining room, through which he could see the staff busy with finishing touches. As he opened the door and slipped through he could understand what was meant by 'the splendour of Kudu'. The room had once been a ballroom and an immense stone fireplace, one he might easily stand upright within, dominated the far end. The blue light of a gas fire drew him closer, and now he could see its surrounds, heavily carved with mythical creatures. Standing in front of it, hand on the warm stone, he turned and looked up. Broad oak beams featured intertwined branches of stencilled roses and the Bedford family crest, now the Kudu resort logo. Set against the high, flat ceiling, a bank of lights glowed indistinctly. The room itself was, he realised now, entirely lit by an army of electrified candelabra that marched in a line down the centre of the largest mahogany dining table he had ever seen, suffusing the room with a soft light. The setting was completed by a set of thirty Sheraton dining chairs, each with carved shield backs and rich green upholstery. Moving off in search of his place card he rested his hands on the back of one of the chairs. Their selection was clever in the way their fine lines countered the masculinity of the architecture. His money was on the choice being Bedford's London architect's and not Jim Stone's.

Joe stood behind his chair, gazing around the room as the other guests filtered in. He and Leo were the last to assume their seats. Leo had been placed on the opposite side of the wide table, just sufficiently off tangent and far enough away that he could see him clearly through the forest of candles but not hear what he might be saying. For a moment the seat to the far side of Leo remained empty. Joe wondered if they had defeated the organisers' attempts to pull off a perfect boy, girl, boy, girl, seating plan but then a few minutes later a young woman in her early twenties, not present at the pre-dinner cocktail party, slipped into the empty seat. Her classic dress and well-chosen jewellery, set off by lustrous black hair piled upon her head, made the older, wealthier women who sat on either side of Joe seem dowdy. He felt a little jealous of Leo.

Leo and the new arrival made a pretty picture. Each time he looked across the table during dinner he found the two of them deep in conversation. Too polite to completely neglect the woman to his right, it soon became obvious, at least to Joe, that Leo had a clear preference. Even without hearing it, Joe could tell it was a different kind of conversation too. In polite mode, Leo's sentences were charming but short and punctuated with silences. However, with the mystery woman, Leo chatted unguardedly for a long time, moved in close to hear her speak, and laughed genuinely and often. With this woman, Leo's gestures were quick and enthusiastic, whereas they were usually laconic and infrequent. Joe was no body language expert but looking at these two, there seemed to be some genuine chemistry.

After a while, Joe immersed himself in small talk with the women on either side of him. They had been chatting for a while then the woman to his left leant in close.

'Do you think we're under scrutiny?'

'Why do you ask?'

'Watts was my maiden name,' she said, gesturing at the place card in front of her. 'My name is Caroline Wilding. Todd Wilding's ex-wife.' Joe could feel his face flush red with embarrassment. 'They're all waiting for me to cause a scene with you.'

'Oh.' Joe didn't know what to say. He cleared his throat and tried to regain some of his composure, although the neck of his shirt felt a little tight. 'Would you prefer it if I moved? My guest over there might be prepared to swap?'

'By the look of him, he's very happy where he is, but as it happens, I asked to be seated next to you.'

'You did?' Joe gulped. 'Why?'

'Because I wanted to see you close up and judge what sort of man you were.'

'And?'

'You're not, I suspect, at all like the other men here.'

'I'll take that as a compliment.'

'Perhaps — but most men wouldn't send a woman to do their dirty work.'

Joe cringed as Jacinta's face flashed into his mind. 'Ouch, but I probably deserve that.'

'Actually, I rather think you deserve a thank you,' Caroline's voice softened.

'Really?' Joe was finding the conversation more perplexing by the minute.

'Not for what you or your assassins did, but for ensuring they were discreet about the whole thing. In fact, to be honest, I admire that it was done woman to woman, although I can't quite articulate why. I hated her at the time. Do you understand?'

'Yes, I suppose. Jacinta has a knack for inciting that reaction in people.' Joe took a moment to really look at the woman next to him. Softly spoken, she had a gamine look about her, with French overtones. He'd been wrong to think her dowdy. Joe continued, 'But you can't be so at peace with the whole thing, surely?'

'Can't I, Mr Wright? Todd was never a very good husband. In fact, he isn't a very good person full stop. It just took me a while to realise that. Don't get me wrong, I had a few ideas of my own long before Charlotte Corday paid me a visit.' Joe looked impressed. She smiled. 'My degrees are in art history. *The Death of Marat* is a favourite.' Joe nodded his approval.

'Is anyone a good husband, really?' asked Joe, surveying the room. 'They all seem to take their wives for granted.'

'I think it's a question of attentiveness,' said Caroline. 'Take your friend, for example. They could all take a leaf out of his book. I think he has attentiveness enough for all of them.'

'So, you met him then?'

'I bought my ticket and stood in the queue for the ride. Who wouldn't? The pursuit of happiness, even momentary happiness, is not a male-only sport. Neither is the appreciation of beauty, *real beauty*.' She stopped for a moment and took a sip from her glass. 'I am here with Ian Reading. I'm sure you know him.' She gestured at a man sitting on the opposite side of the table, as far from Caroline as Leo was from him. As she did so he caught her eye and smiled, raising his glass in reply. 'He's a good man, or he seems to be so far.' Returning her gaze to meet Joe's, she said quietly, 'You and I are not dissimilar. We see things other people don't, but we can't either of us see everything.'

'I think that's most people.'

'No, there you're wrong. Most people don't see anything at all. Taking another sip of her glass, she continued in a considerably brighter tone.

'We, Ian and I, have just come back from Vietnam. It's wonderful and so very beautiful. Have you been?'

At the end of the evening, the party began to dissipate. Couples took their leave and headed for their rooms while the hardcore drinkers headed back to the bar. Joe suspected Leo might be feeling a little worse for wear before conceding that he too was feeling the effects of a lot of expensive wine. He motioned to Leo that he was heading up to the room, but Leo showed no interest in leaving his conversation. Joe filled his glass one more time and headed for the entrance hall. Looking up at the largest of the Kudu that had greeted his arrival, he offered a toast.

'That was a good night, thank you. Here's to the veld.' Craning too far back, he lost his balance and fell awkwardly, hitting one of the wooden chairs arranged in a formal line against the wall with a wallop.

'Are you all right?'

'Yes, quite all right, thank you.'

'Can I fill your glass?' Joe looked the waiter up and down, noting his sleek torso, and then remembering the mess he got into last time.

'Take it away.' Joe said as he handed the waiter the glass. Sitting, his head back against the wall to stop it spinning, he noticed a carved door lintel, reading *Library*. He got up and walked over to it. Opening the door, he peered into the dimly lit room and waited for his eyes to adjust. After a moment or two he could make out an immense book-lined space, the only unhappy intrusion into which was a large screen television mounted high on one wall. The fire was unlit but walking over to the hearth he noticed a panel of buttons. Pushing one, the gas fire in the hearth roared into life, casting a warm glow in an arch around Joe's feet. He pushed the second button on the panel and lighting concealed in the top of high bookcases flooded the ornate coffered ceiling with a soft light. Joe threw himself down on a leather Chesterfield couch and gazed up at the ceiling.

In the middle of each recessed square was a plaster medallion containing a relief portrait of one of the greats of English literature. There in front of the fireplace were the obvious starters: Chaucer, Shakespeare and Milton. Then a man in an unusual cloth turban he assumed was Alexander Pope. He recognised the image from the engraved frontispieces on the opening pages of books leafed through in second-hand bookshops. As he rested his head against the low back of the Chesterfield, he extended his legs out in front of him towards the fire. He looked straight up. Directly above him, he met the plaster stare of William Makepeace Thackeray. He raised his hand to his temple in mock salute.

'Mr Thackeray, I presume?' He relaxed into the seat and now staring into the fire said quietly, 'When I look at him, when I think of him, I am in paradise.' He glanced back up at the spectacled face staring out from the ceiling. 'Apologies, for the gender mangle, but mate, I think you owe me.'

When he got to the door of their room, Leo was slumped against the doorframe in a half squat that Joe recognised from long ago.

'No key,' said Leo as he struggled into an upright position.

'I thought you were staying with your new Chinese friend for the night,' replied Joe, not caring if he sounded bitchy. Leo's face lit up.

'She's amazing. Her name is Nor. She is Malay but grew up in Hong Kong. Even went to the same school as me — years later though.'

Joe rested his hands on Leo's chest. He felt his heart beating steadily beneath the thin cloth of his shirt. Standing close together in the open doorway, only a few inches apart, they looked into each other's eyes.

'She's part of the hotel management team here. Beautiful, wasn't she? Not to mention super smart — double degree in hotel management and classical Chinese poetry.'

'Told ya — Chinese.' Leo ignored him. As Joe put the key in the door, Leo leant in closer as if about to kiss him but stopped a few inches from his lips. Joe could smell the sweet tang of Leo's breath. Reaching out, up, running his hand lightly across his chest, Leo pulled Joe's bow tie undone — leaving the two ends to fall.

'Better,' Leo smiled. 'You know, you look pretty good for a man your age. You were definitely the cutest guy there tonight.'

'Second cutest, I'm pretty sure. Rugby always beats soccer.'

'Do mine,' Leo whispered, his face still close to Joe's.

'What?'

Leo gestured at his tie. Joe pulled the two ends, and the knot fell.

'Best part of the night that, like pulling the Christmas crackers.' Leo blinked slowly. Joe leant on the door handle, and as they stumbled together through the open doorway, the bed loomed into view.

'Fucking thing.'

'Yeah, fucking thing,' repeated Leo, clearly mocking him. Laughing and smiling broadly, he took off his jacket, stumbling slightly in the process. Recovering, Leo walked across the room, placed it on the arm of the leather chair and headed for the bathroom. Returning a moment later, he began unbuttoning his shirt, pulling it off over his head and placing it on his jacket. He sat down on the large deep-buttoned leather chair and undid his belt, unbuttoned the top of his trousers and then unzipped his fly.

'Shoes.' He gestured at Leo's feet. Leo looked confused for a moment, and then his eyes slowly traced the direction of Joe's extended arm and then finger.

'Thanks.' He unlaced his shoes and took them off, taking a moment to admire them before placing them on the Persian rug in front of the fire. Taking off his socks, he stood up, pulled down his trousers and for the second time that evening stood nearly naked in front of Joe, the firelight flickering across his muscled body. 'That's better.'

'Much better.' Still dressed in his suit, Joe placed his hand on Leo's shoulder and took a close, appreciative look at his friend. He sighed and placed his lips gently on Leo's other shoulder. Leo wobbled a little.

'Bed!' He smacked Leo on his rump as he turned away. He searched the upper shelf of the wardrobe and pulled out an embroidered quilt and a pillow. 'I'll sleep on the chair in front of the fire. It'll be fine.' Joe watched as Leo climbed into bed and then began undressing in front of the fire. He plumped up the duvet, ready to make a nest of it in the armchair, at the same time contemplating whether he should push the two heavy chairs together. Leo threw back the covers of the bed.

'Get in.'

'Really?'

'Just get in.'

Joe climbed into the bed, leaving a gap between the two of them.

'Come here,' Leo commanded, but before Joe could move, he placed his hands around Joe's torso and deftly turned him to face away from his own body while at the same time pulling him close. The two of them nestled tightly together. Leo wrapped his arms around Joe and placing his mouth close to his ear. 'Joe, I love you. I'll sleep with you, but I can't fuck you. You understand, eh?' Joe quivered. He felt the warmth of a tear well up on his lower eyelid, but he said nothing. 'Good. You're a good friend, Joe. The best. Now sleep.'

Joe slept. He didn't know if it was the effect of the wine or the luxuriousness of the bed but when he awoke the next morning Leo's arms were still around him and the strawberry field of the embroidered cover lay undisturbed. It took Joe only a moment to realise that he had awoken to the less-than-subtle protrusion of Leo's automatic morning erection. Desperate to turn over so that they might touch, even through the fabric of their underwear, but not wanting to break this new bond, Joe instead got out of bed, leaving Leo to sleep.

Making for the bathroom, Joe turned on the shower and stepped into it. For the second time that weekend he began jerking off under the hot massaging jets of the water. As Joe, cock in hand, reached the moment of no return, the bathroom door opened and silently Leo walked in. Joe, eyes half closed, shot an emphatic load across the marble tiles of the shower floor.

'Looks like fun,' Leo croaked.

Joe snapped back into consciousness. Dismissing any attempt to disguise himself as pointless, he smiled sheepishly before reaching for the soap.

'I'm next,' Leo said, removing his underwear, and through his half-hard cock pissing a steady stream into the toilet bowl. 'Great night, last night.'

Leo had never told Joe what it had cost him to spend that weekend at Kudu. He had wanted to go just as much as Joe had wanted him there. He wanted to see the house. He wanted to see what the latest car could do and listen to some good, loud music on the drive. He wanted to spend a weekend away from his wife and kid. Just one. For once he wanted to have an uninterrupted conversation and to talk about ideas. He wanted to read a book that wasn't about dinosaurs. He wanted to play a game of billiards on a full-sized table. He wanted to drink too much and not have to drive anywhere. He wanted to sleep in the next morning — that he wanted so *very* much. He wanted his breakfast cooked for him. He wanted to eat food that hadn't already been chewed by a two year old. Just once. Just for this one weekend. The pleading had been heartfelt and the bargaining hard, but in the end he'd told her she 'just had to trust him'. Now, as he carried box after box down the corridor to his new apartment, he had a lot of reasons to be rethinking that weekend.

The bed hadn't meant a thing. Well, not much. It was annoying, but he half suspected Joe would try something on. It wasn't the first time and it wouldn't be the last. Joe always left extra shirt buttons undone so that he might flash his pecs when Leo was around. After their occasional game of squash, Joe usually had a matter that needed to be discussed while he stood naked in front of Leo in the changing rooms. Joe was, Leo knew, always hoping he would be convinced to cross the line he'd so willingly crossed once before. He knew how Joe felt about him. He knew the sacrifices he'd made.

Brendan, the rugby player, closeted, not bright, but sweet, had worked hard to please while trying to deal with his own stuff. Drew, the kid from the firm, had seemed devoted. But somehow Joe had rejected them both, perhaps afraid of the hard work involved, or just tone deaf to the potential in the youthful innocence of their desires.

Leo also thought — well, he knew really — that Joe was still unwilling to give up his feelings for his first love, himself, so that he might commit, really commit, to another man.

'Sorry mate.' Leo smiled pleasantly at the young guy waiting for the lift, as he moved his boxes into the hall, all the time trying to hold the door open with his leg, while the guy checked his phone. The lift door closed and the guy disappeared.

Nah, it had been the suit that had got him mad. It was expensive, *extremely* expensive. The bag hadn't just contained the shoebox but a belt, socks and a box of underwear. The shoes were English, clearly handmade. The small and careful artisan stitching around the buttonholes on the shirt suggested it was too. In the pocket of the jacket, he had discovered engraved silver cufflinks.

He hated it when Joe did stuff like this. It wasn't the money. Joe had money, *too much* money. He liked to spend it on other people. That was okay. What bugged him was that Joe was packaging him up and putting him on show. Jesus, he'd even bought him underwear. Guys just didn't buy each other underwear, no matter *how* close they might be. Obviously Joe hoped to present him to the dull couples downstairs as if he were a trophy beast, a prime slab of beef, no different from the show cattle that surrounded the lodge. Leo had been tempted there and then to derail the plan because Joe was pretending Leo was his, but pretending most ordinarily. The truth was, Leo was and always would be Joe's, in a unique way. If only Joe would stop playing games long enough to see it. That was it really, what bugged him, Joe's stubborn delusion that they had some sort of future as lovers, because in that hope there was a danger Joe would never find the happiness he deserved.

He opened the door of his apartment and, propping it open, started moving the mound of boxes from their pile in the corridor down the hallway to the little lounge. The place wasn't big — a kitchen and bathroom, a small lounge and a bedroom for him and a smaller one for Tay. He had chosen it because it had a tiny and distant view of the sea and because it was all he could afford.

When Joe had turned up in his life again, Leo had at first thought him unchanged. If it were not for a small scar on his lip, which he refused to discuss, he looked much the same. Except that *this* Joe was now businesslike, every aspect of his life ordered and controlled, whereas the kid, the one he still considered the *real* Joe, had been all over the place, romantic, trusting and capable of great happiness. It was as if, keen to convince the world that he had his act together, Joe had dismissed his real self as too untidy and locked it away from view. The thing was, Leo knew exactly what this locked place contained and yearned to see it again.

As soon as they'd entered the bar at Kudu, Leo had realised what he faced. The men were to the last dull, balding and self-obsessed, their suits were either tired or hired. Their jackets flapped open over corpulent stomachs while they tugged at the collars of tight shirts. Their wives ranged from long-suffering firsts and savvy seconds to dewy-eyed thirds, but they were all united in one thing — they were at heart bored by their current situation. The game had soon gotten tiring — being the most charming man in the room wasn't much of a challenge when so many of the husbands seemed to have forgotten they'd even brought their wives. Even Joe had figured it out and was busy chatting with future clients and contacts.

What he hadn't counted on was Nor. The seat next to him had been vacant. He was pleased about that. She had slipped into her seat at the end of the table just as the staff had begun serving the first course. His back had been turned but, sensing her arrival, he had excused himself from the conversation with the woman to his right. Turning, he had unexpectedly come face to face with her. His immediate reaction had been to stand but, caught between chair and table, he had half-stood in his seat and leaning forward in a small bow, extended his hand.

'Good evening. My name is Leo Bridge.'

She nodded. 'I am Nor.' Placing her hand delicately on his, he noticed for the first time that she was wearing long satin evening gloves. Noting his attention to this particular detail of her dress, she looked at him worriedly. 'Too much?' she asked. 'I didn't know.'

'No, not at all. Very, very beautiful.' He took the opportunity to follow the line of her arm and look directly into her eyes.

'You look like a very old racehorse,' she said with a smile.

'Old?'

'Of *old* family. An old family racehorse, black and white. You too are very beautiful.'

He smiled, hoping she meant thoroughbred. He knew immediately that Nor was Malay. He also knew that to everyone else in the room she was simply Asian. By default, they would assume she was Chinese. She was dazzling. She made the other women in the room seem dull. She was sophisticated, politely refusing the wine offered to her by letting her gloved hand hover gracefully over the glass and smiling kindly at the steward. She spoke assuredly but quietly. She listened attentively and laughed softly but honestly.

Coincidentally, Nor's parents had sent her to the smart Hong Kong girls' boarding school next door to the boys' school that as a ten year old he had attended briefly to prep for Auckland. They talked food and distant memories of places and buildings. He struggled to recall a few words of Malay, and she corrected him gently and kindly. By the end of the evening, he was as happy as he'd been in a long time.

Then, suddenly, Joe had indicated he was heading upstairs. Leo had followed soon after — it was time to mend a few bridges. As he'd excused himself, Nor had looked a little embarrassed.

'I have neglected the other guests. I must go too. I hope to see you tomorrow.'

'Oh, are you here tomorrow?'

'You silly thing, I work here.'

Leo knocked his hand against his forehead, mocking his own forgetfulness. A look of distress suddenly crossed Nor's face. She reached up and took Leo's hand in hers. Lowering his hand onto her lap, she said, 'Don't hurt yourself.'

When he got to the room, Joe wasn't there. At first, Leo wondered if, pissed off, Joe might have locked him out, but, listening, he sensed the room was empty. Eventually, Joe appeared at the end of the hall, wobbling slightly, the fingers of his extended arm tracing a line along the wall to steady himself. He grinned when he saw Leo. As they stood there in the doorway — Joe struggling to get the big cumbersome key to turn in the lock — Leo decided Joe looked good. He looked good in his suit. Later, lying under the covers of the room's big bed, looking down at Joe, he looked equally good out of his suit. Joe was a decent guy and, when it came to Leo, was only doing his best with a messy situation that had, after all, been Leo's making. There and then he decided to reward Joe. He had not intended to tell him he loved him, but of course it was true. There was no other name for all this. He'd felt Joe's body tremble as he tightened his grip on him and within moments they had both fallen asleep.

They had spent a leisurely Sunday at the lodge before heading home after a late lunch. He could sense the feeling of dread returning as he stepped into the Audi. As Joe backed out of the parking space, a figure came running out the front door and stopped at the passenger window. Leo fumbled for the controls and eventually lowered the window.

'Sorry, I not see you. Very busy today.' Nor handed him her business card. 'I hope you had a nice time?'

As they drove away, Leo hoped Joe hadn't read too much into the fact that he placed the card in his shirt pocket rather than leaving it on the dash. He wasn't sure he'd do anything with it but it somehow reassured him to have it. Not feeling he could risk a wave, he'd looked straight ahead as the car crunched across the gravel and touching slightly on his pocket, to ensure the card was still there, he thought about the woman who had given it to him.

The fallout began as soon as Leo stepped in the door early on Sunday evening. Joe's car wasn't even out of the front gate. The lawns needed mowing. He'd promised to do it before he left. The neighbours had complained, or at least she expected they were about to. It would be dark soon. He'd better do it now. He needed to feed Tay. She was exhausted. She needed to lie down. There were bills to pay — much more manageable if he was in partnership with Joe. Had he asked? Wasn't that what the weekend had been for? If he wanted clothes for work tomorrow, he had washing to do. His lunch would need to be made, and he couldn't expect her to do that, not after having had Tay all weekend. Lying in bed that night, in the distance between himself and his sleeping wife, he understood one thing clearly. Dani didn't trust him.

Even now, as he dumped the last box on the floor and kicked the door closed behind him, he thought, if only he had been able to share the splendour of Kudu with her. He'd liked to have taken her there. After all, it was a hotel. Joe would have arranged it. He'd like to have told her about the bed mix-up. Laugh about it. He'd like to have shown her the suit, the suit he'd left in its bag in the back of Joe's car. He'd have put it on for her. Hell, he'd have liked to tell her they'd slept together, innocently, in each other's arms, like brothers. He knew none of this was possible, not in his wildest dreams. The thing was, when something as important as that couldn't be spoken about, he wasn't sure what might be said in its place. He realised that inside himself something had begun to unravel. Not because he'd slept in the same bed as Joe, but because sleeping with Joe reminded him he had once been his own man, an honest man who had made his own choices. That weekend marked the beginning of his retreat from the tatters of his marriage. A year later, a year of trying everything he knew to keep things afloat, he decided there was no other option but to end it.

He knew now that he hadn't lived up to his wife's expectations on multiple counts. Or his father-in-law's for that matter. That he was a good husband and father was far too low a rate of return to satisfy an ex-bank manager.

The thing was, Leo stayed on the tools well after most of his contemporaries had their own firms, or at the very least headed construction teams. Making things made him happy. Managing people did not. He had no wish to tell anybody what to do any more than he wanted telling. He couldn't make small talk. He didn't network. He wasn't Joe. He was a builder.

Years ago, he'd bought a section dirt cheap. It was the only real asset he brought to the marriage. When Dani's father offered to fund the house, she'd convinced Leo it was a good idea. What he didn't realise then was that his retired father-in-law, perpetually parked in front of *The Living Channel*, had big plans through which he might, at last, realise some potential in Leo. 'A second chance,' Dani had said to Leo, after he'd been 'rooked' by Joe. From the day she met Joe, Dani had believed he owed his approach to property development to Leo, but that wasn't how it had been at all. Leo never understood how she'd arrived at that idea.

Left alone to design his house, he had been happy. In the beginning he'd worked on it every evening and every weekend. He collapsed into bed late at night only to lie awake considering every detail of its construction. He would then rise early to get to work ahead of the others so that he might accumulate hours. Those he took at the site of his new house. For a while Dani drove out with his meals, spreading a blanket on the long grass. The construction took a year, halfway through which she'd stopped coming. She stayed home instead and bought furnishings for the house from English firms with whose promises of quality she was familiar. When the flat-pack parcels arrived, they were never quite what he'd had in mind for the home they were creating together. But it didn't matter. Eventually, they moved in. Then the baby came.

Leo was happy because he loved his son as he loved nothing else in his life. He worked long hours to pay bills that accumulated alarmingly after Dani stopped working to care for Tay. Dani became suspicious that every late night meant an affair, every early start a prearranged rendezvous. She eyed the receptionist at each new building firm with suspicion, inventing reasons to travel to the office unexpectedly. After all, he'd 'done it before', but she didn't seem to recognise her own role in that initial affair, so long ago. The choice to leave was Leo's, his first independent decision since deciding to go away to Kudu Lodge. It hurt that divorce meant leaving his house behind for this tiny city apartment but it was the realisation that he'd see less of his son that broke his heart.

Leo returned his phone to his back pocket and looked again at the small patch of sea on the horizon. For the last thirty minutes he'd been on the phone while at the same time imagining himself on a small boat as it crossed that distant shimmering blue triangle. He knew his marriage was a 'failure' as she so delicately put it. He knew this was 'not the best situation for his son'. He knew he had made a mess of it all. It was the third time this week he'd been told. That didn't count the emails.

Bending down, he opened the next box. More books. *Androcles and the Lion, The Woman in White, The Old Curiosity Shop, The Adventures of the Black Girl in Her Search for God*. That last one could go. However, opening the little hardcover and flicking through, looking at the illustrations, he knew he'd keep it. It took a lot for Leo to dispose of a book. Some of these he might reread now he had more time. He looked around. The apartment was beginning to look something like the tennis court flat he'd had all those years ago. So, this was what starting over looked like? Glancing back into the box at the next layer of books, all neatly face up, he spied a yellow cardboard envelope tucked down the side between the books and the wall of the carton. He pulled it out.

Written on the front in thick black felt pen were the words 'Leo and Joe', which appeared to have later been angrily scored through multiple times with a blue ballpoint pen. He turned the thick cardboard envelope over in his hands and looked at the back, then again at the front. He couldn't recall it at all. He opened the little brass split pin that held the envelope closed and, opening the flap, tilted it. Out came a series of photographs and scraps of paper, the rush of which, too much to be contained in his unsuspecting hand, fell to the floor.

Pulling up a chair, he bent over to examine the pile. Mostly it was sentimental stuff — cinema stubs, an old driver's licence, a tape cassette insert with 'Songs for Joe' written on it in his handwriting and other odd things, none of which he remembered keeping. There were a few photos, mostly innocent — one of them on their bikes. Odd photos of him Joe had taken. One of him naked on the beach, taken with a little disposable that weekend they'd gone to Rangitoto. There was another of him doing a handstand. A couple of photos of Joe washing his ute, parked outside the old flat. He smiled — Joe had loved that ute, fussing over it like an old chook. Joe with a stray cat that had adopted them for a week, only to disappear again. A letter or two — not love letters, notes really. He unfolded one — a recipe for pancakes with 'Joe's Mother's Recipe' written along the top. He unfolded another. It contained various different handwriting styles, depicting the signature 'Joseph Wright of Auckland'. Leo remembered finding that. It had been just after he'd given him a book on the painter Joseph Wright of Derby. The detached dust jacket flap of a book on Jacques-Louis David. Most of this stuff really belonged to Joe — the scrap of paper on which Leo had first written his address, the paper wrapper from a set of chopsticks from their first meal together, a birthday postcard signed 'Love Leo' with three big kisses. It was all evidence of another life. The archaeological scraps of a domestic life, one long left behind.

The photo in his hand was of Joe in his underwear, wearing a pair of headphones. The photo had been taken their first week together. When Leo asked Joe to move in, he hadn't thought it through beyond it being a way to avoid Joe's flatmates. There was scarcely enough room for the two of them, but it didn't matter — they usually just tumbled into bed. Leo had been surprised by the sex. It was harder, more visceral, more exciting, than any sex he'd had previously. He found he instinctively knew what another man required and desired. He learnt fast how to mix desire and requirement. He discovered that the things Joe did to him worked for him when he did them to Joe. He enjoyed the lack of complication. Their sessions together were long and the pleasure derived from them intense. Joe had made him feel good.

His phone buzzed in his pocket — he ignored it, he knew what it would be. Instead he leant down and picked up the black paperback copy of *The Old Curiosity Shop* and slipped the photograph into the centre of its pages. He'd keep this one. Joe looked so entirely innocent in the photo, but back then he'd wondered at first whether Joe wasn't some con artist, in part because of the sudden interest in reading.

Unsure Joe was doing anything more than paying lip service to his own love of books, one day he had come home in the early afternoon to collect something from the lock-up at the end of his veranda. Surprised to find Joe's ute parked outside, Leo parked behind it and walked quietly down the driveway.

There was Joe, sitting in a patch of sun against an oak tree by the old tennis court. Unmoving, he appeared asleep. Joe had not seen him, Leo realised, because he was crying. Not just crying, but sobbing hard and moaning softly to himself, rocking slightly. It looked as if he'd been there for a while. Joe only noticed him as he crouched down. When he'd asked, 'What's wrong?' Joe just shook his head.

'She's dead.'

'Who's dead?' he looked at Joe's face. 'Not your mother?' Joe shook his head. Stumped as to who it might be, Leo asked again. 'Who?'

Joe, sniffing hard, passed him this same old worn copy of *The Old Curiosity Shop*.

'I was reading it at lunchtime and told the boss I needed to go home.'

'I don't understand.'

'Little Nell . . . *Little Nell* . . . she died.'

'What?' Leo felt suddenly relieved. 'You're screwing with me, right?' Then, looking at Joe, he realised he wasn't kidding. Joe had asked for the afternoon off because a character in a novel, written more than a century ago, had died. Leo laughed. He looked at Joe and then again at the book in his hands. He rolled back onto the lawn and laughed even louder.

'You knew. You *saw* me reading it.' Joe was suddenly outraged. 'You *knew* and you didn't tell me. Joe jumped on top of him and started pummelling his chest with his hands.

Leo grabbed Joe by the arms. 'Of course I knew. *Everyone* knows Little Nell dies. Oh, Joe, it's all right. Do you know what Oscar Wilde said about it?'

'No.' Joe looked up, momentarily hopeful.

'Well,' Leo spoke soothingly. 'He said, "One must have a heart of stone to read the death of Little Nell,"' — he stopped for a moment for effect — '"without laughing."' Joe let out a cry of anguish. He again started flailing at Leo's chest with his hands. Leo pushed him off then reached over and grabbed the abandoned book. 'Where are you up to?' He opened the book and started reading. Neither of them returned to work that day.

The thing was that Leo had also, in the moment of reading, lived and felt every story with intensity, just as Joe had come to do. Leo believed he perfectly understood, as near as any modern reader might, what the author — be it, Dickens, Thackeray or Gissing — had intended his reader to feel. Later, however, he could rarely quote passages from memory. Even in the next moment, the exact words always lay outside his grasp of recall. Knowing they dwelt somewhere within a particular book he would be led back to search its pages, favourite ones singled out with a marker, anything to hand, like the photograph that now lay between the open pages of this book. Books dwelt within Leo, never before had they been something he had shared with another. Joe had somehow walked not so much into Leo's life but into Leo's inner world and put an end to the perpetual loneliness.

Their first months together were great. By summer, Leo was as happy as he'd ever been. Joe began to shed the restrictive skin into which he'd been born. He emerged as someone altogether different — someone more imaginative, more interesting than the building site dropkick upon whom Leo had stumbled. No longer lonely, no longer alone, Leo hadn't meant to tell Joe he loved him that night. It had just happened. He didn't regret it. The words came naturally without pre-thought. There and then, in that moment, they were true.

As their second six months together began, it became increasingly clear to Leo that Joe wanted a life for them, and to explain him to his friends, and to introduce him to his mother as his boyfriend. On all these things, Leo was unable to negotiate.

The end came abruptly. There was a job in Christchurch. The restoration of a big, old Victorian house, the new owners of which had known his English boss. It was too good to turn down. It was supposed to be simple. He'd move away for a while. He'd think about things. He'd see how they were when he got back. Or Joe might join him. He just didn't know. He had practised the words so they would not hurt. In thinking how he might tell Joe, the time he had left ran out. Then, when he delivered his words, something harsher took over. He knew he was breaking Joe's heart and it hurt like hell. He regretted almost everything he'd said that night. He regretted most of all that he didn't get around to telling him about Christchurch. Joe moved out on a Sunday morning. On Monday he was on a plane and was gone. He knew he had disappeared and, to Joe, he had vanished. He had been cowardly, but in time he told himself it was for the best.

Even now, sorting through their old things, which he'd probably pass on to Joe sometime, when thinking about how *they* had happened, he didn't get very far. The women in the pub on that Friday before Anzac weekend were playing a familiar game of seduction he knew well. Joe was playing the same game, same rules, same outcome. At that moment it had been to him as if the players were interchangeable. A door had opened. He walked through it only because it felt like the most natural thing in the world to do. The best he could do to explain the end was to say the same door that opened on a Friday night in one pub slammed shut almost a year later in another.

Leo knew he wasn't gay, not the way Joe was. It wasn't that Leo was afraid to come to terms with anything. He'd fallen in love with Joe, simple, but he wasn't in the closet. Even now, he wasn't struggling with anything more significant than how he might continue to love the one man whom he had once loved in quite a different way. He knew for most this would be inconceivable — a step far outside the norm. In taking that step, he supposed he had transgressed. It would forever make him different from other men.

Other builders talked about their prowess in the sack, always connecting their professed abilities to allusions of size and power. He wanted to tell them that submitting to another man, allowing him to move inside you according to his will and for his pleasure, would make any one of them a better, more considerate lover when and if they returned to girlfriends and wives. As for himself, he tried to be honest about his past. However, once his marriage had begun to fall apart, his honesty didn't help one iota. Every true word he'd ever spoken was hurled back at him loaded with accusations, including that he was queer.

Bending forward to scoop up Joe's stuff, before finding a new envelope for it, he stopped. Looking up for a moment, he wondered how this collection could have come together in the first place? How had they gotten into an envelope? He hadn't done it. He knew for sure he hadn't. Most of these books had remained in boxes for years. They'd been stored in Auckland all the time he'd been away and then moved to his shed when he returned. Only a few books had ever made it into the house. He'd never quite got around to building enough shelves. He stopped for a moment and looked again at the envelope. The handwriting wasn't his — it was Dani's.

Dani must have gone through them all. She must have found something in a book in the house and then moved on to the wall of boxes in his shed. He could picture her there, hauling down dusty boxes, cutting the tape, opening them one at a time, searching every book, every box, repacking, retaping, restacking each one. She must have searched *every* book for any scrap of evidence of his relationship with Joe. She would have looked at each item, piecing them together, creating toxic images in her head, reading too much into every object, every image, making herself miserable, all this making her paranoid until — shit. He leant forward and ran his hands through his hair. He wasn't sure, even after everything they'd been through, that she deserved that.

Standing up, he remembered the buzz of his mobile. He looked at the message: *I hope you took that on board!* He looked again at the patch of blue sea. The yacht had gone. Due to meet Nor at 3 p.m., he was late.

CHAPTER 16

'What *are* you wearing?' Leo pointed at a pair of luminously bright yellow leather gloves below the neatly turned-up cuff of Joe's blue checked shirt and pale grey jacket. Joe ignored the question.

'Not only are you late but you are delightfully presented.' Joe indicated Leo's clothes with a sweep of his gloved hand. Leo bent over and gave Joe a peck on his cheek before taking the seat opposite him. He didn't do that often but he could see just by looking it made Joe happy.

'Here.' He handed Joe the envelope.

'What's this?'

'Ancient history. Look at it later.' As he looked through the glass window into the depths of the café, he caught their shadowy reflections. They looked like a couple with history. They'd known each other a long time now. Leo knew Joe would prefer to be at one of the flasher cafés in Ponsonby or Jervois Road. One day he would indulge him in that too, but today Joe would have to make do with this place. Leo liked it here. He liked the way the café was ageing and settling into the street. He was feeling good about things. The long weekend was shaping up to be a good one. Joe motioned to the waiter, who came over to the table.

'A trim latte for my friend. Not in a glass, in a bowl.'

'Full milk.'

'Trim,' Joe repeated. 'I'm paying.' The waiter looked at them both. 'I'm paying,' repeated Joe slowly and deliberately. As the waiter began to turn away, Leo spoke again.

'But I'm drinking it.' The waiter turned back as Leo dropped a random pile of coins into his hand. The waiter grinned.

'It seems this one's not going to be told what to do,' said the waiter. Leo laughed but Joe seemed determined to ignore the intrusion. He turned to face Leo.

'So, what's up?'

'Why is there necessarily something up?'

'These sorts of things — coffee catch-ups — you never arrange them. I do. So, tell me, how are things with the hot, newly solo dad?'

'Well, that's kind of what I wanted to talk to you about.'

'See, I know you too well. Talk away but remember, no babysitting.'

Joe seemed in a pretty good mood, and so it was with only the slightest hesitation that Leo continued.

'You see, I've met someone.'

'What? That was quick.' Joe's voice was unexpectedly sharp.

'Yeah, I've met someone. Well . . . more than met.'

'It's been — what — six weeks?'

'You know her actually.'

'Who?'

'Nor.'

'Nor?' Joe shook his head slightly to indicate his lack of recall.

'You met her at Kudu Lodge, that weekend. So, in a way, *you* introduced us.'

'You mean the Chinese girl?'

Leo was annoyed. 'Malay.'

'Shit and you've been . . . ?' Joe's question trailed off, but Leo knew full well what he had been going to say.

'No, I haven't *been* anything. We connected up on Facebook afterwards.'

'You're on Facebook? When did that happen?' Joe's demeanour had shifted dramatically from a few minutes earlier.

'I felt it was time to, you know, make some changes. Nor popped up. A friend request. We reconnected. I've seen her a couple of times.' Joe sat there silently sipping his coffee, a dark expression consuming his features. Leo had wanted to tell Joe sooner rather than later because, since the separation, Dani had gone a bit crazy. He needed Joe's friendship. It was only Joe and Nor who made his horrible cramped apartment, the separation from his son, his current lack of a job and everything else bearable. Somehow though, unexpectedly, Joe's reaction had turned things on their head. Leo suddenly felt as if, rather than looking for advice about navigating a new relationship, he now had to reassure Joe. Leo had seen Joe sulk like this before. He knew this was going to take a while.

Leo sighed. If this weekend was going to be about Joe, it was best they got a few things sorted once and for all *before* Joe opened that envelope.

When the waiter skirted past the table, Leo asked, 'Can you put those coffees in takeaway cups please?'

'What's the hurry?' Joe scowled.

'Bugger this place. Let's go for a walk.'

'A walk.' Joe's tone was flat, his voice distant.

'A drive then, if you prefer. What monster are you driving now?' Without speaking Joe gestured at the sleek, top-of-the-range silver two-seater Mercedes parked directly in front of them. Only Joe would get that park. Perhaps that was it, that was the problem. Joe had never really learnt how to handle life's small disappointments.

'Should have guessed that was yours — not big on brand loyalty are you? Let's head to the beach,' said Leo. Once seated, he leant forward, fiddled with the stereo and found the music he wanted and turned it up. Relaxing back into the seat, he said, 'Drive. Let's go to Muriwai. A big beach for a big problem, okay?'

As Joe climbed out of the car, he stood for a moment in the maw of the door, looking out at the beach. Heavy grey clouds moved slowly across the intense blue of a sunny April sky, making the beach alternatively inviting and miserable in turn.

'Hey, Joe.' They had hardly spoken a word on the way out except to disagree briefly as to the right direction at a turn-off. Joe took his time to turn around. 'Lose the gloves.'

'Why?'

'Because this is a beach and you look like a total dork.' Joe pulled his gloves roughly from his hands and, flipping forward the car seat, placed them on the small rear shelf on top of Leo's envelope. Taking off his jacket, he piled it on top.

'You might need that.'

'Fuck you.' Joe slammed the car door.

'So,' Leo spoke almost as soon as their shoes hit the black sand beach. 'I take it you're still pissed off?' While waiting for a response, he pointed towards the far end of the beach. Joe took an exaggerated wide arc before rejoining Leo to head in the same direction. He remained silent. 'Joe, when are you going to get real about this?' Leo asked softly.

'About what?'

'About us.'

Joe shrugged. 'Oh, suddenly we are an *us,* are we?' he asked sullenly.

'Don't be a prick. Yes, of course, we are.' Leo let his despair colour his tone. 'We have something good — but it seems it's not good enough for you.' There was another long silence. They walked side by side about a metre apart. A cool breeze swept between them. Leo suspected that Joe, dressed only in his shirtsleeves, was getting cold. 'Good beach for misery, this one.' No response. 'Joe, I'm out on a limb here. What do you want from me?' He stopped. As his shoes sank into the wet sand, a thought suddenly came to him. Catching up and looking over at Joe he asked, 'You didn't think . . .' he paused a moment and then continued, a little more gently. 'You couldn't have thought we were back on again?'

Joe winced.

'Oh shit. Dani, Joe, Dani, Joe. Is that what you thought? You think I'm that predictable? That my entire life is all a repeating pattern?'

'No.'

'Screw you. You did.' Leo thrust both hands deep into his jeans and bent over against the sharp wind. 'When are you going to get it through that thick skull that carrying a torch for me means you're missing out on your own life?'

'What life am I supposedly missing out on? Because from where I stand my life looks pretty good. It's yours that's shit.'

'The life where you get to be your own man and find real happiness beyond a line-up of pretentious BMWs and dorky yellow gloves.' Joe looked down at his bare hands. Leo could see the blue tinge of his skin.

'Your own man? You're a great one to talk.'

Leo decided to take up the challenge. 'At least I've spent my life *trying* to be my own man. You know that, and do you know one of the best things about it? Do you?' Joe's expression was blank. 'It led me to you. So, things between us didn't work out textbook, but look what I got instead.' Joe looked up as if expecting to be shown something. 'A friend that drops everything to drive me all the way the fuck out here — in his stupid silver car without once querying it. Just did it — because I asked.' They resumed their walk along the deserted beach in silence for some time. 'Interesting house up there.' Leo made an effort to break the silence. Joe responded sourly.

'Yeah, if you have lots of money and no imagination. She's what? About twenty-four?'

'Twenty-seven. Are you about to get all moralistic on me?'

'No, it's just that you're almost fifty.'

'I am *not* almost fifty and, even if I was, how many twenty-somethings have you dragged home from bars or clubs in the last six months?'

'It's not the same.'

'No, it's not the same. Nor actually means something to me. I'm giving this a chance, Joe. You reject every opportunity you get for anything that comes close to something meaningful.'

'I have plenty of opportunities.'

'Yes, you do, but you're too fucked up to even recognise them.'

'What does that mean?'

'Brendan.'

'Brendan was a munter.'

'He was a good guy trying to sort out his shit — for you as much as for himself. You know, sometimes love is about taking a whole lot of shit and still hanging out for more. Figure it out. Who else has been hanging around — waiting, wanting, asking, practically begging to take on all your shit?' Joe ignored him and, as they walked, the thin end of the waves trickled across the sand towards them. The ones with the longest reach lapped Joe's expensive shoes. He flicked the wet sand off them, but Leo ignored the performance, deciding instead to use his bulk to hem Joe in, shifting emphatically each time in order to block his way to the upper side of the beach whenever Joe tried to gain dry ground. Joe could afford new shoes, and for the moment he just needed him to stop and listen.

'Look, Joe,' Leo stopped and turned toward him. 'My marriage failed because of me. It seems I can't change enough to be the man other people want me to be. I couldn't do that for *you*. I couldn't do it for *her* either. I certainly couldn't do it for her prick of a father. I want to be my own man, not someone else's creation. Live your life by someone else's ideals and success, even love, remains elusive. Finding someone who loves you for what you are is near impossible. In this world, people love you for what they can make out of you. People love you for what you don't tell them about yourself. I know that better than anyone.'

'And running off with a twenty-something when you're forty-five, that's original, is it? That's finding yourself?'

'Who said I'm "running off" with her? Come on, Joe.'

'They're called MSM's now?'

'Who are?'

'Men like you. Men who sleep with men but are not gay-identified.'

'Screw you, Joe, I can't believe you just said that. I'm not a man who sleeps with *fucking* men. I was the man who slept with you — years ago. That was the originality you're looking for so hard. Right there. Everyone wants a label for me. I'm simply a man who found you and every fucking day — except maybe today — I'm glad of it.' Right now he just wanted to beat some sense into Joe. The all-purpose option men had once called upon to settle disputes seemed appropriate at this moment. Leo started walking again. A moment later Joe followed. When he caught up, Leo glanced over at him with a little smile and continued, his voice now barely audible over the wind. 'Don't ask me to explain how I feel. I don't have the words. It is as simple as that. I never did. I've never had words for the emotional stuff. Shit, why do you think I spent all those years with other people's words? When I was a kid, I wanted desperately to be a writer, but the words don't come, Joe. I'm a failure there too.' He paused before continuing in a new, slightly more conciliatory tone. 'Look, Joe, I'm trying to tell you something important and I feel like you're not even listening.' He pushed himself into Joe's line of vision. 'Joe, you are as frustrating as hell. I am not coming back to you because I've been here all along. I never left you, not once.' He knew immediately he'd said the wrong thing. Joe raised his eyebrows quizzically and spat it out like a poison.

'Christchurch.' There it was — the sting. The one thing they had *never* talked about — his disappearance.

'Fuck, you're an arsehole.'

'Probably.'

'Probably what?'

'You're probably right.' Joe shouted into the wind: 'JOSEPH WRIGHT IS AN ARSEHOLE.' Then, regaining his usual voice, he continued, 'The property developer arsehole. That's the profile, isn't it? That's the billboard you're all waiting to see? I'm the arsehole, and you're the nice guy everyone's in love with. But face it, Leo. You're the one who walked off. You just disappeared. You left me with nothing, *nothing* to go on.' Joe was yelling at Leo now. 'You tore out my heart and left. I didn't know where the fuck you even were. For ten *fucking* lonely years, I didn't know jack shit about where the only man I've ever loved even *fucking* was.'

Leo stopped and faced him. Joe's eyes were wild, glistening, his face distorted with the pain of his words. Leo reached out to take his hand. Joe pulled back his fist as if he were about to punch him. Employing an old rugby trick, Leo placed his foot behind Joe's ankle and, with his hand, shoved him hard in the middle of his chest. Tripping over his foot, Joe fell sprawling backwards into the wet sand, landing with a distinct thud. Before Joe could get up, Leo placed his foot squarely in the middle of his chest, pinning him down.

'Listen to me. When I left for Christchurch — which was a prick of a thing to do, I admit — you got off your twenty-two-year-old arse and made something of yourself.'

Joe squirmed under Leo's foot.

'Get off me, you oaf. Are you suggesting you did me a favour?'

'Listen to me. You've made a success of your life. You're a hell of an interesting guy, complex, smart and successful. You are nothing like the randy, vacuous kid you were. You did well, but in your hurry to prove something, you left the best bit of that kid behind.'

'Oh yeah, and what the fuck was that since you suddenly know so much about it?' Joe was still shouting as he struggled pointlessly against the weight of Leo's foot.

'That kid was committed to loving someone else other than himself. Totally committed. Shit, Joe, I was lucky to be on the receiving end of that. I'm still looking to get back to something even close. But I'm not the only person you can share things with. I am not the only man who is capable of loving you.'

'I suppose there's Gerald,' Joe said sarcastically. Leo pressed down on Joe's chest. Joe coughed and struggled half-heartedly.

'I see you almost every week, and I see the big part that's missing. I see the real you, the whole you. Self-pity is not hot. Is this what you want from life, Joe?'

Leo leant harder still against Joe's chest until he could tell it was hurting. Joe didn't answer. Eventually Leo let up on the pressure and bent down to look Joe straight in the eye. 'If you tell me this is turning you on, I'm going to cut your dick off.' Joe laughed at last — a small, constricted laugh.

'Look, Joe.' Leo returned to the conciliatory tone with which he started. 'Believe me, I didn't set out to give you a hard time here. I'm the screw-up. I'm the one who's just walked out on my marriage, one I made a commitment to because I want to be happy. Yes, I'm a middle-aged man looking for happiness. I'm the cliché. I want, I *need,* to be my own man. I've got a kid I am not going to see much. He's going to be brought up Monday to Friday hearing that I'm a prick and a loser. I've got to trade that for something, Joe. Something really big. Got to take a risk, like you did.'

'What does that mean?' Joe looked unconvinced.

'I gotta jump, take a risk. Find something — or someone — that can throw me off orbit again, before it's too late.' Leo looked down at Joe's expensive clothes, now a crumpled mess and covered in clots of black sand. His hair was matted, his face dirty. Then, at that moment, a substantial wave rushed up the beach, thoroughly drenching Joe in the process.

'Fuck, Leo!' Joe yelled. As surprised by the sudden dousing as Joe had been, Leo took his foot off Joe's chest with a start. Springing up, Joe stomped off towards higher ground — comically holding his wet trousers away from his legs. Sitting down on the dry dune, Joe tucked his knees into his chest and lowered his head onto them. Leo walked slowly up the beach towards him. There was a long silence as they sat together in the morning sun. It was a little more sheltered here. It was warm. After some time, without looking up, Joe spoke into his knees.

'You're a fucking arsehole.'

'I'm sorry.'

'No, you're not,' Joe raised his head. His eyes were red — he had been crying. 'What day is it?' he asked.

'Saturday, why?'

'Weekend. What *weekend* is this?'

'Anzac weekend. You know that.'

'Exactly.'

'Exactly what? Come on, tell me.'

'It was *exactly* twenty years ago.'

'What was?'

'Us.'

'Can't be.'

'Was.'

'Shit.'

'Anzac weekend, 1994. Kurt Cobain had just shot himself. You were supposed to have been doing something with a borrowed trailer.' Leo put his head in his hands.

'Oh, Joe I'm *so* sorry. This is an anniversary. Of course, you thought . . .'

'I didn't think, but I hoped. You rang. You *never* ring. Told me you had something important to say. You chose today. Then you turn up with an envelope — ancient history, you said. You kissed me — *in public*. I've always hoped, and I always will hope. That's who I am.' He stopped for a moment and stared out at the sea.

'I don't feel one bit different, Leo. Not one. I get it. You're not supposed to feel at forty what you felt at twenty about things, but inside here,' he tapped at his chest, 'nothing *fucking* changes.' The tears welled up in his eyes, and as they trickled over his lower lids, he brushed them away.

'I get that, I do, but you have to let it in. Let change mess with you.'

'Why, Leo?'

Leo looked at Joe and, reaching out, put his arm around his shoulders. He didn't need to ask what Joe meant. He recognised a question Joe had asked before.

'Because you were cute, because I'd had too much to drink, because it was just sex and because I wanted you. There were a thousand reasons, none of which will ever be good enough. You deserved more, I know that.' They both stared at the sea silently for a long time before he spoke again. 'Joe, what I feel for you, it has no other name — this is love. It's the sort of love for which you were always looking. It's the lay down your life, fight and die on the barricades kind of love. It's that stupid Rolf Harris "Two Little Boys" song kind of love. It's the love you always wanted, but love isn't fucking, Joe. That's not the endpoint. It's not the proof of love, the way you seem to think it is. The love between men is not just getting your hands on the other guy's dick. It's better than that. It's being next to each other the way we are right now.' As Joe brushed his forearm across his nose and sniffed, Leo continued. 'You're struggling with stuff you don't have to. It's simple. I love you, and I assume you still love me?' He smiled and looked into Joe's red tear-laden eyes. 'What we have is the best, Joe. It's solid because it's a foundation. You know as well as I do there's a lot of different houses built on the same set of foundations. Love isn't the house. It's the foundation. You and I can add to it without either of us hurting each other because we know we're in this together. I told you at the start that I didn't know what this was but that we were in it together. The love that we have should free you up, not hold you down.' He took a deep breath and slipped his hand onto Joe's thigh. 'Joe, I wanted to tell you about Nor.' He waited but Joe gave no reaction. 'Not the details, Joe, but you see, for now Nor suggests to me the possibility of a happy future. That's what I'm letting you in on, Joe, the possibility of a happy future for both of us.'

Leo stood up. Reaching down, he pulled Joe up into a standing position. Placing his hand behind his friend's head, he guided him into his chest. He held Joe against him for a long while. When he had stopped trembling, he took hold of Joe's chin, and, raising up his head, softly but firmly kissed Joe on the lips.

'What was that?' asked Joe.

'Something I promised myself I'd do twenty years ago but somehow forgot to do — or to do properly — what with everything else that happened.'

Joe smiled. 'Nice.'

'Come on, let's go home.' As they walked back down the beach, Leo slipped his arm around Joe's shoulders. Joe turned and smiled weakly.

'Never a BMW. If *that* happens, smother me in my sleep, like any real friend would.'

CHAPTER 17

Betty had set the small table for lunch under the old jacaranda tree at the far end of the garden. As Joe placed the heavy wooden tray on the table and took up his place on the bench seat, he resumed the conversation they had started in the kitchen.

'Do you know what he said to me at the café?' asked Joe in a conspiratorial tone. 'He said I had no "brand loyalty". He was talking about the new car, but I knew what he really meant.' Betty lifted the heavy stoneware pitcher and filled both their glasses with water. At the same time, Joe reached over and poured a buttery yellow wine into their glasses.

'Thank you for this.' She held her wine glass up to the sun as it shone through the leaves of the tree. 'It looks very nice, quite wonderful, in fact. You are very good to me, Joe.' Joe was a frequent guest for Sunday lunch but today had been a last-minute arrangement. She suspected when he rang, rather late on Saturday night, that he had been a little worse for wear, but he showed no obvious signs of it now.

It was the Sunday of the long weekend. Sitting under the tree, she wondered why she hadn't thought to arrange a lunch herself. The garden was looking soft and feathery, and the weather was warm. Auckland wouldn't see many more days like this over autumn. It appeared Joe and Leo had had an argument, a fight really, at the beach the previous day. She got the gist of it. He had already relayed it word for word from the beginning and was now starting his story all over again, it seemed.

'You see, Betty,' Joe spoke as if revealing something new. 'I fall back in love with him every time he walks into the room, again and again, day after day, week after week, over and over. Every time I see him, it's like he's walking into my life for the first time. I have no idea what to do to change things.'

Betty didn't respond. Not yet. It was best just to let Joe talk until eventually he reached a conclusion. He usually did, nattering away to her over lunch about something or other that she only barely caught. He was 'processing'. So, while he did that, she would have lunch. She unfolded her napkin and, placing it on her lap, helped herself to the salad and sipped from her glass as he talked. The wine was lovely.

'When he walks towards me, I'm happy. When he walks away from me, I am devastated. I see those weird but beautiful eyes. I see him, the way he walks, the way he looks at me, the way he avoids looking at me, the way he speaks, his silences, his moods, his kisses and I—'

There, something required her attention. Interrupting the ready stream of consciousness, she risked her question. 'You kiss?' Joe, his thoughts derailed, waited a moment before answering.

'No. Not really,' he sighed.

'Joe?' She was trying to sound as stern as she could manage on a beautiful Sunday morning.

'No, Betty, he doesn't. That's just it. I fall back into a familiar world. Barred from ever re-entering, I can see it all from where I stand — just beyond the gate.'

'Barred from Paradise with no way back to the Garden of Eden?' she asked sympathetically.

'Yes, precisely, but where was the snake? Who ate the apple? I just got chucked out. The door got slammed in my face without warning.' She wondered whether Joe had ever had a door slammed in his face but decided to let it pass. Kindness was the best approach, at least for the moment, but at the same time she was beginning to feel a little guilty. This wine was expensive and, as she'd heard many a time before, there was no such thing as a free lunch. She assumed, like so many things these days, it now also applied to Sundays.

'Oh, dear boy, we all have problems with love. Most people never find even half of what you've had.' He looked over at her. It was only then he noticed the salad in front of him.

'You did.' He picked up the servers from the bowl and began to help himself.

'Well, yes, I did.' Betty paused for a moment. 'I suppose.' It was a test to see if Joe was listening. As he placed the green leaves onto his plate and searched the table top for the little bottle of dressing, it seemed to her he'd missed his prompt. She smiled a little when eventually he spoke.

'What do you mean, suppose?'

'Oh well, all marriages have their moments. All marriages have their ups and downs.' She was hoping to sound a little mysterious so Joe might, at last, begin paying her story some proper attention.

'Yes, but you *had* a marriage. You had Joseph there with you day after day, night after night.'

'Yes . . . yes, I did . . . but . . .'

'But what, Betty?' Whether it was the wine, the sunshine or the situation, Betty didn't quite know, but she decided there and then to tell Joe something no person still living had heard before.

'Joseph, my husband, wasn't my first love affair.'

'Really?' asked Joe, a little too casually for her liking.

'Yes, *really*.' The emphasis was sufficient to pull Joe up. 'So I *do* know what I am talking about. And Joe?' She leant in. 'Listen to me, this thing with you two, with Leo, it was a long time ago now. You're a lovely boy. Don't take this the wrong way, but other people your age, they've been in and out of love three or four times since.' Joe was gazing at her, and she tried to read his face. She had a sense what she was saying was too much, she risked overstepping, but now she had gone so far in, she had to keep going. 'Don't you think it's about time you started seriously considering number two before it is too late?'

'Number two? That's just sounds like code for a poor substitute if ever I've heard one,' said Joe dismissively.

'That's where you're wrong. It's that first love of which you need to be wary. More often than not it's just a test, sent to see if you're ready for the real thing.' Joe wasn't listening, Betty could tell. 'Oh, doll, where do you get these ideas from? Comic books or television? You seem to think — no, you seem to believe — just because you saw someone across a crowded room on some enchanted evening it will all work out the way you want it. Life isn't written by Rogers and Hammerstein you know.' She looked down at her knife, turned it edge up and then lay it flat again on the pink bamboo placemat. Somehow the conversation had returned to Joe's situation, but to Joe's credit he steered it back to Betty.

'So, this affair you had before Joseph, was it a teenage thing, a crush?' Betty bristled a little.

'Well, a first love might be more accurate.'

'But you were very young.'

'Yes, I was young, but age has nothing to do with it. Your relationship with Leo was perhaps more adult, but I know the territory. I know it well.'

'Come on, Betty Strauss, spill the beans.'

'Not if you're going to be flippant.' She reached over and took a bread roll from the little cane basket. Picking up her knife, she cut it open vigorously. When she'd finished, she looked up at Joe.

'Sorry, Betty.' She could see he was contrite, but she chose to take a few long moments before taking up her story.

'We met when I was a teenager. I had just left school for secretarial college. I was just a baby. We met on the tram. He was older than me. A handsome medical student, and I fell for him, head over heels. He was the loveliest chap — kind, considerate, charming and very good-looking. He had a quiff of jet-black hair that wouldn't stay down, and in those days every man's hair did exactly that — stayed down, I mean. He had flashing blue eyes and dressed so nattily.'

'What happened?' asked Joe more eagerly. She wondered if it were the flashing blue eyes, the quiff or the natty clothes that had suddenly hooked his attention.

'We fell in love,' Betty stopped for a moment and toyed with a piece of bread on her plate. 'But he was going to England to study medicine — a lot of people did in those days. I was going to follow him when I'd saved up.'

'And what, did he meet someone else? Did you get a Dear John letter?

'Not quite.'

'What happened?' He leant forward.

'He disappeared. Got off the boat and vanished. He never arrived at his lodgings. They never saw him at the teaching hospital. His family didn't hear from him. None of them did — well, not until thirty years later. His sister filled me in.'

'Do you have a photo?'

'No, I burned them all. I had to for my own sake.'

'Wow, Betty, that's so sad.' They sat in silence for a moment. The conversation was taken up by a bird sitting in the branches of the big tree above their heads — its opinions harsh and discordant. They both listened until, having finished its song, the bird departed. Joe's voice was soft when he spoke. 'Did you ever find out why?'

'It doesn't matter.' She meant it. Having long since put this episode of her life behind her, it was now proving unexpectedly painful. It was as if a long-forgotten mortification, the shame of being utterly abandoned, had come flooding back into her life uninvited with the telling of the story. 'When I met Joseph I was working in the secretarial pool of one of the big importers, saving for a passage. I'd start at Tilbury docks, and I would find him somehow. It was all I thought about. Every penny went towards it. I put up with last year's winter coat, a big thing in my day. I imagined him hurt or wandering the streets of London with no one to care about him. I didn't know whether he was alive or dead. The police here couldn't do anything — or more likely wouldn't. He meant everything to me. He was my whole world, my only hope for any future.'

'And you never saw him again?'

'No.'

'And Joseph never knew?'

She reached into her pocket and took out a small, white linen handkerchief. 'Yes, Joe, he knew,' she dabbed at her eye. With the handkerchief still pressed to her lower eyelid she looked at him directly. 'Joe, I was pregnant.'

'Shit.'

'Joe, a little respect.' She lowered her hand and placed the small, white square in her lap.

'Sorry, but hell!'

'Joe, I was very young, very young indeed.' Betty wasn't sure he entirely grasped the fact she had been barely seventeen, but she couldn't even now quite bring herself to say it out loud, not after all this time. 'I knew I'd have to leave my job. You did in those days. I tried everything to disguise it. Then, I started to show. It was hopeless. One night when I was working late, he found me crying. He asked me what was wrong. It all came out. He didn't say anything — he just listened. Then he offered to pay my passage — lend me the money. But he knew before I did that Paul — that was his name — wasn't coming back. He sensed it. He knew I was in love with another man, but he eventually asked me to marry him. Me, a Gentile. Joseph loved me, but I married him to give my child a father. I resisted for a long time. I'd rather have been an unmarried mother, rather be ostracised, than marry someone else other than the man I loved, but you know what, Joe? I would have missed so much.'

'So did you adopt the baby out? What happened?'

'I miscarried.' She dabbed at her eye. 'Joseph and I wanted children but after that it just wasn't possible.'

'That's so sad.'

'Yes, but I eventually found I had a husband who loved me.' Betty let that sit there. 'So you see, Joe, life works in mysterious ways. What we think is the worst moment in our lives may just be the moment before the door opens onto a wonderful life.' Joe looked at her for a long while. He had a curious expression on his face. It was, she decided, the look of deep affection with which cats stare at their owners, and she imagined how a devoted son might look at his mother. 'In time I realised that Joseph and I loved each other. It just crept up on me. After that, every moment I had with him was precious. Those years were too short.' Joe poured them another — large — glass of wine. They both paused before reaching for it. The sunlight through the trees dappled the table and, hitting the bottle, sent rainbows of colour dashing across the tabletop.

'My point is, Joe, you can moon over Leo just as long as you want, but it will only make you lonely. Eventually, when the end comes, you'll have only bitterness.' She said the word emphatically, and it made Joe sit up on his bench. He reached for his wine and took a deep gulp. 'If you want, we can go on a tour visiting the spinsters of Remuera all cocooned in gin and their own brand of bitterness. We could hire that nice bus driver — it would be a long day, though.'

Betty thought for a moment about the day she'd met Joe. How she'd watched him through the weeks of the course sitting there alone and miserable. How eventually she just couldn't stand it any longer. She smiled, remembering the boy who had come to her all those years ago when she'd felt Joseph's loss so strongly. He had been like a visiting ghost, his face drawn, his eyes dull, barely moving, barely talking and never eating, all skin and bone. Then how they'd seen Drew on that tour — just a little boy then. Drew, who the previous day had been to mow her lawns and sat in the same place Joe was sitting now with the same hangdog look on his face. She'd watched Joe grow like she might her own son. She was now very, very, fond of him. He had, as promised, made her a wealthy woman. Not that it mattered, she'd leave it all to a good cause one day. She was happy, happier than maybe she'd ever been, but she felt exhausted too. The aches and pains were taking their toll. Soon she'd have to consider leaving this old house and its lovely garden.

She pointed at Joe's lunch, barely touched.

'Eat! I'm not having you waste away on my watch.' As he poured the last of the wine into their glasses, she thought having more to drink was perhaps unwise. As Joe emptied the bottle, shaking the last drops from the rim into her glass, she decided she too would empty her thoughts. She would say the rest of what she now knew needed to be said.

'Joe, you are a very dear friend to me.' He smiled and tilted his glass towards her.

'What Leo said, what he said to you on the beach, it seems true enough to me.' Joe looked suddenly hurt. 'Oh, don't look like that. Yes, he disappeared, but he came back. He worked with you on something good. Something you wanted, and he needed — a friendship. He looks at you so kindly, the two of you are more like an old married couple than most. Joe, your view of love is perhaps a little simple. Love is not one person getting what they want. It's two people coming together knowing they want the same things. Yes, you and Leo want a lot of the same things. I am sorry that some crucial parts are missing, but they always will be, doll.'

'But Betty—' She was in no mood to be interrupted and held up her hand, still clutching her handkerchief.

'Joe, do you hear yourself? It's been twenty years — to the day, you tell me. You were twenty-one. That means you're forty-one now and, on paper, to anyone looking at this, it appears you've spent those years with an obsessive boyhood crush on a man you can't have.' Lowering her hand, she rested it on the tabletop midway between the two of them. 'Arrested development it's called. I've Googled it.'

'Leo's on Facebook, you're Googling things, what's happened to everyone suddenly?'

'They're moving on, Joe. You're the one standing still. That's called anchoring.' She looked at Joe. 'That is when—'

'I know what anchoring is. It's when a buyer reads somewhere that a one-bedroom apartment is the best investment, so they refuse to look at a good studio or something with a decent flexi-room. It's when you're told it's good to buy in Grey Lynn and so you won't even look at Arch Hill or the back end of Herne Bay.'

'It's when you fall hard for a first love and refuse . . . oh, Joe. You decided on love when you were twenty-one. You're a grown man, but you've let your crush determine your entire life.' Joe looked annoyed, and she knew why. She'd chosen that word because it was a word he had tried on her earlier.

'It's not a crush.'

'Is that all you heard?' She reached across the table and took his hand. 'Forgive me for saying this, for saying *all* of this? I've gone on and on I know, prattling away, but you're spoilt. You can read all those things in the paper about how successful you are, but you're a wimp.'

'Betty!'

'Well — sometimes these things need to be said. I'm old, so listen to me, doll. Leo loves you, but you can't leave your life in his control.'

'I don't.'

'Oh yes, you do. Most break-ups occur because couples fall out of love. Leo still loves you, and he's come to terms with his "unusual" past. You're the one not healing. It's eating you up. Leo loves you more than you love him because he requires nothing of you and gives you all he knows how to give.' She had reached the end. Not because she had nothing more to say but because Joe wasn't going to take any more home truths. Not today. 'Joe, you are a dear, dear friend. You have been very kind to me, like a son, but that is all I have to say on this subject. Look at me, Joe.' He looked up. She felt sorry for him and so very, very, tired. 'I mean it. That's me done. You've gotten some excellent advice on this subject from both Leo and me. So now it's time you took some of it but I've had enough. Do I make myself clear?' Without waiting for a response, she continued, 'Good. Be a sweet boy and go and make us both some good, strong coffee. Then we'll look at the garden together.'

CHAPTER 18

Gerald was basking in the sun on the little deck Joe had built for Betty years earlier. She had found his number in the book that morning and was now getting her first real look at him. In a crumpled white linen suit, a pink shirt and a large white straw hat with a lavender band, he reminded her of Truman Capote. She placed a tray with two glasses of gin and tonic on the small, round iron table and sat down in the chair opposite Gerald. He removed a pair of pale blue gloves and placed them carefully on the table, then lifted his glass and took a sip. He looked surprised and, holding the glass in front of him, looked at it suspiciously.

'Anything wrong?' Betty asked.

'Delightful. Light and refreshing. Tanqueray?' he asked.

'Gordon's.'

'Oh yes, that'll be it,' Gerald said charmingly. 'I'm Bombay Sapphire. Never mind. Cheers.'

'I'll dispense with any further chit-chat, if you don't mind, Gerald, and get to the matter at hand. Joe, our Joe, is in love.'

'Oh!' Gerald was clearly somewhat relieved. 'From your call, I was thinking something much worse — cancer or the Global Credit Crisis.'

'It *is* worse. Joe has been in love with the wrong person for far too long. Don't get me wrong. Leo is a lovely man. You'll meet him in a minute.'

'Oh?' Gerald tinkled the ice in his glass. 'A raven of conspirators, how thrilling.' Betty chose to ignore Gerald's massacre of the commonly used collective noun and tried a new word combination of her own.

'He is, as they say now, "straight-identified".' She seemed to be testing the term as if for accuracy.

Gerald showed no indication she'd misspoken but instead said ruefully, 'They usually are, the problem ones.'

'That's where I hoped you might come in. Some previous experience perhaps?' Gerald smiled a noncommittal smile. 'But he hasn't, it seems,' she paused again. 'How should I say this? He hasn't always been,' she spoke tentatively.

'Tell me more.' Gerald clinked his gold signet ring loudly against the side of his glass as he lifted it from the table.

'When they were young they had a romance, a very good one apparently, but it ended as things often do when we're young, and Joe has, shall we say, never moved on.'

'And the other boy has?'

'Yes. Girlfriends, a wife, a child, now separated.'

'A phase?' asked Gerald knowingly.

'I suppose so. One Leo successfully exited, but Joe . . .'

'Has never found his exit?'

'Precisely.' Betty gently wiped the condensation from the bottom of her glass on a small, square paper napkin. 'Joe is ironically the one trapped in . . .' she hesitated momentarily, 'the phase.'

'Ironically?'

'Well, you know, he's a high-profile gay man on the television and magazine covers. Joe is outwardly very successful, but inside he's like a child sulking over a prize toy in the shop he can't have. It is as if Joe is frozen in time. It is as if his emotions have seized up.'

'Ahh and you brought me here to get him all oiled-up again?' Gerald shot a quick mischievous glance in Betty's direction. She ignored him.

'The thing is,' Betty continued. 'I'm used to a quiet life. Don't get me wrong — at my age any attention is nice. I love all these young men — but it's a bit like a downtown tram stop here every weekend. Joe comes on a Sunday to moon over Leo. Drew, that's the other one, comes every three weeks on a Saturday intending to mow the lawns but instead moons over Joe. Some weekends Leo, who did up my shed, brings his little boy Taylor to play in the garden. Leo just looks desperate to escape the whole mess. Though, obviously, he's not happy either. I think he worries Joe might do something stupid.'

'What? Suicide?' asked Gerald, a horrified look on his face.

'Oh no, not that,' Betty said quickly. 'At least I don't think so, though you can never know how another human being thinks. I do worry what will happen once the bitterness sets in, and there's no doubt that it will.'

Gerald nodded his agreement. 'What about you? Where do you fit into this colourful menagerie?'

'I find myself the adopted mother of three handsome but moody boys . . . or, rather, men.' Betty stopped for a minute and looked out at the view. 'Do you think perhaps some boys never grow up?' Gerald did not reply to this. 'I believed the chance of having children was long gone. I'm certainly too old for them now. I just want them all to be happy and to get on with their lives.' She sipped at her gin and tonic. 'Then they can all come to lunch together once a month.'

'Does Joe know?'

'About?'

'You, Leon and this Drew getting together about all this.'

'Leo,' she corrected him. 'Does Joe know? I don't know. He should. He certainly introduced us all, but he can be surprisingly unaware. Sometimes he can't see what's in front of his nose. Take Drew, for example. I mentioned him, didn't I? I rang him one day, asked him if he'd like a job mowing my lawns. I wanted to know where he was, so I had access. I just know how good he'd be for Joe. If only Joe could see it for himself.' The two of them sat in silence in the warm sun and sipped their drinks. 'Have you ever known true happiness, Gerald?' Betty asked.

'Ah. Now that subject requires another gin.' Gerald downed the contents of his glass, and Betty went to get up.

'Allow me,' Gerald said, taking her glass and placing it on the tray. He disappeared into the house.

'Happiness, Betty,' said Gerald as he returned, placing the tray back on the table, 'is relative. As I'm sure you well know. Years ago, in the Seventies, when those young men started protesting in the streets with placards about GayLib, we hated them because we thought we'd lose every scrap of misery we'd cobbled together to resemble happiness, but in the end it was a genuine happiness they were after. This generation, they're going all out for all the happiness they can get. Life is hard. Here's a toast — to the young ones.'

Gerald raised his glass high in a dramatic salute. Betty nodded and, lifting her glass, took a sip of her fresh drink. Alarmed, Betty touched her lip as if the glass had bitten her. She ran her finger around the rim looking for a chip or crack — nothing.

'I found another bottle in the cupboard. Three fingers — always three fingers.' He held his three middle fingers on the side of the glass in demonstration, covering, what appeared to her, most of the glass. 'And then a splash of tonic and, of course,' he paused for effect, 'the Meyer lemon. Freda Stark, *the darling*, was a customer, she taught me to make a drink. Heavenly, don't you think?'

As Betty took a second, smaller sip from her glass, Leo and Drew rounded the corner of the house together. Turning towards Gerald, she placed her drink on the table and smiled a welcome.

'This is Leo, our problem.'

'Hmm,' Gerald quivered, giving Leo the full inspection. 'I can quite see why.' Gerald stood up, holding his hand out. She thought for a moment that Gerald might be about to take a bite out of him, but instead he said, 'How do you do, Leo?'

'Nice to meet you, at last, Mr Gilmore,' Leo nodded politely.

'Gerald, please.'

'And this is Drew.'

'Oh,' Gerald chuckled. 'Our very pretty solution. How do you do, Drew?'

'Um.' Drew, seeming to regard Gerald as some creature from another planet, waited a moment before saying, 'Hello, Gerald.'

'Drew, go and help yourself to a drink from the fridge. There's beer for Leo.' When Drew was out of hearing range Betty turned to Leo. 'So, you and Joe have had an altercation?' Leo looked at her and then at Gerald uncertainly.

'Don't mind me,' said Gerald. 'I've been briefed.'

'On the beach. You thumped him apparently, and then you tried to drown him?'

'Not quite.'

'Oh, don't look so distressed. A little rough and tumble is a good thing between boys.' Gerald seemed excited. 'No one got hurt, right?'

'No . . . no one got hurt.'

'More importantly, did he listen to you? Did it sink in?' Betty asked.

'A bit, maybe.'

'Yes, I think a bit too.' Drew reappeared with two beer bottles in his hand and, handing one to Leo, took up a position next to him at the top of the steps.

'He'd think this was treachery if he ever found out.' Leo indicated the four of them sitting together. 'Whatever Joe's faults, he's unswervingly loyal to those he loves.'

'No, he wouldn't like it, not one bit, but things can't go on like this, not for any of us. Well, excluding you, Gerald.' She nodded in his direction.

'Oh, don't exclude me. There were *four* musketeers, you know — not three.'

'So, what *exactly* is this?' asked Drew. 'Is it like an intervention? Because if it is, isn't Joe supposed to be here?'

'Oh, I think the intervention has already happened,' Betty looked across at Leo. 'Some things have to be done one-to-one by the lead players.'

Gerald looked directly at Leo with an expression of penetrating seriousness. 'Leo, are you queer?'

'No!' replied Leo indignantly.

'But you sleep with men?'

'Betty!' pleaded Leo, looking over at her, squirming uncomfortably.

'Just answer him, Leo.'

'No. I've only ever slept with Joe, and that was good but . . .'

'Not for you?'

'No, not for me, well . . . yes, but a different me, a different part of me. Not for me now, if that makes sense. I loved him, though. I still do.' Drew flinched.

Catching the movement, Gerald turned his attention to Drew.

'And you, Ganymede, you love him too?'

'Since I was eight.' Betty and Leo exchanged a worried look. 'Okay, if you prefer, since I was sixteen — but, truthfully, about eight.'

'You've told him of your feelings?'

Drew hesitated. 'I might have.' He looked shifty.

'What do you mean? Surely you'd remember?' asked Gerald incredulously.

'Well, the first time I was high, and the second time, well I *might* have told him that second time but I was possibly too subtle, and I'd been drinking. So, no, *not sober*, not properly. My bad, I know.' Drew lowered his gaze so as to avoid any disapproving look in Betty's eyes.

'Well, it seems to me to be simple enough,' said Gerald, taking a moment in which to gather his thoughts. 'Leo, have you done anything to let Joe think he has another shot?'

'Definitely not. Quite the opposite.'

Gerald turned to Drew. 'What's the problem then?'

Drew looked up. 'He doesn't know I exist,' he replied mournfully. 'I've tried. Heaps. Even once on the roof of your old factory before they pulled it down—'

'If I could intervene?' Gerald interrupted. 'What Drew says is quite true. He has tried, but he's worried Joe thinks he's too young and therefore doesn't really consider him as a romantic prospect. Am I right, Drew?' Blushing, Drew nodded.

'Haha, oh my,' laughed Gerald slapping his hands on his thighs. 'There's never been a man, gay or straight, who let that worry him.' Gerald looked directly at Drew. 'Have you done your maths, schoolboy?'

Drew smiled. Betty glanced at Leo, who appeared similarly confused by the comment.

'Yes, everything's good,' Drew replied.

'Well, it seems we just have to find the right place and time to open our absent friend's eyes to certain truths. It sounds to me like you've all got him well primed. We just need a plan.'

The four of them sat quietly for a while. Drew got up and walked to the bottom of the stairs and picked distractedly at the leaves of a camellia bush.

Eventually, Gerald spoke. 'You all know him better than I do. What does Joe love most of all, what is it he can't resist?'

'Leo.' Drew was dejectedly tearing at a leaf in his hand. 'We all know that. Maybe if I changed my name, dyed my hair and went on steroids?' He gave a half-hearted laugh. Leo glared at Drew.

'Oh *Drew*, that's not like you — buck up,' said Betty. 'Good idea though, Gerald, let's make a list. Drew, there's a bridge pad and a pen by the telephone in the hall. Let's all think!'

Drew returned with the pad and pen and placed them in front of Betty.

Turning back the cover, she selected a clean page. 'Leo, you know him best. You go first.'

'I can't think. Joe's an authentic guy — it's not about stuff.'

'Come on now.'

'Well, expensive cars, yes, those stupid cars, definitely.' He looked at Drew, who was settling again on the top step. 'You're a rich kid. Maybe you could buy him a Maserati. I'm pretty sure it's next on his shopping list.'

'Not helpful.' Drew screwed up his face.

'He had a ute he loved once. Pity we can't get it back for him, but that would have gone to the wreckers years ago. Not booze, he never could drink more than a glass or two, although I think he's got a little better these days.'

'No, not booze,' Betty agreed. 'He still gets squiffy on one glass of sherry.'

'He likes going to the opera and the ballet. Ferrier,' she added, scribbling it on the pad.

'Yes, definitely music. Echo and the Bunnymen. The Teardrop Explodes.'

'You've lost me,' Betty murmured as she recorded Leo's suggestions.

'Think Sinatra and Mathis.'

'Now, those I do know.'

'Also Oasis and Blur.'

'Really?' asked Drew, looking worried.

'Well, he *used* to like them.'

'"Blue Monday", it's almost our song,' said Drew.

'True, although that was mine first.' Drew's face fell. Betty could tell Leo regretted what he'd just said.

'All good if he were a radio station but none of this is getting us anywhere,' said Betty.

'What about you, Drew?' Gerald asked.

Drew thought for a while. 'Arts and Crafts houses, old buildings. After that I'm stuck.'

'Well, don't worry. After all this I feel I don't know him at all,' Gerald smiled. 'You're all doing very well.'

'He does like to read.'

'Of course.'

'And he loves a good laugh,' chimed in Gerald.

'Gardens,' Betty added. 'He's always loved this one, and he liked your mother's, Drew.'

'He loved the garden at our flat — he loved that it was a garden in Mount Eden,' Leo added. 'It was his idea of paradise. Silly, but if you saw where he grew up you'd understand.'

'Thackeray — or is that too obvious?' Gerald asked.

'No, that's good.'

'"When you look at me, when you think of me, I am in paradise",' said Leo quietly.

'What did you say?' asked Gerald.

'Forget it, something private. I shouldn't have spoken.' Following Leo's lead, the little group went silent and for a while they simply rested up in the sun. Betty tapped her pen against the pad.

'I'll read the list and see if we've got anything,' said Betty. 'Cars. Opera, ballet, Ferrier, Mahler, Echo and the Bunnymen and The Teardrop Explodes, Oasis and Blur. Have I got all those names right, Leo?'

'Cross off those last two.'

She crossed them out and continued. '"Blue Monday".'

'That's music too.'

'Yes, I gathered that, but thank you, Drew. Arts and Crafts houses, old buildings, gardens, books and Thackeray.'

'Quite a list.' Gerald raised his eyebrows at Drew. 'Sure you still want to take him on?' he asked.

'More than ever, but what can we do with all this?'

Leo stood and then, pausing for a moment, as if struck by something, rushed back over to Betty and crouched down to read the pad in her hand.

'What is it, Leo?'

'I've got it. It has been staring us in the face all the time.' He gestured at the city skyline. Joe loves Auckland. Years ago, I gave him a book on the painter Joseph Wright of Derby, and he loved it. Later I found a pad. He'd been practising signing himself *Joseph Wright of Auckland* over and over again. I found the page again the other day.' Sitting down on the top step, Leo continued, 'In fifteen years as a developer he's never done a thing to harm the city, hardly ever pulled anything down and provided people with great homes.'

'That's true.' Betty looked at Gerald. 'It broke his heart to demolish Gilmore Gloves.'

'True, they did everything they could in the office to work with it but they were sort of caught in planning regs.'

'I wanted him to do it. I'm glad it's gone,' replied Gerald. 'But I am interested to hear more about this rooftop tryst.'

'Hang on. I've got an idea.' Jumping up, Drew looked at the three of them in turn. 'No. Wait.' Drew took a few steps up the stairs, so he was eye to eye with the seated Leo. 'Promise me one thing, that you're never going to want him back. That you will never take him from me? Because we all know you could.'

'No, Drew, I won't do that. But I need you to promise me something too.'

'What's that?'

'That you won't take him from me either,' replied Leo. Drew pondered this silently for a moment. Eventually, he extended his hand.

'Deal. Let's shake on it.'

Leo stood up to shake Drew's hand.

'I'll need help. Can you get him to a café for me, sit outside, say 10 o'clock the Saturday after next? I'll take care of the rest.'

Leo shrugged. 'Sure. Which one?'

'Best, Bib and Tucker,' replied Gerald.

'That's not one of the Italian boy's coffee shops?' Betty asked but no one answered.

Instead Gerald said, 'It's where those young café people took our old glove counters.' Leo winced at the thought of fronting at such a busy weekend destination.

'Okay then.' Drew turned to face Betty. 'Mrs Strauss, I know this,' he gestured at the group, 'was your thing and I . . . well, I appreciate it, and guys, thanks for everything — but,' grinning broadly he said, 'please understand some things have to be done one-to-one by the lead players.'

'Wait, before you go — there's something you need to know.' Leo led Drew away from the others where he spoke to him quietly for a moment.

Then, with a cheerful 'Goodbye everyone,' and a bow, Drew skipped off around the corner of the house.

'Do you know what he's up to?' Betty asked Leo. 'What were you two talking about just now?'

'I'd rather not,' mumbled Leo.

'Oh, come now, there are no secrets between conspirators,' said Gerald.

Leo cleared his throat. 'All right then. I told him to forget convention and take every risk going. To be, if you like, the *man* in this.' Leo looked embarrassed, 'At heart I believe Joe's looking for someone who will take risks in life.'

'Doll, I know *exactly* what you mean,' Betty said with a sigh.

Unexpectedly, Leo strode over and hugged Betty. 'Thank you, Betty. You are a real lady and such a wonderful friend to Joe. I'd better be off now. Perhaps I could bring Tay to play in your garden again sometime? Gerald, nice to meet you. It has been a real pleasure.'

When he had gone, Gerald turned to her. 'Now, what *exactly* happened on my roof?'

CHAPTER 19

The phone rang at 9.30 p.m. on Saturday. It struck Joe as a strange time for a call from an unknown number, but he answered all the same.

'Joseph Wright.'

'It's Andrew Campbell from the café this morning.' The connection wasn't great. Joe reached over to turn down the amplifier.

'Andrew?'

'Drew. We met . . . I mean . . . I used to work in your office.' The penny dropped. Now Joe remembered, the redhead architect, who'd popped up at his table as he waited for Leo. He'd asked for his number, said he had something he thought Joe would want to see.

Joe continued in a friendlier tone. 'Yes, of course. My apologies. How can I help?'

'This thing, I'd like to show it to you. Would you like to meet for a drink?'

'Ahh . . . when?'

'Well, how about now? I mean . . . if you're not busy. I'm in the little house bar at De Brett's Hotel. There's no one else here. It's very stylish.'

'There never is, and it always has been,' Joe replied.

'Sorry?' said Drew.

'There *never* is anyone there, and it *always* has been stylish.' As if sending Joe a signal, the concerto he was listening to finished. He looked at his empty glass of wine on the table and made a decision. 'Give me twenty minutes.'

Two salesmen in shiny black suits and candy-striped shirts perched on stools at the otherwise empty bar. At the far end, Drew sat in the corner of an upholstered bench, nursing the last of a glass of wine. He was wearing a grey t-shirt that strained across his chest, over which he wore a once-expensive black evening jacket. It fitted perfectly, but he suspected it predated its wearer by a couple of decades. Drew was looking out the window but, seeing him, turned and jumped to his feet, his leg knocking the table in front of him. It wobbled alarmingly. As it began to fall, Drew grabbed the table and steadied it. At the same time Joe snatched up the glass as it began to topple from the edge. Clearly it wasn't the kid's first glass of wine. His words came in a rush. 'So glad you came. So glad I ran into you today. I mean, what are the chances? I've been hoping to see you again. I've got something to show you. Do you want a glass of wine? I mean, what would you like to drink?'

'I think a drink would be good.' Joe gestured at Drew's glass, 'Another for you?'

Drew had worked in the architectural team for six months a few years earlier straight out of architecture school. There had been a couple of redheads, but Joe felt sure he could place him. He listened as Drew described what he'd been doing since he left Thackeray Makepeace. Having finished his professional qualifications, he was now a junior architect with the heritage department of a large firm in town. He referred to it as 'the factory'.

'Hang on, were you with us when we did the Virginian?'

'Yeah, in the early days.'

'You came to the party — picked up Betty for me?'

'Yeah, that was me.' Drew was suddenly grinning a little too broadly.

'On the roof?'

'Yep.' Joe stared across the table for a moment without speaking, both men reaching for their drinks. Eventually Drew's voice interrupted the hum of the background music.

'Well, perfect timing, now we've established joint history, we come to what I wanted you to see. It's not far — shall we walk?'

'Are you all right to walk?'

Drew laughed and standing demonstrated his ability by walking nimbly to the end of the bar and then, as the two businessmen stared, turned and sashayed back, more male model than architect. Joe laughed and, leaving their half-finished drinks on the table, they headed for the door.

'Come on then, follow me,' Drew said with a wink and they headed down the back stairs and out onto O'Connell Street. At the corner of Shortland Street, Drew led Joe towards the top of the hill. They spoke very little as they climbed the rise, Joe appreciating the exercise and the fresh air but mostly trying to recall the rooftop conversation, which remained a blur. Crossing at the small Art Deco building, just below the brow of the hill, they then veered off the footpath by the old, converted flourmill. Crossing the road, they walked beside the park, leaving the road to carry on down the hill. Suddenly, Drew stopped. Taking up a position on the low bluestone wall, he touched Joe on the arm and pointed to the other side of the street.

'This is it.'

There, on the other side of the lane, sandwiched between the ever-imposing Brooklyn apartment building and a low-lying commercial building of similar age but very different intentions, appeared a small, grey concrete structure. Two stories in height, it was set back from the road, almost disappearing into the night. It might have slipped away entirely was it not for a deep-set porch, resembling a self-important bus shelter, which projected out from the ground floor and lapped the asphalt footpath. In front, two columns were thrown into high relief by the raking light of tall streetlights. Inside the porch, on either side of the solid panelled front doors were two built-in seats in a weathered green paint, each large enough for someone to lie curled up. Joe knew this from experience. He'd once huddled on one of those seats, miserable and drunk, lost on his way to find another pub. Looking around, he realised that, like him, this building had survived. He turned to Drew.

'I know this building.'

'It's a honey.' Drew's eyes were shining. 'I love it. It's Edwardian, built in 1910 by two German doctors as a centre for new medicine.' Squeezing Joe's arm so that he instinctively turned towards him, Drew gestured towards one of the large ginkgo trees running down the eastern edge of the park. 'Come on.' Without turning, he repeated his bar room sashay, this time moving backwards in the direction of the tree, beckoning Joe to follow. Then, tripping on an unseen tree root Drew fell sprawling on the ground.

'You okay?' Joe asked, leaning over to help Drew to his feet.

'Of course,' he said, grinning as he brushed the seat of his pants. Suddenly animated, he removed his evening jacket and folding it neatly placed it on an exposed knot of tree roots. Standing in front of Joe in his jeans and t-shirt, Drew inserted one hand inside the lapel of Joe's jacket and with the other turned him slightly, peeling off the jacket in one continuous move and placing it over his own. Joe, suddenly embarrassed by his compliance in this unexpected undressing, asked, 'What are we doing?'

'Up there,' Drew indicated the tree that towered above them and turning away placed his foot firmly on the trunk, and hoisted himself up into the tree. Once positioned, each foot on a large branch, he leant down and held out his hand to Joe. 'You've got to see it from up here.'

'Are you crazy? Get down. I'm not climbing trees in the middle of the night.'

'Oh, come on. Trust me. It'll be so worth your while — but of course if you're too old to have fun anymore — I get it.' After a moment trying to conjure a suitable reply and coming up with nothing, Joe took Drew's extended hand and scrambled up into the tree.

'Follow me.'

'Where to now?'

Hoisting himself up to the next substantial branch he positioned himself so there was space next to him for Joe. When Joe had clambered up, anchoring himself, hand on Drew's shoulder, Drew spoke.

'Now, look.' Joe peered through the foliage. There, on top of the building, too far back from the road to be seen, was the shadowy form of an elegant little rooftop apartment. Along the front, unusually deep-set doors opened out onto a broad, entirely private, terrace. 'It's the original owner's apartment. The front was offices with four other apartments at the rear because it slopes away into a steep garden. It comes out on the street below. The whole back is a faceted wall of glass — sort of a Pierre Chareau meets Saint Kevin's Arcade type thing but three stories high.'

'Five apartments?'

'Four or five, it's hard to tell. The other doctors never came. Experimental German medicine wasn't so hot once the First World War started. It's been different things since.' He pointed towards the ground floor. 'There's a weird Fifties office through there, but it's been closed up for years. The last tenant moved out about twenty-five years ago. The owner is ancient. It's going to come on the market soon, and I thought it would be perfect.'

'Perfect?'

'For us,' Drew smiled, before adding, 'Oh . . . well, I mean for *you* really. A development!'

'Ah, now I get it! And you'd like to be the architect on this?'

'I have a few ideas.'

'I bet you do.'

'But only one excellent one. Only one I have any real commitment to.' Drew wrapped his arms tight around Joe's waist and pulled them both against the trunk. There was no time to object before Drew kissed him firmly on the mouth. As a wave of unexpected pleasure surged through him, Joe quickly released an arm from the embrace to steady himself on an adjacent limb, even then unsure what had just happened.

Joe chuckled softly. 'I suspected you had a plan.' He pushed Drew away slightly, pressing him hard against the trunk.

'Of course I did. I'm an architect. Plans are important to me.'

Drew moved to kiss him again and this time Joe met him halfway. Foreheads still touching, Joe spoke.

'Plans that involve getting me into bed?'

Drew ran his hand down Joe's chest towards his belt.

'No bed required. Here is more than acceptable.' He tugged at Joe's belt buckle.

'We're in a tree, unless you've forgotten?'

Drew grinned. 'Whatever, but you need to know I'm a man of many talents, able to sort any situation, you know, a risk taker, able to take control when it matters.'

'You *do* have a plan then?' Joe repeated, feeling bolts of electricity radiate forth from Drew's hand, his warm body against his. Joe asked, 'How do you know this place is coming on the market?'

'Not here. Some propriety! We're in a tree, remember?'

Joe sat on the wooden chair, cradling his coffee in his hands. He had gotten out of bed early, brushed his teeth, sprayed on cologne, massaged his hair back into place and put on new underwear straight out of the box in his wardrobe. He'd even made the coffee without waking Drew. He felt prepared. He considered for a moment whether he should turn his chair around, Christine Keeler style, hiding his lower abs to make the best possible impression. Glancing down, he decided he looked pretty good the way he was. He'd done stomach work yesterday, and the results still showed.

He looked at Drew asleep in his bed. He was really quite startling: his translucent white skin glowing against the pale blue sheets; the messy mop of red hair, which had last night been so carefully slicked back in the current style. Freckles cascaded down the back of his neck only to stop halfway across his smooth, white shoulders. They started again in a distinct band across his biceps as if he were wearing long gloves woven together from caramel brown freckles. The sparse auburn patches of morning stubble were clearly never going to produce much in the way of a hipster beard. Joe liked what he saw but even now there seemed something else, something less tangible, about this man's appeal. Last night the man in his bed had been sensual and self-assured. They had been a perfect match in body shape and size. They fitted together physically *and* mentally. If anything, they fitted too well. The sex had been good, *really* good. Yet somehow it lacked the element of feverish exploration but — just then Joe's thoughts were interrupted.

'Are you looking at me?' Drew asked, his eyes still closed. 'Is that coffee?'

'You want one?' Joe murmured. Interpreting Drew's responding groan to be a yes, Joe got up to make another coffee. When he came back, Drew was sitting propped up against the pillows, the sheets tossed to the side of the bed, exposing his full naked glory.

'Something wrong?' he asked as he took the coffee.

Gazing intently at the man in front of him, he asked, 'So, Drew . . . are you a daddy-chaser or just a good old-fashioned gold-digger?'

'Yeah, I get where you're coming from, but it's okay.' Smiling, Drew leant over and picked up Joe's cell phone from the bedside table. He tapped at the screen. 'You should have better security than this . . . here,' he tossed him the phone. 'Call for you.'

Joe caught the phone and looked at the screen, which displayed the words: *Nick Lawyer mobile*. He looked at Drew with a questioning look.

'Tell Nick to draw up the prenup, bring it over, and I'll sign it now.'

Joe pressed 'end call' and tossed the phone back on the bed.

'Prenup? Aren't you rather rushing things?'

'Nah, this is the real deal. We might as well face up to the big stuff immediately. It may take you a while but I'm here to run things in the meantime.' Drew looked at him for a moment. It seemed as if Drew knew he needed to wait for the mist in Joe's head to clear a little before proceeding. 'Awww — I'll give you all the time you need but this is it: I am what you've been looking for, same as me really, something meaningful, a deeper connection with someone who is right for you. Call it true love if you will.'

True love, did anyone even say that anymore? Thing was, Joe was good at spotting conmen but somehow nothing this guy said seemed obviously fake. Drew's words seemed to possess a kind of truth that made him want to hear more. Because of this, the curtness of his own next words surprised even him.

'We've only just met.'

'Good deal for you then. I sign the prenup. If that's the best fun I get and it's all downhill from there — then it really is win-win for you, isn't it?'

'You're a cocky little number.'

'You didn't mind that last night,' Drew said with a wink. 'And any rate,' he crossed his ankles and placed his hands behind his head, exposing the glorious tufts of red hair in his milky armpits. Then, as if suddenly rethinking the obvious provocation of his attitude, he pulled himself up into a sitting position tucking his knees into his chest. He began to speak with a new seriousness. 'Joe . . . you believe in history . . . I mean . . . you think it matters?'

'Yes, I do really.'

'Yeah, me too, you know I could see that last night when I showed you the building, your eyes lit up but the motivation wasn't profit.'

'No . . . I saw an outcast, caught in the wrong time and place . . . in need of rescue.'

'Yeah, me too. Joe, I don't need to be in on that project, not if you don't want, but . . . it is probably time you knew ours.'

Joe looked at him with an expression of obvious confusion. 'Ours?'

'Our history . . . see, I fell in love with you when I was eight.' Joe's eyes widened with alarm. 'You came on a tour of our house with some old ladies from the university. The big Gerald Jones house in Arney Road. Do you remember? I was in my soccer gear. You were so hot.' He smiled. 'That night I told my parents.'

'Told them what?'

'That I was gay, Mr Wright.'

'Don't call me that — this is getting weird enough . . . is this bullshit?' Joe took only a moment before answering his own question. 'This *is* bullshit.'

Drew continued dreamily, 'You were wearing blue jeans, a black Unknown Pleasures t-shirt, and a blue jacket. You had on steel-capped boots you hadn't cleaned. Your hair was longer then, sort of a surfy look—'

'Hang on. No one tells their parents they're gay when they're eight.'

'Well, I did,' Drew hesitated for a moment. 'Well, I told them I liked boys and that I had a new boyfriend. You said you loved me.'

252

'I would *never* have told an eight-year-old boy I loved him,' Joe spoke emphatically.

'Well, you said "like", but I knew what you meant.'

Joe buried his head in his hands for a moment.

'So, is that why you came to work in the office?' he asked suddenly.

'That *was* a total coincidence. John said Thackeray Makepeace would be good for me when I graduated. I threw myself in front of you a couple — well, more like a hundred — times, but you never noticed. You seemed preoccupied. I decided you must have been working through something and that I could wait for you.'

'What did they say?' Now, for once, it was Drew's turn to look confused.

'Who?'

'Your parents?'

'Oh. What you'd expect. They ignored it. Until I was sixteen, then a school friend and I snuck off to Mardis Gras in Sydney with my cousin. That's where I met you the second time — we danced to "Blue Monday". Remember that now? My aunt ratted us out, more about the ecstasy than the gay thing. I was confronted with the usual parental hysteria, but they got over it. They're all good now.' Drew moved over in the bed nestling into the stack of pillows, at the same time displaying his backside, quite intentionally, Joe suspected. Drew lay back, patting the bed next to him to indicate Joe should join him. He rose slowly and lay down beside Drew, his arm across the younger man's hips. Drew placed his right hand in the centre of his chest spreading his fingers out like a fan and lightly teased the hair on Joe's chest. 'Don't worry.' He pulled Joe closer. 'I'm not a stalker. If you think about it — it was fate that delivered you to me every time, like again and again, reminding us of each other, until last night — that's the first time I've come to you on my own terms because it was the first time I really ever could have.'

'This is a lot to get my head around. How do you know I'm not taken?'

Drew looked startled and dropping his hand to the bed he sat up. For a moment the two men repositioned themselves a little further apart.

'*Is* there someone?'

'No,' said Joe emphatically. 'Well, there was once. A guy called Leo.' Even as he spoke, Joe had no idea why he'd said that. In all these years he'd never mentioned Leo to any partner, let alone what might, despite the way he was feeling, yet turn out to be an ambitious one-night stand.

'Yes, I know Leo. We met at the launch party, for the Virginian project, the night I collected Betty in your car. I quite like him. He's one hell of a handsome guy. In fact, full disclosure and everything, I had a drink with him just the other day.'

'What?'

'Aww, it doesn't matter for now,' Drew murmured as he ran his fingers through Joe's hair before pulling him into the first slow kiss of the morning.

As the waiter placed a cooked breakfast with extra fried eggs in front of Drew, Joe felt again as if he might throw up.

'Reckon I burned a few calories last night and again just now.' Drew took a mouthful of bacon and egg and closed his eyes with the sheer delight of it. 'Hmmm, as I was saying, there's a young guy in the engineering department at work, ugly as sin but the dirtiest fuck you'll ever . . .' Joe raised an eyebrow. 'What? I'm not a virgin, you know. I've been waiting a long time for you to get your act together. I had to develop other sideline interests.' He grinned broadly while under the table he gently brushed his leg against Joe's inner thigh. 'Anyway, he got in. He's doing a structural assessment for this douchebag client, some ex-bankrupt making a comeback. He said it was really great. Asked me if I wanted to see it.' Drew took another mouthful of his breakfast before continuing. 'He, the client, the developer, is charming the owner with all this stuff about respecting the building, but he's commissioned an engineer's report.'

'Nothing unusual there.'

'No, but the engineers have been told the report must say it needs to come down.'

'So, he'll buy it, then the report will appear, saying there were no options other than demolition.'

'Right. Then the report gets peer-reviewed offshore. That makes it all but unarguable. International best practice it's called. There are a couple of independent heritage architects who'll say the building isn't exceptional. Historic Places will snooze through it as always. Tangata Whenua won't give a shit because it's not Māori. The Council are always pro-development. The developer is planning a huge apartment block — the plans are already going through the office. We, they, do this all the time. It always works. Meantime, in heritage we are busy designing "sympathetic" access ramps and handrails for the façades of old buildings that they've torn the guts out of.'

Drew was attacking his breakfast again while Joe moved the muesli around his bowl with his spoon. He knew what the kid was saying was right, though he wasn't sure he'd call the Council pro-development. He'd seen it before, too often. Drew, having cleared up his plate, leant forward suggestively as if about to kiss him but instead swerving away took another piece of toast to wipe up the last of the egg yolk. Grinning, he rubbed his knee against Joe's crotch.

'Sorry, that was a bit of a rant, but Auckland doesn't deserve this, and I figure you're probably the only one who can do anything about it.' Joe looked around conspiratorially, half keeping an eye out for the competition that might be eavesdropping, half hoping someone he knew was seeing him get felt up by a hot twenty-four-year-old.

'Can you get me, *us*, inside?'

'Probably.' Drew looked sheepish.

'Without whatever his name is, the dirty engineer.'

'Oh god no, that's well over. Besides, I'm taken,' he pointed to the finger of his left hand and then feigned surprise at the absence of a ring.

The green front doors were resolutely bolted. As a further precaution against entry, additional strips of wood had been nailed across them. An old sign hastily tacked up long ago warned against trespassing. Joe could tell the doors weren't going to open in a hurry.

'This key is for a side door at the top of the fire escape.' Joe followed as Drew climbed the old iron stair treads, deeply etched with rust. Reaching the platform at the top, they came to a solid door with a brand-new padlock, to which Drew had the key.

'This is more of a shutter than a door — it opens out. So, you need to back down the steps a bit and swing it around and latch it over there.' Joe did as instructed. The door moved slowly, grinding on its hinges, but the catch fell quickly into place, securing the door against the wall. Regaining the platform next to Drew, they encountered another door — this time lead-light. A new hasp and staple crudely bolted to the exterior indicated this, a window rather than a door, had once opened from the inside.

Jumping down from the window ledge onto the floor inside with a thud, Joe looked around. Now their entry point made a little more sense. Ahead, on the opposite side of the building, a pale light glimmered through an identical window richly decorated with the same geometric motifs. Together this and the window through which they'd entered acted as the terminal points of a graceful elliptical hall. Joe turned and scanned the space. Into each quadrant of the room were set frosted glass doors. Each with sets of cast bronze handles descending in an arch from the middle to the bottom, in a trio of parallel lines, mimicking the descent of a waterfall. He inhaled deeply.

'My God, Drew.' He looked at Drew who, smiling, took a torch from his jacket pocket and began using its beam to point out various architectural features.

'This floor was the doctor's private suite.' Opening the first set of doors, they encountered an empty room heavily laden with dust. Footprints across the room revealed the path of its two previous visitors. The wall of doors and windows in front of him were those he had first seen from the branches of the ginkgo tree. In the centre was a tall door in its own veneered entablature but on either side the arched windows stopped short, meeting a line of radiators each set into deep boxes covered with ornately gilded grills of geometric design. The ledges these created terminated in demi-lune vase stands at either side of the door. The vases were long gone but above the stands hung a pair of long, thin, mirrored, pier glasses. He had never seen a room quite like it, and he sat down on the window ledge for a moment to take it in. A moment later Drew positioned himself next to him.

The corners of the room featured small built-in seats, covered in turquoise-blue silk upholstery. Their leading edges were variously torn and gaping. Above each, a small deep sculpture niche was recessed into the wall. The veneered walls were in a pale timber. Lemonwood or maple? Joe wasn't sure.

'Maple,' said Drew confidently. 'They brought these rooms crated up from Vienna. I found an article in an old medical journal — no illustrations though. The inlays are in mother of pearl and ebony.' Joe walked over to the motif Drew was pointing at. He reached out and ran his fingers along the teardrop pendant in the upper centre of the panel. Turning back to survey the room from this different perspective, Joe thought it had a delicate feminine feel, an ethereal nature, best expressed in the finely ribbed plaster ceiling that curved elegantly towards an elaborate centrepiece, from which the light fitting had long since been removed. To one side of the room appeared a small fireplace, flanked on both sides with panels of green-veined marble, in it a cylindrical heater. The grills echoed those under the windows. Above it, an allegorical relief represented Eve in Paradise. Walking over, he ran his fingers over the surface of the carved stone.

'Adam's next door,' said Drew as he opened a pair of tall doors in the wall and turned to announce, 'The dining room.'

Joe, stopping in the doorway, slipped his arm around Drew's waist and looked. This room was masculine. The ceiling was deeply coffered in severely regimented recessed squares. In the centre hung the spine of a chandelier now denuded of its crystals. A discoloured rectangle on the parquet floor suggested a rug had done service for a long time before being removed. He looked back through the doors to the previous room — a pair of carpets, he suspected. The windows in this room were treated identically and looked out onto the same terrace. Except here the corners were closed out on either side by a pair of imposing built-in cabinets with low, flat ziggurat tops.

'Cocktails?' asked Drew, as he opened the door to reveal green velvet lining and an interior fitted out to hold bottles and glasses.

'Perhaps later — together out there?' As Joe reached up to pull aside the curtains to get a better view of the terrace, a large section of fabric ripped and fell into his hands, covering them both in a shower of dust.

Drew coughed. 'Don't worry, it's nothing that a good hot shower won't get off.'

'Drew, these are the most beautiful rooms I've ever seen. They are mesmerising.'

'Wait, there's more. You ain't seen the free steak knives yet.' Drew took him by the hand and led him back to the hallway. There he opened the matching set of doors on the opposite side. 'Master bedroom,' he announced triumphantly. Joe was given only a moment to take in the empty bedroom's most apparent feature, a wall made up of floor-to-ceiling mirrored doors, each set in silver gilt frames, before Drew ushered him through the central mirrored door in the wall and into the adjacent bathroom.

Here, Joe stopped, wholly incapable of movement, his breath gone. The room was windowless and dark with only a little light filtering in from the chamber through which they had come. Standing next to him, Drew lit up elements with his torch. The roof was curved in a half cylinder like that of an old railway carriage. The marble walls were illustrated with inserted plaques depicting mythical fish executed in pink and green majolica. At the far end, a sunken bath, in the same marble that made up the walls and floor, took up the entire end of the room. A small set of steps descended from a starting point, midway between door and bath, delivering any would-be bather into the waters at a leisurely pace. Joe immediately thought of Cleopatra being lowered into the Nile. Over the centre of the bath, a shower nozzle protruded down from the roof like the rose of an ancient watering can. A cage of thick nickel-plated metal pipes surrounded the whole ensemble, looking something between old plumbing and the railings of an ocean liner.

Jumping down into the dry bath, Drew turned to face Joe. 'Come here — there's plenty of room for two.' Placing Joe's hand with his on the railings, he said, 'There's a switch on the wall, the pipes heat up, a sort of early heated towel rail system.' He aimed his torch beam either side of the doorway to indicate a matching pair of heavy white porcelain sinks, each standing in front of enormous mirrors.

'Impressed?'

Leaning back into Drew, he nodded. 'Oh Drew, *very*.'

'You should see the size of the wardrobes — dressing rooms, I suppose. Behind those other mirrored doors. This is just the top apartment. The business was done downstairs. The other hall door is a service space, a little pantry from which the butler could serve dinner. There's a food lift to the kitchen downstairs. The other apartments are out the back overlooking the gardens.'

'Gardens?'

'Yes, you know the bottom of Anzac Avenue? There's a little carpark and then a stone wall with an iron gate that's always been locked up.' Drew waited for a moment as if allowing Joe time to consider the landscape just described. 'The one with the wooden panel over it covered in posters?' Joe searched his mind but realised his map of that part of town was twenty years out of date. He shrugged. 'Well, it was the old driveway for this place.'

Drew led the way past the first floor without comment, and before Joe could ask its purpose, he got his first sight of the ground floor foyer. He could tell immediately this was not the work of the same architect. Still, Auckland didn't have many rooms that looked as grand as this one. He could forgive the use of mere oak panelling. As they stopped in the middle of the tiled entrance floor, light filtering in through the large front windows meant he could see the surrounding offices had been re-clad sometime in the 1950s and painted rich plum, pale blue, and even paler primrose yellow. Leaning against the wall were a stack of cut-out decorated crowns, curling at the corners, with *ERII* and the date 1954 emblazoned across the front.

'No real damage here.' Drew motioned him over to a chimney breast. Pulling away the gaping pinboard linings, he exposed a glimpse of an impressive black and white marble fireplace. 'They put in a giant electrical heater instead, go figure.'

'Hang on, what's that desk over there?' Joe asked. Drew pointed his torch to a large pale blond tawa desk. Its broad, elegant top hovered dramatically on slender columns over two banks of drawers. Walking over, Joe stroked the top of it, his fingers making broad lines in the dust.

'It's fifties — looks local.'

'Very smart. Exactly the kind of piece I've been searching for for my office.' At the other end of the desk, Drew smiled and leaning forward wrote JW + AC in the dust before circling it with a heart. Joe laughed.

'What? Gotta act my age sometimes.'

Joe laughed. 'You sure do but don't you think it's strange that this is the only piece of furniture in the whole place? Just got left here.'

Sitting on the edge of the desk next to Drew, Joe looked at the ceiling. The ornate pressed zinc panels had latterly been painted black. It would be a mission for a team of painters to bring those back to what they'd once been, but already his mind was buzzing with possibilities.

Drew opened a door behind the staircase. 'This way — but now it gets tricky, this back bit hasn't been used in years and maybe never was. It's been leaking for a long time, I understand. There's rot everywhere, so watch where you step.' Through a second door, the building opened out into a narrow U-shaped atrium, around which ran a balcony framed with a wide, open geometric iron balustrade. Hands on the wooden railings, careful to keep his weight on the structural parts of the floor, Joe peered over the edge. Below he could see a second, almost identical, level.

'Sort of like an old prison,' said Drew.

Joe looked up. Curved iron supports held up a ceiling, the central panels of which were a glass skylight. 'A very glamorous prison.'

'These are the other apartments.' Drew gestured either side. 'Two on each level. They're locked up — so I've never seen them. And that,' he said, pointing at the tiled floor below, 'is, believe it or not, the parking garage. The floor heats up — or at least it did — to keep the cars warm. Can you believe it? A heated floor with space for nine cars in 1910! There's a boiler room, and little apartment tucked right under, probably for a husband and wife, cook and chauffeur.'

Looking straight ahead, the entire end of the building was a wall of faceted glass made up of long, narrow metal-framed panes. Down it, water from a degraded gutter had been running for a long time, and patches of green slime adhered to the window and ferns grew in the mullions. The central part of the window wall jutted out, rather like the central part of a bay window.

'See, I told you, just like Saint Kevin's Arcade, but better — can you imagine the engineering required back then? We can't stay long, but you need to see this.' Turning, Drew started walking along the boardwalk towards the glass wall, his hand trailing behind indicating that Joe should take it. Obliging, Joe followed, careful to step where there was a joist, but almost immediately, reluctantly, let go of Drew's hand. When Drew got within a few metres of the window, he raised his arm to identify a detail high above their heads, while at the same time turning back to face Joe. The complication of his manoeuvre made him stumble. With his footfall came a loud crack. Arm still above his head, expression frozen, he disappeared through the floor in a cloud of splintered timber and plaster.

It took a moment for Joe to realise what had happened. He peered through the dust cloud to see a big hole in front of him, with Drew lying on the floor below surrounded by debris. Dropping to his knees, he called out, but there was no response. His heart beating loudly in his ears, Joe looked around frantically for the way down. Thankfully, in the gloom he could make out the staircase they had previously ascended. Joe made his way along the precarious inner edge of the balcony as quickly as he dared. Inexplicably, as he made his way to where Drew lay, certain memories came flooding into his brain like sunlight. Joe realised that everything Drew had told him had been true. By the time he got to Drew's side he realised, without a shadow of a doubt, that before him lay the little red-headed kid in his soccer whites; the sixteen-year-old dance party boy in blue speedos; and the philosophical architecture student looking to define love on a rooftop. None of whom, until that very moment, he had *entirely* remembered.

Still trembling with fear, his throat tight, sweat beading on his forehead, Joe started to lift Drew but thought better of it. The boy's face was scratched. There seemed a lot of blood. How much blood can you lose? Somewhere in his brain, Joe recalled it was a lot. Perhaps this wasn't so bad. He must not lose focus. He put his head on Drew's chest and felt him breathing. Thank God.

'Drew?' He shook him gently. 'Come on, kiddo. Come on.' After what felt like an eternity Drew opened his eyes.

'I fell.' The words came out in barely a whisper. Joe suspected the air had been knocked out of him. Drew's head collapsed back on the floor and into unconsciousness. Reaching out for his hand, Joe found Drew's shirtsleeve sticky with blood.

Shaking, Joe said, 'Stay with me Drew, I know everything now and I need you more than . . . I'm calling an ambulance.'

The occupants of the neighbouring apartment building were gathering on the footpath. Having dealt with two agitated police officers by summoning his lawyer, Joe now turned to the ambulance driver. Drew had been winded — it was mostly minor cuts and scratches. The gash in his arm needed attention. There was, the St John's man said, 'the possibility of a fracture.' His wrist didn't look so good. On top of all that there was, he added cheerfully, 'always concussion.' As they lifted the gurney into the ambulance, the driver asked him if he wanted to ride in the back. Joe didn't hesitate.

Drew lifted the oxygen mask from his lips. 'It must be love if you're here.'

'Sssh.' Brushing Drew's hair back off his forehead he said, 'We have a lifetime for all that. For now, temporarily, let's just call it mentoring.'

CHAPTER 20

'You seem distracted,' commented Betty as she took Joe's plate.

'That's why I come here, isn't it? To be distracted from my crazy life.'

'A nice young man perhaps?' asked Betty hopefully.

'Yes, maybe, but,' he hesitated, 'I suppose it's business that's on my mind today.'

'A nice young man is the only business you need,' Betty smiled and patted his hand. 'I've never known you to think business on a Sunday, except when it was something very big.'

'Quite the opposite, Betty. This time it's a small building I want. The owner won't sell, not to me, not to anyone, it seems.'

'Why do you want this one so badly?'

'Because it's the most perfect little building, just melting away at the moment because some crazy old German lady won't sell it, yet she can't afford to maintain it either.'

'It's because she loves it. She doesn't want things to change. Love comes in many forms. You know that.'

'She probably does, but so do I and I am—'

'Sick of not getting what you love?' Betty interrupted him.

'Hmm, sick of coming second perhaps? Or something like that,' Joe hesitated. 'No, this is different. This building, its potential, it makes everything I've done in life make sense if you know what I mean. This is my purpose.'

Betty turned and looked out into the garden. 'By any chance are you talking about 62 Emily Place?'

Joe sat bolt upright in his chair. 'Betty, how . . . ?'

'I am not as out of touch as you think. Maria Klein, the crazy *Austrian* lady, and I have known each other for sixty years. Emily Place, Joseph and I rented the ground floor for more than forty years. That was where we had our giftware business.'

'So, it was you — the pink and blue colour scheme?'

Betty sighed, 'Yes, doll, it was me. Well, it was Joseph actually. I've told you once before, he did it for me, the Royal Tour, official colours you know. It looked so lovely. He decorated the front of the building with cardboard crowns and bunting. Funny, we went to all that effort. She didn't come anywhere near us, just Queen Street.' Betty stopped for a moment and then continued. 'Maria will sell it all right, to the right person.'

'Yes, but *who* is the right person?'

'You are, because you have a weapon.'

'Weapon? What weapon?'

'The past.' Joe looked at her, perplexed. 'Men aren't new, you know, you're all recycled. You've all been around before, which is funny given how long it takes any of you to learn anything. Women, we're different. Those they make from new cloth, smarter, stronger, every time. Men, men keep coming back just the same. Some just keep turning up like bad pennies. Others, the real diamonds among men, well, we're always waiting for those to return. Do you want Maria's building? Invite Leo to my house for lunch next Wednesday at 1.30. Don't explain anything — just tell him to trust me and to go with what happens. Tell him I'll sort it all out with him after. Oh, and dress him up a bit. Be there at 1 o'clock sharp with Andrew. Then we'll see.'

'Andrew?'

'I wasn't born yesterday. Don't you remember, Drew and I go back years, to the Virginian launch party? You sent him to me. He may have overlooked to mention that afterwards I found him in the book, rang him and offered him a job mowing my lawns. He's done that for me for years while mooning over you. How do you think he knew where you were that Saturday morning, what was it three weeks ago, at the café? And yes, before you ask, Leo was in on it too. Gerald too. Now remember, Wednesday, midweek. Time to get moving, Joe — no one is getting any younger, least of all you.'

Joe had spent many a lunchtime at Betty's, but he'd never seen the dining room used. He recalled taking a sneaky peek in there on that first day he visited — back then he wondered if he'd strayed into a place caught between *Oliver Twist* and *Great Expectations*. Today the table was laden with polished silver. The glassware gleamed as if promoting a new brand of dishwasher.

'Drew came around early to help me.'

'He didn't mention it. You two are becoming very chummy.'

'He's a wonderful young man.'

Drew blushed.

'I know. It just took me a while to notice.'

Through the windows, they all watched a taxi pull up to the kerb. A moment later a tiny woman stepped out. That she had any presence at all from this distance was due in substantial part to her impressive backcombed hair, elegantly streaked with grey and black.

'Ninety-four,' whispered Drew as Betty ushered the woman into her front room. Joe and Drew glanced at each other, surprised to find they had automatically lined up, side by side, as if prepared for inspection. Betty too took on a new formality he had never seen before.

'Mrs Maria Klein, I'd like to introduce, Mr Joseph Wright and Mr Andrew Campbell.' With pursed lips, Maria extended her hand to Joe who shook it, noticing the large diamonds covering her long, thin fingers.

Drew raised his bandaged hand in acknowledgment and offered his left hand instead. Maria turned to him and, with an imperious tone still heavy with German pronunciation, hissed at him.

'Ah, the trespasser.'

'I am so sorry, but I just love that building and simply had to see inside,' Drew stammered.

'You have a funny way of showing your respect. Breaking and entering is not love. Not to me.' Maria leant forward to inspect his face at close range. 'And now,' she said, pointing her jewel-encrusted hand at Drew, 'I have a you-shaped hole in my floor. What do you propose to do about that, young man?'

'If I might intercede?' Joe asked politely. 'It is true that Andrew is young and can at times be a little impulsive but he is certainly not some young hoodlum. Rather, he is a very talented architect with a bright future ahead of him who has a deep love and respect for beautiful buildings. Mrs Klein, he meant no harm. He means what he says. He, or rather *we*, simply adore your building. It is so beautiful that we couldn't resist the temptation to look inside. We certainly never meant to cause any damage.'

'And you, Mr Wright, you are the developer? The one who wrote to me, cooing sweet things. You think you are *my* Mr Right? Well, we shall see about that, won't we?' She leant forward. 'You would do well to remember, Mr Wright, I am no fool.' Betty, who had popped out of the room unnoticed, came back in with a small silver tray of drinks.

'Brandy?' She looked at the two men. 'Mrs Klein has a medicinal brandy before lunch. I'm sure one will do us all some good.' When everyone had taken a glass, Betty turned to Drew. 'What do you think of my tray? My husband brought it back from Italy after the war.' Joe noticed Maria flinch slightly at the sudden mention of the war. 'Probably pinched it from some villa they looted — a lot of that went on, you know. Anything they could carry, those Kiwi soldiers, they were famous for it. There's a house in Remuera with a little Botticelli. Where do you think they got that?'

'Ah, yes. So much was lost during the war,' said Maria quietly.

'Yes, but a lot was gained too, and I don't just mean silver trays. After all the horror and ugliness in the war, my husband Joseph wanted a job where things were always pretty. That's why we set up in giftware. And that's how we met Maria. The tray is *very* pretty, don't you think, Drew?'

Drew cleared his throat. 'Yes, very pretty. You are so lucky to have such beautiful antiques and such good memories.'

'Not all memories are good, of course. You young people, you have it too easy.' Maria lowered herself down on a chair and held her empty glass out to Drew. 'Get me another, thank you. You have some repairing to do.' Drew hung his head and disappeared down the hallway. Joe suspected he would linger out of range for a while.

The three of them continued the conversation. Betty seemed determined to remain on the war theme, although it was clear the conversation was unsettling Maria. Joe tried to steer the subject in other directions but didn't seem to be having much luck.

'Where is that young man with my brandy?' grumbled Maria. Just at that moment the doorbell rang. Joe started to get up.

'Stay where you are. Drew will answer it.'

'Who is it? Another homosexual, another developer?' On another day Joe might have laughed at her characterisation of Leo, but not this time. There was too much at stake.

'No, just another guest. Better late than never.'

Leo entered the room and Drew followed close behind. In a single tick of the mantle clock, the colour had drained from Maria's face. She suddenly looked very, very old.

She turned to Betty, a look of pure astonishment on her face. Betty simply smiled, took the glass of brandy from Drew and handed it to Maria. This time it definitely seemed medicinal.

Drew slipped in behind Joe and whispered, 'It seems Leo is Betty's secret weapon. Apparently Leo looks remarkably like Maria's older brother — missing in action in the war. And, on that note, haven't you noticed that you look a lot like her husband, Joseph? Especially in that photo on the wall of the hallway of him in his uniform.'

'No, I don't.'

'Oh, *yes* you do.'

'Not now.' The thought rattled Joe, but he dismissed it for the moment and turned back to the others.

Betty had done the introductions and now Maria was holding Leo's hands and staring deeply into his eyes. She was speaking quietly to herself in German, and a tear welled up on her eyelid before tumbling over onto her cheek.

'Oh, please don't cry,' said Leo softly. He reached into his pocket and took out his neatly folded handkerchief. 'May I?' he asked before gently dabbing her cheek. Then, slowly and deliberately, Leo spoke again,

'Ich habe Dich nie verlassen und werde es nie tun,' before refolding his handkerchief and pressing it into her hand.

'Did you know he spoke German?' asked Drew under his breath.

'Ah, yes. From university, but I doubt he's got too much more than that.'

'I wonder what he said? Actually, it doesn't matter what he said, does it? It seems he's worked magic on Mrs Klein.'

Joe squeezed the fingers of Drew's unbandaged hand and leaning in kissed him gently on the forehead. 'Sssh.'

Over lunch, Maria's mood seemed quite transformed. Even Drew appeared forgiven — although Maria still treated him like the hired help. She told them all stories about her grandfather who had come from a Viennese banking family. Her parents, both doctors, had known Freud. They believed they had found in New Zealand a new world of possibility. She explained how they'd relocated their apartment out here in its entirety. They'd had the interiors, designed by Bruno Paul, refitted into the specially designed upper floor of the new building. When Maria said they'd brought all their art and furniture too and that it was still either in storage in the lower apartments, or at her house, Drew made a sign across the table, indicating that his head had just exploded. Joe gave Drew a look to silence him, but inside his chest, his heart raced.

Maria talked about how her uncle, a doctor who had returned to Vienna in the 1920s, had died in the gas chambers along with most of her extended family. She talked about her brother Richard and how he had kept the family's hope of a life here alive after the venture had failed. Richard had avoided internment by going to the States just before the beginning of the war. In 1941 he had enlisted in the American Air Force. As she talked, she gazed at Leo across the table, clutching the handkerchief in her hand. Drew got up and discreetly removed their dirty plates, balancing Betty's best china on his bandaged hand.

'Coffee in the front room, I think,' said Betty. Without a word, Leo got up from the table and came around to Maria's side and took her hand. He led her through to the other room. The secret weapon indeed, thought Joe.

'Did you brief him,' he whispered to Betty, as soon as he got a moment.

'Not a word. Isn't he fantastic? So chivalrous.' Yes, Joe thought, Leo at his very best. He now sat beside Maria on the couch and rested her hand on his.

After the coffee was served, Maria finally turned her attention away from Leo to Joe. 'So, Mr Developer, what does your enterprise want to do to my building? Pull it down? Blow it up? What?'

'Oh no,' said Joe quickly, sitting forward in his seat. 'No, Mrs Klein, you are misinformed. My company, Thackeray Makepeace, doesn't want your building.' Betty and the others were obviously taken aback, and for a moment he relished the look of surprise on most of the faces in the room. 'No, not the firm. It is simply me. A house hunter looking for a home. A very special home in which to live. I want to restore it faithfully to its former glory. Return it to what it once was, what it still is, the most beautiful building in all of New Zealand. And in time, I would like Drew, Betty, and Leo and Nor to think about coming and living there with me. If any of them want to, that is. In apartments of their own — or perhaps with me.' He shot a quick glance at Drew before continuing. 'A beautiful building for a beautiful extended family just as it was designed to be.'

'Go on,' said Maria.

'I'll offer you a price now that is more than fair. I'll then sign it over to a trust with you and me on the board. You'll appoint one other trustee and I will appoint another. Professor John Sims of the University of Auckland's School of Architecture will chair. There will be no unauthorised work. We'll start the restoration immediately — so there are no more unpleasant accidents.' He winked at Drew. 'You will be able to see the work we do for yourself. We'll need you every step of the way to tell us how it once was. Then, when I die, the Trust will have it — a residence for visiting medical staff, perhaps? Somewhere for those people who want to get a glimpse of your parents' vision of a land of opportunity.

The Thackeray Makepeace Charitable Trust will set it up with the University's Medical School and the hospital. They will make sure that part is funded. We can talk through all the details at your convenience.' When Joe finally finished, there was silence in the room. Maria took a slow sip of her coffee.

'That all sounds most interesting, Mr Wright. Yes, you may say I am interested in what you have proposed.'

Leo had taken off straight after Maria, but Joe and Drew had whiled away the remainder of the afternoon at Betty's, helping her tidy up, and dining lightly on what remained left over from lunch. Nobody had said much and, when Joe could see that Betty was starting to get tired, they once again expressed their profound gratitude and said their goodbyes. They headed off down the road, walking side by side, along the narrow footpath.

'Thanks for helping with the dishes.'

'That's all right. I *love* washing up,' Drew replied.

'How can you? You're just *not* normal.'

'We covered that topic once before — do you remember?'

'Yes, I do. You said you weren't a very normal architect.' Joe smiled.

'See, the thing is, I've never lived in a house without a dishwasher. The big house has three. It's so old school, so romantic, washing dishes. You just have this incredibly real, quality time together. I feel sorry for people who have never had that.'

'I've never considered it that way.' Joe slipped his hand into Drew's.

'Wow, look.' Drew pointed at the evening sky.

'Where?'

'On the horizon, low and bright, what is it?'

'Probably a satellite,' said Joe, then stopped in his tracks. 'No, hang on, I remember now. *That's* Venus.'

'The goddess of love?'

'*In the sky over Auckland, it's another summer of love,*' said Joe in his best radio voice with a tinge of irony.

Drew laughed. 'Do you believe in that stuff?'

'Perhaps. Funny . . . that reminds me of something else you once asked me.'

'What was that?'

'"Do you believe there's one person for each of us?"'

'And do you?'

'I did, and then I didn't, and now maybe I do. I used to think the universe's job was to line up the elements of my life as soon as possible. I know differently now. I know sometimes the universe absolutely *has* to wait — sometimes for years — before it can deliver. That can be hard on those of us doing the waiting.'

'And in our case?'

Without replying he tightened his grip on Drew's hand, releasing it only as they reached the door of the house so that he might slip his arms around his waist. 'Drew, you asked once if history mattered to me, and it does, but you know there comes a time in a man's life, in any life, when you've got to leave history behind and create the future.'

Gesturing at the sky, Joe continued. 'It's not the orbit of a planet that matters, the key is allowing ourselves to be thrown off orbit, to find new paths. At least, that's how it was once explained to me.'

Opening the door, Joe pulled Drew in closer. 'Do you know what I really see up there? The sky above Auckland — and to me, day or night, that's always meant a beginning, *the* beginning, I hope of something big, a happy future for both of us.'

THANK YOU

Writing a novel would be an almost impossible task without the support of friends. In particular, I'd like to thank Fenella Tonkin, Lucy Hammonds, Ian Watt and Stephanie Johnson, all early readers of the manuscript, for their support and encouragement. I'd like to thank Stephen Salt; our walks around Auckland at night in the 1980s have stayed with me my entire life and reappear here. I'd like to thank Harry McNaughton, Emily Writes and Jeremy Hansen for their early support. Thanks to Charles Dickens and Evelyn Waugh for novels worth quoting from. Thanks to Louise Russell who was both editor and mentor, and to the whole team at Bateman Books, who together brought *Shelter* to life. Thanks to *samesame but different* for the opportunity to read from the novel at their festival. Finally, thanks to all the smart, stylish, independent, older women throughout my life who collectively inspired Betty Strauss — to you I owe an enduring thanks.

ENDNOTES

1 Dickens, C. (1838). *Oliver Twist*. London: Richard Bentley.
2 Waugh, E. (1945). *Brideshead Revisited*. London: Chapman & Hall.
3 Ibid.